Praise for Elisabeth Cohen's

The Glitch

"Takes a hard look at the definition of work-life balance. Through hilarious antics and sensational story lines, Elisabeth Cohen encourages readers to slow down, take a breath and consider the perspective of a younger you. Would that person think you are living your best life?"   —*The Washington Times*

"Elisabeth Cohen has given us one of the most unforgettable characters in recent fiction. Shelley Stone is a workaholic CEO who is 'leaning in' so far she might just be losing her mind. This debut is a smart and delirious ride through a world of TED Talks, tech start-ups, and efficiency junkies. I tore through *The Glitch* with delight!"   —Jennifer Close,
author of *Girls in White Dresses* and *The Hopefuls*

"Sometimes you read a book because it sounds really good, but then it turns out to be way, way more strange, original, and thrilling than even claimed, and that's what happened for me with Elisabeth Cohen's *The Glitch*."   —Elizabeth McKenzie,
author of *The Portable Veblen*

"Shelley Stone is a genius comic creation, and her story—one where she's struck by lightning, drives a potentially haunted car, and meets her doppelgänger—is as madcap as it is fabulously relatable. She's a spreadsheet-crunching, yoga-practicing, flexitarian CEO overachiever who is so utterly hilarious, I couldn't help but love her."   —Lucy Sykes,
author of *The Knockoff* and *Fitness Junkie*

Elisabeth Cohen

The Glitch

Elisabeth Cohen majored in comparative literature at Princeton University, and her work has appeared in *Conjunctions, Mississippi Review, The Cincinnati Review, McSweeney's,* and *The Millions*. She has an MA from the Johns Hopkins Writing Seminars and an MLS from the University of Maryland. She worked as a librarian before her current career as a technical writer. She lives outside Philadelphia with her husband and two sons.

The Glitch

THE

Glitch

A NOVEL

ELISABETH COHEN

ANCHOR BOOKS

A DIVISION OF PENGUIN RANDOM HOUSE LLC

NEW YORK

The Library of Congress has cataloged the Doubleday edition as follows:
Name: Cohen, Elisabeth, author.
Title: The glitch : a novel / Elisabeth Cohen.
Description: First edition. | New York : Doubleday, 2018.
Identifiers: LCCN 2017054208
Subjects: LCSH: Women chief executive officers—Fiction. | Working mothers—Fiction. | BISAC: FICTION / Humorous. | FICTION / Contemporary Women. | FICTION / Satire.
Classification: LCC PS3603.O3464 G57 2018 | DDC 813/.6—dc23
LC record available at https://lccn.loc.gov/2017054208

Anchor Books Trade Paperback ISBN: 978-0-525-43464-1
eBook ISBN: 978-0-385-54279-1

www.anchorbooks.com

Printed in the United States of America
1   2   3   4   5   6   7   8   9   10

To James

Part 1

CAP FERRAT, FRANCE

✦✦✦✦✦✦┼✦✦✦

Chapter 1

Like a lot of successful people, I have problems with my sinuses. I was digging in my bag for a tissue when I felt my phone buzzing. It was work. And so between the call and my nose, I didn't notice our child had gone missing.

First things first: we were in France, on the beach. We had stopped beside a little café with a red awning and a menu board advertising moules marinières and dorade grillée and a kind of wide-topped ice cream cone in which the two scoops sit side by side, competing for your attention. The café had an astonishing number of little tables on the pavement surrounding it, suggesting that its gross revenue per square foot was high for the local market, thanks to the competitive advantage of its beachfront location.

But nobody was eating there now. It was too late for lunch and too early for dinner. People were catching up on email in their hotel rooms, or running out of their offices to do an errand, or coming home from nights out that had stretched into the next afternoon. And then there was us: Rafael and I, both on our phones for work, and our two little kids—well, one of the two. I was thinking, Nova would like those double ice cream cones, and I was about to show her, and then I thought, where is Nova?

Have you ever been to Cap Ferrat? It's very nice. A little trashy, not exactly what I expected, but nice. We were beside the café and a parking lot, at the edge of the beach, with the sea beyond. Rafael had his phone against his ear and our baby, in a carrier, strapped to his chest. The baby looked placid and content as Rafe rocked from one foot to the other, murmuring in the soothing voice he uses to discuss leveraged buyouts.

Our daughter too had just been there with us, and all at once she was not there. I stood up and blinked, thinking that might rearrange things, rematerialize her. I hoped to reboot the situation.

She was not very tall—she was four, but even for four she was shrimpy. That comes from my side. She has dark hair, a pale dress, legs, feet, sandals, big pockets bulging with grass stalks and little walruses and pieces of sea glass, which get put into a bin in our laundry room. She's not that musical, but she does sing. She plays soccer, though she hasn't shown any special aptitude for it. She hasn't mastered her Chinese tones. She likes drawing. She draws spirals that look like concepts for product logos, often going right off the edge of the paper. "You have to stay on the paper," I'd told her just that morning at the hotel. "Look, you're making marks on this table. Stay on the paper, don't wander off."

It was good advice. She was the type to hide under the table-cloth in a restaurant or fall behind, transfixed by a fountain. I thought she must be nearby, even if I couldn't see her.

Tall, thin cypresses lined the road, and olive trees. There was a breeze off the water that smelled of fish and lavender. Unrealistically blue water slapped at the hulls of the sailboats in the marina.

It would have been very enjoyable had she been there. Planters with blue and yellow flowers. That strikingly legible European signage. Just a few minutes before, we had walked along the road and stared at the Plan du Port (I think I can translate that: Plan of Port) and a little sign pointing the way to the Ship Chandler.

"That's the person who sells candles to pirates," Rafael had explained, and Nova had looked up at him quizzically with her cloudy little expression, as if she wasn't sure if it were true or he were joking. That cloudy look was often on Nova's face. Earlier. Twenty minutes ago. Before we'd lost Nova.

The boats' masts cast long pointy shadows across the pavement where we were walking. The shadows bobbed and dipped as the boats stirred. Nova, who had been in a good mood for once, had run along the sidewalk jumping over each one.

"Take a picture!" I'd said.

"Good idea," Rafael said. "In a second. I have to take this call. It's Zach."

I was overwhelmed, as I often am, by the tidal currents behind my nose. My sinuses were giving me trouble. I dug for a tissue and from the depths of my bag saw the bright glow of my own phone trying to summon my attention.

"Yes?" I answered, cupping my ear. I struggled to maneuver the tissue out of my bag and deal with my nose without altering the crisp, resonant timbre of my phone voice.

I'm not sure how many moments later I noticed she wasn't there. I got into Rafe's line of sight and lip-mimed (because we were both still on our calls), *Where's Nova?*

He gave me a distracted thumbs-up. Without missing a beat he said, out loud, "There's a lot of opportunity there, yeah."

I mimed confusion. Into my own phone I said crisply, "Brad, yes! I met with them just last week. They're putting out feelers. They want to get in on the action. It could be huge for them. Haptics are an exploding field."

I turned, expecting her to have appeared. She hadn't. *Rafe,* I signaled, *Nova?*

Rafael put his finger into his ear and shook his head. He was on a call with an investor and he seemed to be straining very hard to hear and pull meaning in through the connection. Our eyes met and Rafe looked away; he had the expression he gets, slightly constipated, when he's doing calculations in his head. Or also, when he's in the bathroom.

"I think it's undervalued," he said into his phone. "For comparison, Mexbol's up a little over two percent this year. I like what I'm seeing. I'm just sitting here looking at some numbers with Pete." Which was not strictly true. "I can just go back a page, hang on, the screen is loading . . . You having internet problems out there . . . ?"

Nova! I mouthed, silently, hugely, inches from his face.

What? he mouthed back, with hand gestures. He began to look around, checking for Nova. His eyes widened.

"I agree completely," I said abruptly into my phone. "I've framed out three different options. We could do it through a merger or acquisition, but a licensing deal could also work, if we could get favorable renewal options. I went over the details with Stefan yesterday, but I'm happy to lay them out to you or the committee—maybe we could do that this afternoon. I'm prepping to go into a meeting in about ten minutes." Which was not strictly true either.

Rafe strode purposefully toward the back side of the café, showing confidence that he would find her. "Who wants to go down there? Not me. But yeah, it would be good to have a guy on the ground. A satellite office, even. I'm looking at some other numbers." In fact he was looking at me, eyes wide, as he came back around the other side of the café, alone, still talking. "I have historical trends right here." His voice was measured and exact, his face contorted with worry. He drew an exclamation point in the sand with his shoe.

Weren't you holding her hand? His expression was reproaching.

I did, I silent-screamed back. *Until the phone . . .*

What?

Until a minute ago!

What?

A *minute!* I pointed at my watch.

How long?

I pinched my thumb and finger together to show a small bit and banged my fingers against the crystal of my watch. Unlike most executives in Silicon Valley, I do wear a watch. It may make me seem older, but I like knowing what time it is. It's just another stereotype I've had to overcome. My fingertips were still stained from the raspberries I'd fed our son at lunch. A *minute!* I screamed it, silently, till my ears popped from the pressure on the tendons along the back of my neck. My Conch slipped out of position, and I pressed it against the back of my ear.

Rafael put his hand over the speaker of his phone. On the edge of audibility, he whispered, "Go that way, I'll go this way."

I nodded and set off. "Brad, sure, no, no trouble at all, sure I'd love to take you through the options, I'll sketch them out for you right now, no, of course, now is fine, now's terrific." I took a deep breath. "So you've got the possibility of a turnkey solution through a straight acquisition of one of the smaller players in the thermoelectric energy harvesting space, say . . . and I think that's a valid possibility for us . . ." Keep it slow, keep it calm, don't give it away, don't blow cred on this because you might need it more tomorrow, you might need it more in ten minutes—and I continued to speak in the same measured way, my breathing even, while I began sprinting along the sand looking for Nova's little sprigged white dress, her red plastic bucket.

There was nobody on the beach or around. Above us, on the cliff that ringed the horseshoe beach, were houses, but could anyone have seen anything from so far above? My heart was accelerating. A little catch in it, like a diesel car on a cold morning. I concentrated on my voice, keeping it smooth and clear and even. You're good at this, I thought. You succeed, every time, what's one more. The previous night, I had set my alarm for 2:25 so I could get on a 2:30 conference call—2:30 a.m. Central European Time, 5:30 in the evening back in California where the main players were. I didn't even have to set the alarm; these days I always wake when I need to. I didn't mention I was away, or that I was at that moment sitting on a balcony with my fingers circling the cold metal railing, looking out into darkness where the sea pulsed invisibly beyond the dark fog, wearing both hotel robes over my pajamas for warmth. I added some vibrant insights to the directors' call, pushed back against a subordinate's idea, assigned some deliverables, clarified the next steps, and then clicked off, stumbled back in, dropped the robes on the floor, and climbed into our palatial bed.

Hang up the goddamn phone, a voice in my head said. It sounded remarkably like my own in a managerial moment. I countered: If I don't find her in sixty seconds, I'll say there's a problem I have to deal with and I'll call him right back. I'll say I'm up against a hard stop. No, new approach, even better—I'll say I can't hear him, that my connection is breaking up. Don't mention a problem unless you've formulated the solution, that's a core principle of mine. Say I'm about to drive into the woods. Let him assume I'm talking about the ones down Page Mill Road. Let him make the excuses for me. Let him tell me the connection's gone bad. That's best. Give it sixty seconds, starting now, and then pretend the connection's broken up. I glanced down at my watch. *You can drown in sixty*, the voice said. True. I appreciate your input and I'm going to act on it. I always appreciate smart suggestions, no matter who they come from. Let's say forty-five.

I looked out over the water, so blue and beautiful, and still. Glimmers of light came and went across its rippled surface. I didn't see any signs of a child, but would there have been signs? I looked for any trace of her. Had she already gone under? I waded out, my socks and shoes wet, hiking up my pants, but what did dry pants matter? With one hand I tried to pull them up, the other clutching the phone.

On the phone, Brad kept pressing for details. "Shelley . . . ?" I knew them cold but it was difficult to recite them, to keep going, to be responsive in the places where he paused and made little harrumphs, little assents. It felt—and I never feel this way about my work—beside the point. Birds flew overhead, their wings splayed wide exactly the way I would draw them, as Vs with the tops bent down. They made bird sounds. Narrow the funnel, I told myself. Fix this, then that. Keep your head in the game, stick to the plan, play your zone, stay focused. Nobody can manage ten priorities at once, or even two. The best managers know this and pick and choose. What to ignore is as important as what to address. Water slapped the hulls of the sailboats, sounding like a little call: *no-va-gone, no-va-gone.* I watched the sweep of my second hand. Thirty seconds. The connection was crystalline, perfect. How could it be this good, on the coast, beside the cliffs? Where was the mute function on this phone? There must be a button. Would it work with my international carrier? "Brad, I'd like to hear your feedback so far," I said, riskily. There was a pause. Let it breathe, I told myself. Don't fill it.

He didn't want to talk, I could tell, but his voice moved into the silence the way human voices do, and footed itself, and one phrase led to another and he became temporarily, agreeably, boringly expansive. I saw the mute icon, and I punched. "Market call line!" I murmured experimentally and there was no response from Brad. Good. "Radicchio," I said, just to confirm he wasn't hearing me. And then, out loud, full throated, "Nova!" I screamed, the syllables breaking into the air, leaping out from my throat, spiraling out as if they had been crushed in there and were desperate to get out. "Nova! Nova! Nova! Where *are* you? No-va!"

Rafe turned toward me from up the beach, covering the end of his phone with his hand so nobody on the other end could hear my screams. He looked the way he did when I came into his home office when he was working, as if the interruption had temporarily thrown him off task, and he had forgotten who I was, and why I had just come through the door and was, bit by bit, like a character in a futuristic spy movie, gradually swiping in and assembling these pieces in the air. He had the same expression of panic, as if he had lost his moorings in space and time and was drifting by on a fragment of satellite. But then I realized it was not that same expression, it was a different form of it, a related panic, seldom seen in Rafael, and that it was not about me interrupting his call, but about his fear of what was happening now, and what would happen next, what had perhaps already occurred.

"Shelley!" Brad barked in my phone, in my hand. "I'm waiting!"

I noticed—rationally, as you notice things outside yourself—that my right hand was trembling as I moved it back up to my phone to unmute it, and that it took me several stabs to hit the right button.

". . . leading to dominance in the global market for wearables," I said, breathless.

"What? What happened?"

"Sorry, was I not clear about how that last one is different? It's not intuitive, I know. Took me a second too. Do you want me to take you through it again?"

"The phone cut out," he said. "Bad connection. I got radio silence there."

"Oh, God," I said. "I was just going on and on, I'm so passionate about this idea I didn't even realize. It must be on your end.

Can I buzz you back from a different line? I'm just about to go into this meeting, but I can touch base following."

"I'll be out of pocket for a few hours," he said, "but we'll connect soon."

It was four in the afternoon in Cap Ferrat, and eight in the morning back in the Bay Area, in the blond-wood and steel office where Brad Barsh swiveled in a leather-upholstered ergonomic chair, hunched over his calculator, figuring and plotting. Brad had a way of stroking his HP 12c when he talked to you, fiddling with it the way someone else would twirl a pencil. In meetings, he caressed the calculator with tender attentiveness, looking over to check its display, sliding it into and out of his pocket. It was like a lover. Except that his relationship with it had so far outlasted all his human ones.

The call cut off. Call Ended, my phone said, and with it a swell of hot worry flipturned in my stomach and I threw up on the ground, a thin hot stream of yellow liquid that made a little divot in the sand. Fennel salad and Chablis, reformulated into something bright and horrible that burned my throat. I coughed and screamed her name again, with the bitterness stinging my throat. Some shirtless men, shiny-shouldered and tanned above their shorts, looked over at me.

"A little girl," I said, my voice choppy, wiping my face. "*Une mademoiselle très petite.* Have you seen her?"

They shook their heads slowly, and looked at me with concern, or perhaps incomprehension. The contours of their chest muscles glistened in the sun.

"My daughter is lost," I said, and they looked at me with amazement. They waited for me to say more. I shook my head, unable to waste time with them, and retreated. They went on with their conversation just as before.

There were boats and fishermen visible on the far horizon where the water met the sky. The tide was low and the sand wet and packed. I looked down at my footprints, fading out behind me. I ran lightly back across the sand looking at the dips and furrows, looking for my footprints, for Rafe's, and for hers. It was hard to see any of them.

"Nova!" I yelled.

Maybe she went to pick up a sparkly rock, a shell, a leaf, a petal. Our nanny's affectionate nickname for Nova was Hoarder Junior. The nanny called herself Hoarder Senior. Rafe and I prefer a minimalistic, well-edited, rigorously curated aesthetic.

Across the street from the beach was a tall pink hotel with white awnings. Rafe was silhouetted against it, tucking his phone back in his pocket.

I ran toward him and our infant son, facing outward from Rafe's chest in his baby carrier. The baby's placidity crumbled on seeing my face—his face reddened, his features slitted up, and his expression twisted into a wail. I reached out for his little gobbet hands and squeezed. His little eyes fixed on me, and I concentrated on looking calmly at him until his sense of serenity reconstructed itself, bit by bit. People need to know their leader is in control.

"Anything?" Rafe whispered.

"Not down that way. Should I call someone?"

"I think we should go up the road," Rafe said. "Maybe she's gone that way." A forced optimism in his voice, unconvincing: "Maybe she saw a cat or something."

I nodded, pretending this was a viable theory, using his attempt to reassure me to reassure him. "Maybe." I looked out the other way, at the boats and the blue water. I couldn't still the spinning disc of my heart. My chest felt tight and sore, as if my heart would break through the wall of my ribs. A liquid seemed to be seeping through me, and I could sense it, dark and molasses-thick, smothering me from the inside out.

"If she went that way," Rafael said quietly, looking out at the water, "then it's already too late. So we might as well both go look on the road."

I looked out again at the sea, so unbelievably beautiful, so tranquil, like a cool solid-state drive withholding its secrets. A huge cruise ship lay like a brown thumbprint on the horizon. I stared at it, hoping it would tell me somehow if she were down there, underneath, if she had slipped through. She could swim a little. She had gone to lessons with her nanny, Melissa, and had a private instructor at the Stanford Aquatics Center on Tuesdays. I had taken her to a makeup class on a Saturday once—the pool didn't look the way that Melissa had described it, which irritated me—and watched Nova scream at the instructor and not put her face in when they got to the end of the song, when she was supposed to. I changed her in the family locker room afterward when she was wet and smelled like chlorine, laying out her little clothes on the bench and trying, ineffectually, not to let them fall in the floor puddles. She shrieked as I dressed her. She shrieked when she got into the pool and then again when she got out. But she couldn't swim very well. I wasn't sure really how well she could swim. She was loud—that was something.

"Who are you calling?" I asked Rafe. "Should we call the police or . . . ?" I was not ready to call the police. If I called the police it might be in the news, even if she were just eating one of those double ice cream cones in the company of a nice lady, just a dozen yards from here, or had found a narrow wall to walk along and was trying it out, again and again. But if I didn't call the police, and Nova was dead . . .

"I'm calling Melissa," Rafe said firmly. "Let's get her back here."

I tried to remember everything I knew about handling a crisis. Every quarter I did media training with an anorexically thin PR consultant whose stylish clothes were all several sizes too big—even her silver watch was sized for a girthier wrist. It slid down her arm to her elbow when she gestured, which I found worrisome but strangely seductive, though it was not a look I would try to pull off. On these occasions our PR director and I went to this firm's offices and spent a morning in their boardroom, where the consultant, ever gaunter, took me through rehearsals of crisis communications scenarios, ever dicier, and what I would say to the board, the press, the police, the investors, the public. Honesty was part of it, and the Four Cs—I couldn't remember, but they would come to me—Clarity (that was one) and doing all you could do to make the situation right (Correction), but making sure that first you'd secured the area, and kept people safe. Was that Care? Was Care one of them or was I just now thinking that it should be? Respond immediately, but defer important decisions until you have the information you need. That was what you were supposed to do. Although sometimes you couldn't get complete information, and in that case you made the best call you could and were straight about why you made it (Candor). People forgive errors if you don't try to cover them up. It struck me that my training, even the intense three days I'd spent when I first assumed my current high-visibility role, was mostly about press conferences, press releases, and staying on message with reporters. I knew it was crisis *communications*, crisis *response*, and not crisis handling or crisis prevention, but all at once it seemed peculiar to me that I had not had more training in how to fix a crisis itself. What if our product's components melted down, or were found to be radioactive, or our servers were bombed and so were our backups, or hacked, or our manufacturer was lying about the ages of those rather slight young-looking women in blue smocks in our Malaysian factory? I had good people in place at work; I had the tools to go forth and convey how sorry I was, and even suggestions for what to wear to look suitably serious doing it (it was all in the tool kit the consultant had made for me, the outfit ideas, the reassuring notes, the mnemonics—but where had we put the tool kit?). I would say how seriously our company took this, how hard we were working to remedy it. Did I also have the tools to make it better? Who would do that? And where was Nova?

"Nova" means new, it's the root of the word "innovate," and it's innovation that brought Rafe and me together, our shared passion for growing small tech companies into high-performing global leaders. Nova is our joint innovation, our first child.

Rafe and I walked along the main road, past a couple of kiosks that sold ice cream cups, inflatable rafts, rude T-shirts, and low, sling-backed beach chairs. We passed a building of pink plaster with an elegant fretwork fence. On its front porch, wicker chairs embraced the rumps of people much less stressed than we were, and above them stretched an awning with the hotel's phone number—a very long set of digits—printed on it in blocky type.

I caught up to Rafael, who was walking faster, ahead of me. The toothpick shadows of boats' masts were still bobbing on the pavement.

"How'd your call go?" I said helplessly to Rafael. You might think, how could I ask that at a time like this? But it was hard to know what to do, it was my reflex, and Rafe and I talked always about work. It was a self-leveling sealant that coated every surface of our lives, and seeped into the cracks and fissures of every moment. It was our hello, goodbye, how are you, I love you.

"Eh," he said. He shrugged. He was laid-back and quick, nimble in business or on the squash court, someone who never worried or stewed, and he seemed uncharacteristically blank.

"Let's focus," I said. "Brass tacks. I'll go this way, you go that way."

He nodded.

"What'd you tell Melissa?" I asked.

He looked surprised, as if he had forgotten he'd called her. "That we needed her ASAP and not to bring anyone with her.

That it wasn't looking good. I told her to get the concierge to get a car and not use a taxi."

I nodded. That's standard procedure when you're doing something in the gray zone—better to use a private contractor, someone you can track down later. Although, were we in the gray zone? This wasn't our fault, really. But I nodded. Rafe was a lawyer before he got into finance and you could tell—he was always thinking of ways to limit our future liability and he never put a damn thing in an email, ever.

We reached the end of the commercial strip, and we kept walking. There was nobody on this part of the road. The houses were small and pastel-colored, smack up against the edge of the road with no front yard or clearance at all. Some distinguished themselves with elaborate white plasterwork rosettes, some with rooftops edged in scalloped red tile. All the houses had a bleached-out look, as if all the saturation had gone into the sky and the water and the smoky-green low mountains across the water, and there was nothing left for the buildings except a bright, cool, glowing paleness. Everything was elegant except us. We so rarely wore casual vacation clothes, and the ones Rafe and I had brought with us didn't look right. My shirt was the wrong style, too boxy—I realized I had been wearing it ten years ago, at a thought leadership retreat in Jackson Hole. My pants, loose, drawstringed, and chic in the catalog, were a little tight. My assistant still thought I was a size four. I had not found the opportunity to set her straight. We looked like any vacationers, which was OK, of course—this was our real life—but my view of the situation was beginning to widen, and I could suddenly see the photographs that might be taken, by the police, and the newspapers, and just how sloppy we'd look, how negligent and flummoxed and pathetic and guilty. How American—that too. I thought of calling Deedee, the crisis communications professional. But that would make me seem guilty, in the event that someone later pulled my phone records.

I could hear the baby, Blazer, whimpering and gearing up for a cry. I nursed Nova for the first few days of her life, until my schedule made it impossible, but for Blazer we used a gestational carrier, which was great because I didn't lose any ground during the pregnancy. But some dormant mammary gland in my chest prickled hard, like an electrical shiver, as if a switch had been turned on, and I could feel my breasts swell into hardness from the core out. I rubbed the left one with the opposite hand, a quick massage to loosen things up and spread the pain around, and then the other. A shiver pulsed up my spine.

"Nova," I muttered, in a slow, grunty, involuntary repeat. I stared at the front of one of the little houses, my eye jerked upward by the twitch of a white curtain in an upstairs window. I walked faster. The sidewalk, which did not deserve that title, which was only blue slates set erratically along the side of the road, ended. The road ahead narrowed. A wall made of stone blocks, like naturalistic Legos, ran along one side. Lichen grew out of the crevices. On the other side the road was open to the coast. I couldn't imagine Nova walking up this narrow road. She likes to stick to the tried-and-true, as her preschool report put it. She's not known for exerting herself. I turned around and ran back toward the town and Rafe.

Something choppered overhead. I looked up and saw a dark spot curve over the water and around the side of the cliff. Slightly strange. Perhaps headed to Nice. My phone buzzed and I looked down at it. I wouldn't answer even if it were Brad. Not now. My assistant perhaps. But it was a new call from an unknown number. The number was long with too many digits to be American. I gazed at it—maybe from the organizer of the conference I was attending in a few days—and sent it to voicemail.

Rafe had gone a long way, but I could still see his tall, lanky shadow up ahead. He was moving away from me, down the road. I sprinted toward him. I hardly felt the effort; the ground surged by as if I were hovering above. I reached Rafe. My phone was ringing again, a buzz I felt spreading across my skin carrying a lidocaine numbness with it. I put my hand on his shoulder and he whirled around. I held up my phone. "Do you know this number?"

He shook his head.

I answered before I could stop myself.

"Hello," a voice said. A male voice, European-sounding, unfamiliar, the kind of voice that evokes armchairs and mustaches. I did not say anything. I looked quickly to Blazer, still fastened into the baby carrier on Rafe's chest. I put my hand over him, as if that would provide an extra level of protection to keep him in there. I could hear my own heartbeat in my ear and tightened my hold on the phone.

"Shelley Stone, yes?"

"Speaking," I said. "Who is this?"

"Are you missing a child?" the voice inquired. I almost dropped the phone. It popped out of my hands and I caught it again. I pressed Speaker. I needn't have bothered; Rafe was right there, his scalp pressed to mine.

"Who is this calling?" I asked, in a very credibly neutral voice. Rafe put his hand on my back to steady it. Shadows of horrors— ropes, rafters, knives—flickered in my mind.

I sensed this had not been what he expected and heard scuffling on the other end of the phone. "Ah, you can call me Enrique."

"Let me speak to the child."

"Of course."

I gulped hard. The period of silence went on longer than it

seemed it should have. I thought, I'll count to five. But there was still silence. I felt hot shocks in my pelvis, like falling.

"Hello," I said, to no response. "Hello. Hello? *Bonjour?*"

Finally the quality of the silence changed, as if someone else were breathing it in.

"Is that you, darling?" I said. "It's Mommy. Mommy loves you. Sweetie, are you there?"

"Eggs," Nova said calmly. Her voice on the phone was high-pitched and tinny. It sounded unlike her, like just one thread of her voice, as if the frequency at which she spoke was untransmittable by ordinary technology.

"Are you all right, sweetheart? Are you there? I love you."

"Eggs," Nova said.

"Did you say 'eggs'?" I said, though I knew that was what she had said.

"Where's Eggs?" she said.

"Eggs is at home," I said, wiping the snot and tears off my face. "Way back home, many miles away. Where are you, sweetheart?"

There was no answer except a thud, as if she had dropped the phone. Rafe and I exchanged looks. Then the man's voice came back on the line.

"I was out walking and who did I find in town but this tiny girl, all alone. Very small and all alone in this large town. Shall I give you our address so you can come to fetch her? Of course — why am I even asking? I know you will be right over. It's not complicated but sometimes visitors have a difficult time, so I urge you to listen carefully." His words rolled out, salted and seasoned, in very burnished though not quite idiomatic English.

"Sure," I said, "of course, thank you." I lip-spoke to Rafael: *Call the police?*

Why?

"What happened?" I asked. "Where did you find her? She was right with us and then suddenly she'd wandered off."

His answer was mumbly, vague. I took down the directions.

I was distrustful, confused, but of course grateful to know she was all right, and holding out hope that my distrust was misplaced and that Nova had been miraculously rescued by this nice person. He hadn't mentioned a ransom. There was nothing hostile about his tone. He seemed avuncular, friendly, possibly a valuable new contact. But it was all very strange and I felt the penny hadn't yet dropped. "Thank you for keeping her safe. We'll be right there."

"Is this some kind of trap?" I asked Rafe.

"This is France, not Venezuela. I don't think . . . but . . . you're so suspicious."

"It's usually an asset," I snapped. And then, and this is very unlike me, I burst into tears.

Chapter 2

We clicked Blazer into his car seat (laboriously, getting my finger pinched in the process), and the three of us sped off in our rental car, the windows down, the mood tense. Nova's sticker book, bright and forlorn, riffled open on her empty booster seat. Blazer, thumb in mouth, eyed it with interest.

Enrique's directions led us away from the coast, into a maze of roads. It was, as he had warned, confusing. We edged down a road wide enough to admit only one narrow car. Stone walls, tall hedges, and the backs of pink and white garages tidily bounded each side, so close I could have reached out the window and touched them with my fingertips. I kept my hands inside the car, though, and tapped at my Conch to get directions, trying to call up something coherent on the GPS. I'd lost track of which direction the ocean lay. The map showed a tangle of blue spaghetti, and none of the roads was named what it should have been. We missed several turns. Then the street we were on ended abruptly with an iron gate and a sign: *VOIE PRIVÉE SANS ISSUE ACCES INTERDIT.*

"It means something about internet access," I said.

"Nope," Rafe snapped, throwing the gearshift into reverse. He's multilingual. We wheeled backward toward the next turnoff and corrected our course. We went by a garage where cars were being repaired and a run-down commercial street where workers were loading pieces of debris into a skip. Across the street a cement mixer churned, as clean and glossy-white as one from Nova's Playmobil set. I consulted the GPS, groaned, and shook my head and Rafe reversed again.

We passed a couple out for a stroll. She was in white linen; he had on a baseball cap and was eating an apple as they walked. I watched them with amazement and a pinch of scorn, and continued to dislike them even when we had driven well past. I could not remember the last time I had meandered around like that. Some people chose a very low degree of difficulty for their lives.

The address Enrique had given us turned out to be an apartment building from the 1960s or '70s, pale brick striped with orange balconies. It did not look very nice. Motorcycles crowded the sidewalk in front of the building, and toylike little cars stared out from their shallow parking spaces with their bug-eyed headlights. I double-checked the address.

"This is it," I said to Rafael.

I felt scared. You'd think nothing could scare me anymore, not after what I'd been through. But there was something off about this. Why, if he had found a child, would he have brought her back to his apartment rather than to the police station or a nearby café? How had he gotten my direct line?

"Does Nova know my phone number?" I whispered to Rafael.

"I've just been thinking about that."

"Text Melissa. Ask her."

We glanced back at Blazer, asleep in his car seat, his little neck creased, his head fallen forward.

We got out of the car, dillydallying with the doors, the baby carrier, opening the trunk to gaze balefully at the stroller, which neither of us could reliably open since we never did it. I looked up at the building and on one of the balconies, about a third of the way up the building, a man was waving enthusiastically. He turned and pulled a little girl out from inside and she stepped out, shielding her eyes from the sun, carrying (but about to drop) a small white dog. Seeing Nova there, looking ordinary, unhurt, my breathing suddenly became labored.

"My baby!" I cried, quite involuntarily. "My baby!" Some shred of me was amazed by this display of emotion, by the fact that I was, quite completely, losing it.

"Coo-coo!" the man cried. "Fourth floor!" He was short and Mediterranean-looking, and wearing a flat cap, which he took off and waved at us.

"Enrique?" I said, and when he kept waving, "Enrique!" Strangely, seeing him waving his cap allayed my fear that this was a kidnapping scheme. It was too corny, and his joy at seeing us seemed too joyous. Rafe inserted a semiconscious Blazer into the chest carrier, threading each fat leg through the openings, and with bemused looks at each other we went into the building.

"Which floor?" I said anxiously, and pressed the elevator button. It did not light up, so I pressed it again and again, even after the elevator stirred into action.

A little way down the hall a door was propped open. Before we reached the doorway, she saw us. Nova shrieked, ran to us, and, as we tried to catch her up in our arms, ran past our legs and into the hall. "Where's my Lissa?" she cried, discovering that the hall was empty. Reluctantly, she turned back toward us.

"It's just us," I said, with a controlled smile at the man in the room. I completely believe it is a good thing she has such a closely bonded relationship with her caregiver, and every child development expert has said that consistency and quality in child care are what create good outcomes. We have an excellent nanny, the best. But it pricks, I'll admit it. There are trade-offs.

Enrique, on the other hand, seemed thrilled to see us. He

welcomed us in. A woman brought out rooibos tea on a painted tray. I did not catch her name nor her relationship with Enrique, which they did not explicate. She had long dark hair and smiled warmly but said very little. At times she seemed his wife, at other times a maid, or perhaps a cousin or business partner or something like that. I like to square things away, but I felt like they might view this as an invasion of privacy. The room was so personality-less and sterile that it gave me this impression. There was one droopy leather sofa in the room, and a pole lamp of a type that I think was banned in the United States as a fire hazard, and a folding beach chair, and a woven blanket that had been spread on the thinly carpeted floor like a rug. Nova said nothing but, resigned to only having us, buried herself in our legs, and I held her across my lap on the sofa. But then we had to sit for a while and nod politely, while Enrique spoke at long length about how he had come across her in the middle of the commercial strip while walking his dogs and asked her where her parents were. He did a long, joyful imitation of her stony refusal to answer, of her constant reference to "Eggs," a word he could not correctly pronounce, which caused me, each time I could feel it coming in his conversation, to squeeze my toes together proactively so I could stand to hear it. The way he said it brought to mind the way I felt about the hard-boiled eggs in the cafeteria salad bar during my pregnancy with Nova, staring at me with their devilish yellow eyes.

A white dog jumped up into my lap; two others yipped and raced each other from behind a louvered door and around the living room.

"Eggs is a dog," Rafael explained. "He looks a little like these guys."

"Ah!" Enrique said, "Eggs is your dog!" and he laughed and laughed while we smiled uncomfortably.

"No," Nova corrected in a soft voice, but he did not catch

it. Nova was correct—we didn't have a dog, technically. Eggs belonged to our housekeeper, and since Jacqui lived in, Eggs spent a lot of time at our house, and for complicated reasons we paid the dog walker, which gave us a certain stake in her ownership. But Enrique was wiping his eyes with mirth.

"These dogs are named Gigot, Gage, Giselle. And in the other room Gevant, and Gillie, and that one, that, you see, is Georges." He pointed.

"All Gs," Rafael murmured instructionally to Nova.

"No accident," Enrique said, and a flash of something in his "No accident" knifed me in the chest, seemed to slip, unresisting, deep into me, and made me straighten up for a moment as if it had hit a reflex between my shoulder blades.

"Why, do you like G names?" I said warmly, inanely, but with the genuine curiosity that is one of my vaunted traits as an executive.

"It was the year of the Gs," he said.

Rafe nodded. "Excuse me?" I said. "What made it that?"

"They are littermates. They were all born the same year. In France it is traditional to name dogs for the year they are born. The year they were born was the year when all French dogs, by tradition, were named with Gs. The next year, it is Hs."

"Really?" I said. "That's fascinating. You know, in America we prize individuality. I can't imagine us all doing that, can you?"

"In America," Rafe said, "all dogs are named Max."

"That's not true," I protested.

"Eggs," Nova pointed out.

"We can't ever adopt a standard," I said brightly. "Not without debating it first. It must be part of our national character to dislike conformity and embrace rebellion. I once read a fascinating article about how America has a long history of 'standards wars'—AC/DC, railroad gauge, Betamax versus VHS." I gestured expansively. It was interesting to consider the cultural differences and the way they foster, or don't foster, innovation in tech. Although nobody present, except me, seemed at all interested.

Rafe was pulling out an eyelash, his signal that he could not wait to leave.

The woman was trying to engage Nova. She had a little doll, orange-skinned and trollish, and was pretending to make it dance. "Do you like dolls?"

Nova's heavy eyelids rose and she stilled herself to stare back. Her expression was cool and condescending. "I'm not that into dolls," she said, clearly. I held her tight against me. I was proud of her. Dolls are so problematic: they reinforce stereotypes and beauty standards of race, sex, age, and body type, plus their hair gets stiff when you take them in the bath. People are always giving Nova dolls—white female dolls in flared dresses—and they are sprawled around like a sordid sorority recruitment party taking place under her bed.

While Enrique turned his attention to the dogs—and suddenly another trotted in, toast-colored but the same size—Rafe slid his phone out from the space between our thighs and turned it slightly so I could read the text. It was from Melissa, and it said, *Nova doesn't know your number. Apologies, will work on it.*

"Really." Enrique smiled. "It is excellent. Very—how do you say it?—*pratique* for studying the . . . genealogy of the dogs. When we walk the dogs"—he mimed walking by walking two fingers along the plane of his opposite palm, for Nova's benefit, I suppose, although she was on firm ground with that concept—"we meet other dogs, and we know by their names if they are the same age, or how old. You see?"

"Interesting," I said.

We all sipped our tea and contemplated.

"Thank God you were able to find us!" I kept my voice light, cheerful.

"The girl told me," he said. "She is very smart."

"Huh," I said. "Very impressive, sweetie." I patted her. It occurred to me that he had not used her name once, and I was avoiding giving it to him.

Enrique, despite his clownish exuberance, seemed to pick up on something in that exchange and suddenly became cannier.

"Perhaps it was not exactly like that," he admitted.

"Oh?"

"You see, I asked her the name of her papa, and she told me but I could not understand it." We nodded. Rafael's name was not easy for Nova to say. "And so then I asked the name of her mama, and she told me. And when she said your name, I said, does your mama run a big company? It is called, um, Conch? With computers, machines?" He wiggled the fingers on both his hands out to the side, to simulate a kind of busy whirring, or perhaps typing on one of those ergonomic split keyboards. "Because I know that name, you see, and I thought you could be the same one."

"It's a very common name," Rafael said, with perhaps a twinge of hostility.

"It is not so crazy that she, the one Shelley Stone, would come here. It is beautiful, yes? There are many meetings at the big hotels."

"You recognized my name? Really?" I have occasionally been recognized in shops or restaurants, only in the Bay Area, usually only right after I've been in the news. Not terribly often. People do double takes, but they don't take my picture. Nobody is that interested in me.

"I am very interested in business," he said. "I read many American magazines." He got up and went through the louvered door, which swung with a creak. Rafe and I looked at each other; I tried to read what he was saying with his eyes and couldn't tell if he was exasperated or just hungry. The man returned with an armload of *Forbes*es and *Fortune*s with sticky notes poking out from the edges. I had a brief glimpse into the next room, which seemed utterly empty—not even a bed. An apartment with nothing but back issues of my magazines? It was like a stage set. My grip on Nova tightened. He held up an old copy of the *Harvard Business Review*, my favorite magazine. "You are inside, right?" He began flipping through it looking for the profile about me. I didn't help him, though I did know right where it was. I just smiled with tense lips and held Nova close.

"I have a business I have started," he said. "I have a business plan for this company. Would you review it for me?" He smiled very delightedly at this idea, and I, reluctantly, nodded. I was beginning to see what this was about.

"Sure," I said. "Do you have a copy? Do you want to email it to me and I'll email you back with some thoughts? I'm absolutely happy to do that for you. Let me give you my card and we'll stay in touch. But we should be going soon. Thank you for your hospitality, and of course for finding Nova—our daughter." I corrected myself quickly, but not before I saw an instantaneous look of confirmation cross his face.

"I'll print you a copy now, and you read it, and then we can talk a little, OK? I think you might be very interested. Maybe you would want to buy the company?" he said. "Are you hungry? I have almonds and oranges for the little ones."

"I'm sorry," I said, rising from the couch, a firm hand on Nova's wrist. "We must go. I have a very important meeting later. *Très desolé.*"

"I would like to speak to the Conch founder," Enrique said. "He is young?"

"Yes, of course. I'll give you his email. I'll shoot him a message introducing you. We are sorry, but we have to be on our way. Please do send your business plan; we'd be happy to give it a look. Maybe I can even connect you with some potential investors. Oh, and, ah, I brought you a Conch," I said, reaching into my bag and offering our signature ripple-patterned gold-and-white box. I keep a few in my bag to give out. He smiled and touched his ear, and bent toward me. I could see the edge of his Conch, small and curved, hugging the little hollow on the back side of the earlobe.

"Oh!" I said, confused. "You already have a Conch. You have your own Conch." I withdrew the box, incompletely, as if I were disappointed to take it back.

"I love it," he said. "I've had it about six months. What I love is how clearly it speaks and prompts me. I hear it right there." He tapped his skull, behind his ear. "Wherever I go, it gives me interesting ideas. To do things I would not have thought of otherwise." He smiled and I felt an unpleasant shiver. "Do you know, there is a feature where when it gets in your presence, it says, say hello to my friend Shelley."

"Oh, God," I said. "How do you know about that? Nobody knows about that. It's just something an engineer built in as a little tease. An Easter egg—do you know what that is? Just something funny. It recognizes when my Conch is nearby. That was Cullen, he was just being cute," I added, for Rafe's benefit. He is jealous of my close relationship with Conch's founder. He thinks Cullen is irritating and gets annoyed I won't admit he is.

"First I've heard about it," Rafe said.

"I must have told you," I said. "It doesn't matter. He threw it in a couple iterations ago."

"I wonder something. I love my Conch. Perhaps I could see your Conch? Just, for a moment, to see the Conch of Shelley Stone?"

With a sinking feeling, I looked to Rafe, who rolled his eyes and tugged another eyelash. I hesitated. It wasn't, I told myself, such an outlandish request. It wasn't like he was asking to share a vibrator or a violin. I looked longingly to the door, and then back to Enrique. It seemed the quickest way to get out. I slipped my Conch off and offered it.

"Thank you," he said, plucking it from my hand. "What an honor." It lay in his palm, small and defenseless, the repository of all my data. A Conch is supposed to bioauthenticate its user to protect stored information, but we've had some problems with that functionality.

"Nova," he said, motioning for her to come closer, "would you like to hold this very, very special Conch?"

I suppressed a groan. "We should be going," I insisted. Rafe raked a hand through his hair and looked intensely pained.

"Have you been to the gardens?" the woman said, and I turned, surprised, toward her. I had forgotten she was there. Her voice was clear and confident, not what I had expected. "At the Villa Ephrussi de Rothschild? The lilies are very nice when they're in season. You wouldn't want to miss them."

I blinked, trying to start an answer. Maybe we would go tomorrow if work permitted, though I was secretly hopeful it wouldn't.

"Nova!" Rafe chided. I looked over. Enrique was getting down onto the floor by the futon, looking for something. Rafe's voice gave away that he didn't care what had happened, he was just saying it to show he was a parent paying attention.

"It's all right," Enrique said, reaching under the futon. "I've got it right here." He came toward me with an odd smile, my Conch held out on his palm.

I took back my Conch from Enrique and kept a tight hold on it as we shook hands and slinked toward the door. I made a mental note to dip it in hand sanitizer.

"It's a great company," Enrique said. "I can't wait to see what you come up with next. I think you would be interested in my company too."

"Thanks so much for keeping our daughter safe," Rafael said, taking the initiative to open the door and let us out.

"I love to do small acts of heroism," Enrique said. It probably sounded better in his first language. "Please don't go yet. I have a gift for *you* too."

"Um, thank you, but keeping our daughter safe, saving her—you've already given us the best gift of all, I can't imagine . . ." And without allowing room for protest, as fast as we could, we piloted Nova down the stairs and out of the building to the car.

Back in our suite I felt exhaustion and soreness in my calves. We ordered room service.

"Nova, baby, do you want some dessert? A boule de glace—that's ice cream? A soufflé citron? That's, uh, citrus. Order whatever you want, all of it if you want to. Are you OK? Were you scared?"

I took an Ativan in the bathroom and washed it down with a third of a cup of red wine leftover from last night. It tasted like the side of a person's tongue but it was fine.

Nova was silent. "Why can't we get six dogs?" she said petulantly.

"That would be too many for Jacqui to take care of," I said. "How would she have time to make *our* dinner?"

That seemed to convince Nova, and she immediately began to dump her little plastic animals all over the bed.

Melissa came in and hugged me. I tried to explain what a terrible afternoon it had been. "Sounds like it," she said. "But, look, ultimately . . . it worked out. Your heart must've been like this"—she rapped her chest. "But here she is. Safe and blessed and protected. Everyone has one of these stories. But you get to move on." She sat on the bed and squeezed Nova. She reclipped Nova's hair barrette, which was fine as it had been. "Hey, Supernova, are you feeling OK?" she asked.

"Yeah," Nova said, not looking up.

"Were you scared?" I asked.

"Enough jibber-jabber!" Nova cried. She mussed up her hair, returning it to its usual state, and continued to line up her animals.

"There was something funny about it," I said to Melissa, but I found thinking about it exhausting. Since it was not a decision-able situation, I stopped investing mental resources in analysis. Anyway, I like to tackle ambiguous problems in the morning.

Melissa got up to close the curtains, to move the shaft of sunlight away from Nova's eyes. She came over and hugged me.

"Shelley, I have to say, I want to take responsibility. It was my fault. I should have been with you."

"It was your afternoon off. That's ridiculous," I said. "*I* take full responsibility. Well, fifty percent. Rafe should have been watching her too."

She snorted.

"I'm not apologizing, it's true," I said flatly. We are fifty-fifty parents, by which I mean that we equally split the percentage that Melissa and her helpers don't do. But I have a closeness to Melissa that Rafe doesn't—for example, when she texts me photos of the kids at their music lessons, I always text back, and I don't think Rafe ever does.

"Look, I'm back on the clock now," she said, "and I'll be with them continuously till we're back at home. You concentrate on getting ready for your speech."

"Thanks," I said, although it was a total simplification that I only had to get ready for my speech. I had to run my corporation while also getting ready for my speech. She touched me lightly on the shoulder and I leaned in, almost as if I were asking her to forgive me, or maybe hug me again (she's a very skilled hugger). She must have just put on her perfume, because it rose from her very fresh, with a parsleyish topnote that I didn't usually smell. I felt that she felt sorry for me. This belief was something I took out occasionally and examined, this sense that despite all

I had she did not envy me. I didn't want to be envied, it would have made me uncomfortable; part of Melissa's appeal was that she never wavered, never gave away that her regular life did not involve Cap Ferrat or private planes, that no matter where we took her or what we did, she was never impressed (or never gave away if she was), but it was still curious to me that there was no part of my life she wanted. My work is very interesting, and in professional and material terms I think there is plenty to envy about my life. I would rather be me than the nanny to my children. It's good for everyone, of course, that the reverse is not true. But it is a little frustrating.

She moved closer, not away, and I buried my head in her shoulder and breathed in her perfume, which I think is actually not perfume but something you buy in tubes at Bath & Body Works. I don't wear perfume, but I like it on her—it's something extra, unexpected. She has a pixie cut and projects an impenetrable asexuality. I think that was part of what the nanny agency liked in her—her southern accent, redolent of a churchy upbringing, and the fact that it is impossible to believe she has ever, or ever would, have any sex life. I'm sure she must, but there's something about her that shuts the subject down, even in your own mind. Like Mary Poppins, although Mary actually does seem wildly sexual, comparatively, all skirty-flirty with Bert. I assume Melissa is a lesbian but I also know that she would never ever tell us this or give us any information with which to deduce it. We know nothing at all about her inner self. Our intimacy is a one-way valve: she knows everything about us, and I mean just about everything—the code to the house's security system, Nova's poor WPPSI-IV scores, the pay stubs in the desk, the stained undies in the laundry—but she herself is a pale fence in a cool, empty field.

The things we do know about Melissa we can count on one hand, and they seem almost staged—she likes elves and detests (theatrically) bananas, which she can smell across a room, even if there is just a tiny bit of one in a smoothie. They give her a particular headache, right between the eyes, which the rest of us are blessed never to have experienced. These seem like traits she chose to appeal to Nova, created for Nova, that will be replaced by new preferences and torments when someday she goes to her next family.

"You're a good mom, Shelley," she said, in her South Carolina accent.

"We lost her," I whispered. "For half an hour. I was sure she was gone. I would only say this to you, but I had actually come to the point where I accepted she was dead. It seemed over. It was real to me."

She looked into my eyes. Her eyes had a film of liquid over them—she was always so emotionally aware that she was on the verge of tears, not for her own situation but for her awareness of my own pain. It was a finely calibrated grief, and mostly for me—she would never have permitted herself actual tears. "It could've happened to anyone. It really could have. It's the age. They have speed but no sense." And then, switching to a wry look that disowned her previous statement, she added, more sharply, with less of the honey: "Does that make you feel any better?"

"You are very kind," I said dryly.

"My job is very safe," she shot back, and I felt tears start in my eyes and gave a sniffy laugh and then I did feel somehow a little better.

"Melissa, I'm not an alarmist" (am I? no—I'm a weigher of risk), "but tomorrow, keep the kids here. The pool and the patio, that's enough. They can play inside too. They don't need the beach anyway, they've had enough of that and Nova's been getting a lot of sun. And let me know if you see anything. You know. Anything off."

"Of course," she said. "Do you want a security detail as well? The hotel can probably arrange it."

"Can they?"

"This kind of hotel? Sure," she said. "Routine for them." I raised an eyebrow. Sometimes she reminds me of me.

"Really? That seems like overkill," Rafe said, coming out of the bathroom with his toothbrush in his mouth. A little foam bubbled out from his lips—I registered Melissa's brief, clinical, nurse-like moment of professional disgust.

"You know, it's probably overkill, but let's do it. Just to be on the safe side. Just until we're sure everything is OK." Rafe rolled his eyes at me, toothbrush still in there.

Melissa nodded. Once Rafe appears in a towel she tends to clear out quickly. She took the children away, mid-dinner, Blazer holding his bottle, and balanced on her arm Nova's barely nibbled-at "plat enfant" from room service. I heard their bath running, distantly, in another part of the suite. Rafael and I were at last alone.

"I am so wiped out I can't wait to crash," I said, setting my alarm for 2:25 a.m. so I could call into the directors' meeting back in California.

"Did you ever get back to Brad?" Rafe said, lying on his back on the big upholstered bed. I groaned.

Rafe tossed a large tasseled pillow up into the air. It hit the chandelier, which tinkled.

"Do you think this is working?" he said.

I had stepped into the bathroom to remove my makeup and I came out dabbing at my eyeliner.

"Do I think what is working?"

"Our, uh, situation." He gestured airily—headboard, you, striped curtains, the sea. He looked at me, with the advance guilt of regretting what he was going to say next. "Our life."

I stopped dabbing the washcloth and closed my mouth, which

was hanging open. "Is this something about Melissa? She's fantastic. I don't blame her for what happened today, do you? I mean, maybe she should have spoken up and said that in her opinion it was too much for us to take both kids for the whole afternoon, but it's our job to make sure she feels comfortable speaking up like that, and for her to manage up takes courage . . ."

"God, no, she's great. She's our fixer," he said. "God, Shell, can you just . . ."

"Do you think we need to hire more help? We've got a good team in place and my understanding is they're feeling a good balance of challenge and capacity, but—"

"Just turn it off for a sec."

"Turn off what? My phone's over there. My Conch is in the bathroom."

"Turn it down a couple notches. Slow down. Talk to me."

"I'm talking," I said factually. "I'm talking about how staffing levels at home might be adversely impacting the ability of our nanny to make decisions—"

"Can you hear yourself? Can you just stop talking like that?"

"What?"

"I didn't mean it like that. I didn't mean it the way I meant it either." He threw the pillow into the air again and we both watched it come down. "Look, if today isn't a wake-up call, what is?" He looked straight into my eyes. "It's all I can think about. She could have died."

I nodded, but I thought he was being dramatic.

"I took that call," Rafe said. "I shouldn't have. But you know what? You shouldn't have taken yours." A glimpse of white teeth, curved creases at the edge to set it off. A smile between parentheses.

"Why would your call take precedence?"

"Because I was already on the phone! You know what? It

doesn't matter. We're living too close to the edge. Our streak was bound to end—that's a gambling metaphor."

"I caught that," I said mildly, unhooking an earring.

"Ugh." He squeezed the pillow. "I hate what this has all become. It's just . . . work." He rolled onto his side and lowered his voice. "Can we keep it going? Are we keeping it going? Think about if we'd lost her today." He looked at me, straight on—his brown eyes, intent and boyish, fixed on this possibility. "This would be a different night. This date—we would remember it forever. The beginning of a horrible new life. Can you imagine? It could have happened. It basically did happen. If she could wander all the way to the street, she could have wandered into the ocean just as easily. God knows what that guy was up to. Who was that? It's only luck that she's here, alive. It's no credit to us."

I came and lay beside him on the bed in silence, considering this. The lowermost crystals of the chandelier moved ever so slightly in the breeze from the open French doors to the balcony. A strand of spiderweb connecting two of the crystal drops sagged nicely, in a perfect parabolic curve, forming a little bridge that a spider could cross.

"We're lucky," I said. But I didn't mean it. We're smart.

"She'd be gone," Rafael said. "We'd have lost her—there's a stunning finality to that. You don't get a do-over. Can you imagine it?"

I tried to imagine it, the way I thought he wanted me to. I pictured the inquest, what they'd say: "So, Mr. Pérez, you were on your phone? Ms. Stone, you were too? You didn't think of hanging up to search for your daughter?" He was right that it'd be awful: the jury laughing, the headlines in the paper, our jobs lost, our reputations, everything, and of course, that was leaving aside the worst part, Nova dead.

"She'd be gone and it'd be our fault," he said.

I shook my head very hard. "Rafe, no! That's the counter-factual, the what-if. We can't let ourselves get upset about that. Everything's like that. There's always a grisly alternative scenario. Behind the worst thing you can think of, there's always a worse one. People don't want to acknowledge it, but risk is always alongside us. Even Melissa said it could have happened with her there."

We both knew this was a lie; it would not have happened if Melissa had been there.

"We didn't have to both be on our phones, though," he said. "Other people, you know, can turn them off. They leave that stuff at home. I call my brother and he doesn't even know I called! He definitely doesn't get back to me. Regular people who are only VPs go on vacations where they don't even check their email except in the morning and at night. They don't have to be on. They don't have to answer every time it rings. They don't have to get up at two in the morning after a beast of a day." He eyed the alarm clock with disdain. "They don't always, always have so much riding on their shoulders. I've got to say: that life is very appealing."

I looked at him with shock. What about it was appealing?

"Haven't you had enough yet? I thought someday you'd have had enough. I thought we were both hard at work building something amazing but someday we'd be able to step back and admire it. I've believed that, all this time. But it'll never be over. You're never going to be finished. You're never going to slow down."

"Well, not yet," I said.

When we were first dating, I didn't really understand why Rafe liked me. I knew why I liked him, and I felt flattered some-one like him was paying attention to me, but I couldn't quite make it out from his perspective. Once I asked him.

"You remind me of my father," he told me then. "The way you work—the way you keep going no matter what people do to you. You're different."

I was touched, because Rafe's parents had a hard life. Rafe's father came to the United States from Cuba as a young man. He'd been an executive at a sugar company in Cuba, and in the U.S. he got a job as a cashier and started over. A few years later his brother died, trying to make the crossing by boat, and he didn't see any of his other siblings for twenty years. He had to redo his education, taking classes at a university. He was always working when Rafe was growing up, gradually rebuilding what he'd lost.

"You seem rattled," I said, getting up from the bed. "It's natural, it was scary. But in the scheme of things, it's small ball. Stuff just happens. People get in car accidents all the time. They get cancer. They wake up on an ordinary morning and there's a lump on their neck, like this woman who used to work in accounting, and a few weeks later she was dead. She went into the hospital thinking she had strep, and they said, no, you have at most four weeks left."

"So?" he said.

"I'm just saying. Likely things don't necessarily follow likely things. What you fear isn't what gets you. It's comforting to think so, but that's not the way the world works. All kinds of things happen. You don't think they will, but they do." I sniffed hard, holding back the tears. "After what I've been through, that's the one thing I know, if I know anything: all kinds of things happen." I shook off the tears and went on, more briskly. "But the flip side is, if something didn't happen, it didn't happen. Count your blessings and put it behind you."

He was quiet.

While I was giving this impassioned speech I was peeling off my underwear and putting on my white ruffled pajamas, the ones that Rafe says make me look like a Swiss milkmaid. "Heigh-ho," I said suggestively, seeing myself in the large gilt mirror on the wall. I brushed my hair.

Rafe kept his gaze fixed away from me. His face was reddened, a little swollen, out of its usual sculptural shape, the lines that, when I brought him to a company holiday party many years ago when we were first dating, made the entire marketing department exchange admiring looks. One of his eyebrows starts less cohesively than the other, more staccato, as if the brow itself is like a deck of cards waterfalling into place, shuffled by a card sharp. It gives him an air of duplicity and intrigue, not at all off-putting.

"We're not good parents," Rafael protested. "We're not used to being with the kids. They need more of *us*, Nova especially. We need to focus more on them. What if I peeled back a little, from my job. I could do some consulting. Focus on supporting you and adding value at home. I'd take the kids to the Exploratorium a few times a quarter. Isn't there a zoo? We could get rid of the night nanny. What would you think of that?"

I blinked, startled.

"You don't mean it," I said. "You'd be bored this fast." I snapped my fingers, but quietly so we didn't disturb the kids.

Rafe, who is always competitive, snapped his fingers louder, inadvertently proving my point. "I want to try something different."

"This is coming out of nowhere," I said.

"I tell you all the time how much I hate my job."

"Yes, but . . ." I thought that was just something he said as a social person, to relate better to other people who did hate their jobs. When he was sad on Sunday nights I thought it was just a different form of the excitement I felt about getting ready to storm out of the gate.

I thought, take a moment before you reply. I felt an emotional response welling up, and my training kicked in and I did not allow the emotional response to determine my statement of reaction. Let your gut have its due, I tell my direct reports, but don't let its voice be louder than the data. "Interesting idea. I might need a moment to process that," I said.

Rafe, who helped refine my patterns, my stock responses, and who knows when I'm using my work persona on him, snorted, sighed, and smacked his stack of pillows to create a dimple for his head. "OK," he said. "You want me to do a SWOT analysis for you?"—which is a basic rough-and-ready strategy and planning tool: strengths, weaknesses, opportunities, threats—"Fine, I'll do it. You want me to get McKinsey in here too? Ask them whether it's optimal to have sex tonight. Or, you know what, don't bother."

"Don't snip at me. All I wanted is to talk about it tomorrow," I said. "It's been a day and a half. And I think of us as a couple where we both have big jobs, and we're both committed to creating innovation and actively changing the world and being at the top of our fields, and it's hard for me to swivel away from that idea, because that's what I want for our family." My voice had gotten, somewhere along the course of delivering this perfectly reasonable speech, whiny.

"I am so fucking tired of innovation," Rafe said. "I'm tired of everything. I just want to sleep without you waking me up at two a.m."

I stared at him.

"Ask me how it's going in Mexico," Rafe said, swatting the tasseled pillow onto the floor and sitting up. The question turned out to be rhetorical, because he kept going. "It'll be a disaster. I can't just mark time and piss in the wind, while going to meetings and pretending it's all great. You wouldn't be happy doing that either. Things are falling apart for me, and I can't do it anymore. Maybe something new, like getting a South American office started, would be OK. But if that doesn't work for us, I'd rather just spend time with the kids while they're young, play games with them, teach them baseball. I don't know. But I can read the fucking tea leaves, darling. This—it's not working." "Darling" is the endearment he lobs when he's angry, as if he thinks it throws a lacy pink tablecloth over everything else.

He got off the bed. His dark hair was a little greasy, luxuriantly curly even in the back where it's thinning and you can see through to his scalp. He pulled off his clothes, jeans, white shirt, tossing them onto the floor near his navy blue slip-on espadrilles.

I didn't say anything. His cock was, for once, soft and hanging slightly to the right, just as tan as the rest of him. I think he goes to a tanning parlor but I don't question him about it. He is muscled, lean, and tall. I am still completely surprised by his physical body, and his interest in me. He is the most athletic guy I have ever been involved with by an exponential factor. Also, this is true: he's the only non-comp-sci major I've ever slept with.

He's not circumcised. I like that. I like the moment when the penis swells and comes uncapped. It appeals to my interest in tracking progress through measurable results.

We have sex every day we're together—why not? If you like something, you should carve out time, or, as I say, copying Beyoncé, put a ring on it, though by ring I mean a Conch alarm reminder. I have it on my personal calendar, purple shaded block, a skinny twelve minutes. I am not saying you need a lot of time. We're efficient. That twelve minutes includes getting redressed and touching up my lipstick. It's a nice release that helps me regain focus. I don't see the point of spending any longer.

"All our days are like this. It's not easy," Rafe muttered. "You think it's not easy for you? It's not easy for any of us." I started to formulate a response. I should validate his frustration and the drawbacks of our situation before moving into a positive reframe and forward-thinking action steps, but I was too tired to flesh out the framework. So instead I lay on my side, my back to him, breathing quietly in the dark.

I felt his body graze mine, and I rolled toward him, feeling tiredness, trying to evaluate a Rafael career retrenchment, hearing Enrique's voice, and knowing that in a few hours I needed to be able to add some insight to a discussion of our acquisition strategy. The currents braided and crossed and I dreamed of Melissa, riding in a speedboat, laughing as the spray curved up into the pleasant air. I woke three minutes before my alarm went off, clicked off the alarm, scooped up my phone, peed in a special quiet way I have developed, took both robes off the hook on the back of the bathroom door and piled them over my pajamas, and went onto the dark balcony to call into my meeting, the phone cupped to my ear. I breathed the carbonated night beach air, gave some sharp commentary on a proposed acquisition, delivered a couple of lapidary one-liners, corrected someone's numbers on the fly from memory, and, greatest triumph of all, when it was over, when I trod back into the bedroom and dropped the robes on the floor and slipped back into bed under the duvet (Rafe moaning as he rolled over), I fell instantly back into a deep and satisfying sleep.

When I was offered the job at Conch, I hesitated about accepting it. It was an unusual and prime opportunity to helm a startup in the wearables space, but I had always been happy in operating roles and believed that was where my strengths lay. Rafe was the one who had urged me to look for an opportunity to jump to CEO. He said I was too talented and would always regret it if I didn't, and while I wouldn't have put it so baldly, even to myself, I knew he was right. We joked that I needed a chance to inflict my vision on a company.

When Brad Barsh, Conch's chairman, called to tell me I'd

gotten the job, it was a dusky evening and Rafe and I were both at home. I'd stepped outside to take the call. To channel my excitement and keep my voice cool and controlled, I did ballet moves while Brad and I finalized the details. I gripped the patio table as a barre. *Développé* (I could still hear the way my ballet teacher said it). *Tendu*. I felt the same full-body itchiness I'd felt anticipating recitals; I'd assumed then it was from the sequins, but perhaps not.

When I told Rafe the news, he seemed genuinely thrilled. He jumped up from the sofa and kissed me. I hadn't expected that, and I was startled, gratified, and embarrassed all at once. He opened a bottle of prosecco. He carried it out into the garden, where he poured two glasses. He handed me one. We clinked. I sipped. The prosecco smelled a little like peaches and tasted like cool radio static.

"It doesn't feel as momentous as I was expecting," I admitted.

"Conch is huge. Their valuation could break a billion."

"It's so not there yet."

"You'll get it there."

I sipped. I was thinking, yes, I will. This thought pleased me. I looked down into my glass—it was already empty. "It'll mean more travel. And longer hours." I held my glass out for him to refill.

"How is it possible for you to work longer hours?"

"I'll have to be more disciplined . . . get up earlier. Less time on frivolous pursuits. Work smarter and harder."

Rafe moaned and covered his face with his hand.

"Hey, you were the one who urged me to do this. I have a lot to do to get up to speed." I combed my hair back with my fingers and rested my head on my hands, elbows propped on the table. I looked up at the magnolia tree. Pink petals lay like snow on the patio. It was spring; I had just noticed.

"You look very pretty," Rafe said. "Success suits you."

I smiled and felt suddenly a little shy. "Does it bother you, me getting a job like this? Do you wish it were you?"

He shook his head.

"I'd understand if you felt a little envious." It's important to give someone an opening to share difficult truths.

He gave me a squinty shrug and emptied the bottle into his glass—a full tip, glug, and fizz. He held the bottle upside down. One last drip. "Maybe now you can be happy."

The words vibrated my cheekbones and set off a warm surge of shame. I was happy. I was ashamed it wasn't obvious. I felt so lucky and joyous to be able to do the work I do. "What do you mean, happy? Do I not seem happy? I'm hitting the cover off the ball where happiness is concerned. I'm knocking happiness out of the park."

I still remember the way he looked at me then. It wasn't just that he wasn't buying it. His face conveyed that it was a silly thing to have said, and that he thought, any moment, I would come around to this view too. His eyes stayed on me, humorously condescending, prolonged, as if he had faith that in a moment or two I would, so we could be amused together. I felt like I had missed something that other people had figured out. Other people could talk about their feelings, but when I tried to do it, it never went well. I used to write down things in my planner like, "Practice being relaxed and relatable," and then one day someone happened to see that note and I realized you can't write stuff like that down, even if that truly is a personal goal. So now I write down other things and think that.

The next day was our last in Cap Ferrat before I flew on to give the keynote at a thought leadership conference in Barcelona. I got up early to exercise and get on top of my inbox and at six had breakfast on the veranda of the hotel with Rafael. We were on deliberately good behavior with each other, a little formal, solicitous, attentive. Croissants on square white plates were set before us, and we tore them delicately and slathered raspberry jam over the white croissant flesh. I watched with satisfaction as my hungry husband finished in four bites. The kids eat so painfully slowly that I could answer twelve emails in the time it takes Nova to take one bite of our housekeeper's Peruvian chicken. Their childhood is fleeting, but when I eat with them or sit beside them on international flights it seems like they will be children for many geologic ages yet to come, that time does not affect them the way it does me, that they are like stones being carved by rivers while I am a flash of salmon on a summer day. I sipped my coffee slowly, or slowly for me, rationing it, because despite the ostentatiously "excellent" service at the hotel, the intrusive bowing and scraping, the frequency with which the hotel staff found it possible to address me by my name, and insert it into sentences in which it did not naturally belong, I had learned from previous mornings with a tiny empty coffee cup how strangely impossible it was to get more.

"There's nothing like trying new cheeses at eight in the morning," Rafe remarked. He was off to tour a *fromagerie* in a cave inland. As an equity fund manager who stripped and resold assets from his portfolio companies, he was very interested in means of production. "You remember that cheese is basically solidified fungus."

I nodded. My thoughts alighted on what it would be like to lick shower grout, my tongue between the tiles. Our shower is very clean, at home, so it's more for the texture, I think, than the taste. Perhaps I am deficient in some vitamin. More and more I have these intrusive thoughts, off-message. I just nodded. It would have been impolite to bring up. It reminded me to take my vitamins. I take a daily men's multivitamin. Why would I take vitamins for women? Because I want less of what's important, fewer nutrients and minerals? I refuse to conspire in my own oppression.

A pale pink rosebud drooped in a vase on our table. It sagged to one side, and I tried to adjust it so it didn't.

"There," I said triumphantly, and then it sagged again. I tried to pretend it didn't bother me by making a little "ha" sound, as if the rosebud and I were in cahoots. But I could tell he knew it annoyed me; that's one of the problems of marriage, the ability to read the truth off each other's face. It obviates all the effort you make to hide how you really feel. I changed tactics. "I'd scrap the flowers, if this were my restaurant," I told him. "With this view, it wouldn't negatively impact the dining experience at all." I smiled cheerfully at Rafe, who dragged a piece of croissant shell through the last of his jam. "I'm thinking not just about the savings from no longer needing to purchase rosebuds," I explained, extricating raspberry seeds from between my teeth with the power of suction, "but even more significantly, the labor costs to source and trim them."

"Pretty though," Rafe said, chewing, giving the impression he had not been listening, a mode that he also adopts when I raise concerns about whether our five-year goals are ambitious enough (his alternative strategy is to immediately jump into a shower, if one is available). He touched my fingers as he lifted the vase away from me and put it back in the center of the table.

As instructed, Melissa kept the children close by. On an ellipse of grass beside the hotel Nova chased a yellow inflatable ball while the beefy man in a linen suit Melissa had hired pretended to read a newspaper. I watched them from the window as I worked. Melissa, wearing Blazer in the baby carrier, was chasing Nova. Blazer's little bare legs kicked the air with joy. Nova was squealing. Ecstasy flooded her face as Melissa gained on her. She dropped to the grass, exhausted and ready to be caught.

Watching Nova frolic, and seeing the man carelessly fold up his newspaper and follow them as they went inside for their snack, I began to feel a little silly. It was a lovely day and trouble of any form seemed very far away. Enrique had been friendly, if a little starstruck, Nova was evidently no worse for the wear, Melissa was so completely and competently professional—wasn't it on me, then, to let the knot in my stomach untangle? We are our own fiercest critic and worst enemy.

The weather was as beautiful as ever, but I'd had enough of leisure and working remotely and was looking forward to moving on. Once I check something off I don't look back—but that morning I had an uneasy feeling that I couldn't file away. I worked in the living room of our suite at an ornate and not very ergonomic desk, my back to the window and my eyes drifting from the screen to the cream-and-yellow striped wallpaper. It was an impressive, attractive room, though as I've said, my style preference is for clean, unfussy lines and no distractions. I made and drank some green tea, and then I called down and placed a lunch order for later: rye crisps and a filet of sole with lemon. I spent a few productive and fulfilling hours reviewing spreadsheets for a possible acquisition.

My Conch buzzed in a suggestion pattern, to let me know it would be an optimal time for a physical movement break. "Avoid blood clots and increase productivity by taking a moment to stand and stretch," my Conch prompted. I took its advice, which is especially valuable for me considering my unusual health history, and I amplified it by doing yoga poses while rehearsing my speech for the Barcelona conference. In warrior pose, I spoke authoritatively to the bathroom mirror on the topic of "Using Reversals to Create Momentum/Leading from a Mind-set of Passionate Curiosity." I fleshed out a version of a stock speech I'd given many times.

I got hungry and opened a tin of Vienna sausages that I keep in my luggage. Rafe thinks they are repulsive. They are, but they are cheap and portable and protein-packed, and they remind me of long car rides when I was a child, and my mother handing them back as snacks. I fished one of the little fingerlike sausages out of the jar and sucked on it while I read slowly. The taste of wet salty meat, like a cold damp hot dog, was comforting. It dissolved in my mouth. Sometimes disgusting things are also the best things. I left the sausage tin out on my desk and completed my most urgent tasks but found it difficult to concentrate on events and tasks further out on my calendar.

My Conch buzzed, alerting me to a new message from Cullen, Conch's founder. *Had an amazing idea for a new potential collaboration,* he wrote. *Gonna revolutionize Conch and take us light-years beyond SportConch.*

woot, I messaged back.

Heading toward even more agile, transparent, boundary-less, and truly seamless artificial intelligence, Cullen messaged. *Connected with great project.*

double woot! I wrote. *When you're ready, I'd love a demo.*

I did a call with my assistant, Willow. The familiarity of her voice was comforting but she seemed so far away. I felt unsettled. Occasionally I looked out the window to see if I could get another glimpse of my children.

At one in the afternoon the bellman rapped on the door. Lunch, finally. I sighed at being interrupted, saw him through the peephole, and then went to the dresser to fish around for some money to tip him with. I prepped the tip, slid the locks, and opened the door, all the rigmarole of hotel life. He had no trolley and no tray of food. I looked longingly down the hall, realizing that I was sick with hunger.

"Madame, a note," he said. I thanked him and glanced automatically to his name badge, "Jules," before I handed him a few euros, closed the door, opened the flap of the envelope, and unfolded the cream-colored stationery with our hotel's crest embossed at the top. The note was handwritten in inky blue.

"It was such a pleasure to meet you, and here is a gift for you." Gift? The note was unsigned. I turned over the paper, which was blank on the reverse, and looked into the envelope unhopefully. At the bottom was a key.

I took it out. Not a particularly *nice* key. It was square at the top, aluminum, with ridges running down its blade and symmetrical notching along both edges. Not a house key, or a key to a suitcase lock—a vehicle key.

I fingered it, tapped it on the dresser, and went back to work, but the key nagged at me. What was it for? It seemed symbolic. But of what?

I called down to the front desk. "Someone has brought me a message," I explained. "Was something else included? Who took the message?"

"Madame, I have no record of a message to you. What was the room number?"

I told them. "It was, yes, ah, Jules," I said, with a little flourish as I said it. It's always a good idea to notice and recall the names of the people who serve you. Once on a TV reality show I saw Richard Branson pose as a taxi driver to see how prospective employees treated him. I thought this was so smart and I've kept it in mind ever since. You never know, the man bringing you your lunch might be Richard Branson. "Ask him."

I waited for him to trip all over himself apologizing.

"The bellman must have misspoke, madame," he said frostily. "Jules does not work until Tuesday. Perhaps he did not state his name clearly."

Perhaps. That must be it.

"I must be mistaken," I said slowly. "Thank you." I put down the phone. I sighed and pried out another Vienna sausage and gnawed on it contemplatively. It gave way immediately under my teeth. Then I went into the bathroom and mixed my nasal rinse, which I always do when I am agitated, to clear my sinuses. Ever since I ascended to the so-called C-suite (it's a metaphor, there's no such thing at Conch), I have had terrible sinus problems. I filled the squeeze bottle with the saline nasal rinse, positioned the injector just under my nostril, squeezed the bottle, and let the water course through my sinuses and stream out my opposite nostril. It is a weird, unpleasant feeling, not unlike waterboarding yourself, and sometimes it creates a searing pain in the back of the head, but when it was over, when all the gross stuff at the back of the sinuses had drained and washed out, there was, once again, a clear spot in the center of my head and a feeling regained of peace and certainty.

Part 2

BARCELONA

+·+·+·+·+·|·+·+·+

Chapter 3

"Good afternoon," I said. I was standing at the center of a stage, in a golden pool of light, with a lavalier mike clipped to my boatneck sweater. I wore pants, sleekly shaped to me, a little tight for sitting but perfect for standing upright onstage, and heels, which tipped me forward so the spotlight warmed my cheeks and collarbone. I basked in the light, clasped my hands, and smiled.

Below me, off the lip of the stage, the audience stirred. Each face carried an expectant expression, lips parted. The air smelled like many people cheek by jowl, the high altitudes of auditoria, the tang of LED lights, like coated paper and coffee and the conference hotel's rosemary-mint shampoo interpreted by hundreds of scalps. Sound rose from the audience like a radio station not quite coming in, like the hiss of a creature under the carpet.

The light onstage softened and spread, and the audience, sensing progress, began to clap. As people, they were barely visible to me in the warm dark. In the first rows I could make out attentive white teeth, faces framed by negative spaces of hair that faded into the darkness around them. The faces were archetypal, ageless, like the masks of a Greek chorus, though this thought leadership conference's target demographic was entrepreneurial women in mid and peak career. As my eyes adjusted and the aisle lights dimmed, I could make out hair—brown, black, blonde, reddish, curled, ponytailed, loose—and faces, lit by a common gleam. They were too smeary at this distance to have expressions, they were mostly flesh tones and the scrawled proofreading marks of features, but I sensed a hum of anticipation, of receptivity, of lipsticks being holstered, airy gossamer scarves coiled, phones quieted, attention directed forward, upward, to me.

I had almost but not totally stopped chewing my greenroom saltine, and I took advantage of the clapping to suck the remains off my back molars and finish it up. Expectation pressed down on me, and my own small, fit body pressed back.

At the edge of the stage were modern boxy planters welded from sheets of copper, with low desert-y plants in them. Succulents. At the cocktail reception last night in the rooftop garden, the conference organizer had told me this venue has the world's largest photovoltaic installation. Wonderful, I said, sipping my mineral water. We had some panels put in at our house in California, I told her. They make enough electricity to power our pool pump. I think these planters were meant to symbolize the future, the vastness ahead. They reminded me that I was thirsty. Someone had provided me with a water glass on the dais, which I couldn't use, because despite many years of practice drinking water out of cups I feared that, with my intense focus on meaningful content delivery, I might this time accidentally pour it down the front of my sweater. That would be eminently GIFable, and also kind of damp. Couldn't risk it.

I was nervous, true. By which I mean exhilarated. Always a little, even after all this time.

They say you should visualize the audience in their underwear. Why would that help? I am less nervous giving keynotes at global thought leadership conferences than I am changing out of my bathing suit in locker rooms. I don't understand how that feels normal to some people. I am no longer appalled like I was as a kid, or traumatized like I was as a young adult, but I still lay out the clothes and, in my imagination, flip them around like Tetris pieces, rehearsing their directions and studying their entry and exit points before I strip. I rarely go into locker rooms, to be honest. I know there are people there who know me or work at Conch, even if I don't know them, or who would be only too happy to snap a photo and send it to the Silly Valley blog. My gym has a no-cell-phone policy, but there are people who might get a righteous sense of satisfaction from knowing they have taken a mental picture of my wrinkly nipples, the dimples of my bare pale cellulite-y flank, all my scars. For a male CEO to go to the gym would be OK, but somehow it's different for me. I'm in good shape, of course. Fitness is so important for image perception and energy, and having the stamina to work hundred-hour weeks. I don't have the time, but I make the time. I shower at home and get to change in privacy. So, no, I was not scared or intimidated by this: an audience of fully dressed people, reaching down to touch their conference tote bags, to steward their freebie pens and five-tip highlighters and ecru cards entitling them to a free drink at the hotel bar.

There were empty seats scattered around the auditorium. Not many. But an opportunity to do better next time. Maybe if my program description had been more concise or incisive I could have filled those empty seats.

"Good afternoon, and welcome," I said, to a satisfying burst of concentrated applause. It crested like a wave just off the edge of the stage. Just over the withdrawing roar (the late adopters), I made a little hand gesture, a little open palm with both hands that welcomed, acknowledged, and turned off the stream of applause. I am good at this, the warmly cool, the coolly warm.

She's so warm, people say. Or cool. Whichever is needed. I am versatilely temperate.

This conference lasers in on challenges for women entrepreneurs, so there were lots of women purse/sunglass moguls in attendance, and so many unbelievably sleek women, with their glossy straight hair, big encrusted stud earrings, "pops" of color, and fjordic clavicles. The venue was thronged with women in close-fitting suits with slim tanned legs. So many high-heeled booties and eye-gouging pointy pumps swinging restlessly, poised to spear actionable key takeaways.

"This talk," I said, "is about that pleasant emotion: fear." There was a smattering of laughter. When I practiced this in the shower it was funnier.

"This isn't how I planned to start," I said. I gestured. "I didn't plan to talk about this, but something happened to me a few days ago and I want to tell you about it." I paused to project gravitas, to let their attention collect on me. I whispered calmly, "It scared the daylights out of me." The silence seemed to hollow out.

"I was with my husband and children. We were on the beach not far from here." (Well, a short flight, close enough.) "A beautiful day. You can imagine the breezes, the feel of the sand, the delight of my children as they toddled around with their buckets, scooping the sand." The audience smiled. The fact that I have children is not unknown to them—I am often profiled as having a family; it's part of my brand. "And my husband and I were having a conversation, just enjoying this time together, when all of a sudden, I look up and there's the sand, and there's one of my children, and the other is . . . gone." I'm getting ahead of this story. I'm getting it out there—just in case. You have to use your material.

I paused to listen, for flicks or rustles of boredom, for sighs. I didn't hear any.

"My son's a baby, my daughter's only a little older, and they're at that age where if you're walking somewhere with them, to a place you want to go, it takes you ten times as long as it should to get there." (Gentle chortling.) "But when they want to go somewhere, they zip off and they can just . . . disappear. That's what happened—one of the kids was gone.

"Just imagine for a second, the open ocean, and a missing child. I know many of you have children, or nieces or nephews, or caring personalities. I don't have to tell you what I was thinking, or how it felt. Pure terror. Fear of the deepest kind." I didn't quite intone it as confidently as I meant to.

"So I walk out toward the ocean, and we go this way and that. Now you can probably guess, by the fact that I'm here today"—I indicated myself on the stage—"giving this speech, that this story has a happy ending." The audience twittered, but they were still a little nervous. Until they'd heard it, it hadn't really happened. That toddler, head tipped up, a look of fear in her black eyes, was still flailing somewhere off the shore.

"And it does, it's very ordinary. I'm incredibly grateful that is so. Just seconds later, we turn around and there's our child, on the sand, safe and sound, not even a drop of water on her. It turned out to be, after all that heartache, nothing, just a sight line issue." What is that? Well, whatever. Don't give them a beat to think about it. "But thank God, right? Thank God." I clasped my hands together reverently but confidently. Religion is fine for currencies and crises. "Because in those moments, and we've all had them, the intensity of fear makes us willing to bargain, willing to do anything, willing to betray ourselves, just to push away the fear. Just to feel ourselves get free of it. Even all these years later, even though I know how important fear has been to me, I still feel it. I still feel it. I'm not going to lie to you about that."

I clicked my first slide and it appeared behind me, so that I was a tiny dollhouse figure in the universe of my own Power-

Point: *260,000 people are struck by lightning each year. Fifty people in the U.S. die each year from lightning strikes.*

"Two hundred sixty thousand people," I said. "Do you ever think you'll be one of them?"

I paused as if I wanted to take time to consider, as if I wanted them to feel shame for not having thought about this enough.

"As many of you know, I am one of them. The odds are about one in seven hundred thousand that a person will be struck by lightning. Not quite one in a million, but pretty close. Those odds don't seem so long when it happens to you."

I shifted from the ball of one foot to the ball of the other, transferring the clicker from one hand to the other, the universal signal for moving on to a new section of one's inspirational thought leadership talk. The place along the top of my toe, which these heels strafe, attempted to claim my attention. I ignored the pain, as always. I ignore it so hard I continue to wear these shoes, even though they leave a sore spot every time, even though it's become an actual lesion. Once I came back from a long day of meetings and went straight into my bathroom and took off my shoes, first one and then the other, and poured blood out of each shoe into the toilet, until my bathroom looked like the climactic murder scene in a multipart BBC detective drama. (Those shoes I had to trash.) Tonight, after all this is over, I will sit on the bed and snip away at a square of moleskin to construct a protective dam to barricade the sore. I transferred my concentration onto this—the comfort that will eventually come, a cognitive behavioral technique useful in situations of physical discomfort—and let the thought float away.

I clicked to another slide: *One out of ten people struck by lightning dies.*

"Not bad odds, right?" I was speaking a little too fast and stepped on my own laugh line. I let it go.

"When I was nineteen—more years ago than I like to count—

you wouldn't have noticed anything special about me. No particular motivation or drive. Nah, nobody would have called me an overachiever. I liked clothes, hanging out with my friends. I'm going to date myself here, but I spent a lot of time *talking* on the phone." I paused, inviting the audience to snicker. "In my defense, this was many years ago!

"Time seemed . . . ample to me. I didn't worry much about the future. I didn't worry much about the present, truth be told. I didn't have big ambitions. I was hesitant, and shy, so sure I wouldn't succeed, convinced that as a girl from a small town in the middle of nowhere, no exciting paths were open to me. Oh, one other thing you should know—those of you who are around my age might remember that, although this seems crazy, it was the style then for girls to wear men's boxer shorts. Sidenote: I have to tell you, my dad found this horrifying. He used to hate it when my friends came over and we were all in these baggy T-shirts and boxer shorts. We used to say, 'Don't worry, they're totally decent. Look, we've pinned the flies closed with safety pins.' Just hang on to that thought.

"My parents were out that night. It was the night before my twentieth birthday. It was a night almost exactly twenty years ago—it will be twenty years, exactly, next Friday. And yet I remember it like yesterday. I had just finished finals and come home from college for the summer. I was excited to get together with my high school friends. It rained a lot in Wisconsin, where we lived. There were storms all the time in Marathon County. It wasn't unusual. So I was outside with a good friend in a rainstorm, just under the eaves of our family's house, sitting on a picnic cooler, just watching the rain streak down the side of the barn. We were catching up, talking, and I was holding a beer can and drinking lemonade (just kidding—you ever heard that line? No? You're not from where I'm from). So. Now. We're watching a big old sycamore tree between the house and the barn and all of a sudden it glows purple. I am not kidding—a purple light surrounds the tree like a halo. That's weird, my friend and I say, and I look over at him and notice that his hair is standing on end. I had never seen that before or since. "Your hair!" he says, because he's equally startled by mine. Or that's what he says he said. I couldn't tell you for sure, because at that moment the purple surrounding the tree surges into a brightness that for years afterward I saw every night when I was falling asleep, and that even now, twenty years later, I can still bring forth when I close my eyes, the exact cut of it, and the next thing I feel is a surging explosion inside my body as if every single piece of it, including bits I was unaware of, were being blown apart, as if— this is the best way I can describe it—my organs were bursting out from inside my skin. The pain rose out of pain into a form of obliteration. It ate the part of me that could feel pain. Then, absolute darkness. I could hear nothing and I could see nothing. So this is death, I thought. I'm dead."

I paused to listen to the audience. They were looking at me with concern.

"But what happens when you die? Who knows, right? I just existed for a moment, and then another moment, with no feeling in my body, no pain at all, nothing to see or hear, wondering what was going to happen. Was this it? There is no backup copy of your life. I understood that for the first time at that moment. There is no backup copy. You run in real time, and soon you are obsolete. You get one little handful of years that you are entitled to, and not even entitled, let's be honest, and probably not as many as you'd want. All this occurs to me in these long moments, as I exist, just this lonely tiny match-flame of consciousness in a vast dark. I wait. Nobody's coming for me. It goes on for a long time. And then I think, maybe I'm the one who has to take the initiative and move. Maybe even in death we have to be the ones who act.

"It sounds very profound, doesn't it? It could be, right? None of us here really knows."

I let the darkness sit with them for a moment. Let them try to imagine.

"I try to wiggle a foot. I can't tell if it's working, but meanwhile something's happening to the darkness. It is, very slowly, lifting, as if a giant cloth over me is pulling away. And after a long time, I can see a shape close in front of me, dimly, on a black field. And I hear something, like a whimpering moan, and I realize it's coming from me.

"Or part of me. The part of me summoning this vague, sleepy awareness isn't feeling any pain, but far away, as if from somewhere else, I can hear someone screaming, and it sounds bad. It's like a moaning scream, sometimes just a moan. There's this girl, and I recognize her voice, and she's screaming. On some level I realize I know this person, and I even know that this girl's voice is me. But I don't even feel sorry for her, I'm that disconnected. I just want her to shut up." (New slide, audience gasps.)

"At the hospital, I was put into a medically induced coma. It would have been too excruciating to be awake, even with morphine. I was under for eleven days. At the end of that time, when I was awakened, I had missed my twentieth birthday. I woke up and nothing was the same. Burns covered the left side of my body. The lightning had arced from the tree to my body, entering near the safety pin, traveling through me, and out near the beer can. And that, I tell my kids, is why you should never drink beer."

Light twittering. They were a little too shell-shocked to laugh. I don't actually tell my children that yet, because they are too young. Also, it's a little flippant, considering the topic. But aggressive flippancy works OK for me; it's a trademark.

Tight smile. I wasn't laughing either. I went on in a didactic, wisdom-earned-through-pain tone:

"When a person is hit by lightning, the shock travels through your body, it perforates your intestine, fries your neurological system, makes holes in the very walls of your cells—it's called electroporation—and it leaves along your skin a very delicate fern-like red rash called a Lichtenberg figure, which looks a bit like a very elaborate henna tattoo." (Click slide. They ooh, and then stop abruptly as if they feel guilty for oohing.) "It's almost beautiful, isn't it? Graceful. Like a fractal, very strange. A manifestation of randomness, stemming from a random event. In almost every case it fades after a few days or a week. But I still have mine, very faintly. Most of the time I don't see it, but it shows up in strange situations, under certain light—I noticed parts of it this morning in the hotel bathroom, under the overhead light. It's still there. I still have a large scar at the exit and entrance sites, also. And some other effects."

I turn brisk, analytical, almost argumentative with myself: "But what can we learn from this? Why does it matter? So what?"

(Click new slide.)

"When I came to from my coma, I was the same yet not the same. Pieces of me were missing. I would try to recall things and there was nothing there. Things like my name. Can you imagine? It was like going into your office and taking the most important file folder out of the drawer, opening it, and finding nothing inside. Like in the old days, remember, when you arrived to give a big presentation, put the CD-ROM into the optical drive, opened the folder, and there were no files, and you realized you'd forgot to burn them to the disc. Remember? Am I the only one that happened to?

"I had to relearn everything. I had lost much of my capacity to taste or smell, or experience sensation. And most of all, I knew that time was not infinite—these minutes, you will never get them back. I knew I did not have the luxury of messing around. I knew that death comes, I knew (or had a pretty good idea) of what it feels like, and I knew that my ordinary, messing-around self would never be able to cope with the challenges ahead. She was the past. She was outdated. I had already wasted a lot of time. I was not ready to die, and I made myself the person I had to be to get ahead—myself, version 2.0. I even adopted a new nickname for myself—I decided to start over with something fresh. The new me was going to go by Shelley."

Sometimes I feel like this part is the weak link of my speech, the connection between this odd and horrible event and the singularity of my later life, of my ability to drive forward a multinational corporation. I sometimes wonder if the connection is there at all, but it must be, mustn't it? The unusualness of the experience, the way it disassembled my brain and rewired it, the way all of my insides were affected . . . it must explain something. Women hold the CEO job at less than five percent of Fortune 500 companies, and that rate only climbs slightly—I think it's five-point-one percent—when you expand that to the Fortune 1000. Women have around sixteen percent of the directors' seats in corporate America. Ten percent of companies have no women directors at all. Surely there's something here that has given me this ability. Everyone sitting in the audience takes it on faith that it does, that the shot of electricity and the resulting agony were what it took for me to get here. Or that I am special, chosen in some way, which is why when that beam of lightning came down, it jumped from the sycamore to me.

What it really gave me is this story to tell at conferences and conventions and in front of people, and privately, in small meetings late in the day, or after dinner, once in a while, when for some reason I am feeling expansive and want to give someone a tiny bit of currency. It gave me something nobody else has, the certainty of being set apart.

"The fear I felt during thunderstorms—that I continue to feel during storms—was debilitating." I click onto a slide of my aunt's bichon wearing a thunder suit and cowering under the coffee table. The audience oohs in a different tone. "I always want to say to Lulu, you have no idea, honey." A needed light moment.

"But when you've experienced true fear, and come through it, you realize that death is always at the door, and fear is only an emotion—it can't protect you. Fear can be the body's way of alerting you to opportunity. If I had feared the storm and gone inside, I wouldn't have gotten shocked. But if I hadn't been hit, I would not be here onstage today. I would not be at the helm of one of the world's most exciting corporations, bringing life-changing technology and actionable intelligence to everyday people like you. I would not be the person I am."

I've told this story so many times, I've written it, I've been interviewed about it. I walked into a boardroom once and some-one said, he's an Olympic fencer and he's a national lacrosse champion and she was hit by lightning as a teenager. And of all those achievements, mine was the rarest and best, the one that made the person do a double take and say, "Really? Wow!" Mine's the only one people really want to hear about. Telling this story has burnished it and peeled the story off the kernel of what happened. At first they were attached, the happening and the telling, and gradually they detached, until, when I try to remember now, it comes already wrapped in my old words. I can only remember my own phrases as I was interviewed, the lights, the mic hanging from the boom at the edge of my periph-eral vision, the sympathetic face of the TV interviewer with her perfectly invisible pores and exaggeratedly interested responses, not how it felt. Even the shape of the light, which for such a long time I could remember without wanting to, and which I tell people I still can.

Instead I talk about risk and failure and passion and what they have to do with success, which is everything. They're all words that the tech industry has co-opted and that are very popular with a certain proportion of a group I have heard called the technofuckoisie and have spent too many hours in rooms with. I explain that success itself, hard work, and leadership as I am now experiencing it, is itself an ongoing experience of pain and fear and nausea, sleep deprivation, and the knowledge that every bit of it is close to being blown away. When I start talking about nausea and sleep deprivation and bone pain, about exercising, about the lesions on my foot, I notice that people pull away. That isn't really the part of my life they covet. They want the Tesla. They are less interested in getting up at 3:00 a.m.

"What can I tell you? Risk is OK. Failure is OK. Disaster is OK. But only sometimes, if you happen to survive and overcome. In fact, sometimes disaster is the route that takes you to the island you couldn't otherwise reach. When Cortés landed in America with his men, his first move was to burn his ships." (Click slide.) "A bold move, and what it says is: there is no going back. I am not advising going out and getting struck by lightning. But I urge you to take that difficult path, because it will lead you to a place very few people can bear to go."

I talked a bit about Conch, Inc., being careful to stay on the thought leadership side and linking it to human potential. I wasn't shilling, which is prohibited by this conference, just connecting it to my trajectory (that's permissible). "Here's a question to think about. In life, are you a cord, or are you a battery? Do you stay tethered to the wall, or are you mobile, bringing your energy with you out to the world?"

Last slide: *It is not because I am strong, but because I am weak, that I am strong.* A quote from a "thinker" because my assistant couldn't find the source. The thing is, none of these speeches hang together all that well if you really analyze them. Mine always scores in the top quintile for inspiration and actionable intelligence in the post-conference evals.

As I spoke I noticed a man in the audience. He was one of just a few men. I'd seen his face before. I kept talking, but I was certain I recognized him. It was not until I was finishing that my mind was pulled back to the apartment, and the fear and relief of finding Nova, and I realized it was Enrique, along with the woman he'd been with. I gazed at them, which I could do because the audience was so big, and I strolled across to the other side of the stage so I had a better view. It was still hard to see much—he was in shadow, and there were so many faces out there, all of them fixed on me, and it was time to wrap up. I smiled and bowed my head with satisfied reverence as the audience applauded.

And it was all over in seventeen minutes, which is the optimal length for a substantive idea talk that challenges preconceptions and stakes out a counterintuitive but motivating inspirational position.

Afterward I went to the private restroom for the presenters and removed the nasal squeeze-pot and my bottle of distilled water from my bag. I pumped saline solution into my nostril with sharp squeezes till it gushed out of my opposite nostril, and cherished the feeling of absolute head clarity and coolness, and an empty place at the center of my head that for once had nothing pressing on it.

Chapter 4

I was tired after my speech, eager to say my goodbyes and fade into a cab for the quick trip back to my hotel. I longed for the moment when, alone at last, I could shoot up the elevator to my room and slip into private-personhood, as into the terrycloth robe with chest-crest on the back of the bathroom door. Kick off my shoes, unhook the unforgiving clasp of my pants, peel out of my slim-cut sweater and knee-to-bra-band Spanx, and pad around the hotel room in jammy pants wriggling and undulating like a sea anemone, which is a technique my yogi, Greer, suggests for loosening the ligaments, preventing blood clots, and inviting conscious relaxation. Watch *Bring It On*, which is my favorite movie to watch after a long day of work, because even though it's stupid I relate to the Kirsten Dunst cheerleader because someone has to show leadership and make it happen when chaos is breaking loose, and the movie is truthful about the hardships associated with that, and also I love the cheer sequences. From the cab, which smelled of cigarettes and clementines, I leaned back and watched the city streak by. Satisfyingly exhausted and lulled by all the treats I had to look forward to, I texted Rafe— *Give kids a kiss for me! Speech went great!* and then my assistant, Willow—*Speech went OK, pls confirm travel and synopsize the tweets.*

I had my evening rehearsed in my head, fully anticipated, up until the moment when I'd slip between the sheets, decide on tomorrow's top three priorities, and flick off the inner light, so it was unpleasant when I arrived in the hotel lobby and a clerk rushed out from behind the desk to buttonhole me. The lobby was set to its "evening" mood lighting, with hyphens of light illuminating every counter edge, making it hard to see if he wanted me specifically or if he was mistaken or simply in my way.

"Excuse me," I said, trying to step to the side of him. He stepped the same way. We both, at the same time, stepped the other way. I once read that this thing, where you both go the same way and then both reverse it, trying to let the other by, is due to unconscious sexual attraction. I don't quite see how that can be true, but whenever it happens I take a good look at the other person, just to see what the option is.

"Ms. Stone!" he said, dashing my hopes that he wanted someone else. "A visitor has been waiting to see you."

"I'm not available now . . ." I began, and then I saw a man waving at me from a leather armchair, a small laptop open on his knees.

"Hello," I said, defeated.

"So wonderful to see you again," Enrique said, springing up with enthusiasm, the computer balanced on his open palm. The soles of my feet hurt in a way that did not leave me room to be kind, so I nodded wanly.

"Speech was wonderful!" he said. "I enjoyed it."

"You came? How nice that you traveled all this way. Thank you again for your kindness to my daughter."

"I have been working on my business plan, in case you are interested." He turned on the little computer so I could see its screen, a gridded spreadsheet. I gazed at it for a moment, and blinked, its oblong light a blot on the dark field of my vision. "Perhaps we could have a drink"—he gestured to the bar—"and I could tell you about my technology. You will find it very interesting. It is a natural complement to Conch."

"Please," I said. "I'm very tired and I have several tasks to take care of this evening. Send me a précis and I'd be happy to look it over." Something caught in my throat, which felt scratchy and sore. My tonsils throbbed in unison. My nose twitched with the effort of holding back the congestion. "Perhaps we could arrange to meet another day," I suggested nasally. Perhaps a day when I would be thousands of miles from here.

The bellman was still beside us, waiting for instructions or a tip. I handed him some money reluctantly. I wanted him to stay.

Enrique closed the netbook and held it in the crook of his arm. He seemed anxious. "You don't have to sit with me," he said. "I just need you to accept a gift. It is for you and is very important. Here—take this!" He handed me the laptop.

"I already have many computers." I shoved it back to him.

"Watch this—just give me five seconds." He opened it again, x'ed out of his spreadsheet, and summoned up a new window. I had stepped back to make it clear I was getting out of there, and then I saw something on the screen that made me step closer to look. It was me. I was speaking.

"There's supposed to be volume," Enrique said. "Your patience please, let me back it up and turn the volume up."

It was me, from the waist up, against a swirly blue background. "Hi, Shelley!" I said too loudly, onscreen, and smiled irrepressibly. My hair looked nice. I was wearing a royal blue V-neck sweater that could plausibly have been one I owned, a useful staple for anyone's wardrobe, but a sweater that, in point of fact, I could not remember ever wearing. My face was looking straight into the camera. It looked pleasant, relaxed. "It's Shelley." I paused, as if unsure what to say next. "Hi. I want to tell you to take this gift and the opportunity it represents. Good things are happening." She smiled, and I couldn't help but smile back at her. "Try it out, imagine, explore: you are in for a treat!" She smiled so warmly that I smiled again—I didn't mean to, it just happened—and the video stopped, on a paused image of myself, looking a little remote.

The real me, in the hotel lobby, was even more remote, trying to remember when I'd made this and why. I couldn't pinpoint it. Perhaps many years ago, for some meeting. I looked like myself, perhaps a little younger. Maybe it was some kind of mash-up we'd done, back when we first amped up our social media presence and we weren't sure how to do it. Maybe it had been reworked from a video chat with employees. Whenever we got a new HR person, they always had these ideas. And then they went away—first the ideas, then the HR person.

"Could I see that again?" I said, reaching for the laptop.

Enrique snapped it shut.

"I thought you were going to give it to me." Now that I'd seen it, I wanted to watch it again.

"You've seen it now. It is convincing, isn't it?" He smiled.

"The video? What do you mean?"

"It looks like you."

"It's me," I refuted.

"It's an app," he said. "It is my business idea. It creates videos of people saying whatever you'd like them to say, whatever you type in. You could sit at work while being—this is a dream of many—a YouTube star. You could make a video of yourself reading a book, for your children when you are not home. You could convince someone you said or did something you did not do." His eyes glittered.

"It was me in that video," I insisted. "It wasn't?"

He shook his head. "Did you notice the pulsing in the background? It is very rough still."

"I make a lot of videos," I pointed out.

"But you didn't make this one."

"I don't know," I said. "I only have your word for that. There is a lot that happens in my typical day and without referring to my Conch and schedule I can't be sure. Maybe a few years ago. No? Really?"

He shook his head. "No, it is the product. My company. But so far, the use of it is mostly for blackmail. That is not my dream, to be a blackmailer."

"You'll have to pivot from that," I agreed. "Can I see it again? It really looked like me." I reached for the laptop, but he held it out of reach. "Let me give it a try. It's an interesting idea."

"That was a taste. It's not ready for you to try."

"You mean it's fake? You haven't actually figured out how to implement it. You just edited some video and are showing it to me in the hope I'll bite."

"No, no."

"I'll give you this, it's an intriguing idea. If you ever get it up and running, I'd be interested in talking to you about it."

Rather than pin me down on this possible meeting, he seemed to change the subject. "I have a gift for you. Just for being so accommodating and keeping my technology in mind. You will like it even more."

"You don't need to give me a gift. You're the one who did me a favor, helping my daughter."

"Then you will do me the favor of taking it."

"I have to go upstairs," I said. "I have work to do. I am intrigued, but unless you can nail down the tech, it's not worth anything. Ideas aren't patentable, you know. And even if you could execute, I see a lot of potential legal pitfalls."

I expected him to be crestfallen but instead he looked

pleased. "It's around the corner, fifteenth space counting from the lobby. You will find it even nicer, I think. It's silver. You already have the key, I believe. Goodbye."

I watched him lope off, somewhat awkwardly, with his raincoat and his netbook under his arms. I felt like, something is happening and I don't know what. It was an interesting, destabilizing sensation.

I went upstairs to my room as I had planned. It was my time for decompressing, but I felt confused by recent events, and unsettled by the thought of whatever was out there in the "fifteenth space counting from the lobby." You have the key, I believe. No, I don't believe I do. I was interpreting it metaphorically, thinking about security keys to websites, hacker attacks, cipher keys, and I was out of the elevator before I remembered yesterday. Jules the bellman. Odder and odder. Had I even kept that key? I really believe in the practice of minimalism and how many benefits accrue from letting go. I jettison unnecessary goods—it's freeing. The universe wants to provide—that's another Greer-ism. But maybe. I went into my suite, which was small, but pleasingly so, with a glossy white TV console wall separating the white bed from the white sofa and chair. There was a balcony shaded by the leafy branches of a street tree, and no art on the walls—I like that, it feels real, like a couple's real minimalist apartment in a Danish film.

In the bathroom—also modern, with a sculptural freestanding white tub, like a teacup—I hunted through my makeup case for the key. Not there. I looked through my suitcase. No. Wait. In an interior pocket of my carry-on, I kept a bottle opener, packets of isotonic nasal irrigation solution, tampons, and a mini LED flashlight. Maybe there? There was the envelope. I took it out and shook it, letting the key shift around inside, making a satisfying thunk as it slid from one side of the envelope to the other.

I kicked off my shoes and changed into exercise clothes. I started the shower, reconsidered and turned it off, opened my laptop on the bed, made a desultory attempt to get on top of my inbox, and sent a tart punctuationless reply to a product manager who was annoying me ("you make the call"). That's not forfeiting responsibility, that's empowering and developing subordinates.

I thought about Enrique. Something about him unnerved me. Why had he followed me all this way? Surely he wasn't involved in the women and entrepreneurship summit. I remembered the strange, spare apartment where he'd brought Nova. Poor Nova—I hadn't thought much about what it must have been like for her, lost and brought there. Had she missed us? Maybe Rafe was right about her needing more time with us.

No time like the present, I thought. I think that constantly. Turn intention into action, otherwise you're a dreamer, not a doer (vote the latter!). So what if I were far away? I could call her.

Melissa, on videochat, looked fish-faced and surprised to hear from me. "Are you OK?"

"Sure, fine. Can I say hi?"

"Blazer's just going down for his nap. Hang on."

The view spun, past ceiling, wall, rug, Nikola Tesla–themed nursery paraphernalia, crib slats, and then Blazer's rump as he was hoisted, then propped on the little chair. He gummed a sippy cup, thrust it out, and smiled.

"Hi," I said. "It's Mommy."

Blazer's face was huge and looming, his skin flawless—I, on the other hand, looked like a pitted desert dweller on this webcam. The sippy cup dropped out of the frame.

"Hi, sweetie. Do you know where I am?"

"Work," Blazer said, or maybe "truck."

"I'm on a trip. Where's Nova?" Her little chair was empty.

Melissa moved into view. "Your husband took her out to lunch. They're out on an adventure."

"Oh," I said. "Oh, right, I remember now, he texted me about that." Melissa gave away that she did not buy that Rafe ever texted anyone about anything. "Let's do our song," Melissa suggested, and unself-consciously began to sing. She's a true professional, my highest compliment.

We did our song, "It's So Nice to See You, It's So Nice to Go to Sleep."

It's been fun and now it's done! Lots to do! Time to go! Clap clap, I love you. It's part of our repertoire, a playlist built over Nova's baby and preschool years, which now includes the Calming Down song, the Being Flexible song, the Wash Your Hands with Soap song, and the recent hit, in heavy rotation now and for the foreseeable future, the Look Me in the Eyes When You Talk song. I waved goodbye as the view went dark.

I sat on the bed, wondering where Rafe and Nova were having lunch. It pricked a little, in a funny way, not to have her where I expected her. It seemed like a foretaste of the time, not that far away, when she would be off doing her own activities, and she'd have a busy schedule of her own that would conflict with mine. If Rafe were here he'd hum that cat's-in-the-cradle song at me.

I turned the television on, clicked out of the TV gulag of pay-per-view options, and watched a green field in which a series of hurdles were surmounted by one bottle-nosed dog, much to the excitement of the announcers. I turned the TV off. On the coffee table lay a plate with three golden apples and a sharp, sharp knife to slice them. A clever touch, really—the hotel leveraging something inexpensive for a luxurious effect. I stabbed an apple into halves, and then quarters, then eighths. I found I had no desire to eat any fraction. Nothing seemed right.

I read the room service menu from beginning to end, settling on chicken salad. The nice thing about an international chain hotel is you know the chicken salad won't contain bones. The same, I'm sorry to say, cannot be said elsewhere. I called down the order, got the key out of the envelope, fiddled with it, chastised myself for indecision (Shelley: you make the call), encouraged myself to connect with my core values (be bold and shrug off fear), put my shoes back on, and went out of the room.

Car bomb? I wondered in the elevator. But who would want to have me killed? I mean, really, I'm a value creator. Kidnapping? That was worrisome—note to self, be careful. Token of appreciation from an admirer? Not impossible, just peculiar.

The video didn't prove anything, even if it did reassure me. That was the point of it, I suppose. To capture my interest. To take me off guard. I should therefore stay on guard. I fingered the key in the key pocket of my yoga pants as I rode down in the elevator.

It was only dusk out, no reason to be afraid, and I was fast and strong and wearing running shoes. The air was humid. A family was unloading their luggage from the car. A little girl pushed a pink plastic stroller beside the car while a bellman hung up a garment bag and her father was digging around in the open trunk, with a suitcase unzipped. A sick-looking woman stood nearby, with very fine, very blonde hair like a doll's and an expression of defeat. She held her hand protectively over the bag she carried, looking wary, as if this was not where she'd thought they were going.

Their eyes fixed on me—was I the kind of person they should fear, and was this hotel all right?—and, just as fast, released me. But I had seen them and they me, and that gave me a feeling of safety.

The hotel was situated on a wide, pleasant six-lane Barcelona street with elaborate buildings lining either side. Yellow-and-black cabs glided past, under very tall streetlights, elegant, decorous, dark. At the end of the block a round fountain shot its plume of water into the air.

Ornate buildings faced each other, adorned with carved statuary, minarets, garlands, and cherubs, and also, looking not at all out of place amid all this fanciness, the familiarly shaped signs for American banks and clothing stores and fast-food places. Strong global brands work everywhere.

I walked down the block. A disconcerting mix of trees lined the street—sycamores, or some kind of trees with dappled trunks in silvery gray, and some palmy things. I saw a palm tree in Ireland once, towering in the front yard of a very small house. You would think palm trees need warmth, but what they really need, bottom line, is for it not to get too cold. I am certain there is a business lesson to extract from that.

Enrique had talked about spaces. Around the corner. There was no parking lot, but when I turned the corner from my hotel, the street had an additional lane with some diagonal parking, separated from the rest of the street by sidewalk. On the sidewalk were dozens of motorcycles. I love agility and individualization in products so you'd think I'd love motorcycles, but I wouldn't ride one because I fear injury, which shows how complex consumer preferences can be.

I noticed people as I walked, hoping they would in turn notice me. I walked by lots of young people who looked like they had just finished sweaty workouts, and people wearing a style of sandal you don't see in the United States. I passed a pale woman wearing khaki shorts, the light falling so that they seemed first to be shorts, then pants as they blended with her pale legs. Then, as she turned into the shadow, for a moment she had one pants leg and one shorts one.

The key was in my pocket and resolution was in my heart. I was stalwart, not trembling except inside. I counted as I walked down the row of cars, peeking in their blank, clean exteriors, their Euro-variation on American cars and their bemusing names, hinting at a different set of marketing preconditions— the VW Polo, Ford Ka, Opel Insignia Sports Tourer, the Toyota Aygo, Citroën C6 Saloon, Renaults, Peugeots, the—can that really be its name?—Nissan Qashqai. And Audis. The TT translated well. I wonder what they do in Cyrillic markets.

At the end of the row, in the fifteenth space—I think—I saw a car that was different. I looked away, worried that it would not be what I hoped. For some reason this prospect upset me. I went back to looking at the buildings. A wall had graffiti stenciled on it. I approached the car at the end of the row with an unusual diffidence, like a boy you meet at fourteen—which is to say, I stayed at the opposite end of the row and barely looked at it, awash in feeling.

It was akin to a sexual undertow. Probably just because I missed Rafe. Maybe because of altitude sickness. Worry. Maybe the high I get from giving keynotes.

I couldn't tell where this feeling was coming from. This—was it sexual or seasickness?—queasy feeling. Did I think a full-on view might dispel its charm? Or perhaps there was something else that made me keep my eyes away as I moved, first this way and then that, lacing my way gradually closer.

The car was silver. That was my first impression. A different silver from the silver of all the other cars, more truly silvery, with a sense of motion underneath, like a one-way mirror in a focus group room, where, when one of the observing executives leaves to return to other responsibilities, the focus groupers turn and glance over toward the mirror, as if they have picked up on some shadowy change. The car's headlights were round, like spectacles. It was tiny, even among the little Citroëns. It looked— what? Cheerful? Sexy? Some other catalog word—compelling. User delight is something we talk about a lot in tech, how to achieve a beautiful user experience, but rarely do I feel it. But "delighting the user" is very 2010. This was two notches up from delight: elation and balming the user's soul.

I slid my hand along the car's flank and felt a shiver of static run up my arm and down my spine. Far away there was the crack of thunder, and I felt, despite myself and all the stuff I'd said earlier, a very unpleasant spasm of fear. I recited some words I say in such situations, paused, and took a few cleansing breaths. Then I bent down to look in, cupping my hands to block the glare. In just a moment I would try the key. I tried the door handle first, and the door swung open. The two front seats were brown leather with rows of scalloped stitching—like the scallops of a conch shell, actually (I can't help but see opportunities for our brand and make the connection. As Greer would say, it's there if you look: the universe wants to provide). The steering wheel was old-fashioned, unpadded, perhaps a little spindly—not a fluid-filled simulacrum of a steering wheel, with the plastic cushioning of old people's toilet seats, but a wheel, a real one, that probably turned all the way.

You might think, don't I already have a lovely car? I don't, actually. Rafe drives a Tesla and it's funny to watch the squirrels eating acorns in our driveway scatter, dangerously late in the game, as he glides soundlessly up. We have an Odyssey for the nanny. I have a car too, but there's nothing interesting about it. Having a driver is key for me, because that way I can work in the car, or could if I didn't get carsick all the time. That's one of the challenges I'm working to overcome.

Also, we like to invest in what's eco-friendly or technically intriguing, efficient or innovative, not in buying things just because they're pretty. Our kind of luxury has to justify itself as being something else. We live expensively but it's all about our work. Not pleasure—pleasure is not something I have much time for, the pointlessness of it, the inefficiency and excess.

My pleasure receptors seemed to get shriveled by the lightning, and now I seek other things: challenge, risk, accomplishment, excellence. I'm not unhappy. I'm never unhappy anymore. Am I ever happy? Yes, despite what Rafe said once, I am very happy, but it's not a leisure-based happiness. If I'm very successful, that's something I can engage in in retirement while mulling over philosophical conundrums and unsolved mathematical theorems. Then there will be time for a more serious yoga practice and more mindful contemplation and adventure travel and serving on scads of nonprofit boards, which I'm always being approached about but don't have the bandwidth to commit to right now: clean water, clean air, curing cancer, helping burn victims, hindering strip mining, opera for the inner city, squash for farm kids—the racquet kind, obviously; they already have the vine kind.

Rafael is a bit pleasure driven. He grew up with so little, and now he gets so much joy out of excess—crazy Christmases and buying four pairs of shoes at a time. Maybe it's because of his family background, their siestas and family meals, or a compensation for all his family had and lost. Whatever it is, I like it about him, his sprawl and size and willingness to take naps and fine-dine, and clients love it, the way he's so warm and socially ept, makes anyone he meets feel like a million bucks. Pleasure doesn't hold the same pleasure for me; I get bored and irritable. It all takes so long, an appetizer's enough for me to feel like I've had the experience at the restaurant, and lying down for five minutes is enough of a nap, and I like to schedule sex for when we're changing out of our clothes anyway. Then I need to get back to work.

And yet. All that was true but. This had my attention.

When I squeezed my hand together the key was in my palm. I got into the car. The leather inside smelled of smoked butterscotch. It was tidy and precise and charming in the way that vintage technology is, with its spiny unsteroided gearshift, its dials with their misguided pretensions of the future, its knob-biness and clock with hands. Even a digital evangelist like me can appreciate the charms of analog. It's like dating a nerd and a football quarterback concurrently (not that I have tried this). The car seemed assembled rather than fused, and made of mate-rials harvested from the world—metal, wood, and leather.

I figured it was all right to take the time to explore this. This was good research for work. We're a wearables company—that's what our marketing director always says. (She wishes she worked in fashion.) I need to stay abreast of design trends. I should drive this car.

It felt right. The seat fit. The pedals were where my feet wanted them to be. The wheel lay a delicate bent-arms distance from my shoulders. The smell was intoxicating, rich—not new-car, not old-car—something concocted specially, rare, rich, library-like.

I made some unnecessary adjustments to the driver's seat, which was already adjusted optimally to my body. I snapped shut the door, and it closed satisfyingly with the dark-toned, vibratory thwack of a successful tennis return. I felt a surge in my spine and looked up.

The sky, which had been twilit, went dark, though it was not yet late. There was a crack of lightning and the sky split like a knifed cantaloupe. Rain pelted the windshield. I sobbed once. Cleansing breath. Then I turned the key.

Chapter 5

I felt the growling of the car under me, the lashes of the rain on the roof. I wasn't sure I'd remember how to drive clutch, but the knowledge was lodged in my muscle memory, and I knew what to do. The car moved with a glide I felt through my body, as if I had merged with the equipment that was making this motion possible, like skiing.

I backed out and drove down the street, past buildings with wrought iron balconies stretched across them like elaborate spiderweb aprons. They reminded me of the buildings in Nova's Madeline books. The decoration adds value, I thought. It might have seemed like an extra expenditure at the time, to order all that ironwork and get it installed, but value is not just short-term profit. Quality creates desirability, which can pay dividends far into the future; i.e., why I was staying on this street, and why my hotel could charge so much.

The storm continued, but I felt less anxious—driving felt too natural, too responsive, too perfectly fitted to me. My father, full of admiration for all well-made mechanical things, would have liked the way this car drove: "Turns on a dime and gives you nine cents change."

I felt a buzz behind my ear as my Conch registered my speed and direction. "Going for a drive?" my Conch asked. At Conch, we call this a confirmation question. It knows what you're doing but it's letting you know it knows. My Conch then vibrated in a suggestion pattern. "For a scenic drive that avoids traffic hassles, head northwest on the A-2 toward Esparreguera." I nodded, accepting the suggestion. Thank God, I thought, for Conch. What a great product. And to think I'm part of its success. What did I ever do without it?

I drove past a sign showing three arrows chasing each other's tails, and then into a roundabout with a rusty piece of public art in its center, resembling a gigantic ice cream cone that had come to a bad end. I followed my Conch's directions, stated plainly, dispensed just as I needed them, as it led me out of town. The bike lanes beside the highway were empty. The road itself was nearly deserted, but even in the dark I felt confident. Lit-up lane markers, like glowing beads dropped in the roadway, showed me the way.

Out of town, past cranes, piers, water—what did they extract here? Mackerel, oil, natural gas? I pressed my Conch in a query pattern. "Local exports?" I asked. In my Conch, and in my ear, something crackled. That was peculiar.

"What are the major industries here?" I said, clarifying.

"Transmission failure," my Conch said. "No data available. Rebuilding database."

I flinched; this was very strange. Conch is not, of course, a perfect product. As I tell our investors, we have a killer concept and are a market leader in the space, but there is still room to improve. That's what makes it such an exciting time to be leading Conch. Our vision for the product is that someday it will be an assistant and a better self, all rolled into one. Who wouldn't want a bon mot, a trenchant line, a translation on the fly, a fact to marshal a floundering argument, whispered into your ear at exactly the right time? *That's the French president approaching on your left. He likes yogurt and he has a corgi. Mention his wife, Brigitte, whom you met last year in Saint-Tropez.* Conch is not quite there yet, we're still refining the algorithm, and most of the time it's just *There's an accident on your route home* and *thundershowers are predicted later* and *your mother just emailed you a photo of your nephew*—but within the near term I can see Conch moving toward much more. But even if what it conveys isn't profound, it usually works. It was strange that it wasn't working.

"New connection established," my Conch said. I'd never heard that before.

It must just be the remote location. I turned my attention to the thought of my chicken salad, which I hoped would have poppy seeds, but probably not, in Spain, and whether it had arrived yet to my room, and whether I should go back to have it. I hoped it would come on a croissant, and then I sharply reproved myself and more strongly hoped it would not, because a croissant is unnecessarily caloric.

I had not driven in a storm in almost twenty years.

"Turn left," the Conch said, clear and present once again; I found its familiar voice soothing, like an old friend's, and I swung the wheel. I am so proud to work at Conch, bringing people the words they want to hear, at the moment they want to hear them.

Rain slapped against the roof. The sky had gone gray. Must be, I thought, something to do with the barometric pressure or the altitude. I'll have to remember to ask the concierge about these weather patterns. It is interesting how when you travel you experience so many different sounds and phenomena not present in North America, or at any rate in Northern California, and that there really is a sense of foreignness to the flora and fauna. Take these gnarled olive trees—their leaves really are olive green, that is *exactly* the color, what a satisfaction to make that connection.

The road pulled me up the mountain and along a ridge. It was a strange feeling, to ascend to the clouds, to drive through them, like navigating a dense fog, and then finally to break through above. It had been loud, and now it was quiet. I had crossed above the rain. Above the clouds everything seemed crisper, colder, more saturated in color. The ever-present lichen between the rocks had a note of clear green instead of mossy brown. The sky was paler, as if it had given up some color to the rock and the hardy wildflowers scrabbling to grow in between. The air was thin and I felt like I could see very far.

Snow dusted the mountains in the distance. On one side of the car was the stony rise of the mountain, where intrepid little spruces grew, and lichens. On the other side was the steep downward slope leading to the city, staked with tall fir trees, the type that bad guys in movies become impaled on while riding their getaway sleds. Some of the trees had lost all their branches and were now just poles, mottled-looking trunks with stubby sticks sticking out in all directions, like antennas looking for a signal.

My Conch guided me around a tricky turn and down the narrow road. The little car thrummed as a motorcycle roared past. I had the sensation that I was stalled, hovering, and it was only the motorcycle that was moving.

My sinuses were streaming. Pressure had built in my head from the ascent. All at once it reached an unbearable level and I sneezed. My eyes closed, and just as they reopened (and in an instant of relief I saw that there was road ahead, and all looked good), I sneezed again. The sneeze shot out snot that caught in my nose and made me sneeze again. With each propulsive sneeze, my eyes closed. A car was coming around the bend toward me. I lifted my arm off the steering wheel to wipe my nose and stop the unbearable tickle. The car came faster and without meaning to I veered, then skidded. Suddenly there was a crack. I felt a bang under the car as the other car whooshed by. I braked fast and hard. My body lifted off the seat as my foot dug down farther and farther on the brake, till my whole body was pouring itself down onto that pedal. My forehead hit the ceiling of the car.

An instant of nothing: an ominous pause in sensation, gravity, and sound. Then nausea, clear and sharp, arrived and knocked me back into the seat. I pulled over on the very narrow road and turned the car off. I rubbed the sore spot under my seat belt and probed the top of my head. My fingers came away wet with blood, but the cut wasn't deep. A car whipped around the curve, and gingerly, after it had passed, I lowered myself out of the car and looked around, examining it. From the outside it looked all right. The trunk—I should have checked before—was empty. I sprang the hood, feeling a pain along my scalp as I lifted it. My hands were blackly greasy before I found the pole to wedge under the hood. I scanned the tubes and pipes and unknown sealed containers for . . . well, anything unusual. Would I know unusual if I saw it? Depends, I suppose, on how unusual. I did not see anything that reached that threshold. I banged the hood closed again. A car came fast around the curve, kicking up a cloud of dust and pebbles. I watched a rock catapult off the edge of the cliff. That was probably it, I thought. Just a stone. Aren't you twitchy. It was nothing.

I stood beside the car and had the strangest vision of a corner of the sky near the horizon pulled up and back like the white duvet of my king-size hotel bed, to expose something underneath. I had a flickering sensation of being on a stage set, or that I was meant to be somewhere else in other surroundings, but it was probably that the atmosphere was thin. I had done too much; it was probably the time change or hunger affecting me. "Navigate back," I instructed my Conch, and was reassured by the confident sound of my own voice.

"Calculating directions," my Conch said. "Rerouting. Nearby café is open till two. Ready for directions?"

I was a little surprised, because I hadn't experienced the Conch suggesting a new location before. But we're adding product features all the time.

"Back to hotel," I said.

"Taking a moment to rest and rehydrate is advisable," my Conch urged. "Let's go!" I've never heard it be so insistent, either, but I was grateful for the input. A drink would be nice. Steadying. Clear the head.

"Sure," I said. A moment of rest. I Conched a note to myself: this would be a great example to share on the corporate Conch-blog about how Conch was helping me. ("On my recent trip to . . .")

The café was not far. It was up against the road, with a tile roof and lights shining in all the windows. I had thought I was very far from civilization, and it was a disappointment to realize it had been there all along, parallel to the road I'd been driving. The building was two stories, and cars were parked close beside it. A chalkboard by the door advertised tapas, and something involving *xocolata*.

"*Hola*," I said inside. I ordered a beer, mostly by pointing.

The bartender turned to me as he poured it. "*Y para tu hermana?*"

I thought of course he was speaking to someone else, so I did not answer. He repeated it, looking me right in the face. "For your sister," he said, this time in English. "What do I get for her?"

I shook my head. "I have no sister." It seemed like a pickup line, maybe—*and for your sister?* Some kind of insouciant inquiry, except that he seemed uninterested in me, so, well, souciant.

He slid a mug across the bar and pointed past me. "She's your daughter?" He shrugged. "That's nice. I had kids young too. All grown now. Nice to finish early."

I gave him the stink-eye and pulled euros from my wallet, not bothering to try to count them out, letting him take from my hand what he wanted. I settled on a barstool. An itch came over me, perhaps better to say a chill.

He gave me a look as if there were something wrong with me, that I was mentally damaged in the part of the brain where family relationships are managed, and he gestured past me to a girl—young woman—standing just behind us. He turned his attention to her, addressed her directly.

Overhead were dark beams with hooks screwed into them, and dozens, hundreds of identical silvery mugs hanging from the beams. The mugs had names on them, if you looked closely—Josep, I made out. Enric. Vincent.

Was it surprising that the bartender spoke English, that he'd known I was an English speaker too? I felt a kind of click in my head, in which an image pulsed forth for a moment and filled my whole consciousness, like a screensaver taking over my field of vision. Then, with the tiniest movement, it fell away. It had been just like a real screensaver, an image of a white snowy field with icy ridges, abstracted by the close and unfamiliar angle. And then it was gone. This was happening more often, these blank moments. I blinked and stretched, rotating my shoulders, drawing infinity signs in the air with them ("Infinite possibility is within you," says Greer, or possibly that is from the tag from my green tea), and I reached to steady myself against the armrest, but it was a stool so there was none and I tipped a bit. The beams overhead creaked, and the dangling mugs struck each other with aggravated, tinny clinks.

The girl had ordered her drink and received it, and then she dug in her pocket and looked to me apologetically. "I don't have money," she said, in English, to me. "You'll have to pay."

It was like a dream in which nothing can surprise you. I held up some bills and coins, silently, and again let the bartender select from my palm the ones he wanted. He took the money and nodded, satisfied. She was my sister, or my niece, and I had conceded it by paying for her. He didn't care why: we all have secrets we like to think we're keeping. She sat next to me in the dark, windowless room and sipped her beer. I watched it slosh back and forth as the cup traveled between the bar and her lips, which had a little foam stuck to them.

She had long, russety hair, a color that mine had once been, until the lightning strike, when, along with every indignity possible, it grew in a nondescript brown. Brown doesn't seem so bad now that it's heading toward gray. I dye it, of course. The perception of youth and energy is crucial in business.

Seeing her made me homesick for the hair I used to have. I looked at it. I felt like I'd seen her somewhere before. She was young, a teenager or young woman. Her lips were chapped and the lower lip was a little cracked at its center. She tucked her hair behind her ear. She had pierced ears with no earrings in the greenish holes (lint? discoloration from cheap earrings?). She had that fleshy, smooth face that you have until your mid-twenties or your first major acquisition, whichever comes first.

I could see a resemblance to someone—maybe a cousin of mine? She looked a lot like, of all people, my brother. *Señor Barkeep*, I could say, *I do have a brother. He is a gastroenterologist in Minneapolis.* It was curious. She was like the female version of him, with his smile and hefty eyebrows. She had bristly, full eyebrows, which if I were being very charitable I could compare to Brooke Shields's—BS has cleverly converted a liability to an asset, similar to what my husband, Rafe, does with troubled banks. There was maybe a tiny resemblance to my son, Blazer, through the eyebrows. She looked like a lot of people on my side of the family, the Stones, but I couldn't place her.

Who did she look like? Someone.

"Do I know you?" I asked.

Did she look at all like me? I did wonder, even at that moment. But I didn't really think so: I didn't think I was ever so messy, so sloppily dressed, with that hangdog expression of pouty indecision. And there was no reason to think she would have any relationship to me. But I could admit there was a bit of a resemblance.

My eyebrows are as shorn as the shrubbery of a newly retired barber, and my skin, with many developing problems I did not realize would assail me at the tail end of my thirties, is rigorously cleaned and enriched with products prescribed by the top-flight dermatologist I Snapchat my skin problems to. I also have occasional laser surgeries, peels, and treatments that are not even cosmetic surgery, just healthy maintenance and an investment in myself in an ageist society. But if I didn't do these things—

"We haven't met," she said. "Thanks for the drink. I didn't think you'd mind paying. You sort of remind me of my mom."

I was nonplussed. "Do I?"

"A little," she said—and then, quickly, indignantly—"It's not an insult. My mom is very attractive. She was the homecoming queen at her high school."

"Mine was also," I said, lifting an eyebrow.

"Mine was in Wisconsin," she apologized, as if that meant less.

I looked back at her. "Tell me your name?"

"Michelle," she said.

"Hi, Michelle. Great name."

"Thanks. I've never liked it much."

I cut her off. "Little advice: learn how to accept a compliment. And, also, it's my name."

"Your name's Michelle?"

"Shelley," I said. "I go by Shell. My real name is Michelle, but

I stopped using it. I like Shelley better. It's snappier. Michelle, what brings you here?"

"I'm on a trip, but the person I was traveling with . . . It didn't work out. Somebody dropped me off here. I don't know where I put my wallet. I'm very tired. Can we get back in the car?"

"What car?"

"Yours," she said. "I can't stay here all night, can I?"

"Where are you staying?" I said.

"I don't have that worked out yet," she said. "I guess I should find my wallet first." She seemed unconcerned. Not unconcerned, but less concerned than the situation warranted. I admired her coolness under pressure, but it seemed mildly delusional.

"Is there a hotel near here? I could drop you off and you could call your parents."

"It'll work out," she said. "It always does. I don't stress." She laughed in a slightly strained way. "If I have to sleep in a barn somewhere on some hay or something, that would be all right. It's all experience, right?"

I gazed at the girl. There was something peculiar about her, about meeting her. My Conch buzzed in an alert pattern. "Say hello," it said, "to Shelley Stone."

"What's wrong?" the girl said.

I pressed my Conch: two light touches, a query pattern. This was very strange. Could my Conch have gone bad? Was it the electrical storm? I shook my head. "Just thinking about something. Sorry. What were you saying? You don't have a place to stay?"

I pressed my Conch to reset it. "Say hello to . . ." it said. I took the Conch out and turned it over, examining it for defects.

"What's that thing?"

"Michelle, are you familiar with Conch and situationally aware technology? It's an amazing way to optimize your experience in the world. It's very simple, very powerful, and it changes lives." I gave her my escalator speech, which is like an elevator speech but ten seconds longer and said a little louder.

She shook her head. "Can I see it?"

She took the Conch from me, looking at it carefully. Crafted from a ballistic polymer to our specifications in our factory in Malaysia, it's an organic shape that looks a little like a shell you'd find weather-beaten on the beach. It's flattish and curved, small, and weighs just a few grams. When people pick up a Conch for the first time they almost always balance it on their fingertip—it sits very comfortably there; users are always delighted by what our engineers call the finger feel. There are different patterns and strengths of vibration for different functions, and increasingly we can communicate more and more just through these tactile patterns—some users hardly use the phone app at all, they can get so much richness from touch.

"If you're interested in trying out a Conch, I can have one sent to you. I'd let you try this one, but it's specially configured for me and runs a next-generation iteration of our software that hasn't been deployed publicly yet. And it isn't working right." I wondered if it could be the high altitude. "I'm happy to give you one to try. Conch is great for busy students, and if you love it as much as I think you will, you can evangelize it to your friends." As the timeless nugget of wisdom on the wall of Conch's sales department says, "Don't be like 7-Eleven—you always gotta close!"

"I'm not religious," she said primly, and then, "Oh! Your head is bleeding!" I dipped my head and sorted out my hair, which was disconcertingly crispy and clumped close to the scalp.

"I'm fine," I said. "The head has many small blood vessels close to the surface. The blood doesn't mean much. Don't worry."

She went over to a different part of the bar. "Here." Some

wadded paper napkins. I took them, dabbed very lightly, feeling it all through my jaw. I touched behind my ear.

"My Conch!" I said, realizing she still had it. "I feel naked without it. I need mine back, but I'll send you one. I usually carry a few extras on me."

"Oh," she said. "Where did I . . . ?"

She reached into her pocket and fished it out. I took it, perplexed by why she had put it there. "There you go."

I slipped it back in and felt instantly more settled. I watched her.

There was definitely something familiar about her. A small pink scar marred her upper arm. I recognized that scar.

I touched my own shoulder, and through the technical fabric of my moisture-wicking, body skimming jacket, I clamped my hand over the spot where I had a very similar scar. I tried not to stare. I got mine from a vaccination. It wasn't strange, was it, that we both had such similar scars in the same places on our arms? That is where vaccinations are given. There must be something about that location on the body that makes it scar easily. Perhaps that spot is especially vulnerable, or the skin there is unusually slow to heal, and something about the muscles of the shoulder creates a scar that curves in that precise way. Probably almost everyone has a scar like that.

Chapter 6

I put her in the car. What else could I do? It wasn't safe for her to wander around, sleeping in barns. If there were barns. It was preposterous and risky. It worried me she was not more worried for herself. Anything could happen to her—did she not realize that?

She did not seem all that curious about who I was or where we were going. She had an air of sedated tranquility, and a few minutes after we pulled away from the café, I glanced over and realized she was asleep, slumped against the passenger door. Apparently, I was not interesting enough to keep her awake. Many young people would have felt differently. I wanted to tell her that. It doesn't sound humble, but it's true. When I went to UCLA to speak, I was *besieged*, as I told several people afterward, by young people reeling off their elevator pitches. A very forward young man even followed me into the women's restroom and pitched while I peed, and you know, while I told him it was over the line, and that that kind of intrusion is unprofessional, part of me admired his gumption. Well, this one didn't care.

She shifted, letting out a drawn-out, soft moan. I glimpsed too much of her thighs as she drew up a knee and resettled herself. Her face tipped out of view, hidden by the cascade of hair, and she submerged back into sleep.

While driving, I recorded my GPS coordinates and sent them to my assistant. I wasn't sure what Willow would make of them, but at least the record was there, whatever happened.

This sleeping girl was a problem of an ambiguous nature. A watch-and-wait situation? An emergent threat? A status quo disrupter? I pondered where to take her. It was getting late, and I had a full day tomorrow. Should I just put her in my hotel? She seemed too lazy and disorganized to be dangerous.

What's a case study I can harvest for insight in handling the situation, I asked myself. I scanned through my mental list: supply chain issues due to natural disasters, disruptive innovations, strategic human capital changes, the introduction of the cell phone touch screen into the mobile market . . . none seemed like perfect parallels. What came to mind was not anything from a business periodical, but something I'd seen in one of Nova's books. This, I thought grimly, was a Goldilocks situation (it's good to have a wide range of reference). What had the bears done? Avoidance. Mostly just talked about it with rising anger until at last she woke up (ineffectual and reactive, not proactive, as I'd told Nova). The kernel of my annoyance came from her deep, rude sleep. I had not slept like that in years. Since I had started working, really. Since the lightning strike, even. Maybe she was a drug addict.

I drove back into the dark city, my eyes addled by all the neon, and I parked around the corner from the hotel.

"Time to wake up," I told her. I said it mostly for my own benefit, to feel on top of things, which does work. ("'Fake it till you make it' is a truism but a true one," my mentor at my old company used to say.) But when I glanced over, there she was, her gray-blue eyes open, glazed and still, like a baby who has

THE GLITCH · 95

opened them and will, any second, if you are very quiet and just keep typing your presentation, re-succumb to sleep. I did that a lot when Nova was small—it worked, though I feel ambivalent about it now.

She became more alert and cheerful as we walked through the glass doors of the hotel into the plush lobby. It was a high space with filigreed panels letting in interesting patterns of light during the day. At night golden light spilled from under the edge of every surface.

"This is a fancy hotel," she said appreciatively. The bellman and I caught each other's eyes. Though we were both, in our way, jaded hotel professionals, we enjoyed her enjoyment.

Upstairs, in my cool white suite, the bedside light was on, the shades were down, and the coverlet had been folded back in one corner. A gold-foil-wrapped chocolate bar had manifested on the plate where the apples had been.

If the chicken salad had come, it had also gone away. I called down to room service and ordered her a cheeseburger and myself two pieces of rye toast, a green salad, and a glass of wine.

My food failed to hold my attention—there were no sesame seeds on the rye bread—but she ate hers rapidly.

"You're welcome to my salad, Michelle," I said. She was eating her burger and fries in an off-putting style, with the hotel bed duvet drawn up over her lap. It was weird to say "Michelle"; it was what I sometimes called myself when rehearsing my remarks for meetings while putting on lipstick.

I opened my laptop and flicked through my inbox. "Ship and iterate," I read. This is one of the Conch mottoes we use on our internal email signatures. We take advantage of that real estate to make every email an occasion to prompt each other to dig deeper, focus more intently, and innovate more. Another one is "moonshot thinking!"

"That's an amazing computer."

I glanced down at my lightweight, titanium, best-of-class, but utterly ordinary laptop.

"And what's that thing?"

"What thing?" I looked, alarmed, out the window.

"The thing glowing under the sheet," she said. She leaned across the bed and pointed.

"It's a cell phone?" I said, in a duh-Valley-girl voice. "I'm sure you've got one too. Yours is probably faster. Kids are always on the bleeding edge with mobile."

She shook her head and whispered, "Where am I?"

"Barcelona," I said. "The City of Gaudí." I had read this in the conference packet.

She nodded slowly, as if this helped. "Why am I so cold? And so, so tired?"

I shrugged. "I'm always tired. Tired is . . ."

"Oh, Vienna sausages! I can't believe you have those. So revolting and yet, I'll tell you something, I actually kind of like them."

I raised an eyebrow, nodded, and gestured toward the jar on my desk.

"I used to buy them at the QuikTrip. They came in handy. That way if my mom caught me doing something worse I could pretend I was hiding out so I could eat gross canned meat."

I turned to look curiously at her.

"Say hello to Shelley Stone," my Conch said.

And then the answer came to me. I was struck still by the simplicity of it. I heard within myself the loud crack of a glacier breaking apart, and with it a bright warmth, as if a shaft of light were crossing a flat rock. Ship and iterate. Moonshot thinking. I felt disappointed with myself for not having thought of it earlier. I had been letting the status quo dictate my range of options. I had been failing to bring sufficient imagination to bear. I had foreclosed the truest, most elegant and simplest option without considering it, simply because it seemed unfeasible, outlandish, and impossible. Nothing is impossible. I had been dismissing a potential opportunity rather than meeting it head-on. That's not how you get to the top. Sometimes you have to face facts, follow the data, and squeeze through the narrow slit of opportunity, however tiny and poorly situated and illogical it is. You must have total confidence in your own vision. This is how I've gotten to where I am.

"Why are you looking at me like that?"

"Because you're me," I said calmly.

Her jaw dropped. She leaned back against the headboard of the bed as if she were stunned, or trying to move far away from me. I had never felt more awake. It's not every day someone who reminds you of you materializes in your life, and it's even less likely (simply because it is more specific yet, and more specific scenarios are always less likely, logically, than more general ones) that it be a manifestation of yourself at a different point in time. Amazing, I thought. Also, how can I leverage this?

The more closely I looked at her, the more I saw the resemblance.

It was curious. Of course I'd seen myself in the mirror. But seeing Michelle, I realized how limited that mirror-view was—not just reversed, so my side part and freckles appeared on the wrong side, but when you look at yourself in a mirror you are always having to *look*. You might catch yourself on occasion out of the corner of your eye coming down a staircase to a mirror you didn't know was there, or reflected in a store window in a posture that doesn't instantly communicate it is you, but you never had the moments I was having, the long stretches of seeing yourself from an outside perspective, from angles the mirror can't reach, taking in yourself not through a flat surface but in three-dimensional space, watching yourself respond and react without creating those responses, those expressions.

It's so odd that normally you never see yourself, except in stipple portraits in the *Wall Street Journal* (not to be vain, but are my lips really that bulgy?) or headshots in conference programs or photos in business mags or in YouTube clips from thought leadership talks. It struck me as funny that you see strangers and take them in all at once in a very quick and informative snapshot, but with yourself there is always the blocked view. In those seconds, seeing her from the outside, I felt I knew myself better than ever before.

I saw her twitchiness, the way her expressions came one against the other, like train cars bumping, the way she blinked, on and on, as if taking it all in. She had a way of languidly leaning back to assess what I was saying that unnerved me, it was so cool and analytic and careless. I had never comprehended the effect before, as I did now, instantly, as part of the package of personality, the way I did all the time with strangers.

I understood all at once some things I hadn't really understood before, like the way people have described me over the years. Handsome (why not ever *pretty*?), intense, restless: certain adjectives the tech journalists like to lean on, certain constellations of specks and lines in caricatures that I never saw the point of, till now.

She was not unattractive, but it was a certain steeliness that was her predominant quality, and I realized that it was effortless, it was always there. Part of my forcefulness was just something about my jawline, something baked into me, the way merit ratings are baked into our compensation calculations at Conch. Along the way I had picked up on how people perceived me, perhaps, and become more and more that way. And she hadn't even yet been through the . . . I shut down the thought.

She was much younger, of course, with the pretty hair I still missed, that had changed abruptly and unfairly after the lightning strike and which I now had dyed to achieve a less satisfying result. She had a different body, sort of, though not, to the eye that knows it so well, fundamentally different—we had the same bones. She had a fuller face, untamed eyebrows, and a lack of the finishing touches I didn't even think of as finishing anymore; they were perpetual, they were little part-time jobs. Her fingernails were bitten, her fingers ringless. Her watch was, surprisingly, digital. A scuff of peeling skin clung to her bare heels, like the whiff of Grana Padano left behind on the microplane grater when Rafe makes pasta.

"You're crazy," she said. "I don't believe it. You're scaring me. I'm leaving as soon as I finish these French fries." When her voice came it was not exactly familiar, but close—low and confident, daring, lively, a little breathy. I almost laughed—I knew it, from voicemail greetings, corporate training videos, webinars, and, in a smothered variant, through my own clogged Eustachian tubes.

"Weird we have the same scar," I said, unzipping my jacket and pulling my T-shirt off one shoulder to show it. Hers was pinker and more prominent, but the same shape. She took a second look at it, and her lips wrinkled up unhappily. "What?"

"It's the same."

"It's sort of *similar*," she said, correcting me.

She obviously did not recognize me, nor see in me any strands of herself. You never think you'll become an old person, and by old I mean a vibrant and ambitious thirty-nine with a BMI under twenty-two and the bone health of a young golden retriever. It simply doesn't occur to anyone to scan a room of elderly people and think, who is the most like me? Which white-haired lady will I most resemble? And yet the elderly do point out young people to each other and say, I looked like that. The ratchet of self-recognition only goes one way. Even Rafe has done it—we don't have many photos from when he was a child, and I'm curious about how much he looked like Nova and Blazer. Once in a while, when we've been out somewhere, he's pointed out a little boy with big dark eyes and said, I looked like him. The resemblance hasn't been clear for me, and each time I've stopped to look back at the child, and felt a little doubtful, wondering if Rafe is right, and what it is he sees.

"It's more than the scar," I said.

She presented a fascinating opportunity. I wanted to watch her, check her out, evaluate her. I wanted to examine her in every particular, every mood, the way I had gazed down at baby Nova, watching expressions flit across her newborn face—adult, complicated expressions, the whole alphabet of mature emotion, from abashed to bewildered to consternated and so on, like a slideshow. I had wanted to know exactly what Nova's infant motherboard was up to, trying to listen to its whirring, the clicks, and predict where it would all lead. Which I couldn't—Nova was a mystery. But this was not at all like having a child. A child is more inscrutable than other people, always becoming something just out of reach that neither she nor you can see emerging. With a child, there is always the sense of someone moving away from you—to college someday, a management training program in a distant city, B-school, corporate relocations, until eventually their connection is fainter and fainter—*come visit at Thanksgiving? Maybe next year.* But I knew what shore Michelle was swimming toward; I knew what the future held for her.

Years ago, after my accident, I had seen a therapist to help me deal with my overwhelming fear of thunderstorms. The therapist had asked me if I ever had hallucinations or saw things that weren't there. I had had migraine auras—always of a few specks and lines, like bits of code superimposed on my visual field, but nothing I'd call a hallucination. "Is that common?" I asked.

"It's not unheard of," she said. "Depersonalization syndrome. It happens."

"Not to me."

"Well . . ." She looked past me to the clock, deftly signaling that it was time for me to leave. "Life is long."

So I wondered, momentarily flicking back to memories of her office and the almost-forgotten therapy, if I were undergoing some sort of psychic collapse, but I didn't think I was inventing this.

I turned my Conch off and on, reset some of the default settings, and pointed it at her. "Say hello to Shelley Stone," it murmured, this time with the bass-xylophone timbre of a famous movie actor's voice. I felt proud and impressed.

"Can you hear that?" I said. "See, it knows you. That's pretty impressive. I'll have to text Cullen. I'm surprised the bioauthentication is that consistent across time. It's tracking off something besides my Conch—what could it possibly be, it's not like you have a Conch?—but it's a great feature to talk up, an example of amazing engineering." But then I stopped, because I realized I could never tell Cullen about this.

"Hate to say it," she said, not hating it. "But I am not convinced."

"OK." I looked around the room, and dug into my bag for my passport. It was old, nearing expiration, with a photo of me taken almost a decade ago. In the photo I have better skin and fewer stress lines in my forehead, and the sharp sleek bob that was popular at the time and now looks like we were all confused about which way was front. "Look," I said, pointing. "See. Michelle Stone. That's your name, isn't it?" I looked into her eyes, and something shifted in her face, and she wouldn't meet my eyes.

She examined the passport with an intensity entirely unlike, in my experience, a passport examiner's. She flipped through the stamped-up pages: London, Singapore, KL, Mexico City, Tokyo. The stamps and visa stickers. I have the thicker (fifty-two-page) U.S. passport, which you have to request specially. When I have a few consecutive weeks stateside I have Willow send it in to get extra sheaves of pages stapled in. It was thick. "You travel a lot."

"Yes," I said. "Flip back to the front. Looks like you, doesn't it?"

"Not that much."

"Not not that much. It has your name on it."

"It's a common name," she said softly. "Lots of people have that name."

"This is your birthday, isn't it?"

She gazed at it, and then at me. Her expression collapsed and swiftly resurrected itself. "Passports are fakeable."

We sat on the bed in silence. I couldn't let it go. There was too much here to leverage, if I could get buy-in. My biggest limitation in life is lack of time, and here was more time, a doubling of time, potentially accessible to me. "What would you like me to tell you? Your social security number? I'm just going to give you the last four digits for security. Where you grew up? Your parents' address: 18 Pond View Drive. Your father's car is . . . a Honda Accord, or used to be." I hesitated. "Or will be soon. It's green. The dog . . ."

She looked tearful. "None of that proves anything!" she said. "You could have found all that out. What's my favorite color? What's my favorite food?" She sighed and blew her bangs up her forehead in a gesture of contempt and defiance.

I sighed and blew upward to lift my bangs, a trick I had not done in a dozen years. I actually had no idea. "Um. Orange. Lasagna."

"Wrong! I mean, I like it, but it's not my favorite."

"I don't know," I said. "But that's a terrible security question. Favorites are so squishy and guessable and subject to change. Let's step back and concentrate on irreducible attributes that stay the same over time. Your mother's maiden name, that's a good one."

"She still uses it," Michelle protested. "That's not hard to find out at all."

"OK," I said, thinking. "Let's drill down. Let me think. Do you want to quiz me about old addresses? Friends, teachers?"

"That's all stuff you could dig up. It doesn't prove anything."

It seemed sufficient proof to me. Names and dates—as data points, what else was there? "We could compare our finger-prints," I offered. "We could go grab a cheek swab gene test—my friend's the CEO of a company that does fascinating things with that. The test tells you how Viking you are, how Neanderthal. I'm slightly more Neanderthal than average, and I was upset when I read that, but I did a deep dive and learned that Nean-derthals were smarter than people often—"

"Tell me something nobody else would know," she said. "Something only I would know. Something I've never told any-one."

My mind flicked to the hospital room where I'd spent months after the lightning strike.

"How old are you?"

"Nineteen. Almost twenty."

So OK, not yet, I thought. What else was there? What other kinds of data existed? "I can't think of anything else."

"There's nothing?"

"Wait." The leaf pile of memory stirred. Something moved underneath. "When you used to fall asleep at night, when you were very little, you used to try to imagine a dog jumping over a stile—a gate. You never could do it. In your mind's eye you'd imagine a path with a gate at one end, and a dog at the other, and then try to imagine the dog running up to the gate and jumping over. Always, at the last minute, the dog would jerk away and go bounding back the way he came. You never could imagine it as you wanted to. Isn't that strange? You couldn't control an imaginary dog. It didn't matter what kind of dog you thought up, it simply wouldn't behave. This was intensely, intensely frustrating to you. You couldn't control it, even in your head, even though it seems like other people, even less self-disciplined ones, can."

She blinked. She didn't nod, but she did seem interested. I went on.

"You can't really picture people's faces. You never have been able to. Only photos of them that you've seen. If someone says, picture your mother, you have to think of a photo you remember, like this one where she's wearing a ski hat. You can't summon up faces from life. Even though you are perfectly good, and this has been borne out on aptitude tests, at spatial thinking."

"That's true!" she said.

"Of course it's true," I snapped. It bothers me that I can't. It seems like a cognitive disability, in a mind that is otherwise very sharp. It's something I've considered bringing up at my annual executive physical.

"More," she said. "Tell me more."

Panes of life zoomed past like computer windows in cascade mode—lake, camp, birthday candles, record player with creaky arm. It all seemed interchangeable, like anyone's past. "Surely that's enough."

She shook her head, but there was light in her eyes.

I heard myself speaking. "You used to pretend there was an owl that lived on the inside of your eyelid."

"What?"

"I really think so. I know. It somehow did. Folded right in there. Anyway, there was a knot in the wood on the inside of your closet door and you imagined it could fly in." I couldn't believe this was coming back to me. It was amazing these memories were suddenly present, as if they had always been there—it was as if I could feel new doors in my mind blowing open, the night breezes sweeping in. "You used to think about the knot when you were falling asleep, about going inside." I yawned, amused. "You were a very imaginative child."

She was looking intent. "I think maybe it's coming back to me. How do you know about that? I had totally forgotten about that. He had a name, right? Tell me the owl's name."

"Oh dear. I'm not sure that's retrievable. Um . . ." I went banging through the empty, windswept rooms of memory. "Louis?"

"Nah."

"Are you sure? What about Osbert? Leonora? Golden-eye? I'm drawing a blank."

"You need to tell me. I need it as proof." There was something swaggering in how she said it; she was starting to enjoy torturing me like this.

I shrugged. I had no idea. What a colossal waste of time all those hours spent imagining owls had been. It was hard to believe I had done it. If only I had stayed up and spent even twenty minutes per night, my God, even fifteen, practicing my tones in Mandarin, how much more effective I could have been.

"One more thing," I said. "It's just . . . never mind."

"What?"

"Even though you're good at lots of things, you don't believe you're going anywhere. You want to do something great, but it seems like it won't happen, that you're stuck, that everyone you know has known you all your life and has written you off as nothing special."

She tipped her head to the side, taking this in.

"You feel like if you only had a chance, you could do something exceptional and prove them wrong." I watched her; she was listening.

"What's that?" she said. I'd taken off my jacket and as I did my T-shirt rode up, exposing part of my side. I pulled my shirt down, but not before she saw the scar, like a red fern, that covers my trunk.

"Are you OK?" she said.

"It's nothing."

"But what is it?" I saw the problem; she was worried it would happen to her.

"It's not a big deal," I said. "I was, um . . . running in a marathon and one of my veins exploded in mile nine." I looked to see how she was taking it.

She looked into me as if she couldn't decide if I were lying. "That's got to be bullshit."

"Swear to God." I could tell she wanted to believe me. "It doesn't hurt, even though it looks like it would have. It was just stupid, I did back-to-back marathons, and—"

"You really think we're the same person?"

I nodded.

"Whatever. I'll just avoid marathons."

"Probably wise," I said. "They are very hard on our knees."

I don't really believe any of this," she said, popping the last bite of her cheeseburger into her mouth, and wiping her chin with the palm of her hand. "But . . . on the chance that you're right, tell me the fun stuff! I mean, if you're right—and who knows?— you can tell me what happens!" Her face shone, not just with grease. "I mean the exciting parts, of course. What exciting things will happen to me? With being in plays or movies"—she cast a critical look at my hair—"or just theater, that's fine, that's OK too, or, um, this guy . . ."

"You want to be in plays?"

She nodded excitedly. "What roles have you had?"

"Roles? Let's see, I was a project manager and then a director, then a VP, and then—"

"I mean, what have you *been* in?"

"In? Are you asking about industries? Well, you know that

American manufacturing is on the downswing and has been for some time, but the tech sector—"

"Acting! Theater! I assume you're an actor, right? In plays, films? That's why you travel and are here . . . isn't it?"

I stared at her. "I'm a CEO of a tech company. I started out in engineering and computer science," I said, "and then I went to a startup after college. Then I moved into a managerial role, and I've been lucky in my career development; my startup went public and dominated the online payment space, and I had some big wins there—"

She interrupted. "So when do you act? At night and on weekends? Community theater?"

"Theater?"

"How do you practice your craft?"

"Oh! Well, that never happens. Oh, don't look so crestfallen. You were never much of an actor. Strong public speaker, yes."

"Never? I must have done it for five or ten years, at least. A few professional roles? Come on, be serious. One? Not even one?"

I shook my head. Huh, I thought. I'd been so different before the lightning strike. Funny how completely we replace old priorities with new ones.

"I never make it into a single play? If I work really hard, won't I make one audition? I'm sure there's something I can be in . . . I was kind of thinking of movies. Not big parts or anything, just good character parts that I'd bring a lot of nuance to . . ."

"No," I said. "Look, don't be that upset. It's fine. Engineering is where it's at. Look, I know this might not seem as glamorous as being what's-her-name in *King Lear,* but someday you're going to have the honor of being selected as one of *Forbes*'s Forty Under Forty."

"Cordelia," she whispered hotly. She covered her face with her hands.

"I don't think that was one of them. There were very few women on the list that year."

She crawled up against the headboard and wrapped her bent legs in her arms, sulkily. "I don't believe you." Her brashness had deflated. "I don't want this. It's not what I want." She waved her arms around at the suite. It reminded me of Rafe, just a few nights ago, in a different suite. "I don't think I like you very much." I've heard variations of that so often you'd think it wouldn't hurt anymore. After a moment she looked up, fiercely, as if she had come to a decision. "It's just a matter of hard work. I'll work harder than you ever did."

"Maybe," I said. I didn't mention my scars. "Or maybe you need to learn what it is you've got to sell."

Angrily, she ate the rest of her French fries. She licked a swipe of mayonnaise off her fingers.

"Want another?" I said. "How about dessert?"

"You aren't worried I'm going to clog up your beautiful bourgeois arteries?"

What a nice way to talk to someone who just expensed you a twenty-eight-euro sandwich, I thought. "Not really," I said. Also, though I did not say this, I'm squarely a one-percenter, not a bourgeois, but I knew this was just her limited frame of economic reference. "Also, I know you smoke."

She looked furtive and her eyes moved to the window. "Only a little."

"Oh, right. Save the lies for your mother."

"Do you?" She pretended to be uninterested.

"Never," I said, bringing my fist down on the bedspread. "My God, never," and she looked relieved. "Well, a few times a year or so, if I have to work for a couple of nights running to close a big deal, maybe, possibly. Just to power through. But very rarely. The important thing, what matters here, is I don't crave it. It's so, so bad for you," I said sternly.

"Was it hard to quit?"

"You'd think, but I have tremendous willpower and I just decided, enough, and that was it." However, circumstances being as they were, I took a pack out of the minibar and went onto the balcony and lit one. I inhaled deeply.

"I do not have tremendous willpower," she assessed, correctly.

"You will when you grow up." This was true enough—I didn't need to tell her more.

She tilted her head from one direction to the other, as if she were weighing this on a balance inside her head, and she accepted it. She followed me out onto the balcony.

For a while we gazed out at the dark street, the yellow street-lights, the invisible people with their raucous voices stumbling home, far below. She was a much more practiced smoker than I was.

"I don't want to get old," she wailed. "I don't want to stop being me and become a boring, corporate shill. And have my hair get so blah and flat and volumeless."

I ignored this insulting construction on the situation. "What's odd is I don't remember this. I should remember it, if you're me, minus twenty years."

"You think that's the odd part?" she said. Finally she said, in a quiet, worried voice: "Does *anything* good happen to me?"

"Sure! Tons of stuff! Just a taste . . . you'll get to launch an amazing e-commerce platform . . ."

"What about a *fun* thing? What about a guy? There's this one, his name is, uh, Tate . . . ?"

I groaned. "Tate Bromberger."

"Does anything ever happen with him?"

I stuck out my tongue. "Ugh. Yes. You could stop that, actually. Don't do it."

"I will totally do it!" she sang out. "When? What happens? What do I do? Do we get married?"

"Oh, Lord."

"Well, do we . . . ?"

"Just trust that enough happens that someday you will never want to hear his name again, or think about him, ever." I pretended to vomit over the railing.

"Yay!" she said. She sighed happily. "Tell me about my other future boyfriends. What about this other guy—wait, are you married?"

"I'm partnered," I said, because I choose the language of equality whenever I can.

"Do you mean I'm a lesbian? Because I am really surprised, although sometimes I do think about—"

I cut her off. "I'm married," I said. I quickly added, "To a man."

"Well, duh. You're married. What's he like? What's his name?"

"I'm not going to tell you."

"Is he somebody I already know?"

"Thank God, no."

"So tell me. Are you worried that I'll meet him and not like him and ruin it for you?"

My thoughts hadn't netted it out that far, but now that she said it, that was a vulnerability I should have anticipated. I thought of Rafael the way he was the night we met: so quick, such nice eyes, such a sharp take on my company's market positioning. When we'd talked, I'd felt a little shivery. I had kept reminding myself that he wasn't that handsome, but I found him very much so.

"He's not your type. He's a wonderful guy, kind, generous, a very capable executive, well respected in the private equity space. But you wouldn't appreciate him yet."

"If you say so. But you're in love, right? It's true love?"

I thought of Rafe now, of the look in his eyes when I got up from dinner to take a work call, or how he left his beard clippings stuck to the sink after he shaved. We were opposites in so many ways, and over time it was harder, not easier, to bridge those differences: he was messy, I was neat. He was charming and good at talking to people, I was good at anticipating their computing needs. He loved Macs, I preferred PCs. He was into squash and I liked to do high-intensity interval training in the office between meetings. He was fun, I was generally regarded as un-fun. He was overpaid, I was probably underpaid. He liked to make and eat delicious meals, and I tried to optimize for protein and speed, which is why I was so seduced by complete liquid nutrition. He'd grown up poor, and I'd had an easy, wonderful childhood packed with ballet lessons, music, gymnastics, and *Little House on the Prairie*–related field trips. But opposites attract, I guess. We were both fascinated by innovation and wanted to work on bleeding-edge technology. We used to talk about advancements in tech the way other people talk about whatever other people talk about. "It's blissful," I assured her.

"Do you have kids?"

"I do." I smiled, thinking of them, at home half a world away.

"Can I ask, is this a terrible question, but is your vagina very slack?"

I ignored her.

"When did you become such a prude?"

"While I have your ear, you should take up running," I said. This was like a meeting getting out of control, and I brought it back to order. "And yoga and Pilates. I do yoga and run and kettlebells and free weights and eat a mostly vegetarian diet, except when on work travel, when I allow myself lean proteins for jet lag—I consider myself a flexitarian—and I do meditation and tai chi and—"

She interrupted me, looking down at the street. "Why are the cars so . . . blah-colored and roundish? They look overweight, like normal cars on steroids."

"That's how cars are," I said.

"Not really."

"It's better this way," I said. "More aerodynamic. More the way it's supposed to be. Progress!"

"Says robo-you."

"It's good you're being so calm about this," I told her.

"It's just a dream," she said. "I'll wake up and be relieved that none of it is real. I saw the future—the cars are all dirty-dishwater-colored and lumpy and people carry tiny televisions and I have become a ballbusting bureaucrat." She yawned. "I'm ready to wake up now."

Inside the hotel room, she sank presumptuously onto my bed. She seemed, finally, a little worried. Or maybe she was sucking up so I wouldn't toss her out into the night.

I stared at her. Doubt prickled my skin. Maybe it was the temperature change from coming inside. "Do you feel completely real?"

"What's that mean? Do *you* feel real?"

I pondered this. "No," I said. "I often feel like an imposter, but this is a common experience of women in power."

"Tell me things I should know," she said. "Just in case? Please? Give me the shortcuts."

"Well," I said, "I think the more coding classes you can take the better, because even though the languages change and C++ isn't cutting-edge anymore, it's still good discipline and teaches you how to think in computer terms. It's exercise for the mind. I would take as many advanced engineering electives as possible and expand your coding skills. And I'd wake up early to spend at least forty minutes first thing practicing character writing in Mandarin, because it's just a tough thing to find time to shoehorn in when you're helming a startup."

"I meant more like, if I go to the Kentucky Derby which horse should I bet on? Give me the Super Lotto numbers. Or, actually, here's a real one, what the hell, it can't hurt: Do you happen to remember if, on your macroeconomics final, there were questions about the Keynesian cross? I have to take econ to fill my distribution requirements."

"Uh, I'm not sure. Wait, I know! There's this green dress—it's a sheath style—and when you go to Hong Kong and stay at the Mandarin Oriental, you leave it behind and the maid claims it isn't in the room, but I am sure it is. Be very careful with that dress."

"It might not be my style," she said, looking me over. She was sprawled on the bed and she laid her head down. Her eyes were closing as she spoke.

"And your retainer. Wear that. Look at this." I showed her my cockeyed teeth on my lower jaw. "My biggest regret," I said, pointing at a tooth. "Just wear it."

"That's your biggest regret?" she said. "That you didn't wear your retainer? Couldn't you get a new one made if you care that much?"

I opened my mouth but couldn't say anything. "Well, I don't believe in regrets," I said. "I believe that working within constraints can be good for creativity and innovation, and that we have to keep our eyes on what's coming. Anyway, you can't sleep there. Here, come." I led her into the sitting area. She lay down on the narrow sofa and seemed immediately asleep, then turned over. She lifted her head and smiled at me very sweetly, and then closed her eyes again. I got her a pillow and a blanket from the closet, but when I came back she was sprawled on the floor, like my indecorous, loose-balled, and brain-damaged childhood English spaniel, Chili.

I hadn't thought of Chili in ages. I felt some kind of surge of happiness. Might as well say it. An experiment, a test. "You look like Chili," I said quietly.

She rolled over. "Chili-dog?"

I blinked. What was that, tears? Funny. "Lying like that. Yeah. How's Chili?"

"Chili's good," she said. "He's a good boy. Is he . . . ?" Her expression changed. "I guess he's dead now, right?"

"He has a good long life," I said. "A really good long, happy life."

She smiled at me and curled around the pillow. I walked to the door and when I got there, I turned. What if I were right about her? This was my chance.

"Couple quick things: Make sure you get coffee with the founder of a biotech startup when he comes to visit his cousin who's in your econ class! Will you remember that? And don't drop your upper division comp sci classes, no matter how hard they are at first!" I said, but she was still and unresponsive. "Make sure you *take* upper division comp sci classes. Go to all your professors' office hours! And floss your teeth. That's the one people always say is a big regret. In movies." I went into the bedroom and closed the door.

I n the bedroom, before I fell asleep, I took out a notebook and wrote down a list of the things I wanted to tell her.

These were things that seemed harmless enough not to upset the broad scheme of her life, but that might make a significant difference in retrospect. I took out a yellow legal pad and drafted a list:

1. If you ever get a gooey eye, don't mess around, see a doctor, even if your schedule is packed.
2. Please don't ever not use condoms. Please keep in mind that it is your own older and wiser self telling you this. It's not propaganda.
3. Try running—you will like it. Has Pilates been invented

yet? Do that. I wish you would pay attention to your laterals. Stay fit. Keep in mind that it will reduce cellulite acquisition.

4. When Grandma gives you a Krugerrand for your twenty-first birthday, have Dad put it in his safe deposit box because you *will* lose it, I promise you.

5. The stock market goes way up in 1999. But get out of tech by July 2000.

6. As discussed, keep wearing your retainer.

7. Sunscreen (60+) and remove makeup every night.

8. Brush up on multiple regressions before the departmental comprehensive senior year. But don't freak out—you pass.

9. Try to maintain good sleep habits. I'm not sure this is possible. But try.

10. Start working on your Mandarin tones.

11. I'm giving you a list of big IPOs—see if you can invest early in any of them. They're not going to let you in easily so show some hustle. Also, these are some great companies for a first job.

12. Remember you won't always have the time you have now, so this is the time to learn Arabic.

13. Remember that greatness is difficult but worth it.

14. There will be plenty of time for boys/men/romance/dating once you're a VP. There's no point before then.

15. Remember, with men, the key quality you need is that they'll put your career first, since it's hard to both be extremely ambitious.

16. But men who don't want to be #1 aren't going to be exciting enough for you.

17. I haven't figured out how to reconcile those two either, but maybe you can.

18. Having a killer work ethic is worth more than riches.

I sighed, looking it over. It seemed paltry. "Things are often for the best," I added encouragingly. "And when they're suboptimal you can work to improve them."

I wondered if I should say something to her about Rafe. "Keep an eye out for a tall, dark, handsome stranger"? If a man comes up to you at a party and puts his hand on your arm and asks you whose party it is, tell him, but when it turns out he's supposed to be at a different party, celebrating the launch of a different company's product, try to get him to stay with you instead. Although I hadn't needed to be told. I had done it without any prior warning. I had even incentivized him to stay by filching him drink tickets. He'd come up to ask me a question, but I just liked the way he looked. That's so superficial, but you know, product packaging totally affects your user experience, and I found him enticing, almost uncomfortably so. It was uncharacteristic of me to flirt, but it had happened. Maybe I just needed to make sure she *went* to that party that night. I hesitated. If I'd known it was going to be such an impactful night, I don't know if I would've handled it so well. I wouldn't have felt so free. There's irony there, in that I've often thought about how, if Rafe had been wearing a Conch that night and had its reliable direction-giving at his disposal, he never would have ended up at my party at all. That bothers me, that I'm helping people operate more smoothly and arming them with the information they need, but sometimes users are going to miss out too. I wasn't sure what to tell her.

But if she met someone else, there would be no life with Rafe. What about Nova and Blazer? I felt a pang, thinking of a world in which they didn't exist. Though Blazer didn't exist eleven months ago, in current form, and I hadn't known what I was missing.

And should I say something about the lightning? Yes. No. I touched the scar on my abdomen and trailed my fingers across my body. The list was missing the one thing that really mattered. When it's a rainy night, and you are with a friend, don't go outside and sit on an aluminum cooler during a thunderstorm. I hesitated. I let my mind skate over the memory, very lightly: the pain, the feeling of tight burned skin, the heavy shuffle of my useless left leg, the boring grid of squares on my hospital room ceiling, the agony of lying in bed and hearing distant thunder as summer arrived and departed outside my hospital window. The Spanish soap opera I watched, every day, gradually gaining a sense of its meaning the way you wriggle on a very tight-fitting turtleneck. The endless hours of loneliness, lying immobilized, with only my laptop for company.

It had been awful. I couldn't tell her.

But when it did happen, when she was lying on the ground, flattened by the surge, would she think of me and wonder why I hadn't? In the days afterward, when she was suffering in the wheeled bed, would knowing I hadn't spared her make it worse? Could it have been any worse?

I thought of her — guileless, unafraid, Nova-ish in her contrarianism and curiosity. It was too bad. It was really a shame. But if she didn't go through the experience, awful as it was, she would not become me. It had been difficult, and yet it had been . . . I prompted myself to finish. Worth it. Hadn't it been? I could not quite say that, even to myself. But this was how it had to be, and difficult calls are difficult; that's why they are difficult calls. Doesn't mean you shouldn't make them, or that you are wrong. I tore the page off the pad, folded the paper over and creased it, and put it on the desk.

This was an interesting development. It was unusual. It could be an edge. How could I use it?

Chapter 7

I woke up that morning in my bed, in the hotel room, fully dressed and with something wadded against my head that I determined, after unballing it, to be Nova's Cannes sweatshirt. I shook it out and gazed at it, surprised to see it. It was stained with dried blood and its small size made that especially gruesome. I held it out in front of me and my mind flicked to a kind of imagined live footage of the kids getting out of bed, starting their day, peeking out from behind large bowls of oatmeal, and then I remembered the time change—they were still asleep; I was ahead of them by hours. Rapidly, I tried to rewind the mental tape. It was no good: the image dissolved, the realness and sense of connection were gone. I gathered the sweatshirt into a tight ball and hurled it across the room. It unfurled in the air and sank into a heap by the wastepaper basket, with an inglorious wave of one arm. Nova wouldn't care. Life was a mystery to her, what she owned, what was going to happen next. Willow could get the festival to send another. Conch is a sponsor.

I gave my scalp a delicate examination with my fingertips (it had acquired a disconcertingly crusty patch, and although I wanted to rip off the scab I didn't let myself) and then got up and started the shower. I got under the stream of water tentatively, but it felt OK on my head. At home, I have switched to a kind of shampoo that is free of some bad-for-you ingredient, which, it turns out, plays a key role in making lather. The hotel's shampoo was the kind that has it. The glop I shook out onto my palm smelled lemony and pleasantly unfamiliar, and when I worked it, gingerly, into my hair, it did not sting and puffed around me like a dream.

The car, the girl, the café, the cigarette—elements of a very strange dream. I did not feel upset by it. I just felt like I was probably suffering the results of overwork, which is a cliff I've been approaching for a long time and have been warned about by Greer, Cullen, and my doctors. Even my 360 review hinted at it: while admiring my prodigious work capacity, an anonymous reviewer said, "It's hard to see how she can sustain this long-term." When I read it I thought, just you watch. And, also, I wonder if I can ID you from your prose style. Yet feeling this fired up felt good. I felt more alive, like I had reached levels of transcendence only available through this path, and that my imagination and dream life were in some kind of overdrive as a result. The feeling I'd been left with was not one of anxiety or distress, just a calm, matter-of-fact sense that it had been interesting and enjoyable, as it often is, to have an intense, weird, vividly rendered dream. I was gratified by my creativity, by the powers of my unconscious. It gave me a sense of contentment, like diving into an absorbing financial model and losing all connection with the world outside Excel for a whole day and night, sustained only by the old wasabi peas rolling around my desk drawer. It reinforced for me that the human mind is truly an exceptional machine, with capacity and potential that continue to awe me.

When I came out of the bathroom in my towel, I went into the living room to find the power cord for my laptop. There was nobody on the floor, nor any sign of a pillow or blanket. I had not expected there to be. Of course there wasn't. I chided myself for even having a part of myself that had wondered, that had invented a pretext when I still had one-quarter power remaining in my laptop battery.

I thought I had left the car key on the table beside the door, but there was no key either.

I checked out of the hotel and got into the car Willow had arranged to take me to the airport. As we pulled away from the hotel, I looked back and thought, for just a moment, that I saw the slimmest sliver of the car, glittering. I thought about whether to have the driver turn down that street, just to take a look. I hesitated—I could inquire at the hotel's front desk about whether they'd noticed a girl leaving, or try to track down Enrique, or even go back to the bar in the mountains. But what would that get me? I had a flight to catch—I'd been invited to fly back with an acquaintance in his private jet, and I didn't want to chance missing the flight and having to fly commercial. There was no time, even if . . . well, it wasn't worth going down that trail of hypotheticals. Paperwork, shipping fees, back-and-forth with my assistant, who could barely figure out which SIM card to switch out in my phone depending on where I was going to be. Why even think about any of it in these terms, as if it were real? And perhaps—not perhaps, *most likely* ("Live in the world of data, not delusion," my mentor in business school used to say)—it had just been another car I was seeing, and something about its shape or color had snagged the hem of my dream and was pulling it back into view—it was not unusual, was it, to have a dream that took place in the foreign city where you were staying? I'd bet it was likely. Almost inevitable, even psychologically healthy. It was probably the mind attempting to synthesize so many disparate threads and create synergies. Perhaps my dream had been too powerfully rendered and the excess imaginative capacity had seeped into my waking hours. The demands on me all day were such that I didn't have time to obsess or worry about the car or—this part I didn't even want to think about, wasn't prepared even to say to myself—the girl. That's the good thing about having such a demanding schedule. Even the most tenacious problems are like barnacles sliced off the rocks by the swift, sharp force of urgency. There's no capacity in the schedule for low-priority emergent items. Those get delegated or forgotten or cast out to sea.

I never thought I'd adjust to living with jet lag, but you do; it's just a chronic feeling of nausea that underlies every other experience. An embellishment, like italicization or font color, that doesn't affect the content. You can get used to anything. I have a protocol of Unisom and B6 capsules to take before bed, which helps. Sometimes I do that; more often I advise others to.

It was a pleasant flight without the usual hassles of having to line up and go through rigmarole. There's a nice man who takes care of everything in the private plane terminal. I would have preferred to work the whole time, but I was socially pressured to drink French 75s and chat with the other fliers on board. On the bright side, I made a promising new contact. Flying private improves just about every part of the air travel experience, but jet lag is still a challenge.

Soon I was back in the United States, alone and striding through a crowded public airport. I visualized/strategized: bathroom, nasal squeeze, listen to voice messages while peeing (my pee streams out twice as fast as other users of the women's bathroom and I listen with pleasure, thinking about the time I save), customs, hydration, car, ten almonds.

I did a standing nap in line at passport control—I didn't close my eyes, just loosened my muscles, concentrated on my breath, and invited the cells of my body to refresh themselves. Afterward I felt totally rested. If not totally, then improved.

Slight hiccup at the passport counter. I couldn't find it.

"It must be here," I said. My wallet fanned out. A stack of cards. License, let's see, ID card for the gym I never go to, pool card for the pool I've been to once, no, credit card, credit card, fancy department store charge, frequent customer card at a noodle shop in Malaysia, punch cards to coffee shops, punch card to balsamic vinegar shop in beach town (one punch), frequent flier cards, crumpled UAE dirham note, fro-yo VIP card, investment bank debit card, a brick of business cards given to me by other people, corporate ID from the old scanner system, aha, oh, dear, that's not it.

"I always leave it in this pocket," I said. My mind went back to the hotel. My body prepared itself for a crisis.

"Actually," I said, very calmly, "I must have taken it out at the hotel. I laid it on the desk. I probably put it down with some papers and it slipped inside." I flipped through the briefing book in my bag, aerating the pages. No passport. "It was here, and it's not. This is very concerning to me." I did not say how much so. "I think it may have been stolen. What do I do?"

Quickly, I conferenced with myself. The missing passport presented a multifaceted challenge. One prong was that it invalidated or complicated my understanding of yesterday's situation. In my dream, I had taken it out of the pocket. The second was that its absence prevented me from crossing into the United States. Of the two problems, only one demanded immediate attention. "What now? I have a critically important meeting in two hours and I have to be there, so I'm motivated to do whatever I need to do. I'm Global Premier Plus Rhodium Elite—does that help? I flew once from Denver without my wallet and was asked a series of questions about my previous residences, which I assume were pulled from government records . . . I suppose this will be similar? And I apologize to you, because I realize this is extra hassle." I paused and looked the customs guy in the eye, to build a connection. He was heavyset, with appraising eyes under smoky-tint glasses and a brown-and-gray mustache. We viewed each other seriously: we were both on the same team, committed to safety and American greatness. Saw myself reflected in the glass divider. I was makeupless, hair pulled back into a severe bun, wearing a V-neck black sweater made of sustainable bamboo lyocell. My face was open, honest, and tired-looking but with a kind of lyrical focus. I looked impassioned and purposeful, like an Oil of Olay ad.

"I'm sorry, ma'am, but would you step this way." Had I really taken out the passport? I must have. Or maybe it was still in there, caught in a fold of my bag.

"How long might this take? I'm trying to make a meeting."

"Might be a while, ma'am, I couldn't say."

"Wait, are you wearing a Conch?" I said suddenly.

"I am," he said. "I just got one from my daughter."

"That's my company!" I said. "Do you like it? Here—see, I'm wearing mine." I lifted my earlobe up to show him. I've had these experiences before, where fellow Conch users—the Conch Community—come together to compare experiences, and yes, you might think that both of us owning the same consumer product is a slim foundation on which to build a personal connection, but in fact true friendship and connection can be forged on such a basis: Disney, Apple, and Jeep are all leaders in this way, in creating strong individual brands that consumers identify with as an extension of their personal values. Why not Conch?

"Do you like it?"

He hesitated. I tried charm, of the direct sort: "Please say yes."

"It's not bad," he said. He rubbed behind his ear. "I'm not used to it yet."

"The voice, you mean?"

"Yeah. It makes fancy suggestions. It doesn't really fit my personality. It gives me a headache."

"That's great feedback. I'll share that with our team. You know what? If you look straight at me, it will say, 'Say hello to Shelley Stone'—that's me. Then you'll know it's me."

"Yeah, it did that a few minutes ago." He shrugged, unimpressed, and scratched around his Conch. "I get some neck sweat right here. It's a good idea, but—"

"We have a new model coming out in October that will address the needs of heavy perspirers. Let me send you one."

"I can't accept gifts, ma'am," he said. "But that's good to hear, I might look into it."

"I hope you will." I studied his name tag, committing the name—Kurt—to memory.

Occasionally I have had an experience where my attention is tugged to some detail, and I realize I should pursue it without really knowing why. It's like a purple glow affixes to some item—a cell in the spreadsheet, certain stock symbols, a suite number in a building's list of occupants, a bullet point in a presentation. "That's an interesting last name, Kurt," I said, seeing his name tag pulse, very faintly, in this way.

It wasn't really pulsing. I didn't really believe it was surrounded by a violet haze. I knew that my unconscious mind, a kind of built-in highlighter, was pressing down a little till the conscious me noticed. But I haven't talked about this phenomenon—not with Rafe or Greer or even my best friend, Christine. It's just too intimate, and perhaps it reminds me too much of that day with the purple glow on the tree, and everything after.

He glanced down at his tag as if he didn't know what it said.

"I knew a Heidi with that last name in high school," I said finally. "That was in Wisconsin, though." Something fluttered deep in my mind. Without the dream, would I have been thinking about Wisconsin or remembered Heidi, a person I'd barely known, and so long ago? It was strange—a new synapse seemed to have opened up.

"Yeah, whereabouts?"

"A small town," I said. "I grew up there. You probably haven't heard of it." Nevertheless, I told him.

"No kidding," he said. "That's where my aunt and uncle were. Used to spend my summers there. They lived right near that square in the center of town."

"Courthouse side or bandshell side?" I asked, the way I'd overheard my mother ask a thousand times, using a special friendly voice that had once driven me batty.

He smiled. "Bandshell. Couple blocks. Big yellow house right by the river."

I blinked, startled. "I think I remember that house. I had a friend who lived next door."

"No kidding. They had a neighbor . . . what was the name? Nice kid . . . Real bad what happened to him."

"That's right."

"Where'd you live?"

I described how to walk to my house from the courthouse in the center of town, down the gridded streets, past the shoe store we went to, with "Bootery" written in script along its brick wall, the turnoff to the ice cream parlor or the windy path along the river.

"Your family still there?"

I shook my head. "My dad passed away last year. You from Wisconsin?"

He was. I already knew that.

"You know, they have fancy food here in San Francisco, but

in Wisconsin they have *good* food." A little bit of a sop, but true. A basket of cheese curds and a nice cold New Glarus Spotted Cow actually would have been very tasty and comforting just then.

It helped, I think. I was through in half an hour. Not bad.

Sven, my first real boyfriend, once described me as wholesome. Being from Wisconsin, I guess. Working hard. Having a sturdy, symmetrical appearance. A center part in my hair. A willingness to eat pizza (then).

Sven was also my boss, but that was how it worked at startups. There was no time for extracurricular social life; you had to make do with the people at work. We were so busy we barely had time to talk, let alone to make out while waiting for databases to rebuild. After we broke up he got extremely rich and now lives somewhere remote and self-sustaining to prepare for peak oil. I learned a lot from the relationship:

1. Peak oil is going to be a big problem.
2. Better to go public too soon than too late (with your IPOs and your relationships).
3. Don't read his email.

After that, I mostly kept my head down and worked. I couldn't say I was lonely, because there were always people around, like the programmer at the next desk. Once he gave me a pierogi. But I was still looking for something more.

I didn't necessarily think I'd find it—there weren't many people who matched my drive to excel. But meanwhile I had my career to focus on. I had a workplace that fed me nutritiously and handed over new power cords anytime I reached into my bag and couldn't find mine. Work also equipped me with a fleece hat and a coffee mug, printed with soon-outdated versions of our company's logo. Work was satisfying, it was frustrating, it was at times enraging, it occupied the full range of emotional possibilities, and it took everything. Sometimes I dreamed of going on vacation, backpacking through Thailand or fly-fishing in hip boots in a cold glacial stream, but no matter how scenic it was, or how much fun an activity was supposed to be, I always felt, away from work, like I was missing out.

Rafe didn't seem like the type of person who would be my boyfriend, which was part of why I liked him. I thought of him as someone I'd remember fondly from a different future.

On one of our early dates Rafe and I went for a walk and got ice cream. It was a nice night, and we walked around in the dusk, cyclists tooting past us, not heading anywhere in particular. I enjoyed it, and I think he did too—he kept reaching over and squeezing my hand. Afterward we strolled to the Caltrain station. I kissed him goodbye and went around the other side to head back to the office. He looked confused. "Enjoy your night!" I called from the opposite platform. He looked startled. My train pulled away, and I watched him standing there licking his ice cream.

The next day he called to find out what had come up. Nothing, I said, I just had some work to do.

On a date a few weeks later we went to a screening of *Dog Day Afternoon* in Palo Alto. During the movie I got a few texts from work and answered them by leaning over with my head between my knees, my phone underneath the seat. After that I couldn't concentrate on the hostage situation in the bank anymore and decided to go back to the office.

Rafe followed me out of the theater and seemed annoyed.

He thought we should watch the rest of the movie and either go back to one of our apartments together (his vote) or, failing that, say goodnight and each go home. I thought this was an intrusive request, and illogical: What made that option superior—why did it matter where I went? "Net-net," I said, "it shakes out the same way: we're not together, but in my preferred option I have better internet and a larger monitor. Why should the time we spend together have to fall at the end of the day?"

"It's the difference between lunch and dinner," he said. "Lunch is a break. Dinner is intimate. You can let down your guard."

"I don't usually eat dinner."

"Don't you want to spend time with your boyfriend?"

I blushed; I hadn't referred to him as my boyfriend, and I wouldn't have done it yet. The thrill of the acknowledgment was dampened by the sense that the privilege might be taken away before I could use it. I looked at my watch miserably. "I gave you two hours," I said. It came out like a whine, but also pleadingly. "We can look up how it ends."

"I've already seen it twice," he said equably. "It's OK." He hugged me.

"It's been nice, and I hope we'll stay in touch," I said, attempting to break up with him—out of duty and decency, not because I wanted to.

He looked surprised. "You don't even want to try?"

I felt like Rafe had lots of options, but when you're the kind of person I am, with jagged edges, a specific sort of puzzle piece, you click when you can. So I tried. I looked for out-of-the-box solutions. "I could get up earlier to work," I suggested.

"We could eat later," he offered, meeting me halfway. "Like, at midnight. Or never." This amused me.

And so I tried, with all the effort and dedication I brought to everything. And I thought he'd try that hard too. It was so good I didn't want to see any problems. Very quickly we started talking about the future, with an implied sense that we would be together. We were inquiring about each other's tastes and hopes and desires—once, exhilaratingly and riskily, the possibility of a baby—after the fact, the same way you'd discuss the thickness of the ice while strolling across a frozen pond. We were already, in a way, far out from shore.

"What's your dream?" he said. "What do you want to do?"

"What do I want to do?" I was surprised he didn't know. "This, exactly this, all the time." I gestured around. We were not actually standing on a frozen pond, we were eating sandwiches he'd brought over at lunchtime, and we were sitting on a low wall in the atrium of my office building, enjoying one of the many pleasant days the Peninsula is known for. "I want to do my part to turn Gorvis into a household word and a billion-dollar industry and an unstoppable force in communications. What about you?"

He laughed. "Right, me too." It was sunny out and he looked sunny, eating a prosciutto sandwich, the sun on his face.

"Really? You want to join Gorvis?"

"Well, let's see." He chewed. It was taking him a long time to think of his goal. I thought of mine every morning when I first woke up. But I loved him and I waited. "OK, this is a good one: I'd like to win my club squash championship this year." A crinkled smile and squint, letting me in on a secret: "I think I've got it in the bag."

And I thought, perfect, he's hungry to win, but later, after we'd been married for a few years, I realized it was about the wrong thing.

Part 3

NORTHERN CALIFORNIA

+·+·+·+·+·+·|·+·+·+

Chapter 8

"3:00 A.M. IS ME TIME"

As told to *C-Suite* by Shelley Stone, CEO of Conch, Inc. *(This interview has been edited and condensed.)*

What's your daily routine?

I get up around 3:30. That's my me time. I'm on the treadmill—it's so relaxing. I love having the chance to just browse the papers—local, international—while pounding out a couple of leisurely seven-minute miles and checking the forecast, catching up on shows on Netflix, doing a little spreadsheet crunching, mapping out next quarter's acquisitions. Sometimes I read classic literature. We can learn so much from the classics. It's not just about breadth; it's about depth. Also, it's such a great time to answer email while doing some high-intensity interval training. I also sip my coffee mindfully while meditating on the tree outside my window, just riding the moment in all its fullness, being open to the gifts of the present with an open heart, and also getting on top of my inbox and gaining global context I can leverage later across all our operations.

I do a couple of phone calls with Europe after I start the shower, while I'm waiting for the water to get hot. We have a big house and a lot of bathrooms—we're really blessed, but even a clear win comes with some cons, though often those don't shake out till late in the game, but anyway, we have this large house, perfect for holding charity events or hosting parties with all our friends, but the downside of the incredible amount of pipeage is that it takes a long time to get hot water to all of the bathrooms. So I punch out a couple calls on the bathroom landline while I'm waiting for the water to heat.

I'm always asking myself, how can I fit in a little more work? What else can go, so there's more time to work? Just because it's 4:30 or 5:00 a.m. our time doesn't mean things aren't really rocking in the Malay production facility, so I like to check in with some of our vendors and retailers. Making that time count allows me to squeeze in a shower, because it's important to take time for yourself. While I'm in the shower I brainstorm solutions to work problems. Then I get out. I have towels I get from a special place in London, extra soaky. I have a system for drying myself in a quarter of the time. Ping me for details.

Wow, so you get up at 3:30 every morning?

It's true, you have to be disciplined to lead this kind of life. Discipline is so important. I'm a grateful hostage to my routines and my checklists. But the truth is, and I'm just going to give it to you straight, that when anxiety is ripping your insides to pieces, it is actually a lot easier to get out of bed than to lie there wanting to die. I can't sleep—it's not that I don't want to. But I need the time, so it all works out. Anxiety has replaced caffeine for me, not to mention a stimulant I was introduced to at TED Ulan Bator. Cut that last part, I'm just kidding.

So you're not just an executive, you're also the mother of young kids. Tell me about balancing that. Is morning when you spend time with your kids?

Absolutely. Sleep is key to kids' brain development, and there's lots of new research about that, but even though I always tell the kids that they can sleep till 6:30 they take after me and they're up in the 5s, so we get a lot of great quality time together then.

In our house piano practice is the first thing we do, and while it was hard to get a teacher to come to the house that early to work with them, the payoff in their skill development has been huge. Blazer's only a year old, but he gets a lot out of it. And it's a luxury, I know, but we have two pianos so when he's a little older they'll be able to practice in parallel. After piano is breakfast, which is usually a hot bowl of ancient/ heritage grains and a gummy vitamin, and our maid speaks Mandarin to them—we aren't tutoring them like some of those Type A parent-loons you meet in the Bay Area, it's just for fun and auditory exposure so they'll have perfect tones.

I take my daughter to school myself. People are always surprised by this, that I do that. You know, some things are important and those are the things I make time for. I can't drive the car myself, of course, because I have calls or I'm on my laptop, but I put my daughter in the car with me and I nudge her with my shoe when she gets loud. Sometimes she goes through my briefcase and plays on my extra phone. And sometimes I can't do it—you can't do it all, I'm telling you, pick and choose, divide and conquer, that's how you win the long game—and then the driver takes her, or the nanny or whoever.

Obviously we are extremely blessed to have live-in help, and every day I appreciate my good fortune. In a position like mine

you need that kind of coverage, because there are mornings—
not many, but once in a while—when neither my husband,
Rafael, nor I can take the kids. Not very often, only a couple of
times a month. Maybe ten.

What's your secret to balancing it all?

If I had to laser in on my most key pieces of advice, I would say
surround yourself with good help, pick a good spouse (which
is basically the same thing), offload everything that isn't core,
and don't lose minutes. I read once that time management is
impossible—what you are managing is not time, which ticks
on with or without you in its own inexorable current, but
yourself. I manage myself, my actions, my thoughts, my goals,
my calories ingested and expended, mood, work deliverables,
and long-range planning with an intensity and accountability
that I know most people could not handle, and which I would
never subject one of my subordinates to because it's too much
to ask, but if you want to know how I've gotten to where I am,
that is how.

What advice would you give to a working parent?

We have this thing in our house called Question Time. We
borrowed it from Parliament. Instead of having the kids ask
us questions all day, which is disruptive and throws us off our
game, we have them save up for Question Time. And then
Rafe and I get out our iPads and the kids ask all their questions
and we can provide real-time answers with factual citations and
multimedia/interactive supplementation.

And if my daughter comes up to us at other times while
we're on our laptops—during the time when our commitments
are to our companies—then we just say, gently, sweetie, it's

not Question Time now. And if she fusses about that I tell
her to Voice Record it and ping me the MP3 and I'll add
it to the queue for later. Or else she goes and asks Jacqui,
our housekeeper, who tells her that bad fairies will bite her
for asking, which usually satisfies her. Jacqui also provides
multicultural exposure so critical in a globalized world.

How do you foster your children's passion for STEM?

Great topic! It's important to start early. I believe pre-K kids
are at an age when they're naturally interested in so much,
including fundamental tech and business principles. To stoke
that early interest, I've set up a program for my daughter
where she comes to work with me one day per month. She
learns from our top people, and that way she'll have a jump
on knowing if her inclination is to pursue law, engineering,
software development, or finance (I'm not gung-ho on
marketing for her). It's totally laid back. My hope is she has
fun and doesn't even realize she's learning about stuff like the
difference between seed funding and a Series C round. It's
a promising model, and I've been trying to brand it with an
acronym because I find that adds a lot of legitimacy and power
to a program. I'm thinking of ODETTE (Offering Daughter
Education and Training in Technical Excellence), after the
princess in *Swan Lake* who turns into a swan, except here
I'm trying to turn my princess into a vice president of systems
development.

*You were struck by lightning as a teenager. How has that
affected your approach to life and business?*

It was obviously something that made a . . . you don't sail
through something like that, I don't care how focused you

are. It's the thing that . . . well, I wouldn't wish it on you, but it made me who I am; does that make sense? That bolt of lightning gave me this energy and focus, indirectly, which I use every day. It's . . . you know, I just don't feel like talking more about it today. Let's get back to work, that's what everyone says I say all the time.

Chapter 9

"Now, Nova," I said, in the car on the way into Conch. It was our special day, official acronym TBD, when I bring her into my office. We both look forward to it all month. Actually, I'm not sure if Nova does—she doesn't yet have the kind of memory that attaches labels to experiences, or knows what to expect, and she is surprised, each morning at breakfast, to hear whether it's a weekday or the weekend. She doesn't believe us, that there's a pattern. And to be honest I sometimes dread her visits to Conch. But I do think it's a good concept. When I came up with the idea it seemed innovative and like a natural fit for the kind of person I am, someone who seamlessly weaves a rich family life around a big job. Also, Rafe had been badgering me to spend more one-on-one time with Nova, so I've been bringing her in with me one morning a month. I'm not sure if it's accomplishing anything, but it's early yet, and that's not a reason to abandon the project: the execution of a new initiative is often a struggle.

"I'm going to whisper a special word to you," I said, leaning toward her booster seat. We were in the backseat of the car together, wedged in with Melissa. "This special word is like a password leading to all kinds of secret information."

"I know it already," Nova yelled. She took out a plastic horse and turned it over, inspecting it from all sides. Nova is allowed to bring a small toy with her to Conch to keep the experience fun and light. Today she was carrying a little suitcase of plastic horses. Bottom line, this is fine, but I feel like overall since we launched this program a few months ago Conch employees have learned more about horses than she has learned about their jobs.

"Listen, darling, I don't think you do. The word is 'data.'"

"It's 'please,'" Nova shrieked. "The magic word. I know that."

Melissa, sitting beside us in the backseat, gazed expressionlessly out the window at a shopping center, even though it was just like virtually every other shopping center between home and work: hot yoga, nail place, dry cleaners. The driver sped up aggressively to make it through a yellow light.

"Well, this might mean more to you someday than it does today, but my magic word is: 'data.' Sing it with me: data! For example, the number of horses you have. That would be data. If you had ten horses, say."

"Thirty-two," Nova said.

"So if you had ten horses," I began. This was the rather clever explanation I had devised while flossing.

"I have thirty-two," Nova explained. "I used to have thirty-five but some got put in the trash on the plane."

"Great!" I said. "Using the *data* you've given me, I know, without even having been there, that it was *three* horses that got put in the trash on the plane."

Melissa, beside us in the backseat, turned to me with an alarmed expression and made rapid, neck-cutting gestures.

"I want it back," Nova wailed. "Daisy, where did you go? Why are you missing me? Why did Daddy throw out the cup?"

"Well, you see, that's a different sort of problem, but for now, let's talk about data. All this information, it's data. And we can use it to . . ." A sort of inner silence settled in me. I felt a deep calm, devoid of the slightest idea of how to finish the sentence. What could we use any of it for?

"Do you understand this?" Melissa asked Nova.

"Yes," Nova said. "Daisy is gone."

"Do ask questions!" I encouraged.

"Data means numbers, right?" Melissa prompted. She looked at me for confirmation.

"Not necessarily," I said. The look in her eyes made me relent. "Oh, all right."

"A number, like two," Melissa said to Nova, holding up her fingers. "Or three. A number is . . . not a letter."

"Not necessarily," I said. Melissa tightened her jaw. Much as I like Melissa, and I'm enormously enthusiastic about the job she does with my children, I don't like her that much in this career-preparation context. She could blend in with the employees at Conch: she's fit, she's outdoorsy, she wears fleece, but she has a totally different mind-set. I'm not sure she's worked in an office, and she doesn't seem to value the skills that would make some-one successful there. This is tricky territory, because how can I tell her I'd be disappointed if Nova became a nanny? And yet she must know that I feel that way, even though I would hardly admit it to myself, because if I didn't, why would I bring Nova to Conch when there is clearly so much potential for embarrass-ment? I want Nova to know that she can do anything, that's the best way to put it, although truthfully I do not want her to do *anything*, I want her to do certain things, and I'm tipping the scales to create those outcomes. Melissa's disapproval annoyed me. I quashed that thought: it's a partnership.

My own private objectives for Nova that morning were for her to greet people politely, shake hands, and initiate a conversa-tion. Also, ask one good question. Some cretinous reporter once implied that I make Nova follow me around and wear a tiny business suit. That is preposterous. This is California; ninety-nine percent of the people I work with are not wearing suits. My only rule is no leggings.

"Nova," I pleaded, "I think you're really going to enjoy this." Nova continued inspecting her horse and ignored me. I once spent half a shuttle flight YouTubing "absence seizures" to make sure Nova wasn't having them, because so often when I ask her a question she doesn't answer. But I think she's just a person of very particular and intense passions; this can be good if channeled productively.

"Aren't you looking forward to being at Conch today?" I asked. Her last visit was a tough morning, but that may have been because she was getting strep.

Nova didn't answer.

"It's OK if you're not," Melissa said.

"Isn't it great for us to spend time together?" I pressed.

"I can't argue with that," Melissa said, evenly, though there was a tinge of argument in the way she said it. Nova looked interested, picking up on this conflict. My driver made the sharp left toward Conch and we all squashed together.

To be clear, I'm not doing this because I'm an overinvolved tiger parent pushing my child to excel. On the contrary. It's the opposite. I've faced a lot of professional challenges along the way, and I want it to be easier for her.

I had assumed my children would be prodigies. But Nova made even being a baby seem difficult. When I look back on her infancy I remember Melissa, fresh from the agency and a stranger to us, always wearing a pair of jeans the style of which you don't see anymore, and didn't see much then either, pacing the hall. She was trying to get Nova to eat. Nova wouldn't eat anything. She'd scream with hunger, but when we offered her the bottle she would twist her head away and scream louder. The idea that we were poking this thing at her, when she was hungry, enraged her. We tried different bottles and nipples of every brand, shape, material, and hole size, and I do mean every, and she didn't like any of them.

It was disheartening, because it seemed like eating should be part of her operating system. She was completely impossible to reason with. I remember watching Melissa jiggling Nova, jiggling the bottle, and making a shushing-clucking sound. I called from upstairs, "Is it working?" My voice lacked confidence, and there was too long a pause before Melissa answered.

"She's tough," Melissa had said flatly, the frustration buried but not hidden in her voice, and it startled me to hear her say it, because it hadn't occurred to me there was so much variability in babies, that you could get one who just might not get it. It was sobering to think that even the most experienced and highly rated nanny could be outfoxed.

Nova did catch on, luckily, just when it seemed like it would be too late, when they were starting to talk about a tube down her nose. (I want you to take the lead on this, I said to Melissa one night, and I didn't say, because this project is making me cry. But despite my clear instructions, the pediatrician's office kept calling *my* phone.)

That's always how it's been with Nova; waiting for her to get it, bargaining, hoping, accepting the failure of it, and giving up, before it finally happens. I looked over at her. The sunlight through the car window lit up the side of her face and pooled in her lap, where she was sorting the horses that were rearing up from the ones that were standing flat. Her ear peeked out through her combed hair, pink around its edge.

"You could ride horses in your office," Nova suggested.

"I like that wild thinking," I said. I tousled her hair. "Remind me to hold on to that one for Wild Ideas Wednesday." That's the time I block out weekly when my team and I try to outdo each other in generating wild and crazy ideas. Nothing is too crazy if it helps us improve Conch, or leads to novel solutions for business or product challenges, though we generally select only a tiny fraction of our ideas to execute.

I know some people take longer than others, but I think she's going to need a little extra time, maybe quite a lot. I put a lot of energy into developing people. And that's why I implemented this program, and why I want to start her early; so she'll have all the time she needs.

Every day I feel such pride and purpose as I walk into Conch. If I'm not at work, I'm thinking about work, so it's satisfying when my mind and surroundings sync. From the moment the lobby doors part obligingly at my approach, till I get back in the car at the end of the day, I rarely think of anything besides Conch. I treasure this gift of focus and these daily twelve to twenty hours of alpha-brainwaves and caramelized, concentrated workflow pleasure.

I stepped into the lobby, Nova and Melissa trailing behind. Overhead was a high ceiling. Gray filtered light streamed down to the concrete floor, where a piece of smooth sculptural art lay, extruded like a giant piece of pasta. I approached the guard cheerfully. "How was your weekend?"

He had close-cropped hair and wore a jacket and tie, making him by far the most formally dressed person in the building. He sat in a chair that spun. All morning long, stuck in the middle of the tide of incomers, he rotated it, a half turn one way, and then back. He used to be in the navy.

"Good, good," he said. "Too short, like always. You?"

"Fantastic, thanks!"

"Thanks, Shell, for the card you sent. Meant a lot to me."

"How *is* your mother?" I said.

"She's doing better. She's out of the ICU and back in a regular room."

"Good to hear," I said. I was glad to hear. I try to spend ten minutes a day writing personal notes to employees about their life events and milestones—it's just a little effort from me but it means a lot to them.

"I was just sending somebody up to see you." He gestured to a woman who was leaning over the counter, filling out the parking registration log. He handed her a badge from a little plastic basket on the desk, of the type my mom used to store onions in her pantry. "She says she's from the *Silly Valley* blog."

"Oh, hi!" I said, suddenly remembering that I had agreed to be interviewed today. I sighed inwardly because although I love to work, this was not the work I love. Also, a reporter plus Nova is a lot to manage.

The reporter was slighter and less bloggerish than I had expected. She had long hair and a pretty but complicated face. She was wearing a fitted white suit and a turquoise necklace. I hoped her outfit signaled an interest in style, not ambition.

She introduced herself, and I activated the mnemonic I use for locking in strangers' names.

"Of course!" I said. "Hi, Cass. Glad to see you." I grasped her hand, employed high-voltage eye contact (if I have a guilty pleasure, it is eye contact), and gave her a handshake of about seven and a half on a ten-point scale, where ten would be the handshake equivalent of eating an ortolan songbird, bones and all.

She gave me a pleasant but assessing look and said, "Thanks for meeting me so early."

She turned past me. "Hi," she said, in the kind of voice people who don't have kids think will engage children. Nova withdrew against Melissa.

"This is early for you?" I said, also pleasantly, with a tone suggesting that it was interesting to get other people's perspectives and I valued diversity in all forms, even the slugabed lazy kind. Then I smiled strongly, so she would like me.

My Q score, which measures likability, tops out in the single digits. My assistant once told me that, according to Q score, I am slightly less likable than Count Chocula. ("But I like you," she added sweetly, and for that I send her a bundt cake every Christmas.) Why am I not more likable? This has been a source of stress and sadness to me each time the quarterly reports arrive, to the point where I don't want to open the envelopes (and for reasons of vanity I can't bear to have my assistant open them for me). I like myself. I would rather spend a day with me, doing exciting, important, and innovative work, than be with other people, who in my observation spend a lot of time eating slowly at restaurants, dillydallying at the front of the line at coffee shops, and dragging their suitcases slowly through the center of airport concourses. I don't think I'm more judgmental than other people, who often strike me as very judgmental within a narrow and arbitrary resonance band, while not really achieving anything of moment themselves. And I don't think I'm less kind than other people, when you net it out—I always do small things like writing thank-you notes and holding the elevator door open for people on crutches.

Still, a more likable CEO might help Conch at the margins, and I felt I had in me the potential, even the obligation, to become an averagely likable person.

"Cass," I said, "so, this is Melissa, and this is my daughter, Nova, who is joining us today as she often does, just so we can spend extra time together. You don't have to wait here for our publicist. I'll take you up myself. It's no problem!"

The guard, Tony, and I smiled at each other, because this was one less thing for him to do. He stood up and, as I went to scan in, came to stand beside the inner door, which was always locked. He held its silver handle at the ready. Other people open this door themselves, but, you know, for me, special service. This is OK, I think.

I aligned my feet with the blue footprints outlined on the floor and leaned forward toward the iris scanner's round black eye. It felt a little like leaning in to kiss a robot. I tensed my core muscles. I use this dead time to practice kegels.

The shutter clicked, the door hissed, and Tony tried the door, which did not open. "Nope," he said.

"Ah!" I said apologetically, as if it were my own skill deficit. We act like we're really high security at Conch. We are moderate security. Some of it is just window dressing.

"She's been like this all day," he said, tapping the scanner. "Mondays, am I right?"

I happen to love Mondays—they are my most productive day and my favorite (thank God it's Monday, I always think when I wake up). It's not that I dread the weekends per se; I love them differently, like a second child. On Saturday mornings, I feel, despite my efforts, a little down at the prospect of temporarily unplugging, and though I never really do, entirely, there's something depressing about pinging out emails and knowing it could be an hour or more before anyone replies. The workweek at Conch is a joy, so it's a nice feeling to have as much of it as possible still to come. I shook my head at Tony, leaned in again, and this time the bell chimed its familiar descending major third, and the door almost jumped open before he could pull on it.

"Perfect. On the money. Have a good one, Shelley," he said.

I beckoned Cass to go ahead. As he does every day, Tony blew me a kiss as I slipped through, into the inner recesses of Conch.

So give me the rundown for the three people out there who don't know about Conch," Cass said with a barky laugh as we walked together. I pretended this was funny, but actually there are tons of people who have never heard of Conch, and that is sad.

"So, Conch—quick introduction: here's mine." I flicked it

out from behind my ear. "See it? The Conch snaps into place in the little hollow on the back side of the user's earlobe, and it clings there in the little chasm between the back of the ear and the ridge of the skull, counterbalanced by the flesh at the hinge of the jaw. It's like a reverse earbud. It's a strategic location nobody else has leveraged. I could talk all day about what makes the location so ideal, as I said on an investor call just the other day. It's out of sight, so it's not obvious you are wearing it, which a lot of our users like. Sound is transmitted right into the ear. And the Conch can measure air temperature, location via GPS coordinates, skin surface temperature, and, because it is sitting right atop the carotid artery, heart rate, from which, using other contextual clues, it infers stress levels. It combines all this data into rich situational awareness it can translate into actionable info provided right at the moment when you need it."

"Amazing!" Cass said. Nova and Melissa hung back.

"We also use behaviometric analysis—which means studying what users actually do and then bringing it to them when they'd like to do it. There are different patterns and strengths of vibration for different functions, and increasingly we can communicate more and more just through tactile patterns—some users hardly use the phone app at all, they can get so much richness from touch. Up this way," I said. "What do you think of our offices?"

"So modern!" Cass exclaimed.

"Design matters a lot, *I* think. Communication, collaboration, transparency . . . those are our values, and our building materials . . ." I gestured, trying to think of a word to say next. Nothing arrived. I looked at Cass to see if she was writing this down.

Our offices are expansive and open, free of artificial boundaries, like walls, which constrain innovation. The ceiling is industrial; the furnishings are corporate IKEA. Bright bursts of color add wallops of fun and whimsy. In the center of the lobby is a curved staircase, which I ascended, past glowing ovoid pendant lights, pickled light wood, and windows framed in stainless steel, toward a big glass-fronted refrigerator containing no sodas, only juice: healthier!

"It chuffs me when people line the bottles up neatly," I remarked to Cass. That was a positive spin on the way they looked today: shitty! I walked through several departments and said hello to as many people as I could. That's part of my role — being present and public and cheerleading. Seeing and being seen. Setting the tone. Steering the ship. "Good morning!" I said. "Greg! Abby! McQ! You're the new intern, right? You're working with Jess? Great to have you aboard. Todd, what happened to your arm? Sorry to hear that." I pressed my Conch in a follow-up notation. I was moseying through — not a hall, there are no halls at Conch, halls are too medieval, too bidirectional, too limiting — but a big open space traversed by long ribbons of desk. The gray carpet was interspersed with occasional darker gray squares, as if somebody digitized the coffee spills at very low resolution. I went the long way, so I could say hi to the maximal number of employees, and pat several of the large, romping dogs. I led Cass through marketing, customer service, and mobile development, detoured around our pesky legal department, and then went through hardware engineering, and finally to my desk.

My assistant, Willow, came sprinting toward my workstation to greet us. Willow grew up in some sort of commune in Nevada, and that experience has given her a passion for capitalism. She is careful and good at catching problems. Jane, my previous assistant, was even better, but Jane only lasted sixteen months. Her name might have been Joanne.

"Good morning, Shelley," Willow said. She always says it in the same intonation, which is boring to me, and I hear it coming before she says it, but routine can also be a time-saver. She took my bag. "How was your morning? Did the call with the vendor happen?"

"It happened," I said. "It was fine. They're a mess."

Willow's expression suggested that she was sympathetic and also flattered to be given a confidential detail she could leverage in the employee cafeteria.

"Do you want me to read off your schedule?"

I nodded. The human voice is very slow compared with my reading speed, but I like to make sure I haven't missed anything, like the time I thought I was going to Building B for a meeting but then I realized the meeting was in Omaha. It was amusing but I fired that assistant.

"So after the Conclave"—our daily high-altitude, top-of-the-trees strategy meeting—"you have your sit-down with the journalist, who I see you already met." While Cass was looking away, Willow whispered, "Elyse called to remind you to stay on message—remember what happened last time! Also, you have a meeting about the Powerplex acquisition, and a one-on-one about the pop-up store concept. Also, Woody, the product engineer, wants to get on your schedule to talk about his ideas for ConchX." I made a facial expression to mean 1) don't talk about Conch's next iteration in front of the reporter, and 2) I was unavailable to meet with Woody. Willow nodded and continued. "Jen from quality assurance is excited to chat with your daughter, so I'll make sure they're set up. Marketing has the new video loop ready. I redid your slide deck for this morning. Also, the SportConch team wants your go-ahead to move forward with the color palette and fabric they showed you."

"I saw that. I'm not willing to sign off on their selections just yet," I said. "Tell them I want to reconvene on that. Any other critical items?"

"Brad might stop by to chat before the board meeting tonight.

And here's a Dramamine for the car, so you can work." I have her staple a Dramamine to the corner of my schedule if the day involves travel, and a tampon if I'm getting my period.

I nodded. "Oh," Willow said. "One more thing." She glanced at Cass and gave me an uncertain look. "This woman called. Her name is Michelle. She says you owe her." Willow looked confused but then she brightened. "She didn't say what."

I looked over at Cass. She was a few feet away, watching one of the fish tanks. An electric eel swam in lazy loops. We have everything at Conch—Ping-Pong tables, free healthy snacks, strongly electric fish.

I came closer to Willow. "Michelle?" I said quietly.

Willow nodded.

"Someone by that name called here, this morning?"

"That's right," Willow said, a little too loudly, and I noticed Cass sliding open her narrow reporter's notebook, fiddling with her phone.

"That was a very common name in the late seventies," I remarked brightly. "Let's talk about it later."

I felt panic but then I got on top of my panic and stuffed it down, like closing the type of hard-shelled suitcase that was also very common in the late seventies. I couldn't fall apart in front of the press. I led Cass over to my desk.

When I got this job, my dad said, "So, Shell, you'll have one of those big offices with a lot of mahogany and stuff?"

I shook my head.

"What about those leather chairs? Did you get one of those globes that sits on the floor?" He gave the air an imaginary whack-spin.

"No, Dad!" I said, laughing. "It's not like this is the eighteenth century or IBM or something."

I thought of this as Cass examined my desk, which is just like everyone else's desk at Conch, and right out in the open, surrounded by other desks. They're just tables, really. "Don't you ever need privacy, for private conversations?" Cass asked.

"Not at all," I said. "I'm not a fan of privacy. I'm all about promoting its opposite: collaboration." In our office, people sit within high-fiving distance of each other. Everyone can over-hear everyone else's phone conversations, even sensitive ones involving investors or other employees. Thus they gain valu-able insight into our business challenges, which will give them a huge base of knowledge when they go on to found their own companies someday. The openness truly promotes teamwork, sharing, and virality. And the proof is that in winter everybody gets each other's colds.

My desk is covered with stacks of paper and folders, plus the bike helmet of the chief marketing officer, whose desk abuts mine (the bike helmet is sleek, Euro-style; the CMO is sleek, Euro-style too), old water bottles, a rat's nest of phone chargers and cords, an open box of antioxidant energy bars, a plastic take-out container, some stray crumbs that Willow shoots out of the way periodically with an aerosol can when she thinks I can't see her, and of course my monitor, laptop dock, and keyboard, which is where, I hope, some of the magic happens.

Mine is a casual office. I thought about instituting a dress code, but Stefan, my CFO, persuaded me that it would get bad press. We were already riding the bad press for my decision to close the on-site day care—it was useless anyway, the hours were so short—so I deferred to him. I think he was wrong, but it's important to let people feel they have decision-making influ-ence, so the ability to leverage that made it a win for me.

So, I'd love to hear about the company and what you're doing," Cass said, pushing her glasses up the bridge of her nose. "OK if I record this? I'm just going to turn it—where's the button?—on! I don't know how much you know about our site, but many of our readers are women, they're moms, they're professionals, they're go-go-go but they also value consumer electronics, fitness, tech, food, culture, beauty, getaways, spa trends—"

I cut her off. "I get it," I said, nodding to affirm this. "After all, that's me too." Although in very broad strokes. The hovering PR person beamed. I happen to know—thank you to whoever tipped off HR—that she has a personal blog called *The Trend Pouncer*, which features her in a leopard print wrap dress, on the prowl for consulting jobs.

"I'm not very media-oriented," I reminded Cass. "I'm not posing in ball gowns or going to big parties like . . ." I didn't name names.

Journalism is a cratering industry and in many ways the opposite of Conch—the content served up may be of zero relevance to a given user, but that's why it's sometimes so relaxing to read about topics like pixie cuts at the hair salon, because it gets tiring always having to be oneself.

"I have a question for you," Cass said, conspiratorially. "We hear a lot these days about the importance of turning off our phones, our devices . . ." Our eyes met, and I nodded, fingers on chin, to show how seriously I took this tough but important topic. "What would you say to our readers about that, speaking as the CEO of a technology company and also a mom?" Oh, the irony. I smiled, as if this were truly provocative.

I gripped the edge of the counter—we were perched atop high stools at one of our Ideas Served Fresh collaboration stations—and leaned toward her. "I'm so glad you brought that up." I talked about my kids, how they didn't have their own Conch yet, how we didn't let them play on our iPads or our laptops, well, only sometimes, talk to me right before dinner, ha ha. I didn't say, because our nanny has them all day and we have a contract.

"It's a struggle some days to balance it all," I said, with a gulp-laugh that I hoped fused wry authenticity and irresistible charm. I also said things like, "I don't have a magic wand, even though I have a lot of advantages." I always acknowledge my privilege. Acknowledging privilege is likable and honest. "It's a challenge to juggle it all."

Willow approached and hovered a polite distance away, which reminded me that I've been meaning to work out a system of hand signals with her, similar to the way baseball pitchers and catchers communicate. "Yes?"

"Your nine o'clock is hiding behind my desk," Willow said playfully.

"What do you mean by that?" I said. "That's very weird. Why didn't you direct that person to the waiting area or get them a cup of coffee?"

Willow blushed. "Sorry to be unclear. It's your daughter."

"Well, perfect example!" I said to Cass. "Life and work aren't two sides of the same coin, they're . . . well, actually, it's that the *coin* is . . . wait, Willow—where is she?"

She was right under my desk," Willow said. She looked stressed, getting down on the floor in her dress to crawl under there. There was a plethora of power cords, but no Nova. "She was just here, playing with those mules."

"She can't have gone far," I said, but with a sinking feeling—she couldn't go far, except of course for that one time she had. But this was different. It wasn't like she could get out of the building, I reasoned, thinking of our iris scanners and security badging. Fortunately—thank God for the open office—it didn't take long to find her.

"We're over here!" Melissa called.

I was more relieved than I expected to see them together, by the fish tanks in the lobby. "Hi, sweetheart!" I called. Nova was standing on her tiptoes, nose pressed to the glass. Cass and I went over. "There you are!"

"Pretty, aren't they?" Cass said. "I like this one with the fins. Which do you like?"

"All fishes have fins," Nova said irritably. She pointed. "I like the seashells." Have I mentioned she's not great with Ss? It's developmentally normal at this point.

"Sweetie, can you shake hands with my friend Cass?" Nova did not react. "Nice strong grip," I scaffolded.

"No!" Nova yelled. The fish, no fools, scattered.

"Ha!" I said to Cass. "She's got opinions all her own." I pretended to be delighted by this.

"Nova, you're being rigid like a carrot stick, not flexible like a gummy worm," Melissa said calmly, stepping between us. "Let's do our rubber band stretches by the window." Nova dutifully followed her over, lifted her arms over her head, and began to undulate.

I gave Melissa a thumbs-up, but subtly, because I knew it would annoy Nova if she saw. When they were done, I gestured that Melissa could go, so Nova and I could have our special togetherness time. I led Nova and Cass over to QA. "Walk tall like a giraffe," I reminded Nova. Cass stood up straighter. I enjoyed the chance to stroll slowly through departments I don't often visit, glancing at people's screens, asking everyone what they were working on, taking a moment to thank them for all they do for Conch. I noticed that the mere fact of my presence, the enthusiasm and energy I exude, seemed to ignite faster typing, intenter expressions, and greater focus. I wear the mantle of leadership even when I'm not aware of it, even when the mantle is a long belted cardigan. Anyway, it was very satisfying.

"So you're going to check out today how we make sure that Conch does what we want," I explained, with a friendly squeeze of my daughter's hand. "Try to talk to people."

"I don't like that smell!" Nova screamed as we passed the kitchen, where a computer programmer looked up from assembling his breakfast. "It bothers me!"

"Eggs can be stinky," Cass agreed sympathetically, whispering.

"Daddy is stinky," Nova agreed, not whispering. "Eggs is very stinky."

"Shush," I said. "Let's go check out the area over here. We have this great whiteboard wall where people write ideas and—well, skip that, it's not so tidy today . . ." I steered us away, because while it wasn't exactly NSFW (I don't mind a little crassness in the workplace if it gets results), it was definitely Not Safe For Family.

"I don't like chocolate," Nova proclaimed to Cass, warming to having an audience. I was pleased she was trying to connect. "Too sticky."

"Chocolate's so good, though," Cass said. "I get a kind made from unroasted cacao beans at my food co-op, and it tastes totally different." She said this as if it would interest Nova. "I bet your mom likes chocolate."

"She likes wine," Nova said.

"Wow, look at that," I obfuscated, with a casual, vague wave at one of our light fixtures. We were getting close, fortunately, to our destination department. As soon as I could do it without shouting, I called out to our perkiest QA manager and introduced Nova. "Hey, Jen—thought. Do we have a Conch she could try?" I'd never thought of putting one on her but Cass had given me the idea, and it seemed an opportune moment to try it. Maybe it could even provide a little prompting and structure to keep Nova focused, or channel some of her conversational impulses. That would be a fascinating application, if it worked.

"What have you got there?" Jen said. She had a camp counselor vibe, with big chunky glasses and pink-streaked hair. "Horses?"

Nova showed off her horses, commenting on each one's special feature (each has exactly one feature — it's not a meritocratic equine society). She began to line them up on Jen's desk. Several QA people gathered to admire this. Jen delved through the drawers in the rolling cart next to her desk. "You know what?" she said, in a Nova-aimed voice, but while looking at me. "I don't have a regular Conch open, but we have a brand-new one that's coming out, it's very special, and guess what? It's pink!" She turned to Nova with a peppy smile. "Bet you'd like that!" She pulled out a plastic box (the packaging is still under review). The special Conch was nestled inside, wrapped in a lint-free cloth like the kind you use for cleaning eyeglasses.

Nova gave me a worried look; she knows I reject pink for her. But in this case I smiled and said, "Sure, honey, put it on, it's OK."

I got so tired of everyone giving Nova things that were pink. I take seriously my responsibility as the mother of a daughter. Once, when Nova was tiny, I saw the maid carrying a basket of laundry and my first thought was that the maid had mixed up the special baby detergent and the red food coloring. I mean, everything in that laundry basket was pink: a striated pile of fuchsias and petals and mauves. It was a wake-up call that we were insidiously setting up a very narrow range of options for our daughter. Pink is a great color; it just can't be the only color. I wanted to see baby Nova as a junior woman of substance, wearing a power onesie, so to speak, and that style shifts over time, à la shoulder pads. Right now I think it's gray and chartreuse stripes.

Nevertheless, a reporter and an employee and a nervous little girl watched me. "Oh, perfect," I said.

"It won't be too loud for her ears?" Cass asked.

"It's very safe," I said, which I think is true. Several QA employees helped Nova get the Conch situated.

"Very special!" Jen cooed. "Beautiful! Do you want it to play you a song?" This attention panicked Nova. She pressed the Conch and her mouth fell open. She held the expression while she climbed into a chair and occupied herself with her horses.

My Conch chimed, reminding me of my next meeting. "I have to go, but this looks fun. Melissa'll be back in a minute. Nova, ask a question, OK? One good question."

"Can I go to the bathroom?" Nova asked.

"Sure, that's a question. Ask another."

"I can take her," someone said quickly. I glanced over: it was a nice QA associate whose chair Nova was sitting in.

"Great, I have a hard stop." The average CEO has only twenty-eight productive, uninterrupted minutes per day and I really feel the truth of that.

When I swung by after my meeting, all Nova's horses were eating sushi from the cafeteria. Nova was getting ready to visit our sensory garden, and the members of the QA team were looking for something.

"This is kind of awkward, but we can't find the pink Conch," Jen whispered.

"I'm sure it's around," I said calmly. "Let's look."

When Melissa arrived, she got down on her knees, eye level with Nova. "Where did you put it?" she asked.

"The seashell is in the potty," Nova admitted.

"Supernova!" Melissa admonished. "You know toys don't go in the potty."

"It's not a toy," I said. "It's a context-aware wearable. Can somebody go check if she flushed? Why, Nova?"

"I was . . ." And then Nova said something warbly, vowely, and unintelligible.

"Say it again?"

She repeated it emphatically, looking up at me. She said it several times, but I couldn't understand what she was saying. I mouthed the sounds, trying to feel out their meaning.

Finally, Melissa decoded it. "Oh! You were *confused*," Melissa said.

"I was confused," Nova said, this time closer to a standard pronunciation, with the sounds in the right order. I'd never heard her say that word before. It was a new word for her, and something about the gravity of this situation had presented it to her, new and unwrapped, ready to be deployed. I felt genuinely pleased for her, and touched. It was a sign of progress.

"You were confused," I recapped. "We're going to help you get clarity on what belongs in the potty." My Conch chimed a reminder of my next meeting, with Cullen and some outside folks. "I'm going to leave you guys to have a little more time together," I said cheerily. Jen looked annoyed. I waved my hands, to let everyone know they needed to move on and focus. "You know what? Not a big deal. Everyone gets confused and makes mistakes. That's how we go forward. You guys can work out a plan for a replacement. Or snake the pipes."

Chapter 10

At Conch, all our office spaces have names that relate to the sea, or eating Conches. Our conference room, where we spend many productive hours debating tiny product details, is Fritter. (Some people find that funny.) Cullen, our founder, who is extraordinary at developing beautiful user experiences and only weighs 115 pounds, was outside Fritter waiting for me.

Cullen has soulful eyes and the aura of a very serious child actor. He speaks slowly and deliberately, burnishing each syllable like a preacher; it's something he's learned, to dumb it down for other people. At times he takes it too far. He grew up in Manhattan, the only child of real estate developers, dropped out of his progressive school at fourteen to found his first company, and by his late teens had become the golden boy of several venture capital firms and the tech press. He is an interesting example of how relentless success can make you a little naive. If you wonder if this has happened to me, no, not in the same way. I am fortunate that I had a period at Gorvis, where I was COO, when we never actually sold any product. And although it didn't really do much to dampen analysts' enthusiasm for our company, that experience deepened my empathy and taught me that even though a lot of people in this sector talk about how great and valuable failure is, they mostly say it later, after achieving stratospheric success. Also, being a woman in this industry, I can't take anything for granted.

Cullen is twenty-six now. I think of him as a kid, even though when I was his age I was already leading a large team. He and I have excellent rapport (we have a special one-on-one once a month that we call Quattro-L, because we both have double *L*s in our names). Privately, I can't settle on how I feel about him: protective, in part; outsmarted, sometimes; jealous, though I try not to be; more grown-up; but also, despite my intense cardio regimen and flexitarian diet, flabby and aging, extra-aware of the lines on my forehead. I am a few inches taller. Sometimes I have sexual dreams about him and wake up feeling uneasy, wondering if he ever does about me.

Cullen's pluses are that he is a genuine innovator and has strong technical skills. His drawbacks include his obsessions with a shifting array of obscure sports and all forms of marine life.

Cullen's eyes widen as he excites himself by talking about the ocean, and his tone becomes increasingly pedantic. At these times he is undeniably attractive yet simultaneously quite boring, and it is interesting that the boredom everyone feels doesn't diminish the attraction. "We've got to save the ocean while there's still time," he says with earnest intensity, while young women hang rapturously on his elbow, buttressing his assertions. Even lesbians and older folks pay attention. A rich man's jokes are always funny. I don't discourage Cullen's interest in the sea, because I think eventually it will be strategic for him to part ways with Conch, and a new passion project and entrepreneurship-for-good venture may be the key to convincing him. When the time comes I am sure everyone will blame me, if I'm still at Conch, but I plan to say that Conch's loss will be the ocean's gain. I like having lines for people's exits worked out in advance—it feels efficient; it feels like, why not? Like the way newspapers prep obituaries for the living, it's smart: we're all going to die. By which, in this case, I merely mean move on to other tech companies.

"Hi, Shelley, you look nice today," he said. I looked down. He always compliments me when I wear something matronly that adds pounds and years, but I haven't pointed this out to him. Cullen wears shower shoes and the same rumpled gray hoodie every day. He is genuinely handsome in the way that a lead movie hobbit is handsome. He reminds me a little of Nova except if Nova had a penthouse in San Francisco and her birthday party at a club in Dubai.

He came over and was telling Cass about his idea for developing a theme park based around math. He envisioned it being both educational and thrilling; there would be a roller coaster called "The Asymptote." Cass murmured appreciatively. Our publicist had promised Cass she could sit in on a meeting to get a sense of how I work and my professional style, although details of the meeting would be embargoed.

"Did you tell her what the deal is?" Cullen said. I nodded, meaning no.

"Powerplex could be a key deal for us," I said. In the way we have of finishing each other's sentences, Cullen and I explained why. Powerplex develops technology to power a device while it's being used. You can print wirelessly. Why shouldn't you be able to *charge* wirelessly? Right now users charge the Conch by placing it on a plug-in charging platform, but the ideal would be to be able to harvest the energy in the air around you—to power the device through your use. Think how great that would be. Instead of having to hand off your devices so your assistant can charge them, you'd be constantly charged up.

"That seems so amazing," Cass said, scribbling.

"You are the power supply," Cullen said, looking into her eyes.

"It feels like I have to charge my Conch constantly," I said. "Of course, I'm a heavy user. Most people don't leverage the product as fully as I do . . . but the point is, that hassle will be gone. Users will *never* have to take off their device. They can have the benefits of Conch 24/7/365.25."

"And there'll never be a reason to take it off!" Cass said.

"You've got it."

"It sounds amazing."

"It does!" I agreed. I'm hoping to make it one of my key achievements. But implementation is, as I keep telling our board, a multilayered challenge.

"I still have doubts," Cullen said. "People are wearing this thing. What about if it's raining and . . . zap? No offense, Shelley."

"None taken!" I said. "Safety is paramount." Also, you have to act like Teflon as a woman in this business. Although Teflon kills birds. So recently I've started emulating graphene.

Willow brought in the Powerplex team, led by their CEO, Phil Furness, a skinny man in a black turtleneck with white centipede eyebrows and a tuft of thick white hair. Phil is very handsome, as CEOs so often are.

"It's so exciting you're here," Willow gushed. "At my cousin's farm, they just installed Powerplex lights in the chicken coops, powered by the movement of the chickens. It'll save so much on their electric bill."

Phil nodded, having clearly heard many similar stories before—at this point Powerplex is primarily used in agricultural applications. He and his team settled themselves around the table.

Fritter, our boardroom, is really no more corporate than any of our other conference rooms, like Gumbo. It's a lot of pickled wood, a chalkboard, whiteboard, inflated blow-up whale, and pull-down projection screen. I like it; it reminds me of a class-room. There's a big window on one side that looks out over the marshland outside the office, and another window on the inside that looks out over the customer service department. From the window, I can watch the reps shooting down trouble.

Our conference room chairs are aluminum. It keeps our meetings efficient. Cylindrical silver air ducts cross the indus-trial ceiling. The air ducts have the texture of those old Jiffy Pop foil pans on the stove, with their expanding foil dome. Some-times when I am frustrated they catch my eye; I want to bite them.

"Great to see everyone!" I said, nodding at Phil and his team.

"Great to be out here," said Phil. Powerplex is headquartered in the Midwest, which is a leading region for energy harvesting.

"Instead of the pitch deck, I thought I'd give you a sneak peek at the new video spot we're developing—this is brand-new, part of our new market positioning, and we're really excited about it. Then we can field questions and talk synergies. Sound good? Great, Willow, can you cue us up?"

Somebody flicked off the light and the screen lowered with an asthmatic wheeze.

Thumping music started, with some little saxophone swiz-zles.

The video hit the aspirational touchstones: beautiful, lush, intercut scenes of starry nights in national parks, a lean adult run-ning across a meadow, a serene gray-suited Caucasian twenty-four-year-old ascending an escalator surrounded by Japanese people, a family pressing their foreheads together ecstatically in a luxuriant rain (although Conch is not recommended to be used in rain). The drumbeats sped up. Clouds rapidly traversed a heartland sky. Two beaming parachutists fell to earth holding hands. A pregnant woman outswam an otter. A horn wailed, plangently. Night fell on a farmhouse as a windmill turned. The earth spun. More saxophone swizzles. The screen brightened.

Cullen added, "We'll be premiering a new tagline: 'The Future Is Hear.'"

"We're still tweaking the creative to bring it all the way to bright," I said, noting their underwhelming reaction. "But what I am personally so excited about is that our new campaign is based around how Conch is for those who want more. Conch makes you more alive, more vibrant, more 'Conch-us.'"

"Or—unconscious," Phil said. He sees himself as a slightly more promising Steve Jobs. In every group, there's always one person like this, who has to prove that he got an allusion, though everyone else in the room has not only gotten it but simultaneously comprehended that everyone else did too. But it's my job, these days, to amuse and seduce Phil. Not literally, just from a business standpoint, because we want Powerplex's technology on terms that are favorable to us.

I glanced at Cass. She was leaning forward in her chair at the side of the room, taking notes. She'd set her voice recorder on her knee. Its "needle"—a digital representation of a needle—swayed between us, flicking back and forth, as if it couldn't decide which of us was at this moment making more fascinating rustles.

"One of the best parts of Conch," I said, "is that it's not tying up the ear. Conch doesn't use up any existing orifices. It creates an additional input jack."

"It augments your life," Cullen said. "It pushes you to expand your consciousness, do more, be more."

"To have the information you need at the moment you can deploy it." I nodded vehemently. "Conch makes all of us more interesting, deeper . . ."

"Richer," Woody suggested.

"Not till we go public, pumpkin," I said dryly. They all laughed.

"Richer in a couple of ways, *including money*," Phil clarified helpfully.

"You know how I thought of it?" Cullen said. "I was at an art museum once and we had those devices that tell you about the art. But other people can't hear them."

I have heard our origin story one million and one times, so I made extra sure to look peppy and attentive. "You can't," I agreed reverently.

"Like a one-way phone. And I thought, what if these told you cool stuff, like funny stories, or the score of the, um, team you follow—" I could tell he was flailing for an example. Mainstream sports are not Cullen's thing—"or how your friends are doing."

"Genius," Phil said, beaming.

The Powerplex business development guy added, "Where are you going with this, down the road?"

"Seamless AI, totally immersive contextual knowledge," I said confidently. "Think about how amazing this would be for someone with Alzheimer's. Their selves would still be there. It's like an external drive, with everything about you on it. Sort of."

"I'm not totally sold on that angle," Cullen said. "I feel like there are some risks to pushing it as far as Shelley wants to go," but then we smiled at each other because we didn't want Powerplex to have any concerns about Conch's management getting along. Already we've gotten attention for the way we pronounce "Conch" differently; Cullen says the *ch* at the end like a *K*, the way people do in the Caribbean. I say it like people in Wisconsin do, with a *ch* like in "cheese." This is enough public discord for any management team, but we're cute about it. Together, we talked about Powerplex, how their wireless charging could work for Conch, and what a great fit we could be together.

The Powerplex biz dev guy broke in. "It's great to hear all this, but what do you guys make of these new, uh, Conch stories?"

"People are constantly discovering new ways to use their Conch," I said. Most of our users use Conch for a narrow range of services—traffic, email, read-aloud texts—but that's not why they buy it. Conch's ability to curate social media posts of particular interest (because of the poster or the content or whatever, based on previous behavior) and read them to you wherever you are, so that while you are in a boring meeting you can peruse the Facebook posts of old summer camp friends, or while brushing your teeth you can be alerted to a new test to determine which type of tooth brusher you are—that's actually one of our most popular features based on user tracking, although it's also become a little bit of a meme where people refuse to admit to using it.

"You're not concerned?"

I glanced at Cullen. "Our users are creative. The Conch Community is a rich tapestry of whisperfeeds." I was pleased to see Cass was scribbling again.

"What about the issues?" Phil said.

"What issues?"

The biz dev guy opened his mouth and then closed it, abandoning whatever it was he was going to say. He and Phil looked at each other.

I felt I might be missing key data. But I just blinked a lot, rapidly, which centers me and speeds up my cognitive processing.

"Our guys are combing through your stuff. Here are the key questions we need resolved," I said, laying it out. "Is the market receptive? Will pricing be competitive? Can we go to market by Q2 next year? Is this technology ready to play internationally, and if not, is that going to chip away at our competitiveness in the overseas markets?"

Phil spoke. "We love Conch, but what we're hearing is really worrying us."

"Are you talking about the charging issue? That's where you guys come in. That's one of the main obstacles our users report to sustaining their Conch use over time."

His colleague had a funny expression on his face. "I'm talking about the news story."

"Be more specific?" I said.

Nobody else spoke. They were looking away. I pushed. I looked at Cullen and Woody. Both looked blankly back at me, waiting for me to do something. Finally the other Powerplex guy spoke.

"The man who jumped off the cliff into the Hudson River? I heard that it was his Conch that told him to jump."

I have a pretty good poker face. I squeezed my toes together to hide any expression from crossing my face. "We're investigating," I said. "But I assure you, that's not Conch behavior."

"There was that other thing," Phil said. "The older woman, the sex thing."

His colleague pinkened around his shirt collar. "Right," he said. "I'm less worried about that one."

Cullen looked up. "Can you recap for the group?"

"Our counsel came across the report. An older woman, single. She was wearing her Conch and one night, she says, her Conch suggested she proposition a guy in a bar. Then she brought him home and they were in the middle of having sex and the Conch called an ambulance."

"That's all?"

"It could have been better. The paramedics broke down the door."

Cullen broke in. "Right. From the product's perspective, that reaction's understandable. It was responding to a divergent health event. Had she been having a stroke the Conch's response would have been appropriate."

"People aren't going to want to buy it," he said.

"It's non-optimal," I agreed.

I blinked, very hard and fast. I hadn't seen anything about this in my clipbook. I was not actually well aware of the issues they were raising. I had, somehow, missed all this. "We're on top of investigating and ensuring quality control," I said with firm, gentle reassurance. "These are highly unusual events."

Cass had perked up and was writing notes in her notebook.

"You know, let's take this conversation offline. I'm interested in filling you in on some of our other initiatives. Right now I'm concerned because we have a journalist who I think is late for another meeting. Is that right, Willow?"

"Oh," Willow said. "Yes. Cass, you have a meeting with our amazing CFO. Let me walk you down."

"Really?" Cass said. "I thought you weren't making Stefan available."

"He's eager to talk to you," I said. "He's here today. Just knock on the windows." Stefan works at home or out of an old Volkswagen bus in the parking lot. He can't come inside the office because he is violently allergic to dogs. "So great to chat, Cass. We'll catch up in a bit."

Willow followed Cass out the door, shutting it behind her. She turned so I could see her through the glass door and gave me a freaked-out look.

"We're excited about partnering," Phil said. "But this a big issue. I don't want to get in bed with a company that is flopping."

"Flopping?" I said indignantly.

"It's not really a problem," Cullen said. "But we have a fix. I'll dive into that with you later."

We walked Powerplex out. Phil was cool, I perceived, in

his goodbyes. As soon as they left I pulled the team back into Fritter.

"What's going on?"

Cullen shrugged. "I have no idea what they're talking about."

"Has anyone here personally experienced any problems? Have the customer service people gotten reports? Willow!"

Willow brought over the customer service manager, who filled us in: "The suicide happened two days ago, but it just came out this morning that he was wearing a Conch when he jumped into the river. It was reported by the local news in Dutchess County this morning. I can't believe they knew about it."

"It's preposterous," I said. "Even if the Conch told him to jump—and why would it?—he didn't have to listen. It's a voice. It's a suggestion. Just as we say in our user agreement, users must exercise independent judgment and use Conch at their own risk."

"It shouldn't have said jump," Cullen said.

"People really like to do what their Conch suggests," the customer service person said. "Not having to make decisions is very satisfying."

Cullen and I exchanged unhappy looks. Our internal research has shown this to be true. It's part of why the product succeeds.

"We're examining our records to look for any cases connected to the incident."

"Such as?"

"Weird stuff. Conches telling people to speed up while driving. Advising them to drop out of school. That kind of thing. Just random stuff that people blame on Conch, to see if there might be an underlying connection. The bad part of the river story is that it's starting to get attention. The OK part, which everybody seems to be missing, is that the guy who jumped was wanted for embezzlement. And now they got him. Thanks to Conch. That part is getting severely underplayed by the press."

I sighed.

"Well, let's deal with it," I said, trying to keep the anger out of my voice. "Let's not minimize it. We need to figure out what's going on. I need you to be the point person to brief me and develop a plan."

Chapter 11

"Shell, can I grab you for a second?" Cullen said. A flash of the iconic smile captured so well in the portrait of him projected above the superfoods bar in the Conch cafeteria. In certain light, and certain moods, even I am not immune.

"I'm always yours," I said, which is truer than I'd like it to be. He's the sun and I'm the lady in the pantsuit. I reflect his brightness; any glamour of mine is but a glint of his. On the Conch org chart, it's like I'm his mom. I want to make it clear that even at the most technical level, I am not old enough to be his mom. (It's kind of close, though—fortunately I was a late bloomer, menstrually.)

"Shall we?"

He pulled me over to his workstation, which is in the same pod as my workstation. Two chairs won't fit side by side at the desk, but I slid over a vivid ottoman, shaped like an enormous Trivial Pursuit pie wedge, and straddled it.

I was replaying the meeting from Cass's perspective, trying to assess what she had observed and how she'd interpret it. "We got her out of there nicely. Willow was slick. I don't think the reporter suspected we were booting her."

Cullen raised an eyebrow.

"You think she did?"

He shrugged. "We'll see."

The engineer at the next desk picked up his phone. "Yes, I'm calling about my soup. I ordered the soup and sandwich special . . ."

I beamed at him and glanced at his desk, littered with light-weight bamboo servingware and cutlery from our cafeteria. "I've been meaning to try that. Is it any good?" To Cullen I said, "I don't see why we keep doing these media things. They always backfire. No matter what I say."

"I don't mind them," Cullen said primly.

"Because they love *you*."

He looked away, almost blushing, and his lips reddened as they do when he gets excited.

"When people say good things about you it's easy to believe they're true," I warned him. "Also, that the people saying them are nice people, not to mention excellent and perceptive judges. But most of the time they're just repeating what other people have said before. They're probably wrong, just as tons of people have been wrong before them. It's possible *everyone* is wrong. If history teaches us anything—"

"Speaking of which," Cullen interrupted. "This guy, this river, the decision to jump in—what the hell was his Conch doing? Look at these customer service summaries. There are a few strange incidents. Like this one: a woman is going to her high school reunion, all dressed up, and just as she enters the building her Conch tells her she's ugly and has never amounted to anything, but for five hundred bucks it can find her a more flattering dress and sexier shoes."

"That sounds like the Conch delivering a poorly timed ad."

"Could be." He made notes in the case tracker. "User perception could be coloring that experience. Conch just wanted to deliver the ad. It wouldn't have said 'ugly.'" He paused. "Right?"

"We have broadened the vocabulary lately. Let's pin that down. Tell me about the river guy."

"Here's another one: two Conch users who hate each other live at opposite ends of Manhattan, but thanks to Conch's navigation they are constantly running into each other. One of them believes his Conch is planning it."

"Sounds like a rom-com plot."

"It's kind of funny. People are crazy." We sighed, scrolling through customer service complaints. Users are our main source of problems.

"Ooh," I said, looking over his shoulder. "I remember this. It's a bad one. A guy says his Conch is telling him to bomb airports. His coworker called us about it. But he has a known history of mental illness. We're working with law enforcement and he's getting help. Crud, it does seem like there are more weird cases than usual."

"Is this weird? Here's a device that was shipped to sell in the Asian market—look at the digits in the serial number—but the report of malfunction is coming from Indiana. Do you think that's odd?"

I shook my head. "It's a global world," I said.

He sighed. "Definitely we're seeing an uptick in unwanted behaviors. I don't know why it's happening." He smiled ingratiatingly, as he does when things are going to shit.

The guy next to us kept talking. "My soup is only half full today. Last time I ordered the special I got a full container. There's less soup." He swished the cup around in front of his eyes as he talked on the phone. It was glossy amber broth slick with fat. Twists of noodle and tiny carrot-cubes spun in the eddy. I can't imagine investing the time during the day to eat hot soup.

"Take it to a phone pod, Tyler!" I snapped. "People are trying to work!" To Cullen I said, "Is it a bug? When did it start? Is it a security problem?" I pulled off my Conch, wiped off a trace of sweat with the pad of my thumb, and examined it. "Is there a risk to me keeping this on?"

"I don't know," he said. "It could be that we're just seeing this now because there are more of them out there. You think that could be it? Just some kind of glitch?"

"I don't know."

We grew fast, at Conch. The typical startup time-lapse movie: cords and monitors snaking across folding tables, a couple of people at first, then more, then many. Better offices, juice fridges, inspiring sayings being painted on the walls. It looked so permanent, but I knew how fast things could go sour. I'd been at Gorvis as our huge office emptied out, witnessed the irritability and tears from employees who could not accept that cutbacks and layoffs were necessary to save the company. Not that they had. I looked across the office toward Nova. She was cutting paper at someone's desk. This wasn't like handing down the family department store. I couldn't give her this and expect it to keep producing revenue for her and her children's children. I had to give her skills for whatever the future brought.

All around me people were clicking through their email, checking their phones, popping open cans of seltzer, expecting their weeks to unfold exactly as their calendars predicted, with zero thought to the precariousness of it all. That's my job, to worry for them. The customer service intranet site reloaded itself, the queue lengthening. New tickets for new problems. I felt a little sick.

"Shelley, you haven't had any weird experiences as a user, have you? Have you noticed any discrepancies, any new behaviors?"

I hesitated, Conch in the palm of my hand, pulling a lock of hair taut and smoothing the cuticle with my fingers. This gave me a reason not to look at him. "Why, have you?"

He scratched behind his ear and made a funny, guilty face. "I haven't been wearing mine as much as I should. I don't like the direction we've been taking it."

"Cullen!" I said, genuinely shocked. "What if someone noticed?" I pulled a gold-and-white ripple-patterned box from the shelves and unboxed the Conch, scattering our attentively crafted packaging all over his desk.

He left it there. "I've noticed that Conch was getting more . . . aggressive."

I nodded. "All data is actionable," I reminded him. "Conch is encouraging people to take on more risk. To live more fully. To open doors! We just have some edge cases where we have to refine the behavior and calibrate the risk."

"When I invented it I saw it more as an entertainment device. Brad wanted to pivot into time management. I thought the Conch would just be for fun."

"It can be so much more."

He made a face.

"Well, either way we need to fix it."

Cullen buried his face in the crook of his elbow, on his desk. "Ugh. Why is it doing this? When we migrated from the old system we racked up a shitload of technical debt. All this junk needs to be cleaned up . . . wait." He straightened up and typed very quickly, long runs followed by lots of long, frustrated backspacing, and then paused, his fingers jittery above the keyboard, diving for another attack.

"How many more of these kinds of customer service reports are there?" I asked. "How long ago did they start? A week or two? What have we done differently since then? Anything with the software?"

"We ship all the time, but . . ." He shook his head.

"Could the Conch be hacked?"

He shrugged. "I kind of think it's something I did."

"With the code?" I could tell he thought I was being slow, needing all this explanation.

"That's not it." He sighed, throwing himself against the back of his chair so the momentum rolled it away from his desk. He clicked his pen over and over, in accelerating cadences. I resisted the urge to take it away from him.

"I let this European contractor do some spec work on a new module . . . I just wanted to see what he could do. It was this guy who got in touch. He had some intriguing ideas and I let him have part of the codebase. I shouldn't have done that, though it's not like he could have *done* anything with it."

"When was this?"

"Last week?"

"You didn't know this person?"

"It's a friend of yours." We looked each other in the eye. "With my personal cell. I was told you gave it."

I nodded, slowly. Oh, crud, I thought. Had I? I had.

"You gave away the Conch code?"

"The ideas were interesting. I just gave him *some*. Just to play with. He couldn't do anything with it."

"But why would he want the code at all?"

"Because it's fascinating." Cullen looked hurt.

The thought of that day with Enrique was almost unbearable, and I longed to take hold of the memory, all of it, and drag it straight into the mental Trash folder. "Don't worry," I said, though I was becoming extremely worried. "We'll fix this. All of this stuff is so diffuse. It might be a glitch that we're only seeing now that we have a larger userbase. It doesn't mean every Conch is going to malfunction." I also believe you have to have confidence you'll be able to do what the moment requires—you don't get assurances in advance.

We went to the microkitchen and I peeled a banana, one of the many healthy snacks we provide free of charge to Conch employees, and I broke off half and gave it to him. "Good source of potassium," I said. We gnawed our bananas contemplatively, watching several marketing people microwave oatmeal.

Back at my desk I began searching online for more accounts of Conch deviance. There'd been sporadic incidents stretching back for months. I was worried about the product malfunction, but even more disappointed in myself. That it had taken this long to uncover it was a failure of leadership. If things don't get reported up the chain, I don't hear about them. I understand why nobody wants to bring me bad news, but that's my own failure as CEO: I have to be receptive and construct a culture of transparency that invites my employees to confide in me and share both their successes and their challenges. I have to offer them approachability by saying things like "I invite you to be candid" and "I would rather have helpful feedback than 'niceness.'"

I breathed deeply.

I searched the web and looked at help desk transcripts. People were tweeting about Conch. It still seemed speculative— nobody had a really damning story of Conch urging them into risky behavior. Nobody who had a platform, that is. But I could see the problem gathering force offshore.

"*Silly Valley* just weighed in," Willow said, rushing toward my desk.

"Send it to me!"

Just at that moment my Conch buzzed. *Great news! You've been mentioned in . . . the* Silly Valley *blog.* It played three notes, rising, cheerfully inane.

"Send me the link," I yelled, and she ran back to her computer, her ballet flats slapping off her heels and against the floor—shooka-shooka—as she ran.

The higher you rise in a company, the better things are going for you, the more your detractors look forward to seeing you go down in flames. They begin to see that you are a threat to their power, and they become increasingly invested in bringing you down. It is hard to realize that there are people who want only to embarrass and discredit you, and that there are an even larger number of people who, while not caring much one way or the other, are so unconsumed by personal passions that they would enjoy the mild novelty of watching you fail. It would amuse them, in the course of their day, to read in a blog about your latest fizzle or view a short video of your humiliating public breakdown. It would give them a few seconds of entertainment before they returned to fucking around and generating more mediocre work product.

I can't spend time worrying about what people think. You can't build a company on Q scores. It's the product that matters.

But is Conch actually a good product? It can be. It will be. It doesn't really matter because the important thing is vision.

Willow's email, ominously subject-line-less, arrived. I gazed at it, there at the top of my inbox, radiating blank hostility. I took a deep breath and double-clicked:

LIGHTNING NOT STRIKING TWICE FOR CONCH'S
SHELLEY STONE

The Conch exec, known for her compelling personal story and her hard-driving leadership style at the context-aware wearables behemoth, is facing new allegations that she's ineffective and in over her head after reports of a glitch that is causing Conch users to endanger themselves and others . . .

I scrolled down. Jesus. Cass worked fast. It had to be her.

An unnamed source familiar with Conch's operations said that Stone, who caught lightning in a bottle during her

successful stints at B2C e-commerce giants . . . has pushed
to expand Conch's behavior into new territory, over the
objections of wunderkind founder Cullen Masur . . .

He's twenty-six, for Chrissakes! How long can you retain your wunderkindhood?

Conch touts its bleeding-edge mix of temperature and
movement readings to bioauthenticate its users, and claims
its suggestions and responses are controlled by a complex
proprietary algorithm . . .

They quoted an "expert" I have never heard of:

"You don't want somebody to be able to pick up your Conch
and tap into your private data. So your Conch not only
reads your temperature and movements, but compares that
to the you it knows, and if they differ it shuts down—that's
bioauthentication. They like to give the impression that the
Conch's suggestions draw on that same data. But what we're
seeing here suggests that they may not be using it that way,
that it's smoke and mirrors."

A harsh assessment. Also, false. Conch absolutely was suggesting actions using individualized data. The problem was that it's very complicated.

Stone, who has been criticized for being culturally out of
touch after she put the kibosh on jeans for employees at
Conch's Mountain View headquarters, is rumored to be
making a play to merge with Powerplex, an Omaha-based
energy harvester. But unnamed sources say Stone's icy

*demeanor, tone-deaf comments, and micromanagement
have . . .*

This was total tripe. (The jeans part.) "Ew," I said. I closed
my eyes and saw reddish horizontal lines, a shadowy curve. I let
the bad feeling sink through me and rise out through my skin.

"Hey, we're leaving now to grab lunch and make it to art
class," Melissa called. I sighed, got up, hugged Nova.

"Thanks," I said, barely able to summon up any expression.
"That's enough for today. I have a hard stop now or I'd walk
you out. Goodbye, Nova." I didn't say goodbye to Melissa. We
just look each other in the eye, intently, in some kind of power
transference.

"The seashell," Nova whispered.

"You know what, let's not say anymore about it." I waved
her concerns away and gave her a thin-lipped smile. "See you
tonight—well, tonight's the board meeting—uh, I'll see you
soon, sweet pea, I'll be thinking of you! Have a great day!"

"It said it to me," Nova remarked, quietly, as if she were talking to herself.

"Yup," I said. "That's what makes it a very special seashell."

"The seashell said, I want to swim in the potty."

"Now, Nova," Melissa said. She was holding out Nova's
quilted jacket, helping her put it on, and trying to change the
subject. "Let's not tell stories. What do you think we're going to
have for lunch? Do you think Jacqui will make us some celery
and wheatberry salad?"

"The seashell wants to swim in the ocean, like I did that
time," Nova said. She seemed to be addressing her comments
to one of her horses. "It told me." Melissa gave me a look over
Nova's head, but I was watching my daughter. "It told me," Nova
said, with wonder, as if she couldn't believe it herself.

There's a private bathroom off one of the conference rooms on Two; hardly anyone goes there. I went in, locked the door, and did my nasal rinse. Forceful gushes of saline solution cut a path through the muck inside my skull. I breathed deeply, with pleasurable clarity, collecting myself. Then I practiced my talking points for the board meeting, making severe expressions in the mirror.

"It's a multilayered challenge," I repeated. I sighed and sat down on the toilet.

I dialed my friend Christine in New York. Her assistant answered. "She's not available," he said crisply.

"I was just calling to say hi," I said. "Not important."

I was skimming a book about the types of electric plugs and sockets in use around the world—surprisingly fascinating stuff—when someone rapped on the door. I sighed. "Willow?" I said. She was the only one who knew I came here.

"Sorry!" she called through the door. "Can I come in?"

I got up, ran the water in the sink, cranked the paper towel dispenser, and squeezed some color into my cheeks. I unlocked the door.

"Is everything all right?" Willow asked.

"I assume not or you wouldn't be here."

"Hey!" she said. She came in past me and leaned back on the edge of the sink. I sat back down on the toilet. "Wow. You look tired."

"Thank you." I yawned. "I'm going to power through. I was just giving myself a brief pocket of . . ." I trailed off. When you don't have the energy to lie to your assistant, things are really bad. "What's going on?"

She hesitated. "I know you have a lot going on and I don't want to add to your worries. You got another phone call . . ."

I tensed. "Who else has picked up the suicide story?"

"It's something else, maybe, um, personal?" she said. "Nothing about Conch. Another weird call. I wasn't going to mention it, but this morning's call wasn't the first. It's getting relentless. I'm sorry to bring it up." She looked at me as if she was afraid I was going to get angry she hadn't told me, or wasn't sure she should tell me now. Her eyes were downcast, deferential.

"Prank calls?"

"Maybe." She looked uncertain. "They could be."

"Obscene?"

"Kind of."

"Threatening? Dangerous? Vulgar?"

"Yes. She uses bad language."

"She?" Despite my own commitment to repudiating gender stereotypes, I had assumed the obscene caller was a "he."

"I didn't want to tell you upstairs," Willow said. "In the office, where everyone could hear. I thought maybe this was something you'd want privacy for . . ." She looked into my eyes anxiously. She knew I'm not a big believer in privacy. I don't have time. It's like the models stripping off their clothes in the back of runway shows. Just no time to fuss. Although I don't change in public, of course.

"I need details, Willow. I'm completely in the dark. I have no idea who she is or what she is calling in reference to."

"Her name's Michelle."

I blinked and felt a pressure, like a hand, against my chest. "Oh, right. What does she want?"

"She doesn't say what she wants. She's someone you know, Shelley. She knows your kids, your cousins, she knows so much stuff. She knew the hotels you stayed at last week. I thought maybe she was your half sister or something."

I felt fuzzy-headed. "I don't have a half sister."

"I know—it's just, in the commune we sometimes had . . . half sisters and they were like cousins we didn't always know were . . ."

"Nope."

"You can't be sure," she said earnestly. "Anyway, she wants to talk to you. She wants your cell number, she's very insistent." Willow unfolded a piece of pink paper from her pocket—a sheet from one of those "While You Were Out" pads. Isn't it odd that we still order those from whatever legacy supplier still makes them? I wonder if it's for the nostalgia value. Certainly there's trivial efficiency savings from not having to bother to write "While You Were Out." And with modern communications, I'm never really Out anyway, merely equally well connected from a different location. She handed it to me.

On it was written, in Willow's loopy, obliging handwriting: "Message: Thanks for the cheeseburger, bitch. Call me." Below, Willow had written, "S, how should I handle?"

I stared at it, turned the paper over as if there would be a clue there, turned it around again, and stared at it. I felt a shiver down my spine.

Willow grew nervous from my silence. "I'm sorry if I should have handled this myself. I know I can't bring every little thing to you and I need to take ownership and make the call myself, it's just . . . I wanted to keep you in the loop in case you . . ."

"No, no," I said. "You did the right thing, you . . ." It felt suddenly very secondary to the situation, to have to say these managerial phrases of reassurance, to pretend to be even-keeled even though I was not. "When did she call?"

"Just now. Just while I was upstairs. This is her fifth—uh, sixth—call today. She's getting angry." Willow's eyes got wet with indignation and she looked away, as if she couldn't bear to look at me. "She called me a corporate whore."

"People will attack you for your sexuality as a woman in this business," I said. "They'll attack anything you do. You can't give it the time of day. Though, don't take this the wrong way, but you might not want to wear that pinafore." I handed Willow a tissue. "Thick skin," I reminded her. While she was blowing her nose and washing her hands I peed surreptitiously and silently via strategic use of my kick pleat.

"She's crazy, right? I shouldn't let it get to me."

I nodded dully. I found it hard to summon up the word "crazy," or say anything. Willow's legs swung off the edge of the bathroom sink.

"Do you have her number?" I asked. "I'll handle it."

"Yeah, it's right on the slip. It's a long one—she's in, like, Europe or something."

A tiny ray of relief burned warmly up my spine. "Thank God," I whispered. Willow looked concerned, and a bit curious.

"Do you want me to patch you through next time she calls?" she said hopefully.

"Not now. I'll handle it. Don't give her a second thought," I said. "You were right to tell me. But I'll take it from here. If she calls again, tell her I will return her call at my earliest convenience. Make it clear from your voice it won't be that early. Do not tell her anything. Got that?"

I could see how much Willow was longing to hear more about this person, about my life. I did not oblige her.

My phone buzzed. A text from Christine: *Everything OK?* I texted back. *I'm having delusions (hallucinations?) and my assistant has entered the fever dream.*

That's not the kind of message Christine and I usually send each other. I stared at my phone waiting to see what would come back. We typically send each other encouraging texts when we're having tough days. We advise each other on clothing, career, and life stuff. She's a law firm partner, which is in some ways all the stress of Conch with none of the creative aspect. We were college roommates. We met the semester I returned to school, after a summer in the hospital recovering from the lightning strike. I was exhausted, frustrated, frequently in pain, and upset by how much I'd missed and how difficult even simple things were to do. It was a hard time, but in Christine I found someone who became an instant and lasting friend. Our bond was based on having similar goals and outlooks, being ambitious, sure, but also having a similar perception of things. We were serious in a way our classmates weren't, but in spite of that, with each other we were able to not take everything so seriously. Now I am so enmeshed in my role it's hard for me publicly to be anything but earnest, results-driven, fun-loving within the scope of my corporate brand, "all about the Conch." It's only with my inner circle that I can continue to be myself, to retain that thread of me that existed before Conch and will continue after. Christine is one of those people who doesn't come across at first glance as super smart or ruthlessly ambitious. She's attractive and pulled together, good at deflecting attention and flying under the radar. But that's very effective for her.

I love Christine—the return text came immediately. A gratify-ingly tall text-bubble. She is an amazingly fast text typist. *Yeah, that happens. I find my assistants very readily reify my reality. That sounds like a Stephen Malkmus lyric. It's the communal brain, under pressure. Plus you're coming up on an anniversary. My therapist says that has got to be hard. Twenty, right? That's a big one.*

U have time for therapy?! I texted back.

I bill the time to my worst client, she wrote. *It's fair, I spend the whole time talking about them. Hang on.*

The phone rang. She was on the line.

"Hi!" I said gratefully. We so seldom have time to talk vocally.

"Hey, I just ducked out of my meeting. Are you OK? Shell,

don't let the bastards get you down," Christine said. In a sterner voice: "Hans, hold that call."

I took a beat to assess. "I don't know. I can't get a handle on the situation."

"It's coming up, right? The anniversary?"

"What? We got married in the fall, in Napa. You were there."

"No—"

"Remember how it had a harvest theme, with the burlap?"

"I'm not talking about your wedding. I meant the anniversary of—"

"Oh, right," I said, cutting her off. "But I don't think that has anything to do with it."

"You don't?"

"Why would it?"

There was silence and I knew she wanted me to answer my own question and admit she was right. I did not. Finally, she said again, "Anniversaries are hard."

"Not for me. Having it happen was hard. The recovery was horrible. But talking about it isn't hard, I do it all the time. I don't see why the anniversary would make it any worse."

Christine didn't say anything.

"Why? You think I should be worried?"

"It might be difficult. I can see it being a time when your mind turns to . . ." She changed tacks. "What about that guy you were with? Do you ever think about getting in touch with him?"

"Walter."

"Have you given him a call?"

Walter was one of my best friends in high school, bookish and irresistibly brilliant. After the lightning strike he was never the same. Not in the same way I was never the same. He still lives in the town I grew up in and works in a tire store. For years my parents bought all their tires there, out of guilt.

"We don't keep in touch."

Christine tactfully changed the subject. "Anything planned for your birthday?"

"No big plans. Cullen's throwing a fundraiser in my honor. For his true love, the ocean."

"Do you have a dress?"

"I do, as a matter of fact. It's beautiful. It's silk, this very piercing blue. With an ocean print, kind of sophisticated and Japanese-ish. Coral, fish. I'm making it sound gaudy but it's not."

"Sounds like it could be all right. Send me a pic. It's not boring?"

"It is boring, if you mean tasteful. It's lovely and unusual. One-of-a-kind."

"Does Rafe like it?"

"Rafe's not into tasteful," I said. "But what can you do? Anyway, that'll be fun." I heard stirring in the background, as if she were getting ready to go into a meeting. "Chris, I just . . . I just . . ." I was still sitting on the toilet and I shifted uncomfortably. "The pressures lately. I am having visions. I'm not even kidding. I can't tell anyone."

"Hallucinations?"

"Sort of. More like one recurring one."

"Of what?"

"Me. But me as a kid. Just before the . . . That a younger version of me is following me around, trying to derail me."

A moment of silence. Then she snorted. "That's really classic," she said. "Don't start psychotherapy, they'll never let you stop. What's it about?"

"It's about this girl following me around. She's not a *nice* girl."

"*That's* the crux of the problem? If only she were nicer?" A pause, as if she realized this was too blithe a response to my angst. Her tone changed. "It's about the anniversary, I'm sure," she said. "It's triggering reflection. Is this person real or a—uh—apparition?"

"Fancy word. No. She resists when a pencil is poked at her. She can consume French fries. She's . . ."

"Corporal?" Christine supplied. Lawyers are so exact.

"Right. That's it. And she's a piece of work. She insulted my assistant."

"And it wasn't you, secretly yelling at your assistant to work out your frustration and rage at her? Which would be so understandable, sweetie, because your assistant sucks. Just fire her and start over. It means three bad weeks, but then it's good. For a couple months . . ."

"I would be feeling crazy in a different way were that the case. She's a separate person. The ghost. That part is clear."

"What makes you think she's you?"

"She knows a lot of stuff about me."

"I know a lot of stuff about you."

"Right, but . . . you were there. I know you. She knows the same stuff but she wasn't there."

"Could she be a sophisticated hacker? Could she have gotten at your data? Could she be a stalker? A new type of scammer or phisher? Somebody hired by Russian cyberthieves? An annoying little cub reporter from the *Stanford Daily*? All of these seem more plausible possibilities, no offense. Hold on. I'm pretending you're a client but that client's on the other line. Let me finesse this."

I sat and thought. Why had I assumed she was me? It seemed so loony. There was such relief in rejecting the idea, refusing to accept it as a possibility.

"I'm so sorry," Christine said, back on the line, her voice accented in my ear. "Mr. Fugiwa, I will respond to your question as soon as I have consulted with co-counsel. I have to go."

Then, in a rushed, different voice. "Talk later, and I actually mean it." I put the phone down. The red circle, signifying the end of our connection, pulsed.

I thought for a second and opened the text app. *She has the same eyebrows I had, before I started getting them threaded.*

There was the immediate bing of a new text. *Send pics!* Christine demanded.

Chapter 12

Christine had to be right. Her analysis was simple and clear, and she was right such a large percentage of the time (about my choice of boyfriends, which job I should take, whether I should get bangs) that it was extremely likely she was right this time too. As a data-driven person, I ought to have been completely persuaded. I wasn't, but I tried to be. The crushing workload and pressure of transactional law had not given Christine much room to be the funny and creative person she once was, and I sometimes felt she had become a little pinched by her job, like a toe stunted by always being in a power shoe. Our grown-up lives hadn't turned out to be what we had imagined, sitting on our twin beds in our dorm room junior year. I had thought adulthood would be a series of viscerally felt triumphs, like the moment when a plane lifts off, and the stresses of our lives merely gnats in the turbines, but stress had turned out to be the airstream in which we flew. I didn't think it would be easy, but I had thought it would be different than it is. Though when I heard about Christine's work life, I was grateful for the latitude of my own, and its inherent pleasures, like making new and better Conches, watching them tumble off the assembly line into wheeled vats, nestle in individual boxes, and stack into cartons bound for ports all over the world. There was something real about that, something gratifying, like when I saw Conch users—part of the Conch Community—at airports or coffee shops or Davos. Plus the external recognition—the interviews, articles, even the silly, gossipy blog posts—that I got from work, which Christine did not. Plus, I live in a beautiful area with unbelievably pleasant weather, and she lives in smoggy iced-over New York and rarely sees daylight. And Rafe is a lot more fun and also better-looking than Jeff, who seems so buttoned-down and angularly serious, with his protuberant nose and his—I'm not supposed to know this—type 1 herpes and predilection for taking clients to strip clubs. (Christine: "It's hard to be single in your late thirties in New York.") Rafe is no saint, but on most commonly accepted criteria he's a better husband. And yet even with these outlets, it was I, not Christine, who was the one having the breakdown. It did not make sense. So taking Christine's advice to heart, I decided to take control and manage the situation.

Clutching Willow's note, I went out of the building to call back the girl. Conch is on a low-slung industrial campus on the edge of the Bay. Across the road is marshland. It used to be a landfill, but now it's a park where paths weave around low hills, and people bereft of full-time employment come to bike, while their curly-haired dogs sprint alongside them. Along the water's edge are windblown fern pines, which resemble overgrown versions of the bottle brushes we keep by the sink to get the residual gunk out of Blazer's baby bottles. Farther in are a few valley oaks, with branches that splay out along the ground, as if in the early stages of their growth there was not enough planning for scalability. It's very pretty, in the foggy way of Northern California.

In the courtyard of our building is the Conch meditation/ sensory garden. A yoga class was taking place on a grassy quadrangle adjacent—lots of lithe twentysomething marketing and communications and product packaging admins in black yoga pants and brightly colored sleeveless tops, their bare feet swaying in the air, their forearms on the mats in front of them. They were the only ones who had time to take full lunches away from their desks and take advantage of the company's wellness offerings. Once a year for Wellness Day I wear a zip-up fleece with my dress pants and emphasize to the gathered employees that I want them to take part, and I do, absolutely, assuming their work is done, because fitness contributes to a perception of competency, and everyone needs outlets for stress, but nobody over a certain level was down there in the garden at lunch.

I dialed the number Willow had given me and tightened my abdominals isometrically as the instructor counted. The number rang and rang. I exhaled and released. I walked in a circle around the garden on the springy mulched paths. In the distance was the mist, and beyond that the mountains. It was cool out, and no one sat on the benches eating Tupperwares of salad or slapdash peanut butter sandwiches. I felt a nervous churn in my stomach and an anxiety that expressed itself in the form of wanting to be closer to a bathroom. It was good I'd just gone— often, I found it hard to remember to. Sometimes I have set a reminder on my Conch, but then I start ignoring it. Not quite ready to have Willow remind me, the way my second-grade teacher used to (I had very focused concentration even then). Nobody picked up the phone. I terminated the call, bit the hard gummy edge of my cell phone case, and tried in imagination to summon up the girl—the length of her hair, the big oblique mouth, her shoulders and flab and presence.

I redialed. This time the phone got picked up right away, before I was ready.

"Hi," a voice said.

I waited to see if I recognized it. It was a female voice. I neither recognized it nor didn't. Her "Hi" faded before I could decide. "Hello," I said, more confidently than I felt, my practiced phrases kicking in. "Shelley Stone speaking. Is this—"

"This is Michelle." She did not seem surprised to hear from me.

"Hi, Michelle, great to talk again," I said, in the assured tone of a thousand investor calls when, quavering on the inside, I projected confidence and leadership and refused to let a speck of doubt infect my speech.

I saw myself reflected in the glass-sheathed skin of the office building. I squared my shoulders and breathed. My silhouette was impeccable in its tailoring and fit. My hair lay smooth upon my head. My expression—to the extent I could see it, shadows on the topography of my face—was fixed, impenetrable. Firmly closed lips, tightened eyes. I felt tense, but my voice still sounded mellifluous, supple, relaxed. Faking it, the same as doing it.

"So you called my office. What can I do for you?"

I heard some breathing on the line. She seemed unprepared for the directness of my question.

"You abandoned me," she said. "I have no money!" Her voice rose. "I mean, a little but by no means enough. Not even any traveler's checks! What was I supposed to do? Where am I supposed to go?"

I held the phone away from my ear and watched a young woman, slim, in black tricot, hold a headstand. Her forearms lay on the mat and her legs were nearly perfectly straight over her head, only a few degrees off 180 at the hip. I watched with satisfaction as the instructor came over and guided her into perfect verticality, which she held a moment, before her legs scissored down. I breathed in and out, paying attention to my breath. I took a moment to regain mindfulness and choose my response.

"Tough situation. However. I believe very strongly that everyone is responsible for their own life. When I said you were me,

I was obviously very tired from my responsibilities in Barcelona. You correctly doubted me; it was a fantastical idea. I had jet lag and hunger and a head injury, and clearly something about you reminded me of me. That's a wonderful, fortuitous connection for us to have. These are the unexpected joys of travel. But it's also a very tenuous connection. In fact, by providing you a ride and dinner, not to mention some informal career mentorship, I would say I've acted quite generously toward you. I'd be happy to go even further and provide occasional—say, once annually—quick feedback on your professional direction as your career develops, but I think that is probably the extent of the relationship we'll have going forward. And of course—it goes without saying—that that's dependent on you ceasing to harass my employees."

I admit that when I finished this speech I felt a kernel of satisfaction at how neatly I'd put it. Especially considering the stresses of the situation. Pride is one of the sins with which I struggle. Meekness doesn't get you far professionally, yet pride can take you down. Like everything, it's a tightrope.

"Ask me a question," she said.

"What?"

"You heard me. Ask me a question."

I hesitated and said the first thing that came to mind: "After this latest round of funding, what will Conch's valuation be?"

She sighed impatiently. "Not that. Something about our childhood or our past. You told me stuff. Don't you want to know what I know?"

"There is no 'our childhood.' That was just silliness."

"All right," she said. "Be that way. You want to bet on that?"

"I have to go."

"There's something I need from you," she pleaded.

"I suggest you get a job. Even if it's menial, you could intern on the side to build your résumé."

"You can't ignore me. You'll be sorry. I'm not a kid. I'm about to turn twenty."

"That wasn't much of a birthday for me."

"Why not?" she said.

Did she not know what had happened to me? I wasn't going to tell her. "Please don't call my office again."

"I know about the problems with those ear things."

"Yes, it's been amply covered by the tech press."

"That's not all I know."

"Well, I should hope not," I said dryly.

"I know about your daughter being kidnapped."

Every muscle in my body tightened; I felt my heart beating in the air in front of me. "She wasn't kidnapped."

My vehemence unnerved me. I blinked rapidly to regain control over myself. Silence on the line. I listened for some clue that she would take this back.

She didn't. "I want one of the new Conches. The ones that aren't in stores yet."

I hesitated. "Do you mean SportConch?"

"The self-charging kind, the ones you're developing—" She hesitated. "Yes, SportConch."

"You do? Why?"

Again, with hesitation. "Because they are the future. Also, it would be cool to have one before everybody else."

I accepted this. Who wouldn't want one? They were going to be a global phenomenon and anyone would want to get in early on that.

"You can't have one. The prototypes are highly secured. Even I don't take one home." I did not tell her that we're a little behind schedule, so they aren't even here yet.

"Please send me one, and also one hundred thousand dollars."

"Are you kidding?"

She ignored this. "I'll make you a deal. I'll take part of the money now, part of it later. Get the ear thing ready and I'll tell you where to put it. For the money, you can wire me the first half. I'm going to give you a number. Ready? Write this down."

"Why do you think I would?"

"I know you can afford it. I read an article about you."

I breathed in and out. "But why would I give it to you?"

"That's not the question I'd be asking if I were you."

"Are you threatening me?" I was outwardly nonchalant, but feeling the cold shiver of a negotiation that is going to flop.

There was silence on the line.

"I knew about Chili," she said.

I said nothing. I'm sorry, being able to name-check someone's childhood pet does not prove a thing.

"Remember that time we sold tickets for the sixth-grade play and charged everyone extra and took the difference?"

"That was profit," I protested. "And compensation for time spent selling tickets." But I was shaken. Nobody had known about that. I'd brainstormed it once for a corporate blog post about entrepreneurship, and then one of the editors said it would reflect poorly on me, so I had parking-lotted that idea. Nobody else had, as far as I'd known, ever found out. I remembered all those nice crisp fives that I'd kept flattened under the plastic kitchen floor of my dollhouse.

"Why don't you just write down the wire number," she said, pleadingly. "You can think about it. I'm going to tell you it now."

"I have no intention of thinking about it," I said. "Zero. Do not call me again."

"Call me back when you change your mind. This number is good. Incidentally, where did all the pay phones go? How do people call each other?"

"Real cute," I said.

"I'll be waiting."

"It's not going to happen."

"We'll see about that," she said.

She had hung up on me. I stared at my phone. The garden was still and quiet. A breeze lapped at the pansies in the planters, and their hundreds of yellow eyes seemed to turn on me, bobbing, expectant, waiting to see what I would do. I gazed bleakly back at them. Why did we spend so much money on pansies? And why pansies? The very name clashes with our brand's core values. We're not pansies here at Conch, and I mean that in the least offensive way possible. Why not impatiens? I would rather see impatiens. How fast could we switch them out?

I tried to do some strategic blue-sky thinking, focusing on our Conch mottoes and corporate touchstones: ship and iterate. Moonshot thinking. Fail better. They were starting to seem extremely tired.

A woman from the exercise class came past me with her water bottle and rolled-up yoga mat. "Hi!" she said, in the upbeat tone that Conch employees I don't recognize use to ask about my weekend. "Hi," I said back, realizing that she had recognized me before she came down the path, that the whole yoga class had noticed me, that everyone at Conch would soon know, if they didn't already (word spreads fast on our intranet chat board, ConchKlatch), that I was doing something sneaky and private on my phone, down in the garden. I looked up at the building. Conch employees in engineering, data-information systems, and sustainable packaging might, even now, be looking out, through the green-glass skin of the building at me, down here and suspiciously alone.

My Conch buzzed in a reminder pattern. "Finalize the board deck," it whispered. "Confirm travel arrangements for your trips to . . . Kansas City, Austin, New York, Shenzhen, Brussels,

Toledo. Schedule one-on-ones. Review employee handbook update and reply to HR."

"Remind me later," I said. I turned back toward Conch's entrance. As I walked, I hummed.

My Conch buzzed in a recognition pattern. "Identifying . . . tune. Do you want to listen to . . . 'Theme Song from *Car 54, Where Are You?*'"

"Yes," I said. "I totally do."

There it was, a song in my ear. As we all say a thousand times a day, what did we ever do before Conch? I strolled across the plaza in front of Conch's main entrance, past our single, unobjectionable piece of outdoor sculpture, a gigantic spring made of powder-glazed red metal. We say it represents the inner ear, but it was here when we assumed the lease. I'm not sure what it represented for the previous tenants. I personally love its coiled energy and extreme bounciness.

I walked across our parking lot and down the sidewalk as far as the stoplight. Across the street was the trail, the marsh, the Bay, and the salty, swampy smell. I have always meant to cross the road and walk down the path to see what is at the far end, but I've never been able to justify the time involved when there is so much pulling me back to our building.

"Make notes from call," my Conch reminded me. I sighed. I didn't want to give it a second's thought. It made me feel awful inside. But I ought to do it, to recap the phone call the way I would if it were a product call or an interview. It was a fallacy to treat this as something different from anything else—that had been my misstep in Barcelona. I had longed for something else, another kind of experience. But there was only one kind of experience, and that was work. "We had a brief convo," I recapped to myself. "She hinted at blackmail and made an aggressive ask. I refused." What was the upshot, the takeaway, the next step? Well, if I'd had any doubt, I knew now it was a scam—her request for money proved that. And so I had put her on warning. No further action necessary. Cross it off. I could move on. Right?

She was just a blackmailer. I felt a little crushed realizing this, but it was an irrational feeling. I was satisfied with my life. It was plenty. It was awesome. I had a feasible family situation and the satisfaction of a challenging number of problems to solve at Conch. My job presented me with a succession of meaty, complex, global business problems, and there was no kind of problem I relished solving more. And yet even these were predictable kinds of problems, variations on existing ones. I had gotten my hopes up that there might be something more. I had hoped her motives were pure. Motives so rarely were. That was basically the definition of a motive.

I tried to remember what she looked like. I tried to recollect her voice, from just a moment before. "Ask me a question," I said to myself, in my own voice. Then I tried to say it the way my mother's sister, Aunt Letty, would have. "Ask me a question!" ("You betcha! Where's the bubbler?") Was that different, or similar? I could have kicked myself for not recording the call.

Why hadn't she requested to spend time with me? If she had really believed she were me—if I, to put it differently, were her—wouldn't she be desperate to know all the things I'd done? I had done well in difficult situations, I had made some tough (but correct!) calls, even the *Silly Valley* blog acknowledged that, or had before the new, mean-spirited editors had come on board.

I watched a particularly joyful off-leash Bernese mountain dog come barreling down the path. Conch was malfunctioning and I couldn't fix it. The code was apparently a mess. My best hope was to close the Powerplex deal, do what I could to pump up the valuation of Conch, and then get out. We'd do better as part of one of the big players—that was a nice way to put it.

I felt a strange indecisiveness in my head, a muddiness to my thinking.

I tried to gain control: I should ignore her utterly and never speak of it again. It was odd she'd brought up the Conch problems. Even weirder she'd brought up Nova. My daughter, kidnapped. I'd told the audience at my Barcelona speech about Nova going missing, but I hadn't told anyone about Enrique. Rafe and I didn't talk about it. The conversation might slip too easily into other things we didn't talk about, like who was to blame that day.

There was a large triangular rock in the park with a flock of seagulls on it. I watched them fly off the rock, swoop through the sky, and come down for a landing. It reminded me of a park at the edge of San Francisco where we've taken the kids, where hang gliders take off, one after the other: a running start and then a satisfyingly predictable disappearance into the blue. Like the seagulls, all the little paper planes of my problems arced through my consciousness, came to rest for an instant on a rock, a promontory, a potential answer, and then when I looked over and regarded them, they flew away, unsolved. I went back inside to attack the rest of the day.

A couple of years ago, I was feeling professionally stuck and was looking for an opportunity to level up and stretch myself. So I put out some feelers to Brad Barsh, the chair of Conch's board, who had been on the board of Gorvis during my time there.

I knew Brad was bullish on Conch. He had been talking a lot about the product and even invited me to beta test it. In its early days, Conch had a program in which a handpicked group of high achievers wore Conches, and not only did it help publicize the product among clout-rich global influencers, but it also allowed the company to gather data on time management best practices. The Conch engineers used this data to fine-tune the product. I was happy to participate, to get a peek at the product, and to share my daily rhythms so other people could benefit.

One day a couple of months after I'd entered the program, Brad called about getting together for breakfast—nothing important, he said, just want to stay in touch, catch up a little, see what you've been up to, have a chat. Well, as you can imagine, this put me on guard.

Brad tried very hard to seem easygoing. His hair was always tousled, as if he'd just walked off a windy beach, and he wore Hawaiian shirts on occasions when other people wouldn't, which was to say, ever. He was surfer-esque, to the maximum extent possible for a nearsighted Jewish boy from Washington, DC. The guy in the office next to Brad's, at their VC firm on Sand Hill Road, dressed better, had neatly gelled hair, and was more punctiliously polite, always conniving to arrive first at doors and make a production out of opening them, but he also kept a speculum on his office windowsill to pick up and ratchet open during conversations with women entrepreneurs. So comparatively, Brad seemed like a prince.

At our breakfast, I buttered my rye toast as Brad sliced his cantaloupe smile.

"How are you liking the Conch?" (We still used "the" in those days.)

"I love it," I said, always the correct answer. Though the way the beta testing program had been billed to me, I thought Conch was supposed to love *me*.

Brad seemed pleased, however. He laid out the situation with his usual concision (typical problems, founder in way over his head), alluded to a search for more experienced management, and said, with a glint in his eye, "If I put you up, will you do it?"

I finished buttering my toast—a little back-and-forth sweep of the soft butter, a satisfying slide back across the brittle surface creating a very fine sprinkle of crumbs on the plate. I thought about it. For a moment I felt scared and worried—what if it was too much for me? But I looked into his eyes and said, "Yes, of course." I didn't say: honored, grateful, me? Those are the things women tend to say. I said, "Thanks for your support. I agree I'd be the right choice." Brad smiled with a little reptilian smirk, signaling that he was pleased.

Later, I made a trip in through the underground parking garage to meet the board, hush hush, and then we negotiated for a few weeks, as their lawyers and mine reviewed the comp package.

I went into the negotiations with an aggressive ask, because studies argue persuasively that women are undercomped for these kinds of jobs. A woman will say, a bonus of x million and y-percent equity is plenty! Why would I need more? A man will push back. And it compounds, because your future comp is based on your current comp.

Pay equity is something you read about sometimes, and it makes you feel guilty about earning so much more than the cleaning people, but by negotiating hard for the maximum package I am fighting the good fight for gender equity, so I can't let myself get distracted by other fights.

When it was all official, I felt anxious, but also excited by all the challenges I was about to take on. I felt like it was a great pick for Conch: I'd hire me too.

I was thinking about this while watching Brad during the board meeting that evening. He seemed unengaged, even though you'd think he'd relish this opportunity for a substantive strategic and tactical discussion of Conch. Cass's article didn't come up till the meeting was almost over. I gave a credible answer, blamed the story on a rabid tech press, and reassured the board that great work was being done all around the wheel.

"So we have nothing to worry about," Brad said. I sensed a glimmer of aggression in the way he said it.

I nodded enthusiastically. "Exactly." I noticed a shadow fall across his face. Brad resumed calculating on his calculator. Or maybe he just turns it upside down and types out the word "SHELLS"; that's what I used to like to do.

The rest of the board seemed satisfied, but Brad's reaction left me on edge. The meeting adjourned, a word I always enjoy for the door-spring action contained in the hinge between the *d* and *j* and also because it induces a temporary, pungent southern accent in Brad as he says it. ("This meeting is now ad-journed.")

One by one the board members left, slinging their backpacks and bags over their shoulders. A few lingered, chatting with Cullen. They aren't as chatty with me. The handshakes I got were springier, faster, and less grippy. I maintain broad and deep relationships with this array of influencers, but sometimes I get the feeling they don't like me much. The room emptied; Cullen accepted an invitation to go out that never quite filtered my way. Brad stayed behind, as if waiting for a chance to talk to me.

Willow came in looking like she'd been asleep at her desk. Her dress—it was odd, she was always wearing dresses—was wrinkled. "Is it OK if I take the sandwiches?"

"I don't think anyone's going to want them, do you?"

She hesitated. "My roommates would." She rushed to correct herself. "I'll put them in the microkitchen for tomorrow."

"Just take them home if you want," I said. Willow had ordered them from a different place than usual. Sometimes risk pays off; it tends not to with catering orders. The turkey sandwiches had an unappetizing smear of pulverized avocado staining the upper roll. (A sad misuse of resources: avocado's strength is its texture.)

"I'll order from the other place next time!" she apologized, flushing. *The other place also has a ridiculously good pasta salad.*

"It's good to try new things," I said, trying to soften the unintended harshness with which my words had come out. It wasn't Willow I was upset with.

The mention of roommates had been a sliver of light onto Willow's life; I never thought about her life outside Conch. I used to try to acquire three key details about my assistant that I could leverage in my holiday cards and future job recommendations, but there have been so many assistants. Now the personal lives of all the assistants plait together into a welter of colleges, unlikely double-majors, first jobs, sisters in Reno; it's simpler to imagine them as solid all the way through, like corn husk dolls.

Then Willow left, and Brad and I were alone. He walked out with me. Even though I got a sinking feeling when I saw his name in my inbox or voicemail, I usually liked talking with Brad while it was happening, even when he was pressing me hard. I felt like Brad and I communicated on our own special frequency, two people who were not frightened or turned off by each other's intensity. He did not even try to be boisterous and glib with me—"brotastic" was how one of my assistants once described him—and I felt like this was a mark of how close we were. But as soon as we were alone, my fear of having disappointed him was confirmed.

"Shelley, mind if we talk freely?"

My stomach dropped. "Of course, I welcome it."

"Something's wrong." He touched my arm. "You're not yourself."

I felt what I think of as the dark star in my chest—a tight, electric feeling on the left side, a concentrated ache, like a cold sparkler turning under my breastbone. I know it's not a heart attack because I have it so often and yet I am still here. So it's benign, I guess: just stress. I forced a smile and shook off his hand, sympathy being the last, unbearable straw. "I'm the same as always," I said sharply, though I didn't like saying this. I'm proud of my commitment to continuous improvement and life-long learning.

"Is something going on?" His tone, concerned, caught me off guard. He squinted at me. "Are you plotting your exit? Because your contract . . ." His voice rose, trying to sound fierce. It didn't work; it's not that kind of voice. But he doesn't have to be fierce. We both know he could get rid of me if he wanted.

"I promise you, I'm not. I'm as committed as ever."

"So don't take this the wrong way but . . . are you all right?" The flicker of worry again. "Are you talking to people about other jobs? Are you bailing?" A pause. "You're not pregnant, are you?"

I took a step back. "Pardon me?" His eyes slid down my body. I pulled up my shoulders and sucked in my stomach, which is, as a matter of record, quite flat.

"Is that it? Seriously? Wow. I guess I have a good eye. Con-gratulations. The timing couldn't be worse, but—"

"I'm not pregnant."

"You want to make sure? I have one of those drugstore testers in my car. Long story."

"It's not that," I said. When I started out at my first job, the payment processor, there was a blow-up doll stuffed into the sup-ply closet where people, by which I mean mostly young women admins, went to get pens. It was there the whole time I worked there, gradually deflating over my two-year period of employ-ment, its facial expression, never very nuanced, collapsing into a leer. A surprise every time you opened the door. The guy who had put it there was, amazingly enough, our in-house attorney. I'm sure he thought it was funny. He was generally regarded as a good lawyer. He helped me get my next job. You had to take the bad with the good, that was the lesson I took with me. You couldn't let it get to you.

"What is it, then? I can help you."

I looked down at the carpet and swallowed, hard.

"Babe, I don't judge," Brad said. "You and Cullen? You have an attractive offer elsewhere? Marriage problems? You fucked up? We can sort it out, but I need you to tell me what's going on."

I didn't say anything. He was getting annoyed that I wouldn't confide in him. "I'm not going to be an asshole and ask if it's menopause." Charming smile held for two beats. "*Is* that what it is?"

I smirked to show that he was kidding, even though he may or may not have known he was kidding. I blinked very fast to keep a neutral expression. "Our valuation is up. Revenue's good. Sport-Conch is very promising. I don't see why you're so concerned about me personally." I laid my hand on his shoulder. "I am as capable as I ever was." As soon as I said it, I knew it was the wrong thing to say. There are certain things that, once you say them, suggest the possibility of the opposite. *I am as capable as I ever was.* It made it sound like maybe I never had been good. I let the words hang in the air. Brad went quiet.

"You can do this," he said, doubtfully, not with the direct, specific, clear coaching you give to a mentee, but the way you cheer along someone you don't yet have enough documentation to fire. "I know you have it in you. I fought for you. I said, she's got the stuff. You can fight your way out of this, but I need you to fight. There are a lot of other guys who would like your job." He halted. "When I say guys I also mean women."

"Understood."

"You're replaceable. I'm not saying that to threaten you. It's just life."

I shrugged. I got it.

"I need you to get the Powerplex deal done. Don't let one bad news story stand in the way of a huge win for us. Do what it takes to get Powerplex."

I pushed back. "But we haven't finished our due diligence. I'm still taking meetings with a couple other players in the energy harvesting space. I don't want to rush into something with Powerplex if—"

"Listen, I'm going to give it to you straight: if you don't close the Powerplex deal, you're out. Get it done or we fire you." We exchanged extremely intense eye contact. "I need you to be the person I thought you were." His voice dropped and became pleading, almost tender. "Don't screw this up for me."

"I hear you loud and clear," I said. But when I took a step forward the floor did not meet my foot at the instant I was expecting, and came up at me too soon, and I felt a hot pain around my knee. Brad offered his arm but I waved it away. I didn't want to give him any evidence I was old and weak. I winced all the way to the car.

I drove myself home with a twinge in my knee, dazed. The kids were in bed. The maid had put all of the lights downstairs on low, and I could hear Bach's Partita in A Minor, its alive flute, coming from Blazer's nursery. I dropped my bag in my office and went into the kitchen to see about a snack. I was sniffling. The seed of a headache was taking root behind my right temple. At least I had all this—my family and the house, warm, comfortable, magazine-worthy. A top performer like me spends seventy-five percent of her life at work, but even so there is satisfaction in having a home life, especially when work is not going so well. It would have been nice, though, right at that moment, if someone had been there to greet me.

The house was dim and quiet. All around was evidence of life lived—toys arranged in signifying ways, a board game still out in the family room, some neatly stacked plates in the sink, a spray of fine crumbs on the table, remnants of a meal I had not been present for. I had the sense I sometimes had at home, of admiring aimlessness: very nice, but what is one to *do* here? Sometimes my employees talk about their "real lives" and I find the concept, and more significantly their preference for it, perplexing. Things had happened while I was gone, of course—the house, while neat and orderly, still made that clear. Atop a bench was a clean, folded stray diaper; some tiny shoes with knotted laces lay near the back door. I don't ever think about what I'm missing at home; why would I, when there's so much that I am gaining at work? Still, my gaze rested on the shoes, the way one lay on top of the other's toe, conveying the diffidence of their small owner, asleep upstairs, who relied on me to provide all of this.

When I first had a baby, I thought it was wonderful that Nova was such a poor sleeper. It seemed so perfect and efficient—success at work during the day and into the evening, quality time with the baby interspersed throughout the night. It was exhausting, of course, but for a few weeks I felt a manic adrenaline, as nights dissolved into days and days into nights and I was present for every single bit of it, the 360 of human and corporate experience. I even suggested to Melissa (whom I didn't know well yet—hard to believe!) that it would be convenient to have a nocturnal daughter. Melissa said no, sorry, we won't be doing that. At the time I was stung (why wasn't she considering my input?), but it was just as well. The tiredness had begun to hit. I had begun to fray.

And so they were on regular child schedules, and now they were deeply asleep, upstairs in their nightlit rooms. Rafe was out with a client. Blazer's night nurse dozed on his daybed, and Jacqui, in her room at the top of the back stairs, watched television. If I went into the back hall behind the children's rooms I might see the thin bar of blue light under her door, the sole evidence that I was not the only person here awake, but I knew that if she heard my footsteps approaching, that bar of light would go dark. Not until she'd heard me go all the way back down the hall would she turn it back on.

I switched on a cone of light in the kitchen. I opened the refrigerator. It was bright inside and stacked with containers. I opened one, but I wasn't sure what it was, or who it belonged to.

If I had no job at Conch, what would that be like? I tried to visualize it. I would wake up in the morning with only my personal email inbox to get on top of. How would I fill the baggy days? I could finally get to the symphony, awesome, but what then? Going to a party, crowding around some other female tech exec, the hot ticket of the moment, hearing her crystal laugh, straining to listen as she talked about her weekend on Larry Ellison's yacht and her merger opportunity and her winking allusions to goings-on—an acquisition, perhaps—she wasn't *quite* allowed to say. I tried to imagine, at this same gathering, a crowd of C-level executives bragging about their companies and asking me what I was doing. What would I say: "I've decided to spend some time with my family"? Could I say it in a way that they would believe? Would they even be polite enough to *pretend* to my face that they believed me? I could see their faked sympathy—they'd have read every detail online—and their deceitful smiles as they tried to pretend they didn't know, and talked about what a brave and exciting choice I had made. Choice—right. They weren't fools, these people.

What kind of job could I get, if I lost this one? Nothing like my current gig. Some smaller company maybe. Or medium-sized but in a downward spiral. A game maker whose hit game had peaked. A toilet company out to manufacture smart toilets. "New challenges": what a noxious phrase. Maybe I'd need to take some time to regroup and fake a passion project. I would have to be my own turnaround coach. My sinuses were filling up again and some kind of snotty water was collecting in the corners of my eyes and wetting my cheeks. Everyone wanted to see me fail, even the people who wanted me to succeed. Just for the spectacle of it, the story, the mild human interest of a human losing her grip. Just to watch me suffer through a power break-fast with Brad, and break down when he reassured me about how happy I was going to be at the smart toilet company.

I peeled off my work clothes, yanked off my bra, and put on a Giants T-shirt of Rafe's as a nightshirt. Downstairs, I made myself a sandwich. We did not have any of the products I wanted, not the right mayonnaise nor turkey nor the bread in the bag with the red label. I don't do the grocery shopping, obvi-ously. I don't plan to start, but you'd think they could sometimes ask me what I want. The sandwich I constructed was a sad little affair, like something you'd get at a third-tier airport on a Sunday morning while everyone else is celebrating Christmas. It made the meeting sandwiches look deluxe. I took a bite and threw it away. I opened the refrigerator and got out the milk to make hot chocolate. A cup of hot chocolate, in an attractive mug, would be comforting. I could take it upstairs, crawl under the sheets, and console myself with optimistic revenue forecasts. It would settle me. But there was no cocoa in the cupboard. There were bottles of mineral water, a six-pack of coconut water pods, pasta made of lentils, lentils not made into pasta, cans of tuna, sacks of farro, unopened containers of sriracha and balsamic vinegar and za'atar, but no cocoa and none of the salty crackers I like. Petty frustration flared. Why couldn't Jacqui keep the pantry stocked? This was a simple issue of inventory. It was logistically untaxing, and yet it happened all the time. I couldn't manage the house the way I managed work—I didn't spend enough time with boots on the ground; I could not, despite everything, do it all. You can't yell at people at home the way you can people at work, and by that I mean reprimand them constructively and make them accountable with a well-structured performance improvement plan. They don't respond right. They quit, or hide your favorite dress, or teach your children to hate you, or storm off in a tiff to go sleep in the guest room. There was a creak from somewhere in the wall as ice cubes heaved out of their mold into a bin. The kitchen was dark. The gasp of a faucet somewhere in the house turning off.

I opened my laptop and tried to work. On the Conch home-page was a video of me. I clicked it idly and realized a few seconds in that it was my Barcelona speech. I watched it, feeling low.

Onscreen, I strode onstage. In my head, when I enter, I take them all in with a wide-angle gaze and this is what I think to myself: hello, bastards! But I think it feeling superior to the bas-tards, not the way I felt right now. I tried to look for the moment I was thinking it, hoping to see everything extraneous fall away and an ascendant, radiant focus shine from my eyes. It was not quite that dramatic, however. I studied my image, shot from just below the lip of the stage. My posture could be improved. I found myself disliking myself. On the laugh lines, I gave away my plea-sure that they had taken the bait; I pressed my lips together to repress a smile, a tell. I wouldn't do that anymore. It was a good exercise to review all this. I should do it periodically, provided anyone continued to want me to make speeches at conferences. There were a decent number of views, likes, and shares on the video, and it repelled me that people had done that. I hated it, and also the part of myself that wished the numbers were higher. There was some redness at my jawline where I had squeezed at an incipient zit in the greenroom, getting nervous. A failure of self-discipline.

In the video, my belt buckle glinted in the footlights as I made dynamic but tasteful pelvic thrusts. I'd been taught to use hand gestures ("Make them bigger than you think, and slower," says my guru, Greer) but couldn't do the ones she'd taught me convincingly. The screen mounted behind me showed a close-up of my head.

Watching myself, not as myself but as a woman in gray pants and a cashmere boatneck sweater twiddling a remote and making big arm-sweeps meant to signal the far reaches of her vision, I saw myself get excited, because I do deeply enjoy it and that comes through, even when I'm speaking from a canned presentation. It was obviously me and yet there was the sensation of being surprised, and perhaps, truthfully, a bit disappointed by myself—these long arms, these choppy gestures, the swell of my ass, the slightly crooked posture, the stupid superficialities. I didn't look like the self I had in mind when I went out there. I seemed a little more disjointed and frayed. You're never as good as you think you are.

One of the things you learn as you go along, one of the interesting revelations of adulthood, is that what you think is attractive in yourself is often not the attractive thing. Maybe Conch had hired me in part because I was a woman. Or worse, maybe they'd hired me because they'd thought I'd be a weak CEO and they wanted that.

Maybe that was what I was turning out to be.

I looked flawed. Sometimes the flaw is what draws you in and serves as a kind of door you can go through. When I met Rafael he had a yellow tooth, revealed only when he raised his upper lip into his fullest smile. Rather than find the yellow tooth revolting, I liked it. It was like a little surprise, a vulnerability he showed only to those whose company he enjoyed most. I took it as evidence of his authenticity. It hinted at the textured life he had had, his range. I found it endearing. In my head he reminded me of an ear of maize, and the nice festive feeling you get from seeing those around Thanksgiving. But it also made him seem gettable. At some point it stopped being so attractive to me and became a flaw that I found ever-so-slightly off-putting—that's the second lesson, that the thing that attracts you often becomes, down the road, the thing that repels you. Another example of this is our attempted acquisition of a digital asset management software company. We were attracted by their asset-sharing component and wanted to do the deal, but once they let us look at the back end we were put off by the patent-infringement issues and the unscalable platform. In Rafael's case, the fonder I got of him the more secondary and irrelevant the tooth became, until it shifted from positive to neutral to negative, though I would never have brought it up. It was noted in a *Businessweek* profile of me ("with a yellowed glint to his smile that evokes the difficult road his family has traveled"), which neither of us commented on, and then a few months later he had it veneered. I told him there was no need, nobody noticed it, well, not anyone who already knew him, but I didn't miss it. Although when I look back at the old photos, I do, a little. Though I also find it a little unpolished and can't believe that it was once a benefit for me — or rather, I miss the old Rafael, the one I fell in love with, even though I love his successor.

In the video I was telling the beach story. I had forgotten about it, about that day, and hearing it again felt unreal. It was nothing, didn't matter, Nova was fine. It could have been such a life-changing day for us, but it had not been, and rather than feel perpetually lucky and wake up each day flooded with gratitude I had forgotten about it and chosen to take my daily good fortune as my due, my zero point. I did not enjoy the sensation of remembering and the sense of precariousness it gave me, when I was already feeling precarious, like a shovel digging out around the ground on which I stood. The data seemed to show that I was unsuccessful on all fronts.

I let the video run and opened a new window to see the house's security feed. I selected Nova's bedroom. It was dark, the transmission was low-res, and I could see little besides the white headboard of her antique twin bed, ghostly visible. Somewhere there in the dark was Nova sleeping.

I knew Nova was there, safe in bed, but I padded upstairs to check. I couldn't see well from the hall, but two steps into her room I could hear her in-sucks of breath and soft exhalations and the slow rhythm of her teeth grinding against each other. I was also a teeth-grinder in my childhood, but I really don't understand what Nova has to worry about. The darkness parted to show her sideways to the headboard, cheeks puffed out, an arm outstretched toward her pillow, upright on the floor. Her hand was open, cupped. She looked like a cupid in a Renaissance painting.

I stroked her forehead and cheek and said, "It's OK, don't worry. Please don't worry. I will worry for you." I picked up her hand, slack in sleep, and it curled around mine. I put it back on the bed. After a moment the grinding paused, her lower jaw still fully protruded, and I couldn't even hear her breaths.

The hall was bright. Nova sleeps with her door open; we close Blazer's. This is the kind of poor operational decision you make at home, with no strategy or forethought, so when we go on vacation and they share a room, somebody is always weeping. Very softly I tiptoed back down to the kitchen.

I opened a bag of potato chips I found in the back of the cupboard and flicked on the TV. I ate the chips, salt and vinegar flavor—"like crotches," my high school friend Walter used to so charmingly say—in front of the TV, licking the salt off my fingers and watching a true-crime program about an unsolved double murder. It was very relaxing. My Conch buzzed with new messages from Cullen and Brad. I just couldn't even. I took out my Conch and dropped it on the rug so I didn't have to hear any more buzzes and ate the rest of the bag of chips, and then I ate all the even crotchier dust at the bottom of the bag and it was absolutely delicious.

Chapter 13

I was drowsing on the sofa with the empty chip bag when Rafael came home from his client meeting. Kind of late. Rafe went to the liquor cabinet, made himself a drink, lolled against the island with the tumbler in his hands. I pulled a blanket around myself and came into the kitchen and gave him the headlines on the board meeting, sounding shrill and pathetic. I told him about how disappointed Brad had been with my handling of the Cass piece, and how cornered I felt on the Power-plex deal.

"They're going to fire me if I don't get Conch working right and get these Powerplex people to sign on. They might fire me even if I do."

Rafe sighed. "They would be crazy to fire you."

"That's BS—they will. Don't lie to reassure me."

"All right, have it your way. They're going to fire you."

"Thanks for your faith in me."

Rafe poured another slug of rum into his glass. He said quietly, "When they do, let's go on a real vacation."

"What?"

"We could finally get time away. We could go to the Maldives. Or Australia. I don't care. Go sit on the beach. Drink drinks." He raised his glass. "How about it? Here's to goodbye, Conch!"

I was white-hot with anger. I picked up a glass off the drain-board and threw it across the kitchen. It smashed against the wall. He eyed the shards on the floor. Then he turned to me and raised his eyebrows. He took a clean glass out of the cabinet, added ice, rum, and a little water from the faucet, and handed it to me. It was not the reaction I'd wanted.

I took the drink, still utterly indignant. "How can you say that? You know how hard I've worked." I felt for an instant the weight of all of that work pressing on my bones.

"That *Silly Valley* piece was rough," he said. "Everywhere I went today I heard people talking about it. But there's always a bright side."

The smash of the glass had been so unexpected that I was chastened. I clung to my blanket. "What?" I said numbly. I took a cold sip that turned hot in my throat.

"So, this might not be the time, but I have some news."

I tightened the blanket like a full-body sling and steadied myself against the counter.

"Had a meeting with all the partners today." He paused expectantly. "They want me to go to São Paulo." The casualness of it, some kind of silvery tone under his regular tone, alarmed me. I thought I heard Jacqui's door open upstairs.

"Fine," I snapped. I went to the closet to get the broom to sweep up the glass. "Get it on the calendar." Our rule is that whoever schedules first gets to go. We try to avoid both travel-ing simultaneously because of the kids, although it happens. We give ourselves a few freebies a year, because being wracked with guilt isn't good either. "What dates?" I didn't care. I was just try-ing to force myself back into normality.

"Like I was saying, São Paulo. Life in Brazil. What do you think?"

"You'll be safe, right?" I said, more because he seemed to be waiting for something more from me than because I doubted this. There seemed to be a catch but I hadn't caught it. I missed him when he traveled, especially at night when I sat on our white bed with my cool metal laptop on my lap and went at the keys solo, without the accompanying rhythm of him delicately picking out a different rhythm on his keyboard. He likes the flatter keyboards, I like the clickier ones where each key has more travel.

"They mean go down there," he said. "Run the South American office."

"Run-it run it? For how long? You mean be based there?"

He nodded—I had finally caught on. He shrugged and took a long swig of his drink. "It could be a year."

I choked a little on my drink. "What else could it be?"

"Two. Three. This would be semipermanent. I'd get the South American office going, kick-start development there. There's huge opportunity—" He looked at me as if waiting for me to say something. "On the plus side, it's beautiful once you get outside the city. It's not a bad place to be, at all. And once you're there the flight to Buenos Aires is nothing." He put his drink down so he could make hand gestures. "Don't you see? This is beautiful. You do your thing with Conch, you withdraw gracefully—'personal reasons'—we move to South America. It's much more relaxed there. We could see my family all the time. It would be a whole new life."

I blinked rapidly, trying to take this in. I sipped. I really don't like rum. "Couldn't you take the new role and commute home on weekends?"

His face fell. "Well, I was thinking we'd all go. Things aren't going that well for you at Conch. You know, I was thinking— Nova's still so young. She would pick up the language in nothing flat."

"I guess."

"New challenges are always good," he said, though there was a tinge of unhappiness in his voice. "Don't you always say that?"

"No question," I admitted. "For sure." I nodded seriously. I really do relish them.

"Look, if you're committed to playing this Conch thing out, you could stay here for a while and see it through," Rafe said, pacifyingly. "We'd move down there and you could join us when . . . you know, the board says enough."

I flinched. He went on.

"I spend more time hands-on with the kids, so I wouldn't want to give that up. If I left them here with you, I don't think they'd get a lot of face time with a parent. You can't . . ." No judgment in his voice, just being honest about our commitments. I get that. I'm very engaged in my career. My ambition doesn't leave a lot of scraps on the table. "You know, it's more relaxed there. I could probably see them sometimes at lunch, for sure most evenings."

"This is a minor setback," I said. "Conch is a great product. Why do you think this is the end for me?"

"Well, maybe it's not," he said, but I could tell he didn't believe it. "Think about it."

My innards spasmed in a way that lifted me onto my tiptoes, and I clutched the edge of the island. "That makes *some* sense," I said, because it's good to show that you understand the opposing side's point of view. "I have reservations, but I want to fully process them." I massaged my nose, which felt very congested. "I see a future for myself at Conch for a long time. This is just a setback." I glared at him. "Don't you think it's just a setback?"

"Do you want me to be honest?"

"No," I snarled.

"You're in a tough spot. I'm not saying it's all your fault. Look, succeed or fail, you're going to end up with a pretty decent payday, and you can use that to figure out your next move. Meanwhile you don't want to be seen schlubbing around Atherton in your yoga pants."

"I don't need your doubt. You know what my talent is? It's my complete belief in myself—and of course also in Conch. That's what it takes to be a CEO. You don't have it."

Rafe gave me a look that wasn't angry, which surprised me. He looked as if this were entirely expected and on some level amusing. "I don't want to be a CEO. I don't even want to do what I do, some days. I'd like to enjoy life. I can't live the way you do."

I hated hearing this so I pretended not to. "I understand you want this great opportunity and I don't want to stand between you and it, but . . ." I sniffed. My nose and sinuses were filling with liquid. I sniffed again to get air in there. "I need to process the implications of you going away, with or without the kids. It seems intriguing, but there might be unintended consequences to the decision, like, just off the top of my head, what if it affects the speed of Blazer's language development?" My sinuses were streaming liquid right out of the corners of my eyes. "Or, what about tropical disease exposure? Nova's immune system is fragile. Her preschool is here. They already understand her unique learning profile."

"It's a city of, what, twelve million people? I'm sure we could find some kind of preschool."

"We have to isolate some of these variables and determine whether they should play into this decision, and to what extent." I tried to wipe my face dry with my fingers.

"Do you want me to say no? I'm trying to make the best of the options I've got. I thought you'd be excited for me," he said. "I thought ambitious men were your thing."

Sometimes I could not believe I had married him. "You thought I'd be excited to have you move away?"

He made a little gesture, a shrug with his hands. He looked seriously at me over the rim of his glass. "You think what we've got here is fun?"

"Well—" I tried to remember a time that was fun. What I remembered instead was how, when we were first dating and he'd come over, he used to bring a grocery bag full of my favorite protein drinks. It was a godsend, because I was always forgetting to eat. I was surprised at the time—it seemed so ordinary and simple, and yet unusually kind. It was like something someone from my hometown would have done, like bringing over a casserole.

"Don't you think it's still fun?" I said.

There was a pause. He did not rush to fill it. I gave him increasingly severe looks.

"Maybe we'd still have fun if you didn't drink so much," I said, and felt triumph as real anger finally flashed across his face. He glared at me and poured a long twist into his glass, emptying the bottle.

I picked up my computer and briefcase and went upstairs into my bathroom. I shut the door, unzipped the main compartment of my bag, took out the distilled water, which I keep in a Nalgene bottle that so far hasn't leaked onto my laptop, and did my sinus rinse, left nostril first. The water shot upward into my nostril with a creaky, saxophonic screech, like in the James Bond theme when the Aston Martin tears off.

Clarity gathered, cloud-like, above my temple and I felt a satisfying rush, as if fresh air had been let in. The salt water rushed out of my nose and out of the corner of my eyes too. I took long, deep sniffs and demolished a dozen tissues, converting them to a wet pulp. Then I sat on my side of the bed, flipped open my computer, and began to type a response to one of Cullen's messages. As I scrolled through the email the hollow space that I had just created, which had felt so good and clear, shrank and was gone. *Don't leave me*, I typed to Cullen, and then I deleted it, and then I typed over that and deleted it too, in case the ghost of the typing could shine through.

Rafe and I have a dear friend who is a filmmaker in Tokyo. Shortly after our designer finished our house, while we were still living in the condo, we rented the house out to a friend of this filmmaker for a video shoot. In the resulting art piece, a woman in a wine-colored bra top and boy shorts, with tight, tanned abs, does advanced yoga moves at the foot of our bed, where her dreamy boyfriend/lover lies sleeping. Dawn breaks through the window behind her while she swims through her yoga routine fluidly. A lot of it involves upside-down moves—headstands and handstands that show off the controlled motion of her sculpted abs. You could see each individual muscle's definition on her bare torso. When we saw the video rough cut, we were like, ha! Just like our life!

Our bedroom now didn't look the way it had then, any more than Rafe and I looked like the people in the video. But looking around, seeing my tired-looking reflection in the mirror, I wondered if I should have made my marriage a higher priority. I try to make time for it, but once I prioritize Conch and my children, it's hard to also prioritize Rafael. How many things can be the priority? Really just one at a time. "Priority" is not a word that can legitimately be pluralized. And Rafe understands, or I thought he did. He has his own work. Of all of them—Conch, Cullen, kids, Rafe—he needs me the least.

I got ready for bed and turned out the light. I heard him coming up the stairs and down the hall. I wondered if he was coming to our room or to the guest room. I wanted him to go sleep in the guest room, but I also wanted him to suffer by lying beside me as I ignored him. I lay in bed trying to gauge the direction of his steps.

The bedroom door opened. He came in. I heard him taking off his shoes, the soft swishing sounds of his clothes parting from his body and getting kicked onto the love seat.

When he was in bed I waited for him to say something. He turned away from me, curled his back, and pretended to be asleep. We lay like that for a long time, awake in the dark. I listened to my own heartbeat.

Rafe spoke first. "You're a solid CEO," he said, unfurling a little. This was as close as he could come to apologizing. "That doesn't change just because you're thrust into a situation where you can't win."

It wasn't good enough.

"I'll win all right," I insisted. "Watch me win." A prick of light on the ceiling smoke detector pulsed green, as if in affirmation.

He made a little noise and pushed away from me. I concentrated on my breath, the way Greer always reminds me to, and seethed. Shouldn't your spouse cheer you on? It was infuriating. "I can do this job, and I can do it better than anyone predicted. I can guide Conch to a billion-dollar valuation, I can make it a product that changes millions of lives, and I can lead a mindshift in this industry. I'm being tested, but I'll fight back and I'll win."

"Do you remember," Rafe said quietly, "when you were pregnant with Nova, how sick you were?"

As a matter of fact, I could remember. Nausea is recallable, even more than pain. I'd had some brand of nausea I'd never felt before—as if there were a veil over my face, or a pillbox hat pinned tightly to my head, and askew. I still wanted to eat even when I felt this nausea, but with strategic selectivity, as if certain specific foods, if I identified and located them, would cure me.

"It was awful. I could only eat thinly sliced extra sharp cheddar," I said finally. The pang of relief to not be fighting.

"And apples, right?"

"Only some days. Only Granny Smiths, so thinly sliced that

each slice could almost let light through, and served very cold. That was all I wanted. I felt so wretched, I've never ever felt so bad." I corrected myself: "Rarely." Extremely thinly sliced foods, managing to both exist and barely exist, were the only foods I could tolerate. I couldn't handle the idea of food—ads for it, seeing people's lunch bags, the concept of restaurants—but I could manage the occasional petite translucent manifestation of it. At work, the smell of coffee roiled me. Also, the smell of the oil on the window sashes in the conference room. I was very conscious of it, sitting in meetings. Or maybe it was window cleaning fluid. In any case it became one of the top five things I was conscious of, along with Gorvis's cratering performance. "Why are you thinking about it?"

"Some people feel like that all the time."

"Gestational carriers," I said knowingly.

"No," Rafe said. "It's a metaphor. It's how *I* feel."

I touched my belly, my belly button. "I'm glad I had the experience of pregnancy. Once was plenty, though." It worked out really well using the gestational carrier with Blazer, since I was able to ramp up to another baby with reserves of strength and energy. The pregnancy was during the time I was managing a major product launch, so I still had the sense of incubating something phenomenal.

"I'm saying: I feel like that about our life."

"It goes away when you have the baby."

"Are you following? Yes. I can't continue feeling this way. I need something to change. We have options. If you hate the Brazil idea, I can stop working for now, and you can do your thing. Why isn't that a compromise you can accept?"

"It's hard for me to respect people who aren't ambitious," I said.

We went silent for a few minutes, our backs to each other in the bed.

"Like me," he said.

"Yeah." We lay in the darkness of our bedroom, with its smell of nice carpet and fresh monogrammed sheets and no other smells, just cleanliness and all-natural, scent-free laundry detergent derived from pistachios.

"It would never occur to me to feel differently about you if you lost your job," he said.

That was so hard for me to relate to I couldn't think of anything to say in response. After a while he seemed to understand this and tried again. "We don't *have* to work like this."

"I have to work like this," I said quickly.

"If things . . . if your work . . . I'm sure there'd be opportunities for you there. I've been pushing for us to expand our operations in that office, so it'd be strategic for me to lead it. It'll amp up my career, which matters to you, and the work would be interesting to me. It comes at the price of me moving away, but it sounds like that's OK with you. I can move down with the kids, and then you can join us if, you know, you . . ." His voice had a funny sadness to it. "You in?"

I sighed. "If I get fired because I can't close the Powerplex deal, then yeah, I'll do it. Sure." That was an easy thing to agree to, as I was determined not to let that happen. Still, it was difficult to say.

"I'll tell them we're thinking about it," Rafe said. The warm brawn of his upper leg fitted against mine.

This was my most intimate relationship, or was supposed to be. Should I tell him about the board meeting, the girl, the caller, whether I should send her the money? I searched for words to begin.

"Something happened. When I was in Barcelona . . ." It was hard to get the words out.

His voice, when it finally came, sounded strained. His leg moved almost imperceptibly, but away. "Yes?"

"I went out one night, to this bar. It was very strange . . ."

"You don't have to tell me."

"I want to. It would make me feel better to—"

"Look, we're adults, we travel a lot, I assume—"

"What do you assume?" I said sharply. I restrained an impulse to kick him. "What are you assuming? What are *you* doing when you travel?"

"Nothing interesting," he said. "Sometimes I order extra bacon for breakfast. But I get the feeling it's different for you. You don't seem to dislike work trips the way I do. When I'm away, I just want to get home. But you—"

"I miss the kids," I blurted out, meaning to contradict him. It came out wrong, as if I meant they were the only ones I missed. I should have added that I missed him also, but I didn't want to have to add it on, so I didn't. "It wasn't an affair, that's not what I meant."

He didn't say anything. His body lay tense beside mine. I knew exactly how he lay even though I wasn't looking at him. I could read his position in the bed by the arrangement of heat. I could tell he was worried by what I'd said and waiting for reassurance. Once I had thought that monogamy might be difficult. But marriage has corresponded for me with an intense career phase, so it's easier than you'd think to be faithful; I'm so busy. I turned my mind over to Barcelona. How could I explain it? What would I say? Would Rafe think I had snapped, or was unstable? Would it make him more likely to pack up the kids and take them away?

"Never mind," I said. "I made it sound too dramatic. It was just a work thing I was going to ask you about. It's nothing."

"Of course. How did I guess? A Conch thing."

"Yes. Sort of." If he was trying to irritate me, it didn't work. Not for nothing have I done all this life-coaching. I spoke as if he hadn't brought up Conch. "Look, if you moved down there with the kids, you *would* miss me."

"I'm sure. But we'll fly back. There's Skype. I just heard about this chat app that's popular with college kids."

"They're known for being so great in long-distance relationships."

Rafe turned over. He wanted to go to sleep, but I wasn't done.

"Do you think that taking this job at Conch has changed me?"

"No, you were always this crazy."

"Be real."

"What makes you think I'm joking?"

I laughed, but he didn't. Rafe did his locking-in-for-sleep maneuver, which I'm sure he doesn't even know he does—a half-roll, a tug on the sheet, a grunt as he moves into position. There was nothing notable about the sequence except that he did it every night. You get used to these things; they become part of your scenery. I gave him a quick kiss. He kissed me back but with a sense of finality, of closing the opportunity up.

"I still feel I made the right decision to take this job. Don't you think?"

He didn't answer. I prodded. "It was an opportunity that wasn't going to come around again. You have to seize opportunities," I insisted. "However you can get them." I heard what I was saying, and I understood its correctness, even though I knew it would hurt to see it through.

Rafe groaned and moved farther from me in bed.

Chapter 14

The next morning, Rafe seemed irritable and distant, but there was no time to talk things over. I left the house early, flew to and from Santa Barbara for a lunch meeting, stopped by the office to tie up loose ends, and then went home to change before heading to the party at Cullen's place in San Francisco. Rafe was meeting me there. Was supposed to meet me there. I had an unsettled, sick feeling that he might not show up as I waited for him outside Cullen's apartment. I practiced my power poses, which Greer taught me, which lower my cortisol levels while helping me emulate the alpha creatures of the jungle. But this time I just felt like a person pretending to be a panther.

The people I network with tend not to have partners or children. They worship their dogs (I view Eggs not as family, but as a housemate liable to eat my socks). Their biggest loves are nonhuman: clean air, clean water, exoplanets, orcas. Cullen's passion is the ocean. (Try saying that three times fast.) He is interested in investing the fortune he's making from Conch in creating nanobots—a kind of engineered bug—that will eat pollutants and clean the oceans. Mechanized krill, or something. It fits his big life project of making technology pervasive. The people I work with also like to mention their big life projects.

I checked my messages. Still no news from Rafe. He hadn't even bothered to make an excuse. It would have been so easy: an unexpected deadline, a client meeting, a problem with his team, a deal unraveling that needed his delicate handwork to stitch back together. I would be perfectly fine on my own at the party, of course. I just felt sad about him not wanting to come with me. I pictured what my life would be like without him: making do with a handful of nuts for dinner, going to bed in a creaky, empty house. Should I start talking about him less in public? I checked my watch again, scrutinized my reflection in the glass of a picture frame, slapped some color into my cheeks, and went in.

The party was in Cullen's loft, in a converted anchovy cannery. Little bronze plaques throughout the building explained that this had been the scaling room, this the cleaning room. There was a carved wooden throne upholstered in tattered mauve silk by the door. At the huge open windows, tall flat curtains flapped. Sea lions cried. Or something did—and I was willing to buy that it was a sea lion when told so. Cullen was converting the loft into a clubhouse for his old summer camp friends. It was vast and gray, every surface polished, lots of concrete. The ceilings were thirty feet above. The espresso machine straddled the kitchen, the size of a mid-century supercomputer, trimmed in brass like an 1880s locomotive.

"Hey, it's the birthday girl! You look lovely tonight, La Shelley," said Cullen's friend Irwin Lee, greeting me. He kissed my cheek, bending into the cloud of perfume that I had spritzed onto my neck earlier, and which now accosted me, sharp and aldehydic, every time I shifted position. Irwin kissed my other cheek too, European-style, which I was not expecting and caused our noses to pass within a pore's width of each other, which is the closest I have ever come to Irwin Lee. How to sum up Irwin? Is it worth the time it will take? He grew up going to summer camp in Vermont with Cullen, where they played guitar together and flew kites (literally chasing the long tail). Now he does something with security and passwords. Cullen says not that well.

I was wearing my blue silk dress—blue like the dirty ocean. Elegant, fitted, just off the shoulders. And earrings. I always forget to wear earrings (I have a checklist on my bathroom mirror to remind me), but I had them on tonight, dangly ones that jingled when I turned my head suddenly, which apparently I do a lot. The little jingle kept making me think it was time for my next meeting. I had made quite an effort. I hoped Cullen appreciated it.

At the moment Irwin and I separated, I touched my ear to be sure my earring hadn't slipped forward. I saw his eyes follow, and I realized he thought I was touching my Conch, prompting it to identify him. Of course I knew Irwin, but at that moment, feeling a little insecure myself, I liked the idea that he wasn't sure if I did. It's so important to stay humble, and the reason people say that is because power-tripping is so seductive. I watched him follow my finger up behind my ear, so I gave my Conch a little tap. There was a flicker of uncertainty on his face. It was a nice little moment.

"Good to see you . . ." I paused just for an instant, just to see discomfort on Irwin's face, as he timed how long it would take to come up with his name: ". . . Irwin."

"I heard about the Clitch," Irwin ventured, as if he were saying something naughty. Willow had told me earlier that this was what the strategy team had nicknamed the Conch glitch.

"Don't like that," I had told Willow.

"Pick your battles," she'd said pertly right back. I am totally developing her.

"Ah, yes," I said to Irwin, as if he'd mentioned a friend we had in common. I squeezed his hand warmly and he looked, I was glad to see, a little scared.

I ate grapes, looking out the big windows at the darkness and twinkling lights. Along the back wall of the loft, large aquariums pumped dark water. In the tanks, lacy clumps drifted and coalesced, forming shapes: maybe they were coral, or nanobots, or krill. I went closer and touched the glass of the tank. The shapes evolved, as if following the motion of my hand. A neon fish pierced the dark dreamscape. A very ugly electric eel lay at the bottom of one tank, featureless except for its gleaming eyes.

A woman glanced from the eel to me and caught my eye. "Reminds me of my ex-husband," she said.

I smiled. I tried to remember who she was: I think a CEO in biotech, very minor.

"Oh, Shelley!" she said, recognizing me as I tried to place her. "You've had a rough week." She said it as a statement of fact, without sympathy.

"It's a good thing I have laser focus, product power, and a team with incredible acumen," I said. "Without those assets, it would be tough."

Her eyes stayed on me a moment, as if she were going to say something and then decided not to. She sipped her wine. "You learn so much through the failing process," she said thoughtfully.

I didn't acknowledge this. Had everyone heard about the Clitch? Perhaps it was my imagination, but as I made my way across the crowded room, people abruptly stopped talking and then started up again in a forced, stagy way. I huddled by the windows beside a table of sustainably harvested seafood hors d'oeuvres. I checked my watch and wondered when would be the earliest acceptable time to leave.

"Greeting you!" a woman said, reaching out to hug me.

"Greer!" I said, melting into the hug, grateful for an ally. I enjoy Greer's bits of wisdom, shared via text, which add an interesting dimension to the present moment, like sucking on hard candies in lavender and oregano–type flavors. At the risk of sounding like Greer, though, there's something transcendent about experiencing her energy in person. I think it might be the gloss of saintliness, or a diet free of additives. Her smile just then was a genuinely balming experience. I feel similarly with Melissa, and, the time I met them, Nova's preschool teachers— next to them I feel bathed in a cool light, and understood.

Greer wore a simple scoop-necked top and gathered print skirt, loose over her small frame, perfect for leaving this event to go teach a ballet *folklórico* class later in the night, or act in a production of *The Grapes of Wrath*. It really didn't matter what Greer wore. As always, it was subsumed by a current of joy, confidence, joint flexibility, fortunate circumstances, and uniquely impactful statement jewelry. She had the posture of someone so used to being beautiful she took it for granted, and it was now beside the point whether she was or not.

"I've been hoping to run into you," Greer said to me, with a warmth that cheered me, but then she went on. "I'm having one of my failure parties next week. Won't you join me?" Greer throws her failure parties a few times a year for her clients. The idea is to defang failure, so it's something to embrace, not to fear. It's like a baby shower except no presents and no baby. The women stand up and give a self-deprecating three-minute talk about their latest failure. Everyone claps. The more major the woman, the more major the failure. In vulnerability, community. I am usually all over this in concept, but I was feeling too genuinely vulnerable.

I shook my head. Greer took my hand, sweetly. "Do come!

You can bring a friend, sister, lover . . ." She lost her conversational balance for a moment, as if thrown off-kilter by considering the possibility of me having lovers.

"Things are a little busy," I admitted.

"Do you find that busyness is the opposite of meaningful focus?" Greer asked.

I wasn't in the mood to benefit from this chastisement/reframing, so I picked up a piece of celery and nibbled it.

Greer leaned in and whispered, her breath in my ear. "I notice you are sharing your dress tonight without apology."

I looked at her, puzzled.

"Appetite is a passion of mine," Greer remarked, with a glance of revulsion toward the snacks, and particularly my celery stick. "I'm fascinated by how we feed our authentic selves. What quenches our true thirsts and hungers."

The celery was stringy but much of it was already in my mouth, so I was committed to swallowing it. I followed through on that commitment. "Great point," I said. Further discussion was postponed by Cullen approaching and scooping both of us up in his arms.

"Two of my favorites!" he said, and favorited me by giving me a crisp and very professional kiss. "Did you try the kombucha cocktail? I fermented it myself." He looked around. "Where's Rafael? So looking forward to hanging out with him tonight."

Cullen doesn't realize Rafe doesn't like him; he assumes everyone likes him, that's been his experience of the world so far.

"He's held up," I said. I changed the subject. "I didn't know you knew Greer."

Greer inclined her head and inhaled in a visible, stylish way. She gave a soft, reproachful look. It was rude to imply there was anyone Greer didn't know. "What a small world," I said, to be friendly, though I dislike that phrase. Seven and a half billion people on earth and I keep meeting the same fifty: it just shows our diversity efforts still have a long way to go.

"Look at Shelley's dress!" Greer said to Cullen.

"Oh, yeah, wow—you're really tapping into the trends." Cullen made a funny face.

What did that mean? I had expected compliments and I wasn't sure what to make of this feedback. When I'd been getting ready for the party I had reviewed, in the bathroom mirror, my not-terrible décolletage, my earrings, how my dress looked from the back. I had made sure nothing showed through the material. I thought back. I had stopped for a moment to lounge on the bed and get on top of my inbox, and then I had been distracted into checking the tech blogs, vile bastards though they were. I'd also had a message from Phil at Powerplex asking for "a couple of minutes as soon as possible." Was Powerplex scared? Well, they could wait. It didn't do to seem like a desperate suitor. I had noticed the time and checked my teeth—and yes, the rest of myself—in the mirror before going out. My dress seemed fine. I didn't know what they were talking about. I looked nice, actually.

Across the room I heard, very distinctly, a young woman say, "It's not a starring role, Irwin, I'm just grateful to be breaking into . . ."

It was as if I were sniffing something strange in the air. And then I heard it again: that voice. It carried across the room. It was so amped up and confident, audible to me without effort despite all the party sounds—it was the pop-up web ad of voices. A cool shiver cascaded down my spine.

"What did you mean, trends?" I asked Cullen.

"It's the second one like that I've seen tonight."

The second one. Another dress like mine. I felt understandably nervous. Not about the dress, about what was underneath.

Not the person's compression sucker slip, I want to clarify, but who the person was wearing it. I had a flicker of a thought, which I tried to suppress, that Michelle was at the party, and she'd dressed as my twin. Of course that was completely crazy. I angled my hand over my eyes, getting a good look around.

"Excuse me," I said, lurching away from Cullen and Greer. I heard snatches of conversation as I wriggled through the crowd.

"They've got to incentivize the millennials."

"Can the opera *do* that?"

I was trying not to listen, but suddenly I was overhearing lots of conversations at the party, and they all sounded ominous and directed at me. "She's a fool to think so." "I couldn't get it to work." "It wasn't what I wanted!" I hoped the people talking weren't talking about Conch.

I scanned the room and saw two men in khakis part to reveal a sliver of blue, like the blue of my dress. I watched, waiting for a better view, and made out a familiar style, seen from the back.

Someone had one hand on my cheek and the other gripping my forearm. It was Greer. "Breathe," she said. "I can see the distress in your alignment. I know how this must feel. Sending you ease."

"You think I'm worried because somebody else has the same dress?" I said, trying to sound breezy.

"It's not just about the dress, is it?" Greer's eyes searched my face. "It's about aging, the passage of time, the decaying physical body, losing your looks . . ."

"Everything's fantastic," I said.

"You have a lot of self-confidence," Greer said. "Good for you."

I approached the person in the blue dress. I felt a glimmer of expectation about who she might be. She had nice shoulder blades.

I tapped her shoulder. "You have marvelous taste!" I said ingratiatingly. She turned. In the hang time before my next heartbeat, my Conch buzzed. "Say hello . . ." my Conch began. My chest went tight. ". . . to Shelley Stone."

"Hi," I said. I looked straight at Michelle.

From looking over my seatmates' shoulders as they read magazines on airplanes, I've learned that if two people wear the same outfit, popular opinion can settle who "rocked it" more persuasively. I wondered, if put to a vote, which of us that would be and how lopsidedly the voting percentages would fall. It always seems to me from studying these pairs of photos for clues about regular people's tastes that the more famous person always wins. If the two people are approximately equal in fame, then the winner is decided by which camera angle is more flattering, although to reinforce the fiction of a meritocratic society, that decision is justified in terms of the person's choice of shoe. But I was too rattled to notice Michelle's shoes.

"What are you doing here?" I demanded.

"Cullen invited me."

I was having a mild psychic glitch. I kept recognizing her dress and having the infinitesimal prick of pleasure the recognition brought (I'd liked the dress so much when I'd seen it on the rack at the store), and then hard on the heels of the pleasure came the dismay it was her. I was too stunned to act; I just stared.

"Come over here," she said, taking the initiative, and also my arm. "Did you see the cake?" She led me over to the kitchen, which looked like a steampunk meth lab. There was a huge, pillowy cake on the counter. The cake was rectangular and covered in whorls of buttercream. Strawberry halves sank deep in the corners. A message looped across the top in strings of dark chocolate, so jazzily written it could hardly be read. I made out an S.

"See, it's for your birthday. It's my birthday too."

I'm losing my mind, I thought. She has the same dress. The same birthday. How can she not be me?

"So I was waiting for the money," she went on. "What happened?"

"What money?" But as I said it I knew. "Oh—the money you asked me to wire. I discussed that with you. That was a firm no."

"This dress was expensive!" she complained. "Although I left the tags on inside so I can return it."

"That's so dishonest," I said, appalled.

I stared at her, taking her in. I was intently concentrating on the way her body moved, the expressions that swept across her face as she talked. She still looked like a relative of mine, like a version of me in which the threads had been woven correctly but not pulled tight. She needed to pluck her eyebrows and do targeted ab work. Also, layers in her hair would reduce the poufiness. I had such a wealth of experience in these areas. Yet there was something about her skin that was simply better, younger, more collagen-y, it didn't matter what she did or didn't do. Mostly, though, she needed to go back to wherever she came from.

"Look, I need the SportConch. Just give me the prototype and I'll go. I'll leave right now, out that door." She pointed at the exit. "You never have to see me again." She lowered her voice. People were looking at us.

I hesitated. I had no intention of giving her the SportConch prototype, even if I'd had it.

She sensed my hesitation, though not why. "We can spend time together too. You know, just us, hanging out."

"I thought you weren't interested."

"I changed my mind. You're fascinating. I can't wait to hear what's in store."

"Well, I doubt it's *all* fascinating," I said, and I couldn't help but preen a little. "As for spending time together, my schedule is very full but I'm sure we can arrange something."

She was looking past me, across the room to Cullen, who was

demonstrating a wrestling hold on Irwin. "I was hoping he'd be more into me."

"He likes fish," I said.

"Instead of people?"

"In addition." Cullen's preferred type, if he has one, has not yet come into focus for me.

"About the money I asked for. How about a small check?"

I could feel my stress level rising; I took cleansing breaths. I needed to get fresh air.

"Look at that!" said someone with a rudimentary gift for pattern recognition, noticing our dresses. "Wow, that's amazing. Get a photo." I was annoyed. I hated that my taste in dresses was apparently just the same as when I was a poorly dressed nineteen-year-old versus a sleek thirty-nine-year-old tastemaker. I tried to remember and implement a three-point plan for handling extreme stress.

I rebutted. "It's an ocean-themed party, and we happen to both be in ocean-themed dresses. I'd say that's not surprising."

"Some women," the guy remarked to me, "would find it upsetting."

I shrugged. I feel like I have very little in common with most women, or men for that matter. I pushed my way outside and stepped onto Cullen's balcony.

Behind me was the bright quadrangle of the glass doors, through them the party, the people who I hoped weren't seeing me out here. The wafting smell of herbs—dill, tarragon, marijuana—from Cullen's pots. A tomato plant, spiraling up its cone-like support.

I clinked an Ativan out into my palm—normally it's calming enough simply to have them in my bag. But at this moment I needed to swallow one. Ativan slows down time for me, slows down my racing heart and makes me feel like I could reach up and snatch a speeding bullet out of the air. I breathed in deeply, taking a moment to take stock, before going back in to face the party.

"Nobody likes me," I said aloud, and felt the full wave of everything behind it, the realization that it was truer than I'd even been able to admit.

It's not just that people are intimidated by you, but also that they don't like you. That's the part your mother doesn't tell you.

I leaned back against the balcony railing. I had hardly drunk any alcohol, but plane travel is dehydrating and the Ativan on top of a few sips of white wine was loosening the relationship between me and the other bits of me. My perceptions were blurring at the edges. Sound and motion were beginning to pull apart, operating at different speeds. Through the window I watched people mill, hug, eat sushi, check their phones, and pick up shards of cheese with their fingers when nobody was looking. Against the back wall, Irwin, egged on by Cullen, was doing a parkour move where he lunged at the wall, windmilled his feet straight up, and flipped himself over to land back on the floor. Or this was the goal. Irwin made it two steps up the wall and then came right back down. I didn't know much about parkour but could tell he wasn't good. As a parent I suspected this activity was likely to end in spinal injury, but as someone with a dotted-line reporting obligation to the person asking him to do it, I just watched. Why wouldn't Cullen hang out with me more? He never invited me to come over to his apartment/clubhouse or go to one of his urban ninja classes across the Bay. Not that I wanted to, but I wouldn't mind being asked. We worked together really well, we had a close, personal, intimate work relationship, sometimes instant agreement on business decisions without a word of discussion; why wasn't it the same thing as being friends?

I texted Christine. *Remember how you said my dress was matronly? Obviously not, because an extremely attractive young person is wearing it too. My stalker, in fact. Remember I told you about her?*

She replied right away. *Sounds like an exciting night. Send pics, I'm stuck at work.* A moment later, she sent another message. *Did you call Walter like I suggested?*

I didn't like that she was referring to him by name. They were from separate parts of my life, the pre and the post.

No, I banged back. Sometimes Christine was right, though. I tried to picture him, couldn't, and tried on the idea of missing him. Then I whispered his name and tapped my Conch to search for him.

"Recent results," my Conch buzzed. "News alert: there's a story that might interest you in the . . . *Marathon County Weekly Reporter.*" I smiled. That's not even a publication that I'd guess would be online. Although everything is going digital now, and that's why this is such an opportune time to be in the aural information-streaming space. The story *was* recent; it was amazing how you could not think of someone for years and all at once find out what they had just been up to. I nodded to confirm. "Sure," I said. "Read it to me."

"Headline," my Conch intoned, "Local Man Remembers Lightning Strike That Destroyed Champion Sycamore."

I straightened up. Lightning strike?

My Conch seemed worried: "Your blood pressure is very high. You may want to sit down until this spike subsides."

"Go on," I whispered to my Conch.

The story was about Walter's recollections of that night. "Send link to my phone," I asked my Conch. I wanted to see the big photo I knew would be there, and it was, in the form of Walter in work boots posed beside a barn. He looked extremely old.

The Conch began reading the article. "*Webster*'s defines lightning as . . ." it began. "Twenty years ago, that definition took on special meaning for a local man when he . . ." I listened for mentions of myself, but the story was about the toll the strike had taken on Walter, and how he'd lost sight in one eye (I didn't remember that). I scrolled ahead in the story. The tree (another victim) was also pictured. Now Walter filled his days with a job at the tire store, and in his spare time made wooden bowls on a lathe. It mentioned me in passing ("Fun Trivial Fact, also with him that night was Shellie Stoner!"). Shellie Stoner, the paper said, had risen to prominence as head of a technology company called the Conch that made personal listening gadgets. She reportedly made millions of dollars per year and didn't spend any of it in Wisconsin. The article continued:

"*You still keep in touch with her?' I asked Walter, an avuncular man whose good eye still twinkles despite all he's been through.*

"*'Nah,' he said, with gentle mirth. 'She always was a—rhymes with witch.'*"

Oh, Walter, I thought.

When Walter had kissed me that night it was with only his lips (the dry, outside part), no tongue, like he was delivering some kind of benediction. Like I was very lucky to be getting this dry Wisconsin-boy kiss on a metal cooler. I thought kissing him would be more exciting, because I'd known him so long, and I liked him so much, but it was a relief to realize even then there was nothing to it. In movies it's more elaborate, but everything is different in movies—the ceilings are higher, the sun is out even at dinnertime, people always hand-wash their dishes when it's time to have an important conversation—movies aren't a good way to know what your life will be like. This was just like a fist bump, but with lips. I'd hardly had time to register the disappointment when I'd noticed a purple glow on the tree and his hair standing on end.

I was knocked out of those thoughts by a bang from inside the loft and a peal—many peals—of breaking glass. I flinched. Way too loud to be a wineglass's festive little fracturing tinkle. Inside, everyone had all at once stopped talking. I let myself in from the balcony. Irwin lay on his back on the floor, surrounded by shards of glass. The aquarium had shattered, and water was flowing across the floor, sloshing across people's shoes, carrying along in its current a toothpicked scallop that floated and bobbed like a buoy. There was a faint violet cast to the water, perhaps a tint picked up from the gray concrete floor. As I moved closer, I heard a thumping, and then I saw on the floor, camouflaged by the concrete, the electric eel.

Cullen crouched over Irwin, holding his floppy hand, checking his pulse. The electric eel (which properly should be called a knife fish—Cullen and I have worked together a long time) writhed in a puddle on the ground. All the guests who saw it backed away uselessly. These were people who paid good money to kiteboard, to adventure-trek, to send their children on Outward Bound expeditions, to have trainers inflict exercise on them, but nobody wanted to deal with the glass or the fish. If you don't pay for it, it isn't valuable adversity, I suppose. The eel raised its head. The ruffle along its belly rippled, starting at the head and moving outward to the tip. It was rather disgusting. It looked like a soft baseball bat, or a long, ropy poop.

Michelle was right there. "Grab it!" I yelled, but she didn't seem to hear. It raised its head toward Michelle, and she screamed. She picked up a serving fork off a cheese platter and threw it at the eel. It missed by a lot. What was her plan, to get into Cullen's good graces by killing his eel? Poor planning is one of the biggest obstacles to success. The other female CEO put up her hands, as if to surrender. She scooted backward so fast her tortoiseshell glasses slid down her nose.

"Oh, for God's sake," I said. Perhaps I thought it. In any case my crisis management training kicked in. I confirmed that I was wearing shoes (Care) and stepped carefully through water and glass shards toward him. Or her—even at this point in my life, after all I've been through, unconscious bias still causes me to default to the male sometimes, such as with certain medical specialties and invertebrates. Whatever the fish's sex, I approached, leaned over, grateful my dress was a practical length, and captured it with my hands. There was an instant when I thought: maybe there will be no shock. That thought squeezed itself into the tiny interval between grasping the fish and feeling the shock itself. Then the shock came: jittery, clean. It felt like a crisp series of jolts, like aluminum foil getting vigorously scrunched around a heap of holiday cookies. I held on to the eel, the experience of shock intermittently blacking out my awareness of the party. When I couldn't feel anymore, raw determination kept me going. Basically, as always. Consciousness came in little slices, intermittently. "Happy birthday, Shelley," wobbled a hologram display on the wall, which I read between jolts. How ironic, I thought. Here I am, again, twenty years later, and this is how I'm celebrating? I wore heavy earrings for this? It was not as bad as the lightning. It was like a minor resemblance; a birthday candle instead of a house fire.

There was no terror, this time, just the execution of responsibility: I knew what needed to be done, so I did it. I didn't lose my grip, even when the eel thrashed with surprising musculature, even when the numbness had reached my chest. I trapped the fish against my body so I wouldn't drop it, was dimly aware that people were watching me, and felt searing pain from the metal of my underwire bra. "Which way is the bathroom?" I asked. I received diffuse direction and tottered toward it. I'm glad I wore heels, I thought. Heels lift you above the fishy aquarium water now smeared across the floor, and they make your calves look svelte and taut meanwhile. I was curious about Cullen's bed, and I got a quick view of it. It was large and low, without many pillows.

I went through to his bathroom and started the tub, the way

you do for a toddler. In point of fact I don't often start the tub for a toddler, since Melissa usually does it, but I have done it before, which is more than you could have said for most people present. The large fish thumped unhappily in my grip, not unlike a toddler. It was heavy, and it was harder and harder to hold on.

Cullen's tub was very clean, deep, and surrounded by brown granite. There was an orchid on the corner, like in a hotel ad, and I wondered who had put it there. Probably he never used it. Or he had good cleaning people. People—women, who am I kidding. I thought this while waves of shock still coursed through me. Who has cleaning men? Even I employ only female household help, and would be, despite my commitment to gender equity, dubious about the motivations or qualifications of male applicants. We have so far to go toward real equality. My arms still had no feeling in them.

When I released the eel it dove rapidly into the water with a very satisfying splash. Its chest must have hit the bottom of the tub. By chest I mean the part under its lips. The eel's big mouth stayed in position, observing, expecting the worst, an expression much like people in my town have at permit variance hearings— dour, disdainful, making it clear they are watching to make sure you don't violate your impervious-surface limits. Of course, this is the fish's expression all the time; it just fit well at this instant.

I watched the water—so clear—swirling in the white tub. Clarity, I thought. That's the final C. Get clarity about the situation. And have confidence. That isn't one of the four Cs, but it's a good one, I told myself. Nobody else picked up that eel, but you did. You can withstand shocks. You aren't scared. You've been through worse. This, my dear (an atypical pet name for myself, but I was feeling tender, the post-electrical afterglow), is a true differentiator. It's good to be tough.

Cullen leaned in the bathroom door. He watched the eel swim in vigorous circuits. "They do pretty well out of water," he said. "They can stay out for hours, even. They secrete a kind of slime to protect themselves."

"You're welcome," I said.

He watched me affectionately from the doorway as I straightened the bath mat. He wasn't going to admit how pleased he was, but I could tell. "Come have a piece of cake?"

Then the world, which had seemed to have turned against me, relented: deep in the service shaft of Cullen's building the elevator gears ground, my phone buzzed, and my Conch read me a text from Rafe in its cool, woman-of-the-future voice (*Sorry, held up, be there in a few*). I dried my hands and smoothed my wet dress, refolded Cullen's brown towel and hung it neatly, and went back out into the party. I wanted Michelle to see me, calm and triumphant. I strode across crunching glass and pooled water; the crowd, deferential and no longer talking about the Clitch, parted to let me pass. I looked around for Michelle. The party had thinned, and people were drifting out. There was no sign of her. For a moment I was disappointed. Then the door opened, and there, coming across the loft, was Rafe, warm, solid, and familiar-smelling as he leaned over to kiss me.

Chapter 15

I couldn't sleep. I was too excited. The shock had been a reminder that I was made of what my ancestors called sterner stuff (never just stern, mind you—I come from a competitive lineage). I lay in bed, trying to extinguish the inner light, but part of me couldn't settle down. I wanted to make use of this feeling of power and competence, this sense of being back *on it*. I replayed the evening, reveling in my triumph, freshly annoyed by the irritating comments. *You learn so much from the failure process. I'm having a failure party, won't you come?*

Get a grip, Shelley, I told myself. You're overexcited. None of this stuff matters. The kind of people whose opinions shift every time *Silly Valley* posts a new story aren't worth thinking about. My arms ached, sore from the shock. That's one of the worst parts of being shocked—the feeling afterward.

She's a fool to think so. The voice that had said that was a woman's—it might not have been about me. But it bothered me, and what-if questions churned in my head. What was causing the Clitch? Why hadn't we picked up the problems earlier? Why didn't Cullen know what was wrong? Why were so many people happy that an innovative product like Conch might be broken? What if Walter and I had just stayed inside that

night, would we be together today, me acting in community theater while he made wooden bowls and knew how to fix things
under the sink?

Beside me Rafe's snore whickered. The cool green bars of
the digital clock on my bedside table rearranged themselves
over and over into new patterns, but it was too early to get up.
I'm an early riser, but there are limits. After a while I knew it
was pointless to lie there any longer, so I got up and went down
the hall. I listened outside Blazer's door and then peeked into
Nova's room. She lay sideways on her bed. Moving very slowly
so I didn't wake her, I reconfigured her covers to keep her warm.
Then I inched downstairs in the dark.

I felt unsettled and uninterested in working on budget numbers. I wandered through the house, putting things in their place,
although most things were exactly where they were intended
to be. My restlessness only resulted in moving the small stone
turtles on the console table into a different arrangement of stone
turtles, less appealing. I rotated a vase of begonias to display
another façade of begonias, with wiltier petals.

The lights were off and I navigated through the house on the
strength of familiarity and the watery light from outside. Everything was calm. I poured myself a glass of water, and mopped
up a little spill with a tea towel that had been a freebie from a
nutrient-pellet company. Their slogan is "Never empty the dish-
washer again." Since fourth grade that has pretty much been my
slogan too.

When we saw the house for the first time, the realtor had
told us that the kitchen would be great for entertaining. Ah,
yes, entertaining, Rafael and I repeated to each other blurrily,
as if this were a startup we'd heard was gaining market share but
whose case statement we hadn't yet had time to pore over. We
looked at her to give us the pitch.

"For holidays," the real estate agent prompted. "Big gatherings. Having people over. Super Bowl parties. Board game nights. Birthday parties for the kids."

"Oh, right!" I'd said. "Family time, or my women's leadership accountability group." Entertaining: I had a firm grasp on the concept but a hard time applying it. It brought to mind an image of faceless people thronging (who? our professional network? our direct reports?). I imagined myself vaulting atop the kitchen island, being handed a microphone, and delivering quippy motivational remarks to the people below, who, because I could not picture friends in such extensive aggregate, I filled in from the orgy scene in *Eyes Wide Shut* (tuxedos and G-strings).

It was a far cry from my parents' brown kitchen, with the checked curtain snapping at the open window, the note ("Eat!") taped to the browning bananas. At my parents', there was always a pile of browning bananas on the counter, and pressure to consume them before even more browning bananas arrived.

A plop on the back stairs, a rustle, the clink of a collar. Hello, Eggs. It was way too early to say that word. I have an ambivalent relationship with eggs, the food, as well as Eggs, the dog. On one hand it (the food) is a great source of protein, but the way it comes out of a chicken bothers me. The dog cocked her ears and stretched into a perfect downward dog pose. Then she turned and trotted back upstairs.

She always was a—rhymes with witch. It was amazing how decades later you could still hear someone's voice in your head, even saying words you'd never heard him say. Walter hadn't used to be a prude about swear words; I could cite examples.

I thought about Michelle, wearing my dress. Nobody who'd seen us had said it was uncanny, or that we looked like twins or sisters (or, thank God, mother and daughter). How much had she looked like me?

In the library is a chest where we store the photo albums people give us, to commemorate our service to their board or org or whatever. Once you get high- (or medium-) profile, people start giving you photos of themselves with you to remind you they exist. I tried to find a personal album, and from the bottom of the chest, I hauled out my baby book. On the first page was a photo my mother had captioned "On top of the world!" I was wearing a diaper and smiling from the top of a bookcase I'd climbed. There weren't many photos of me later on. This was before phone cameras, so we took pictures rarely, only on occasions when we looked least like ourselves: Halloween, formals, sprawled on the beach in sunglasses. It was hard to tell.

Dawn approached eventually, and with it a hangover of tiredness. Normally when I wake in the morning I restrain myself in bed for ten seconds and spend them bullet-pointing the most important things I will accomplish that day, and it fills me with joy to consider and then spring out of bed to act—to make a plan and know I'll see it through. But that morning I felt sandbagged and nauseous.

I went to the kitchen to make tea. I shook cereal into a bowl and chewed an oat cluster contemplatively. In the back hallway near the kitchen we have a conglomeration of family photos, selected and hung by our decorator: parents, grandparents, old people who may not be our genuine relatives but add gravitas (I believe one of them is Thomas Edison). I was suddenly aware of one photo. A faint but familiar violet glow. I went over and knelt down for a closer look. It was one of me. I was in my early twenties, wearing a bathing suit and standing on a dock fishing for walleye. In an Adirondack chair behind me, my father holds up a copy of a magazine and points at it—it's an issue of *Forbes* with a squib inside in which I was quoted. (Can I still remember the quote? Yes.) It was a funny picture, nostalgic the day it was taken. I knew then my first appearance in the business press wouldn't be my last.

With a rush of emotion I leaned in to study the photo now,

the furry pine trees, the lustrous lake, and me looking cheery, slim, and optimistic about my future (but not irrationally so, as time has borne out). I remembered being proud and a little embarrassed that the quote in the magazine hadn't been bigger. I had been pleased to be spending a weekend with my parents, because work was going well and I was excited to tell them all about it.

My parents were extremely hardworking, though their ambition confined itself to hopes of affording retirement. They grew their own vegetables and recaulked their own bathroom. My newfound relentlessness worried them. They treated it somewhat like a urinary tract infection I'd picked up in the hospital: likely to go away, awkward to talk about. They encouraged me to see my doctor and eat a lot of yogurt. Inquired delicately from time to time if the burning was still there.

My father looked young. I squinted at the photo now. I can still play back his voice, though only certain phrases now (the throat-clearing hmph he used to do every time I called him on the phone). Time went by, economies grew and shrank, companies were founded, bought, and sold, got funding or didn't, went public, went bust. A person stayed the same but not really. I had been the girl on the metal cooler who'd wanted to kiss Walter, and now I wasn't. I thought about how lucky I was, to have come so far.

The girl in the photo didn't look as much like Michelle as I'd have thought. Reminiscent. Similar. But not to an amazing degree. How had I not noticed? It was suddenly impossible to see us as the same person.

I try to avoid bombarding Willow with emails in the middle of the night (it's not as satisfying when she doesn't respond ASAP), but I sent her one instructing her to order me four sets of tires from a certain tire store in Wisconsin for our corporate hybrid fleet and have them shipped. Also, there's a man there who makes hand-turned wooden bowls, I think his name is Walter. Please purchase fifty, I want to do something unique for our corporate holiday presents this year. If he can't make fifty, that's fine. Pay in advance. Thanks!

I hesitated. Ask if he can do a hundred bowls, I wrote, and please don't use my name.

Blazer's rooster cry pierced the quiet house. I went upstairs. The surprised night nanny gasped when she saw my shadow in his doorway. She put down her knitting needles and handed him over reluctantly.

"Should I go get him his milk?" she asked. She said it clearly hoping I would say no (which I did).

I took Blazer downstairs, gave him his milk, and sat him on the carpet with a basket of intellectually stimulating toys. He threw himself into building a tower with the joyous energy of someone who had been in bed since 6:30 p.m.

I lay on the sofa, gazing at him, watching the multicolored tower ascend. It wasn't just that Michelle had looked like me, was it? It was because my Conch had said—and kept saying—she was me. And she knew things about me, all sorts of things. It was as if she had had a rich trove of current and archival data about my life, available to her in real time: Tate Bromberger, the name of our dog, my tendency to steal cash in small denominations from my classmates.

"It's going to fall," I warned Blazer. He smiled sagely and added a stacking cup. The tower (briefly) held, before it collapsed.

I thought of the two dresses, and how you could mistake one thing for another. Double and doubt. They were not dissimilar words. You wavered between two things.

Could they be etymologically linked? I went to Conch that question. Just as I was about to tap my Conch it fell into my palm.

Blazer had crawled over. He pulled up to a stand between my legs, balanced on his own feet, and reached imperially for my Conch, as if it were a squished blueberry. I moved it out of his grasp. He said something I couldn't decipher, probably an idiomatic expression in Mandarin. I didn't repeat it back so I wouldn't throw off his tones.

"Mine," he said, reaching for my Conch, undeterred. "Miney mine mine mine." And his declaration dissolved into a puddle of desirous consonants and a sharp, agonized squeal. Blazer is extremely smiley right up until the moment when he switches over to rage.

"Nope, buddy, these toys are yours. This is mine." I looked down at it again. My Conch. I gazed at its soft silicone housing.

It was as if she'd had my Conch, I thought, or been able to access all the information that was on it. I squinted at the Conch and, thinking hard, rotated it between my fingers, too distracted even to notice its finger feel, or that Blazer was about to eat a penny off the couch.

It was almost, I thought, as if she'd had a copy of my Conch.

Chapter 16

"Hi there, Tony," I said, entering the lobby at Conch. It had been a long night, and despite a pot of coffee and some sun salutations I was feeling about ten percent human. That morning in the car I'd had another panicky voicemail from Phil. The *Silly Valley* blog had doubled down on the Conch river-jumper story and run a follow-up. I'd have to call Phil back. But first there was the lobby to cross, Tony to greet, the brushed steel doors to part with my gaze.

"How's it going? How are you?" I said wearily to Tony.

"Not bad!" he chirped. I nodded and he turned back to a conversation he was engrossed in. I went up to the scanner and leaned in, widening my eyes so the camera could get a clear view. I waited for the usual chime. Instead there was a quick, jarring triple beep. I flinched (odd numbers make me wait, on edge, for a final bell that doesn't ring). I looked over at Tony, but he didn't seem to notice the aberration. I tried the door myself—locked. God, now I couldn't even open the door with my own irises. My skillset was decaying rapidly indeed. Tony stepped over to yank at the door for me. It didn't open.

We tried again and the door stayed closed.

"Get someone out to take a look at this," I said. "This

254 · ELISABETH COHEN

is ridiculous." I leaned in again. A triplet of staccato beeps, all on the same note, issued from the box. I cringed and audiated a fourth matching tone. Tony, who'd gone back behind the desk, made a long, low whistle. He came over with his tablet.

I tried the door again. Unbudgeable. "Tony, I need you to work your magic. This thing—"

"Hey, you're not wearing your Conch today. What's going on?"

"You noticed."

"I always notice. I have an eye for it. I check everyone."

"I'm having a problem with it. It's totally my fault. My daughter was eating breakfast and spilled . . . well, you don't need the gory details. I need to pick up a spare. Can you help me get in?"

He looked at the tablet and then up at me. "Now this is interesting. I've never seen this before."

"How hopeful that sounds."

"Look, Shell. A fly in the ointment. Something's going on."

"What?"

"It says you already entered."

I didn't understand.

"It says you're in the building. It thinks you're inside your office."

"What? But I'm here."

"I've never seen this before. You jump out the window last night on your way out?"

I shook my head, still not seeing where this was going. "Nope," I said curtly. My interior timer was going off. I had exhausted the time allocated for lobby conversation. Banter is fine, it serves a purpose, I enjoy these brief interludes of hearty back-and-forth with Tony, they give me a semblance of a social life ever since my women's accountability networking group fell apart, but I'd had enough.

"Hang on. There's got to be a way to override it, since you're clearly right here . . ."

There was a problem with my Conch, and now there was a problem with the door. Someone could be forgiven for wondering if we were really in the technology business.

"It's not like there are two of you," Tony joked.

"Of course not," I said. A tiny shiver ran down my spine. Of course not.

"Can you tell on that thing what time it thinks I came in?"

"Yeah, that's what it's good at. See, we just need to go down here, a little more, oops, not that much. There! You left the building last night at seven thirty-four and you reentered at seven twenty this morning. Twelve hours to rest, twelve hours to work, and all may be . . . how's the rhyme go? Socialist shit, pardon my French. Came back in at seven twenty on the dot. And now it's seven fifty-six and you're entering again. But—two entries, no exits: you see the problem."

Distant thunder. No. It couldn't be.

"So it shows me coming in this morning?"

"Exactly. The machine likes a one-to-one ratio between departures and arrivals. That's how we know you aren't sleeping in here, like that guy Arnold in QA."

I looked blank.

"With the"—he did a thoughtful little finger-chin stroke— "goatee? They said he smelled but they never knew why. I guess he wasn't taking advantage of the showers on Two. Maybe they didn't tell you about that. Never mind, it's been taken care of."

"I'm not sleeping in the building. And it's obvious I'm not in there now. Must be a glitch with the system." God, the glitches. I'd been elected mayor of Glitch City.

"Yeah," he said agreeably, but the light in his eyes was guarded, as if he sided with the tablet.

"Were you here then—at seven, when it thinks I came in?"

He hesitated.

"Don't lie to me," I said.

"Shell, come on. I'm your guy. You think I'd lie to you? Just give me a second to think. I'm thinking. The days they do blur." He held up his hands. "I was here. I've been here all morning, got in around six thirty."

"No breaks?"

"No."

"Did you see me come in?"

He shook his head.

"You're sure?"

"Yeah. What, did *you* see *me*?"

"It's a good point. I'm thinking." I looked over at his desk. "Where'd you get that coffee?" It was in a Conch compostable cup. "That's not from home."

His eyes moved over to it. "Oh, that. My tea. I can't drink coffee, it irritates my throat. You know, my dad would only drink Postum, same reason. Yeah, that's possible. I forgot about that. Just five minutes. Quick pit stop." He hooked his thumb toward the southwest, thirty degrees up—the cafeteria. "I'm sorry. I'm truly sorry."

"Doesn't matter now. Just get me in the building," I said. "Get my assistant. Tell her I'm coming up. Why do you think it thinks I'm already in there?"

"Somebody else with the same eyes must've come in earlier. Bet it's . . ." He kept talking but I couldn't listen.

Someone with the same eyes? I felt a flicker of nausea. It was so *impossible*. But I try never to say something is impossible. It stifles innovation. It is my job to solve it regardless. It's when you move beyond the possible that you—oh, Lord.

"Tony, get me in the door and see if you can pull the surveillance tapes. We may have an intruder. Don't say anything to anyone yet."

"So I shouldn't call security?"

"No."

"You want me to come up with you?"

"Just stay here."

"Shell, are you firing me? I'm sorry about the tea, it just didn't—"

"Just stay here in case I need you. I'll call down."

"Phew, I had this feeling you were about to fire me."

I gave him a look. "Your supervisor would be the one to fire you, were we doing that, but that's not on point right now."

I hurried in, past mostly unoccupied workstations. There were Conch-branded fleece jackets and ribbed sweaters smoothed over the backs of swivel chairs, meant to suggest their wearers had just ducked into a meeting, not gone home for the night. On the desks were monitors with bright, expectant lock screens, framed photos, insulated coffee mugs, bags of bread (our cafeteria doesn't serve simple carbs, only quinoa and parsnips), and open boxes of every food product that can be reconstituted with hot water—instant oatmeal, soup, hot chocolate, ramen—their competing brand elements clashing with the spare Nordic futurism of Conch's decor. Fortunately there were very few people in at this hour to see me. When their heads popped up, smiling— *look, here I am, working hard so very early*—I couldn't manage even a nod, and the heads withdrew, looking worried, as if they connected my expression to some minor screwup they had made, some poor run of circumstances in which they were the central, deficient player. At the top of the steps I walked faster, almost running. My heels skimmed the carpet. Just around the bend, Willow was waiting for me, notebook pinned under her arm, her attention fixed on her cell phone. She looked up as I approached. She didn't have to say anything. Her panicked expression told me what I needed to know. I touched her lightly on the shoulder and she recoiled.

"Who's here to see me?" I croaked. "My half sister?"

Willow shook her head.

"There's nobody here to see me?" I asked hoarsely. I took a deep breath to steady myself. Maybe the girl was hiding somewhere, like under my desk.

Willow looked on the verge of tears, like the least competent edition of herself. I remembered suddenly the slightly pathetic but vehement Willow who'd shown up for her job interview, her white slip hanging lower than her skirt. "It's snowing down south" was, according to my mother, the correct way to tip off another woman about her problematic hemline. Though I just ignored it and figured that the slip-wearing would work itself out in time, which it seems to have. If anything, it had made me feel like here was a person who needed this opportunity.

"Nobody's here to see me?" I repeated, incredulous.

"Brad is on his way over! Phil's saying"—a huge sniff here, to pull back some snot that edged out of her nose—"that you misled him about the functionality of our flagship product!"

I gazed into her eyes to restore her trust. "Powerplex wants a better deal," I explained. "People will use anything as a negotiating point."

Willow's expression melted into relief. "Oh, I forgot, you have a visitor who's not on your calendar. She was waiting by your desk when I came in."

"Where is she?" The carpet-tile floor seemed to jounce, ever so slightly, under the balls of my feet. I engaged my core.

"Is she our new intern? I sent her over to Making Waves to get breakfast."

"Are you kidding me?" I said. Although that is in fact the name of the cafeteria. The Arctic char is excellent; the zucchini fries are to die for. New hires, we joke, get Conch's version of the freshman fifteen: ConchPaunch. However, this was not the time. Willow and I entwined ourselves in eye contact: hers curious, mine anxious.

"What'd she look like?" I said. "This intern. What was your first thought?"

Just then the phone in Willow's hand rang. She answered it: "Hi, this is Willow at Conch." *It's Powerplex,* she mouthed.

"I'll take it."

"Yes, she's available. Please hold for Shelley Stone." She silently counted off three beats and passed the phone to me.

"Shelley, I have been trying to reach you," Phil said, his voice sounding smushed, as though his mouth were too close to his phone. I envisioned him in his Omaha penthouse, pushing aside his plate of breakfast steak, fortified to harangue me. "I know I'm the last person on earth you want to talk to right now."

"That's not true," I said. "You're at least the second to last." This amused him, and while he chortled I glanced around for my visitor.

"I want to ask you a question," Phil said. "Have you ever had a time when you're just going in circles in your mind, plagued with doubt?"

"Uh," I stalled. How had this visitor, this "intern," gotten through the iris scanner? Was it because she was the younger me after all?

"Maybe you haven't, but I sure have," Phil protested.

"Every person is unique," I murmured. I squinted at my reflection in the glass of an inspirational poster and studied my eyes. They looked ordinary, like anyone's eyes, but what were the chances of someone else having the same irises?

Phil said he'd had a bad dream about the deal. He'd dreamed of a lobster going after a golden retriever. He'd woken with a sweaty pillow and guilty thoughts of his fiduciary responsibility to his shareholders. "But that's not what bothers me most," Phil said. "Are you aware that this person, this—"

"User."

"Let's call him by his name," Phil insisted.

There was a tiny pause, which grew into a medium-sized pause.

"Mr. Lee Beckett," Phil announced, as if he'd won a moral victory. "Did you know Mr. Beckett called Conch customer service, twice, in the week before he jumped? He may only have needed a little warmth and human sympathy. Not to say the obvious . . ." Though Phil always said the obvious. "But Conch had an opportunity to make his life better, not worse. You guys could have cheered him up."

"Yes, absolutely, every day is an opportunity to show kindness and compassion, I couldn't agree with you more." I thought: maybe I should arm myself in case Michelle ambushes me.

Phil went on. "He told your customer service people that his Conch wasn't working right"—that was what his mother had told Phil's lawyers. He'd been getting headaches ever since he started using it. Instead of sympathy, Conch's customer service reps stonewalled him and said they couldn't find his serial number.

"Kill 'em with kindness," Phil said. "That's what I always say. You're not literally killing them. What I mean is, be nice and then they think you're being nice, but you're not." I looked around to see what I could use to defend myself against Michelle, if it came to that. Certainly not the inflatable whale. Perhaps a pen with a sharp point. You'd think I worked at a preschool, with the lack of sharp objects around.

"Agreed," I said. Also, rope is always good. I picked up a coiled USB cord. You can secure someone's wrists with USB cord (I mean, I think you could).

Phil pressed. "Mr. Beckett was part of an online community of people who believed that wearing Conch had made them sick. There are tons of them, reporting their experiences in a chat room, did you know?"

"Of course," I said. "If your product were more popular people would be complaining about you too."

"It's tragic . . ."

"Phil, they're just looking for a scapegoat, though it's very sad and I feel for the family," I said. "I reached out with our condolences. But we're making the safest, most disruptive technology ever here. It would be silly for this to make us skittish." Delivered with the supreme, cast-iron confidence of a tanned television news anchor chatting with you at a cocktail party: whatever dumb thing you say, she or he'll whack something friendly-smooth right back.

"My company has an unblemished reputation in the agricultural sector, going back to the time when my grandfather Philip Milliken Furness the first, God rest his soul—"

I broke in: "This is how we know that Conch is a life-changing product. That when it fails, it actually matters." Willow pursed her lips and looked doubtful. I'm not sure I buy that line either; I'm just trying it out. If you say something brightly, with enough sheen on your words, it is hard for other people to find indentations to cling to, to respond to. They look helpless and relax their grip and slide right down the mountain, while you smile down at them. In general, other people are not as confident as oneself, and if you fix your gaze on them, they will look away or back down. "We'll have the self-charging prototype at the end of the week, and I guarantee you, Conch will never be working better. We're crossing the digital-physical divide here. That is not an easy chasm to bridge. It's natural to expect some hiccups. But who wouldn't trade places with you right now? We're going to have a solution to these minor—and I'm not trivializing them by saying that, just that I want to take a big-picture view here—we'll have a solution by the end of the week."

"The end of this week?"

"A real solution, I promise you. Let's hang up now."

"We're supposed to sign this deal on Friday. That's only a couple of days away."

"For sure. Let's talk again in a few."

"A few what?"

"Perfect-o," I said, and hung up. "Willow," I gasped. "The visitor! Go find her! Right now!"

I logged onto my computer. It seemed, even as I did it, like a pointless activity. I lacked the appetite for work. Email was not, right then, as Greer would have put it, the nourishment my authentic self craved. To type in my password correctly took multiple attempts, fortunately not so many that the system locked me out. There was a tremor in my mouse hand that jerked the cursor around like a kite on the windiest, though not quite windy enough, day of a beach vacation. Then I heard the sound of people approaching and Willow's upbeat voice explaining our printer codes and I turned to face the beanbag area.

There she was.

I took in a quick impression of her: button-down shirt a little too big, jeans a little funny-looking (but young people's jeans often do look funny to me), the slope of her hair as it bridged her ear and skimmed her shoulder. The overall impression was nondescript. There was a patterned cloth bag over her shoulder and a babyish convexity to her belly. There was something about the curve of her spine that I recognized from store dressing rooms, when you catch sight of someone's back in a mirror not realizing at first it is you. She looked younger than I'd remembered. I'd been thinking of her as a threat and was surprised by how unthreatening she looked. Like some neighbor's babysitter. I put the USB cord away. I already knew this wasn't that situation.

But she was a threat, I reminded myself, because she did not have authorization to be in here, she was not a Conch employee, she should not have been given a badge, and yet she was here, approaching my desk, carrying a mauve cafeteria smoothie.

"Hi," I said.

"Hi," Michelle said.

Willow asserted herself between us. "This is the new intern. I don't think you'll be working *that much* with Shelley. Now, Shelley, should I move your ten o'clock out a smidge? Also, the Clitch is definitely affecting my Conch today. Every time I see her it says, 'Say hello to Shelley Stone.'"

"Put that in the bug tracker and label it high priority," I said sharply. "Ask engineering what their time frame is for a solution. Then say nothing but look at them unhappily until they revise it downward."

Conch employees were streaming in, unloading their backpacks, unclicking the chinstraps of their bike helmets, preparing their elaborate microwaved breakfasts, husking off fleece quarter-zips from their ropy runners' bodies, cheerfully greeting each other and stopping mid-greeting to surreptitiously gauge my mood. Did their Conches, every day, announce, "Say hello to Shelley Stone"? Every time I rounded the corner or approached someone's back at their desk? How obnoxious that must be.

"I'll talk to her," I said to Willow. "Tell her a little about how we do things round here."

"Hold this notebook," I whispered sharply to Michelle, thrusting one at her. "People are watching us. I need to shift the optics."

It was reassuring to be at work, in familiar surroundings, scene of a million previous less-personal disasters, most of which I'd dispatched with fairly good results. I could do it again, and I would. I was fully myself in my workplace, I brought every bit of me to bear on challenges, and I drew strength from all of it:

the activity of the teams around me, the channel that opened up as I propelled myself through Conch, the enthusiasm with which everyone greeted my feedback, the vigor and whimsy of our decorating strategy.

All I needed to do was stay loose, agile, nimble, incisive, visionary, adroit, detail-oriented, upbeat, and tastefully humorous, or, as I remind myself for short, LANIVADUTH.

I was at my best at work, no question, my family would have said the same, and this confidence bolstered me as I hustled Michelle into Fritter.

From inside, I examined the door. No lock. I went to close the blinds so the customer service department couldn't see us. Willow was loitering on the other side of the window. She gave me a curious look through the glass and seemed a little crushed to be excluded. I pulled the blinds all the way closed. Sometimes there are occasions for privacy.

"OK," I said, not bothering to sit down. "Who are you?" My voice had so much edge I could have cut myself.

"My name is Michelle," she said, as if there could be no question.

I sighed. "How'd you get *in* here?"

"Into the building? Through the lobby."

"What about the iris scanner downstairs?"

She shrugged. What was there to explain?

"How?" I was steely.

"I just went to the scanner and . . . did what everyone else did." She mimed leaning forward with wide eyes and gaping mouth. Her eyes caught mine. "We have the same irises, I guess." She said it defensively, looking uncertainly at me. She tugged down on her lower eyelid so I could assess this. There was a little goo in the corner.

"We must," I agreed, but I could hear the note of doubt in my voice. Be as persuasive as that time when you met with Conch's board for the first time, I told myself, and slayed them with your acumen. Let her believe you still believe. "That's fascinating. Of course. I'd like to see you do it. I'm very interested in how security systems work, especially in use cases like this one . . . especially how they'd handle you. Let's go downstairs and try it."

"I'm in here, aren't I?" She glowered.

"I'm more than a bit curious about it." I tried to keep my voice in the register of curiosity, not suspicion. Curiosity is one of my core leadership traits.

"I need something from you."

"Money? It won't be forthcoming."

"That, but first I really need the SportConch prototype. I really need it."

Someone rapped on the door and it swung open. "We have this room now," a male voice said in an officious tenor. Then he saw it was me. "Oh, hey, I didn't realize! We're just getting together for a quick confab to talk about the SportConch product package and Holly's *great* idea of making the instructions fold out like this . . ." It's sweet how Conch employees always assume I am deeply interested in their minute decision-making.

"Awesome to hear!" I said. "Can't wait to see it when you hammer out the details. We're having a productive meeting; hope you do too. Just give us five minutes. Sorry for sniping your room rez." (A provocative topic on ConchKlatch.)

He gestured magnanimously, letting us have it. Employees always concede to me, when what I crave is a little fight.

We watched the door close.

"Why are you here?"

"To pick up a SportConch."

"Why?"

"I need you to give me SportConch. The prototype. You offered to fill me in on all kinds of stuff. I think this would be very helpful."

I gave her a long, searching look. It didn't make any sense. "You don't want the damn prototype. You *barely* care about haptics and energy harvesting."

"Don't you want me to care?"

"This is bullshit," I said, in a soft, understanding, empathy-filled voice. "Tell me what you did to my Conch."

She looked surprised. She put her finger to her lips. *Are you wearing your thing?* she mouthed, tapping her neck.

"What are you saying?"

"Shh!" *If you are, take it out.* She mimed the removal of something from the neck area.

"I'm not wearing my Conch," I said. I brushed back my hair and lifted my earlobe to prove it.

"You're so smart!" she cried. "I knew you were smart."

A rap on the door. It opened and Willow leaned in. "Hey, Brad's on the phone."

"I'll call him back."

"He's on his phone, in his car, turning into our parking lot."

"Give me a minute."

"Do you want a Cobb salad for lunch?"

"Um, sure."

"I'll replace the egg with one I hard-boil myself in the micro-kitchen." Willow made a show of saying it, though she does this all the time for me, it's NBD. "I know you don't like the ones that come pre-peeled—"

"I can live with that today."

"Is it because you don't like the gray around the yolk?" Michelle commiserated.

That's not why. Willow and I both ignored her. Willow left. Michelle and I looked at each other.

"Do you want to go to prison for fraud?" I demanded. "For breaking and entering, for identity theft, for probably other things I can't even think of? I'm going to call the police unless you give me a full explanation, right now."

She covered her face with her hands.

"Oh, please, don't cower. The way to my sympathy is to be clear, concise, and give a sharply drawn overview of what is going on. I'm not into shrinking violets."

She pressed her temples. "Ask me questions," she suggested. "You know, about what your father does for a living, or your favorite kind of ice cream sundae. Butterscotch, right?"

I shrugged. I really didn't know what my favorite sundae would be. Maybe peanut butter for the protein.

"I didn't mean for this to happen," she said. "I can be useful."

"When I showed you my Conch back at that bar, what did you do with it?"

"I gave you a different one. I switched them."

"Why?"

"I don't know. Because they told me to."

"Who's they?"

"The people I worked for. They told me to switch your Conch and I did it, but I don't want to keep working for them. Can you help me?" Plaintive pause. "I liked you."

If she thought this would resonate, she was wrong. I would rather be respected than liked. "What kind of job was this?"

"As a sort of . . . actor. I was cast in a role. To meet you at a bar and exchange your Conch for a different one."

I went tense inside. "The one I had on last night?"

"I guess? They all kind of look the same to me. My part was just to take the one you had and give you that one."

I blinked hard. My mind went back to the bar. It was an elusive memory. Swaying, clinking mugs overhead and a paper napkin splotched with blood. "You switched them?"

"Remember, you showed it off to me?"

I often showed off my Conch to young people, as a way of stoking interest in the product among a demographic that's a bit squishy for us, but I did remember.

"I told them what a good job I'd done," Michelle went on. "I might have bragged too much, because—"

"Women tend not to self-advocate as much as men, but it's a complicated issue because they pay a social price when they do," I said knowingly.

"They wanted me to keep going, do more. I didn't know how to get out of it. I didn't want to get typecast either; I feel like I have a lot of range. They want that new thing you guys are making. SportConch. I told them to send me here, and I would do it. But I was having doubts, and you know, I'm done. I'm not feeling it anymore. It's not a role that stretches me."

"You put something in my Conch to intercept data and track me."

And then her voice got very definite. "*I* didn't."

Cullen opened the door and leaned in. "Shelley, sorry to break up the party but we need you out here."

"Just wrapping up."

Cullen raised an eyebrow, looked at her and back at me. He hesitated in the doorway. "Everything OK?"

"Excellent," I said, with a waver in my voice that he took as a joke.

As soon as the door closed she brightened. "What's he really like? Do you think he likes me?"

I shook my head. "I need proof. I need to know how you got in here."

"Uh . . ." She emptied her bag onto the conference table: a scrunched receipt, some loose dollar bills, a plain-Jane kind of business card with a wave-shaped logo on it and a long Malaysian address, and a U.S. passport. I snatched up the passport and opened it. For one second I thought, wow, she really does look like me. I looked back at her, and then back at the passport. There was a truly disorienting second when I couldn't figure it out. To be fair, I had a lot going on.

"It's yours," she said finally. "Duh."

"Oh."

"I took it at the hotel. Remember, you showed it to me? I'm sorry."

I tried to remember, but the memory squidged out of view. It's not that I'm repressing it, exactly; it just isn't there, as if someone forgot to run the backup. It's as if data is missing, or—to be analog about it—as if the film were spliced with Scotch tape, and I'm spinning back and forth across the splice, trying to land on a frame that was taken away.

"So how'd you get in here?"

"Into the building?"

"Yes. Through the scanner. Was the guard there?"

She looked shifty. "I might have waited till he wasn't."

She sorted through the pile of crap on the table, then lifted a finger in a weak give-me-a-moment gesture and reached down into her bag. I watched her and wondered if she had a gun. I doubted it. I had a brief faint extraneous thought-flicker: If she shoots me in Fritter will it be A1 in the newspaper or just inside the business section?

But when she withdrew her hand, it was with a small, folded-up piece of paper. She handed it to me.

I unfolded it. "What is this?"

"This is what I used," she said.

In her nervousness, the area under her eyes had gotten thin, veiny, and shone with sweat—a glint of fear. This happens to my friend Christine too. I thought, people are similar even if they aren't the same. Then I thought, what a fucking fascinating insight, Shelley, you'll have to remember to put that on LinkedIn, where it will attract dozens of sycophantic comments, albeit in substandard English. I tried to make sense of the paper she'd handed me.

It was a photo of a pair of eyes, so close up that the image had pixelated. There, composed of tiny squares, were blue irises flecked with green and gold, and black pupils. The eyes were surrounded by a cropped-out face.

"Eyes?"

"They're yours."

"You used that to get in?"

"You can do it if the photo's good enough. Iris scanning is not that secure," she said. "You know that, right? The scanner isn't even heat-sensitive."

"It works?"

She did her devastating bang flutter. Voila.

I rubbed my own actual, heat-sensitive, bloodshot eye and raked a lock of hair away from my face. I gazed at the photo. My eye doctor, was he in on it? My official-events photographer who sprinted around with deeply bent knees recording official Conch milestones? I tried to recall the last time I'd had my photo taken. The problem was I had my photo taken all the time.

I practiced my calm breathing. My bladder was beginning to twitch in a way that it had never, despite whole days without bathroom visits, twitched before; I was having a new stress reaction just when it seemed like my body must have no emergency flags left to fly.

"You've fallen in with some bad types," I said. "Infiltrating a company is a big deal. You need to listen to me."

Willow knocked aggressively on the window, and I opened the door and leaned out to see what she wanted. "I'm sorry to bother you, but Brad's here."

"Shelley, what the hell were you thinking?" Brad called, striding toward us, past the door to Gumbo. He was wearing a Hawaiian-style shirt with a pepperoni pizza pattern; is it a joke to satirize his love of Hawaiian shirts or a genuine commitment to the Hawaiian-shirt format regardless of content? I don't know, but it makes me want to vomit.

I came out of the conference room, Michelle following, and nodded at the group from marketing who'd been waiting for the room. I gave them what I hoped was a cordial, taking-care-of-business smile. I caught up to Brad in the beanbag/collaboration area. "Wait, what?"

"You could've been killed out there."

"What?"

"That video." He must have noticed how genuinely puzzled I was, because he pulled out his massive phone (Rafe: "Please don't ever say phablet, I can't stand that word").

"Not out here," I said. "People are working." People were all too willing to stop working to listen to our conversation, is what I meant. Brad, Willow, Michelle, and I jammed inside a pitch pod, which is where PR people go when they're annoying each other. We were squeezed together, Brad pressed against me.

"So what's this video . . . ?"

"Watch," Brad said. He cued up the video on his phone and held it out so we could all see.

You're making me nervous, I mouthed. Willow wouldn't meet my eyes; she must have already seen it.

"Wow, that's a crazy number of likes," I said.

"The people I worked for make videos too," Michelle remarked. Brad was cupping her shoulder, ostensibly for support.

The video started out with me addressing an audience. It looked vaguely familiar. I recognized my outfit, colorful jacket over neutral pants, and the setting, perhaps a graduate classroom at Stanford. Then a cut, and I was bicycling on a path through a field, lightning crackling all around me. I had a fiendish look in my eye.

"That's Photoshop," I said.

"You can't do that in Photoshop," Brad said. "Photoshop's for photos."

Look how skinny I am, I thought, and then I thought, social conditioning is such a powerful force, and then I said, "Well, some other program then, that's what it is. It's fake. I would never do that."

Later in the video I said, "I am a brave leader!" and cycled through a river in a storm to the tune of a catchy pop song, which I am sure they did not have rights to use.

"So dangerous!" Brad said. "A totally unnecessary risk."

"You can't believe that's real," I said. "It's not."

"I'm not sure," Brad said slowly. "I've seen you make that expression."

I thought back to the hotel lobby in Barcelona and Enrique's app. He really did it, I thought. He made it all look real. It was stupid but innocuous. "Who cares?"

"I care," Brad said. "Conch's investors care. A CEO shouldn't take risks like that. We don't have a succession plan. Nobody wants to ally with a company whose CEO is endangering herself."

"It shows poor judgment," Willow said, emboldened by Brad. "There could've been a twister."

The last screen of the video was just a title card: "So proud of you and your company!" It was ridiculous. I noticed with casual, detached surprise that my left arm was trembling. Sometimes this happens after very intense strength training: I wake up the next day and the muscle twitches and flutters. I can type through it, but when I'm not typing my arm levitates briefly on its own twitch-muscle power. But I had not done especially intense lifting yesterday. I grabbed the arm with my other arm, steadying and squeezing. "It isn't real!" I said, and my voice came out more loudly than I intended. Willow opened the door of the pitch pod, and one of the office labradoodles ambled up to me, lifted its front paws sympathetically, and, standing on its back legs, gave me a soft, curious, only mildly judgmental look.

"It's not Shelley in that video," Michelle said sharply.

Brad raised his eyebrows.

She went on, dismissive. "I can't believe you guys are so uninformed about this. This is not a brand-new thing. It's an app that is totally common in my age group. Aren't you familiar with it?"

Brad shook his head and took a second look at the screen.

"It's catching on with older people like you," Michelle said crisply, "but it's so lame, I hate it. I stopped using it months ago." Michelle went on, telling Brad about this purported app, and he listened and softened.

"I guess we just have to contextualize," Brad said. "Just treat it as the bizarre thing it is. Make clear it's parody or register a complaint and get it taken down."

"It could happen to any of you," Michelle said. "You should see what people did with it at my high school."

I looked at her in admiration.

She was infuriating, sure. It was alarming she'd been able to get through security at Conch, but watching her cut through Brad's objections and make the video into a nonevent, I couldn't help but feel a connection. It was like something I would have done, back when I was doing well. Have you ever read your own email message, tacked onto the bottom of someone else's reply, and thought: that is awfully strong, decisive prose, I'm intrigued by this person, let's LinkIn with him/her, and then been disappointed—all in a sliver of a second—by the realization that there was no such other person to network with? Have you ever read the minutes of the board meeting and thought, what on-point questions that person is posing, glad somebody was asking that—who? Oh yes. Me. Or stumbled across your own dictated voice MP3 and thought, what deft phrasing and crisp, clear signposting. I'd had that experience all the time, and it was so nice to recognize ability in someone else. I knew she was a fraud but couldn't help but be impressed. Had I been interviewing interns, I would absolutely have chosen her. I could even see going to a happy hour with her, as an end-of-summer intern-executive group thing. I wanted to mentor her, even though a large proportion of my mentorees have left the workforce to become stay-at-home moms.

"It's just sloppy," Brad said. "The last thing we need is for you to look unserious about Conch's future or take silly risks. I don't care how it came about, it's not what we need right now. I just want a day with no more problems coming out of Conch. You guys are taking up too much of my time."

"Do you think Phil's seen it?" I asked tremulously. "I feel like Powerplex is the only one who would really care."

"Jesus, Shelley. You're slow today. He's seen it. He sent it to me."

Let's go somewhere," I said to Michelle once Brad had taken off. "I want to take you someplace where we can talk alone. Willow! You need to manage things. I'm not taking calls. I'll be back later." I ignored the many backs of heads that were listening to me while pretending to work.

"But you have an eleven o'clock to talk about new product features. Do you want me to move it?"

"Tell the team I had to postpone and run home. Say that a family thing came up. I'm sure they'll understand."

Willow frowned. "Is that a joke? This is the team that stayed up all night getting the demo ready for you."

"Tell them whatever you want to tell them. Make it work— it'll be a good challenge for you."

Willow cowered as I steered Michelle out.

"You're very hard on her," Michelle said. Not as hard as I'm going to be on you, I thought.

I took her down the stairwell. I didn't want to risk seeing anyone in the elevator. Our footfalls reverberated off the concrete stairs and walls. The back stairwell at Conch lacks innovation because the fire codes in our town stifle creativity; without the suspended opalescent panels and pops of color, our building's stairwells are just as utilitarian as any insurance company's, which disappoints me whenever I use the stairs. I scanned us out a back door and we went out to the parking lot, through the misty fog and to my car. I started it and felt the thrum underneath me and made no motion to move. It was like the last time we had been in a car together. I didn't know where to take her.

Chapter 17

It's important to remember that being a decisive leader doesn't require having all the information. You just have to be comfortable managing through ambiguity. I thrive on it. "We'll drive around while I decide where we should go," I said candidly. After a couple of stop-and-go lights I realized I was driving toward home. It seemed the best place to go. Home is the place where, when you don't want to be seen in public with someone, you take them for lunch. Your lawyer's office is also an option.

But home would work. Rafael would be at his office, Blazer and Melissa on one of their educational morning outings to the science museum or the zoo or one of Blazer's music, foreign language, art, pre-chess, or preliteracy classes. Afterward they would pick up Nova at preschool. I had done it a time or two myself. Nova's teachers, Clay and Vanessa, had been beamingly glad to see me, and touched my forearm gently as they shared their gladness. It made me feel nice when they looked into my eyes and touched me, like they could see, deep down, what a lovable, fun, and special person I was, but then I had to stand there as Nova changed out of her school peace slippers and put on regular shoes. Adults weren't allowed to help, not even Clay and Vanessa—it

was all part of the school's process. The time I went, it was difficult to stay peaceful, watching it unfold.

I revved the car down the main road, past the Chinese place
where we get takeout, a hair salon, nail salon, exercise studio, and
the clothes shop I have wandered into on weekends and briskly
exited, where everything is cream or brown or gray except for
one coral scarf and the iPad they use as a register. The looks I get
in that store make me feel unlikably corporate. It was weird to be
in my neighborhood in the middle of a weekday. There were an
astounding number of people just moseying along the sidewalk
with their dogs or strollers or—a popular configuration—both.
We glided past a corner shop that has, on a ledge inside its long
front window, four big cards, each with a letter on them. Every
time I'd been past, they spelled "N-O-P-E." Now they had been
rearranged to spell "O-P-E-N" and I was so jarred that I almost
missed the turn.

I turned onto my street. It's narrow, woodsy, and gently winding, tucked behind a private elementary school I am already
mentally prepared for Nova not to be admitted to. My street is
bounded on each side by hedges, fences, and walls, with wide
gates that crest over each driveway: ornate or expensively simple,
wrought iron or wood, according to the owner's taste. A very
plentiful number of garbage cans and recycling bins were lined
up outside each gate—today was, I suppose, garbage day—and
the sheer number of cans (seven, eight, more) hinted at the
extent of the operations behind the fence.

There was a perfectly trimmed hedge, along which a stocky,
short, dark-skinned man dressed all in white walked, plucking
out every last fallen brown petal.

"This is where you live?" Michelle said.

"Up ahead."

I'm not sentimental normally. Nor nostalgic. So much of my
life is about looking forward to the future, when we'll all wear

Conch and the Clitch will be a funny story in our company legend. But sitting beside her, feeling vulnerable, I felt a kind of connection. I knew what it felt like to get in over your head.

I drove slowly. Twenty-five is the speed limit. I stayed well under it, slowed by thought.

"Do you like it here?" she asked.

I nodded. What's not to like?

The street is one of the loveliest in this lovely town—the crazy zoning keeps it stratospherically expensive, but everybody's liberal, complicated stuff!—but it's as if the houses are too shy to be seen by strangers. They demurely turn away from the street, shaded by their deeply inclined roofs and the layers of plantings that screen them from view. Transparency at work, deep privacy at home.

She had taken my Conch. How could I not have noticed her taking it? She knew things about me that even I didn't remember anymore, like my love of butterscotch sundaes. The thought was strangely exciting.

As you drive down the street there's the occasional whiff of some large piece of outdoor sculpture—a Calder, say, on the back lawn, surrounded by trees. At my neighbor's house, their kids' tree house is glimpsable through the lacework of leaves. It is a beautiful little tree house, buttressed underneath by four thick columns, barely needing—not needing, basically irrelevant to—the tree it abuts.

Michelle had gone silent, watching out the window. It's not showy, this street, although that's a technicality: it's covetable. Every sconce, house number, gate hinge, and paving stone has been carefully chosen, though these details are hardly visible among the foliage, the lush plantings. I watched her take it in.

"These cars are kind of . . . normal," she remarked. She meant the ones parked along the road, outside the fences.

"It's a very down-to-earth community," I said. What I meant

was, those cars belong to the housekeepers. Or the babysitters, the arborists, the professional organizers, the carpenters, the personal chefs, all the people whose hard work keeps these households going.

We approached the wall bordering my property. It's a thickly ivied brick wall, with a row of laurel bushes planted in front. In front of the laurels is another layer of ivy, this time as ground cover. There's one spot with a perfect oval carved out of the ivy for the yellow fire hydrant set there. In an ideal world we could replace the fire hydrant with one that's more European-looking and better designed, and more in keeping with the naturalistic setting, but I haven't seen any in the catalogs.

Graceful ornamental trees frame our driveway's entrance. I turned the car, stopped in front of our closed gate, and rolled down my window. Into the keypad (subtle, metal, on a single curved, cantilevered leg) I punched the code, shading it from Michelle's view with my hand. Though for all I knew, she already knew it. Silently the halves of the gate opened wide.

"Not bad," she murmured, looking subdued, perhaps embarrassed. It's not bad. A very low-key kind of grandeur. Artistically arranged boulders. Careful, tasteful landscaping. A turn in the driveway as you approach the house, with a gnarled madrona that comes suddenly into view, like a present you unwrap with your eyes. I parked in front of the house and turned off the car. "Come on in," I said. The wall, the gate, the plantings: it wasn't enough to protect me. Anything could get you, could leap out of an open sky, if it wanted to.

When I imagined being here, it was warmer," Michelle said, wrapping her arms around herself.

"That's a common misconception about the Bay Area," I said, leading her down the path and through the kitchen door. I hustled her through the dark, clean kitchen into the dining room. I don't spend much time in the kitchen, less since they started making yogurt in tubes. "I need the contact information for the people you've been working with. I'll also need a detailed accounting of the dates, times, and places you met with them. Start organizing your notes so you can go through them with my lawyer. Are you listening? Here, sit." Our dining room table is round to facilitate the exchange of ideas between high-level peers. A large abstract print on the wall depicts aggressive swooshes, like the unstoppable upward trajectories of the kind of people we invite to dinner. I got out some paper and a pen, an obsolete technology still useful in niche situations like this one. "You can make a list. Or a grid. I prefer grids myself. I like that extra dimension."

"Nice house," she said. "Don't get me wrong, but I thought it would be fancier."

"It's a very nice house," I said factually. Our realtor had said exactly that (with a slightly fishy look, as if she thought Rafe and I were likely to dispute her assessment). The editors of *Sunset* once put our pergola on the cover. "Now, come on. Give me some names and dates."

She picked up the pen. Well, good. First step. Break tasks into manageable chunks, that's the way.

"So what I need to know is, first: Who were you working for? And what did you do for them? What was that card you had, the business card?"

She produced it. It had a blue logo, like stylized waves, from a logo genre often used for spas and dental offices. It had an address that looked like the Conch factory address. Although of course that's the only address I know in Malaysia, so probably they all look quite similar.

"How long have you lived in this house?"

"A few years. I really need you to focus and answer my questions." I spoke in a low, authoritative, yet gentle voice. It was the tone Rafe used the time a bird flew into the house. The bird had whizzed around the downstairs, into and out of the fireplace, and then hit the dining room wall and fallen dazed in the corner. Rafe murmured to it while getting it into a box. He drove it to some kind of bird repair farm, where they took it in, accepted our charitable donation on its behalf, and later sent us a postcard to tell us it had died.

"So, to summarize, you stole my Conch and replaced it with another one, at the behest of someone, whose name you will write right here." I drew a line on the paper. Best to treat her like Nova. She was closer in age to Nova than to me—that was a startling thought.

"Right, I switched it back."

"What do you mean, *back*?"

"They'd already stolen it to copy, I guess? Anyway, I didn't really get the woman's name."

"Michelle. Let me quickly remind you that I have grounds for prosecution. You stole my passport! You trespassed at Conch! If you can't be straight with me I'm going to call the police."

"I think you would have called by now if you were going to," she said. "I'm not avoiding, I just don't know what to tell you. I needed the money and I didn't want to ask too many questions."

"So you came today to get SportConch. We don't even have the prototype ready yet."

"They want it. But I just want to be done with them. I came to see you."

"Me?"

"I felt like we hit it off," Michelle said. "I read some stuff about you and thought I could give it a try, being you. If I got rich I could build a theater of my own and star in the productions. Just a thought." At the office I'd thought she was appealingly fresh and effective, but now I was horrified by her deficits in drive and focus.

She drew a free-form star on the paper, which was otherwise blank. The sketch looked a bit like a storm cloud. "I thought I could live in your pool house."

"We don't have that kind of pool house."

"I'm starting to see that."

Some insistent burbles from the kitchen and then the very low early shriek of a soon-to-boil teakettle. It rose in pitch, asserting itself.

"Coming," a voice shouted, and Rafe strode in. "Holy shit, you're home," he said. He went into the kitchen and emphatically twisted a dial on the stove, ending the drama. "I thought you were Jacqui. What happened, did you get fired?"

"*You're* home," I said, trying to strain the surprise from my voice. I noticed Michelle noticing him, taking in his height, his casually scruffy T-shirt, and the sly pleasure he was taking in the possibility of me having been fired. He was a man, I thought, who looked better in jeans and T-shirts than in suits. That bothered me. Just doesn't seem like my type. "Sorry to disappoint you. Wasn't fired. But why are you home? Are the kids OK?"

He came back into the dining room carrying a mug. "I'm going in late. I had some stuff to take care of." Something in his body language made me look past him to the hallway, where there were some flat, unassembled bankers' boxes leaning against the wall. He was looking steadily at me when I looked back at him; he knew I'd seen them and was waiting for me to react.

"You haven't even been into the office yet? It's almost eleven! When are you going in?" I was conscious I was speaking differently than usual, that having Michelle present had inflected my speech with a bright, insincere quality, as if I were a corporate trainer.

"Hi," Rafe said, turning to Michelle. I decoded all the data compressed in that syllable: ignoring my surprise that he hadn't made it into the office, the implied rebuke that I hadn't introduced him, the pride in his own good manners. The efficiency of marital data compression algorithms rivals that of the most advanced internet software. "You the new assistant? Lucky you. She doesn't usually bring 'em here." A deft dip of the tea bag. It was like a secret life he had here.

"We met in Spain," I said.

"That so?" Rafe said. He gave Michelle a second look.

"At that entrepreneur conference?" I prompted.

"So what's your billion-dollar idea?" Rafe asked her. "What are you working on? Autonomous self-driving suitcases? Dog underwear? Sorry—I've been around all this crap too long." His voice was light but I sensed he was including me, the house, and Conch in that "all."

"We connected over some shared passions," I said. "Feel free to chime in here, Michelle."

"I was doing a study-abroad," she said. She spoke tentatively, wary of the tension in the air.

I nodded vigorously, approving of this direction. "I interned abroad. Very worthwhile experience and even more popular now, I understand, with the U.S. government's restrictions on what constitutes an unpaid internship."

Rafe said something to Michelle in Spanish. She replied, slowly.

"*Bueno!*" he said encouragingly. He asked her something else and she stammered a reply. I didn't know what they were saying. They continued to speak, and I felt left out. Can Conch insta-translate? Maybe someday, but that's hard to do.

"I found your jump drive," a voice called from another room.

"Thanks, Jacqui!" Rafe yelled back. "Can you throw it down here? Your tea's ready."

"I got out all the suitcases," Jacqui said, coming through the doorway.

"Where are you guys going?" Michelle asked.

"Ho ho," Jacqui said. She got her tea from the kitchen and let out a guttural laugh. Then she came back into the dining room and whistled. She totally disapproved. Jacqui's uncompromisingly judgmental—I love that about her. "He's moving away," Jacqui confided. "With the kids."

"To Brazil," Rafe said simply.

"Oh, wow," Michelle said. "I didn't realize. This could fuck up my pool house plan." She turned to Rafe. "So you speak Portuguese too? Why'd you guys decide to go there?"

"I'm not moving." I couldn't bear to hear more. "Rafe's taking a new role at work and will be in Brazil for the foreseeable." "For the foreseeable" was a Rafe phrase I sometimes overheard him use on the phone, and by adopting it I felt like I was proving my loyalty, making it seem like this had been my idea. "Just for the near term." There was consolation in that phrase. The near term, the place in which I happen to live, looking out on the smoky vistas of the medium and long term.

"Not to pry, but . . . you're getting divorced?"

"No, the opposite," I said with the insistent, delusional brightness that my life kept calling for. I made some gestures as if I were testing the elasticity of a long rubber band, to simulate the stretchiness of Rafe's and my geographically unbreakable relational bond. "Listen, my sinuses are blocked. I have a lot of trouble." I waved at my face, explanatorily. "I have to take care of this. Excuse me."

Such a relief to close myself in my bathroom, so tasteful, so serene, so spa-like, with its textured grass cloth wallpaper. The grass cloth is a diamond pattern in which alternate rows of diamonds shine subtly for reasons not clear even after careful daily study while brushing my teeth. When I am nauseous the pattern makes me more nauseous, and I find my eyes following individual fibers as they wend inward and outward to form diamonds, the way as a child on long car rides my eyes followed telephone wires.

I saline-rinsed, and a fiery pain rose in the back of my head. The pain burned down to nothing, like wadded paper ashifying in the fireplace on a November night. The experience was somewhat cathartic. When Rafe was my boyfriend I used to call him from the bathroom at work. It was the only place with privacy. We had a lot of intense early conversations, including one of the first times he said he loved me, while I sat on the counter by the sink, examining my hair for split ends, riveted by his voice, embarrassed when the cleaning person came in with the cart and broke the mood. That bathroom was always empty because there were very few women at that company.

I went back into the foyer. Through the archway I could see them in the dining room, still talking. Rafe had sat down with her. He was leaning back in his chair, gesturing. I could tell he was talking about himself, possibly São Paulo (a variation on himself). He combed his hair back with his whole (large) hand and flung out his arm. Showing off. Occupying the maximum space he could occupy. He hadn't had to be taught power poses; emulating forest predators came naturally to him. Michelle looked annoyingly rapt. I felt like, how could I have felt such a sense of connection with her? How could I ever have thought she was me?

In our foyer is an alcove with an art piece. We have a special little spotlight that picks it out at night. It's a fulgurite. They're these things that form underground during a lightning strike.

Mine looks like a mess of tree roots. It was created from sand and soil fusing together, when the sand becomes superheated and turns to glass. I was given it by a board I served on, as a leaving present. I didn't know what it was at first either, but I have since learned. A little printed card that came with the sculpture explained it. It's a piece that is unique and obviously has special resonance for me. Something similar happened on a larger scale in the desert when they tested the atomic bomb—glassy sheets formed out of the fused sand.

Normally I just enjoy the piece for its unique look, its symbolism, the fact that it fits very nicely into this preexisting alcove in our house that I wasn't sure how we were going to fill. I ran my fingers over the bumps and troughs of its tubey surface.

In the e-newsletter of an octogenarian futurist who once made a pass at me in an elevator, I'd read about something called the Zeigarnik effect. This is a phenomenon in which people experience intrusive thoughts about a task they've begun but haven't yet completed. A tiny piece of cognitive energy is devoted, continuously, to maintaining the knowledge that you need to go back and finish up. This idea itself has stayed with me like an uncompleted task, awaiting its eventual application: a commencement speech, maybe, or a provocative op-ed. I thought of it now, how the lightning strike had sparked something inside me, setting me on a new path, but left something else unfinished.

I ran my finger over the surface of the fulgurite. The fulgurite seemed like evidence that you couldn't go through something like I had and come out the same as before. The intensity of it had to change you at some basic level, the way sedimentary rock turned into that other kind that's harder. My life had taken such an abrupt and irrevocable turn; perhaps deep in the skunkworks of my brain, part of me might want to revisit who I used to be.

Even if she wasn't there, my inner voice said.

I heard this, as if said by a voice inside me. Not my Conch, but a different inner voice, the one fond of violet highlighter. In my experience it isn't inner at all, but heard ("heard") from above and outside the body, in what medieval painters would consider, in a better person, the halo area.

I'd heard a version of this voice the day I was knocked to the ground by the lightning strike. A girl (me) was screaming, and over her screams came a different voice (also mine), which said, with a dismissiveness that would have been rude, had it not been so reassuringly in control: "Oh, give me a break, it's not *that* bad."

People, especially people like Greer, talk about one's inner voice as if it's like a Conch but so much better. But if it were that great, people would not be buying Conch. One's inner voice definitely does not provide real-time guidance customized to every situation, not to mention traffic and weather. It's unreliable in a way that can be even more frustrating than the Glitch. It doesn't speak when you want it to. You can wait and hope, pray for a decisive answer (guidance on what to do about an attractive job offer or your daughter's poor spatial awareness or which Asian market to roll out in first), and then when, or if, it comes it's iffy and lacks authority. You don't get a message in the clear, resonant voice of an actor who counts among his previous voice-over credits the English-language version of the Taj Mahal audio tour; instead, you have to extricate it from your bones and it's mangled in the extraction. You're not sure if it's real or what you want to hear, truth or delusion. It speaks in ways that often seem completely sideways to the topic. And sometimes it's wrong. There's nobody to complain to then, no customer service number to call, no corporate social media team to tweet at and expect immediate, groveling resolution.

You can see why consumers trust Conch.

Rafe's voice broke into my thoughts. "Hope you don't mind sharing the room with all my boxes." I looked up to see the two of them walking toward me. "Shell, I was just telling your friend that if she needs a place to stay, she can crash on the couch in my home office. She was talking about sundaes, and I had this great idea that we should all go out to the Creamery, Nova's never been and it'd be a fun—"

"Rafael—"

"I totally don't mind about boxes, that's no problem, thank you!"

"It's not a bad couch at all, I sleep there a lot myself." So much subtext.

"Sounds perfect!"

"I'm not sure that's a good—" I began.

"So we're on for going out for sundaes tonight?" Rafe asked. "Maybe a walk afterward?"

"Absolutely," I said. "Can't wait, but Rafe, babe, I need to—"

"What's that thing?" Michelle said, pointing at the fulgurite.

How bad was it?" she asked, in the curious, inappropriate way young people inquire about devastating trauma. A pale butterfly looped between us and settled on a lilac. We were outside on the patio.

Backyard: bluestone patio, burnished silver grill, koi pond with arbor, lap pool, modern chaise longues, eight of them, distributed along the pool's edge, each one more expensive than the monthly rent I used to pay at my first place. That's before the cushions. The roar of neighbors' leaf blowers, always present. When they turn off the leaf blowers they start jackhammering to replace the Belgian block in their driveways with some other kind of Belgian block.

I exhaled deeply. "Bad," I said. I was crafting an email, and I shifted my laptop to move the heat to my other thigh.

"You're lucky it didn't damage you."

I hesitated, trying to find a simple way of responding to that. "The damage was mostly internal."

"You guys must have a lot of fun out here," she said, looking around. I nodded. The shade was cold; I was aware of something out of order in my knee, a shooting cautionary pain.

Tons of fun! But not really. We're pretty busy. But you could, if you had time. It's definitely very seductive when you see it for the first time, when you come to see the house for sale, when you imagine the life you would lead, if you lived here, kids in bathing suits hurtling off the diving board, your spouse with a spatula in his hand, slaws heaped in bowls on the table, friends coming out the back door with corkscrews and bottles of Rioja and compliments about your kitchen renovation: a kind of magazine life, of lazy days and friendship and warmth, an illusion that has wobbled and disappeared in the surface of the pool. But nobody lives that way really, do they?

"Except for that rash, you seem totally fine," Michelle said.

"I've moved past it but it's part of who I am. You don't go through something like that and come out unscathed. It was a difficult experience and the unfairness was hard for me to—"

"But you know what's funny? You didn't tell me," she said. "When we met. Your advice list—I recall there was something on it about a green dress."

"An emerald sheath," I clarified.

"That's the thing you thought was the most important thing to tell me. If you lost your favorite dress, why didn't you just order a new one?"

"It's the principle," I said. "There has to be a consequence for carelessness. Though I blame the maid."

She said, thoughtfully, "Did it feel like getting a shock, or different?"

I felt the nausea and throb in my right temple that I feel when I think about it, or even when I guardedly approach the topic with the intention of considering thinking about it. "Both."

"So I can assume from this that you would have let someone else get hurt if you thought it would help them in the long run?"

"Of course not." (Yes.)

"That's awfully cold."

"As *Forbes* once put it, I'm a pragmatist."

"Have you ever killed anyone? Or had anyone killed?"

"Jesus. No." ("Axed" is just an expression.) I went back to typing. "I'll be done with this in a sec. Then I want to talk."

I hit Send and my email went off to its destination, as impalpably as the butterfly taking off from the arborvitae. "Look—I'm sorry. There were a lot of problems in my chain of reasoning when we met. I privileged data over other inputs." My voice wavered and I strengthened it. "I realize that now, and I've put some work into compensating for my biases. I'm a data-driven decision maker so I'm particularly susceptible when the data is flawed. But I'm sorry. Luckily you have only the regular odds of getting hit by lightning. Which are quite small—two hundred fifty strikes or so a year, in this country, among three hundred eighteen million people." I nodded vehemently, because she ought to be reassured by these numbers.

"But why wouldn't you just mention it, just in case? Like a normal person would. Here was something horrible that happened; here's how to avoid it."

"It's just that—while awful, it was the best thing that could have happened to me." Was it? I had the familiar sensation, which has become more familiar since I ascended to my current role, of feeling one thing while saying another, of being amazed by the audacity of what I was saying. I felt some murky, hard-to-articulate truth I wanted to convey, but in the course of speaking about it, it took on a shape of its own. Some people would call this lying but I think it's more complicated: maybe the feeling is a lie.

"Not very nice."

"No," I conceded. This was an easy concession; I don't value niceness much.

The Tibetan wind chimes hanging from our porch gonged and a burst of wind freed tiny blossoms from the tree overhead, carried them across the lawn, and scattered them on the surface of the pool.

"Maybe you were always going to be this way," she said.

I thought about this. I've thought about it before. "I don't think so."

A grinding noise startled us both. Michelle covered her ears. For no reason other than the crazed pursuit of optimization, home edition, the very nice house next door had been demolished by its new owners to make way for a new one. A bulldozer parked by the property line blighted our view (Blazer liked it— he was the only one). From my bedroom upstairs I could see the huge concrete-lined pit that would become the new neighbors' commodious basement, and the small steel-lined outline of their future panic room. The new neighbors were a young family with obscene wealth, small children, and no qualms about the thousands of jackhammer hours needed to take down the old house and put up a new one. I liked envisioning them huddled in there against weapon-wielding maniacs.

I'd brought out a new Conch in the packaging we were going to launch next quarter. I'd left it on the patio table. Michelle picked it up. She lifted off the top of the box and pulled out the Conch, turning it over in her finger.

"Can I?"

"If you want. It won't work on you. Willow set it up for me. It only works on its owner."

She installed it behind her ear. "It's working!" she said.

I shrugged. We've had some hiccups with the bioauthentication.

She took her hand away slowly as if she expected it to fall, and a moment later, when she realized it was not going to, she made a funny expression of pleasure (I've seen that same expression before, in focus groups), tossed her head, and smiled. Her hair rippled over her shoulders.

"It's in." She smiled. "It just gave me the weather report. Storms later in the week. It tickles."

"Surely it's not your first Conch. Isn't that how you knew so much about me?"

"No."

"I thought you must have been wearing a duplicate." Eggs was doing something ecstatic and dervish-like on her back on the grass.

"Just flash cards," she said. "And instinct."

I pushed down my laptop lid to give her a serious look. "How did you get the job?"

"I thought you might ask that." She started out softly, eyes cast down at the ground. "I'd gotten new headshots done, for my acting. And then I got this call for a job. Would I come talk to this casting director? Sure, of course. You don't say no, you know?"

I nodded. At her age, it was wise not to reject a professional opportunity out of hand.

"This woman met me at a coffee shop. I kept asking what the part was, and she said she wasn't sure which one I was right for yet. She said it was for a commercial job. She seemed friendly, but very professional, not chatty. She told me what I needed to do. It was all very straightforward, and I said, sure, I'll do it. I wasn't scared. She showed me videos of you and I practiced talking to you. I felt like I really got to know you, even before we met."

"Please, can you get me this person's contact information? Any details would help."

"I don't have much to give you." She swung one leg over the side of the chaise and sat up. "I did it for my résumé. It's better than being an understudy. I was an understudy for Irina in *The Three Sisters* but I only got paid if I went on."

I sighed. "They must have picked you because of the resemblance."

She looked surprised. "I don't know. I wasn't expecting that you'd . . . identify so closely with me. I think they thought you'd be nice to me because I was young and lost. You know, because you're a mom."

I didn't know what to say to that. I glanced back at the house, at the windows, where inside lunch would soon be served, a cube of avocado in Blazer's newly developed little pincer grasp, Nova inspecting her edamame for flaws, bean by bean. Then, lunch cleaned up, the children taken upstairs for naps. Someday we would all eat nutri-pellets and we wouldn't need to hire a cook anymore. Did Jacqui realize how tenuous her occupation was, how likely it was to be disrupted by new nutritional technology and robot cleaners or relocations to other cities? It seemed not.

What was I going to do about Michelle? What about my Conch? I'd put a new one in—I could hardly go without one, in my position. I gazed at the wobbly surface of the pool. Something sinusy was happening again. The clarity doesn't last like it used to. I was looking at water through a haze of water. I inhaled sharply till salt came down my throat.

Michelle lay back, lounging, oblivious to how troubling I found her story, and how much personal and professional distress she'd caused me. How naive was she? Who was she working for and what did they want?

Michelle giggled, breaking into my thoughts. She touched her ear. "It just spoke to me again!" That joyousness, that's one of the things that makes me feel it's all worth it. Having your own Conch is like being in the in group, the A-list. You're the alpha girl.

"What's it saying?"

"Willow's been trying to reach you—the SportConch proto-type just came in. Oh, and Brad's coming over."

I've been doing some research," Brad Barsh said, placing his laptop on the lounge chair next to him, lid at half-mast like his heavy-lidded eyes. He was wearing a pool blue shirt spotted with palm trees, and when he lay back it looked like an inlet of pool water had risen up through his chest. He took off his glasses and wiped off the sweat, replaced them and wriggled his bare feet at the relief of seeing clearly. His toes were long and the joints seemed more functional than they were supposed to be, like a flying monkey's. I found this erotic.

"I've reached out to some contacts about the crisis."

I blinked for one moment, processing this. The crisis. That would be? Oh, right: Conch's failure. The Clitch. I ought to consider a color-coding system for my crises. The ivory drapes of the pergola snapped in the breeze and billowed like sails, as if the whole thing were about to take off.

"We can't leave aside stochastic factors," I said slowly. I blew my bangs upward while he thought about this. I find this a useful suggestion to make in many scenarios. Because one should never leave aside stochastic factors. And nobody except me really is clear on what I mean by that. I sighed. I flipped through my notes. We'd confirmed that the bridge-jumper's Conch had told him to jump. This followed weeks of constant suggestions that he pursue higher education, exercise more, change his diet, give blood, and register as an organ donor. The Conch had also suggested he make dinner reservations for Father's Day (his father was dead). "One Conch, behaving erratically. Which happened to be sold to a man with mental health issues who couldn't handle wearing a Conch. The product malfunctioned, sure, but . . ."

Brad shaded the display of his calculator from the sun, bright overhead. "In other words, you don't know. Why would a Conch make these suggestions? What data is it acting on? Could we have a hacker?"

I twiddled my top lip with my bottom teeth. "I've considered that," I said. "It doesn't seem likely based on my analysis of the situation, but Cullen is mystified. And it's not a good thing when he can't come up with an answer. The team is reviewing the last couple of weeks of code changes."

Brad looked at me intently. I thought about what it would be like to climb on top of him. I felt like there was a chance he was thinking the same thing.

"Has any of the code changed?"

"We ship all the time, but we haven't made any changes to the algorithm. I'm pulling info on that right now from the team." I touched the brand-new Conch in my pocket—it was the Powerplex prototype Brad had brought over. I couldn't wait to try it out.

Michelle, coming out of the house, caught Brad's eye.

"Hi!" Brad waved, sharply. He squinted at her, then at me. "Au pair?" he diagnosed, and looked to me for confirmation.

"She's my cousin. She's in town."

"She's attractive." I enjoyed the implicit compliment.

Michelle took this as permission to approach the pool's edge. She raked up the water with her bare pointed toes. I was the only shoe wearer among the three of us.

"Maybe your smart young mind can solve this puzzler for us," Brad said. It hit me squarely in the cringe zone but she looked intrigued. Brad wriggled his long toes. Brad likes them young. I have succeeded, for long stretches of our working relationship, in forgetting this.

"What's going on?" she said.

"We're having some issues with the Conch," I said. "Weird

messages to vulnerable users. Prompting them to do things they shouldn't."

"How'd this happen?"

"We don't know."

"Are they new ones?"

"Some are," I said. "Some aren't."

"Long story," Brad said, patting the spot next to him.

"Where do they make them?" She came over. She did not sit down, which pleased me. She looked straight at him.

"Malaysia."

She looked thoughtful. I touched a spot of pain where one of my eyebrow hairs takes root.

"Could they be using bad parts?" Michelle said.

"It's a possibility I've considered," I said, though I hadn't. A software problem was more likely. "What if someone is sabotaging them at the factory?" Malaysia, it had said on the address on the card Michelle had had in her pocket. "It's worth investigating . . ."

"We have that guy in Penang," Brad said. Brad and I looked at each other, reading each other's thoughts as seamlessly as Conch reads its users' data files, when it's working correctly.

"I'll go myself," I said, saying it before I even knew I had made the decision.

There's a concept in Buddhism called Beginner's Mind, which I've read about in business periodicals. The idea is that there is a clarity and openness that comes from encountering experience without preconceptions. I've used this successfully to leverage the lack of knowledge of a sharp new hire—I meet with her at thirty days out, sixty days, and ninety days and listen to all her questions about why we do things as we do. And some of the questions stem from misunderstanding or confusion, but sometimes we get a fresh look at a legacy process or outdated workflow, and we're able to take the insight and apply it. New eyes on a problem can be useful even if the new eyes don't know very much. The experienced eyes can fill in the gaps. Sometimes not knowing is its own form of knowledge. That sounded very good—I could see it going viral.

"Can you spare the time to go, Shelley?" Brad asked.

"We have no choice. We have to get to the bottom of this before anything else comes out. And it'll show Powerplex how committed we are to a solution." I admire commitment hugely. In point of fact, though, I am not sure commitment by itself shows much; it depends what you commit to. Conch's earliest employees, who have basically created entire jobs out of retelling stories of their first months at the company, don't understand this. The fervent loyalists think their stories have intrinsic value; they overlook that the value of their past is indexed to the level of our present and future success. But me going to Malaysia would reassure Phil about how seriously we were taking the Clitch.

Brad nodded.

"I'll make arrangements. If I leave tomorrow, let's see, Wednesday, and I go through Hong Kong, I can be wheels-down on Friday." I hesitated. I thought of the ice cream outing, the Creamery, whatever it was I had committed to. "Or I could leave tonight." We could reschedule. There were other nights. I knew this to be true but felt internal friction over telling Rafe. Sometimes that's a clue you're leaving some factors out of your analysis. He'd be annoyed. Would Nova be upset? It was hard to know.

"That seems smart," Michelle said, looking beadily at me.

So it wouldn't be a quiet night with family. Was it ever really going to be? There was a flight around 10:00 p.m. I did my mental packing, in which, Claymation style, I envision certain neutral suiting basics inchworming their way into my spinny suitcase, the belts coiling, the socks rolling like hedgehogs. A blouse slipping itself off a hanger. And then I text the maid and she puts the stuff in.

Michelle glanced back at the house and I felt a stab of uncertainty about leaving. How many more nights did I have here before Rafe and the kids moved? Quick jump cut in the mind to upstairs: the children, so vulnerable and fleshy, with their soft wrinkly fingers fresh from the bath, smelling of their calming calendula baby shampoo. I glanced at Michelle—could I trust her here? I remembered the orange striped balcony of the apartment at Enrique's and the nausea that memory brought up; I didn't even want to remember. I thought of Rafe and the kids with Michelle and imagined the four of them eating ice cream and strolling around Stanford.

"I do think it's best," Brad said.

"I agree," I said, privately thinking, two days to get there, the rest of the week shot, and I'm doubtful it's a supplier issue. But I couldn't not go.

Brad knew that if more accounts of Conch failure hit the press, investors and consumers would become leery of our company, and most pertinently in the short term, the Powerplex deal wouldn't go through. Worse, it could destroy Conch's reputation in the consumer market. And mine. My reputation hung in the balance too. It wouldn't be an atmospheric, prologue-y failure like Cullen and Irwin's first company in middle school. It would be news, probably not at the television evening news level, but definitely worth a couple of pieces in *Forbes* (cue the alarming infographics), zillions of blog posts from people who had never even run their own lemonade stands, and maybe even a couple of *New York Times* op-eds ("Why Stone's Failure at Conch Is Not a Gender Issue"). The *Journal* would cover it. The Gaggenau ("It's a nice refrigerator but I wish you had gotten the other one" —Jacqui) would go to auction and Johnnycome-latelys building megamansions in the exurbs past San Jose would bid on our kitchen appliances. I'd have to take Rafe up on moving.

All of this shouldn't scare me, of course. Fear is no reason not to do something. If there's one axiom the Valley has adopted unanimously, it's that failure is an excellent thing, a sign that you're trying.

I know that I have to retrain myself not to be averse to failure, instead to reprogram myself to like it, welcome it, embrace it—I *know* this, I have fucking made a brand out of it—but the reality of what it's like to really fail, when your own job is at risk, when three hundred Conch employees' jobs are likewise on the line (so many mortgages and college tuitions and water bills, all balanced on my shoulders), and by fail I don't simply mean to have a marketing campaign go bust or make a bad acquisition or hire a polarizing COO, paralyzed me. It's not fear, like Greer insists: it's just that I didn't want it to happen. Was that so wrong? All this striving to fail—bigger and better—strikes me now as the most preposterous bullshit, propagated by people who have gone on to achieve mammoth success and are only ready to reminisce in extravagant retroview. There were only a couple of days to fix things with Conch, and time was running out.

I had no choice but to go. What could I do? Conch needed me to.

Part 4

PENANG, MALAYSIA

+ + + + + +⊹+ + + +

Part 4

Chapter 18

I don't meditate as much as I should, but there's peace to planes: the endless immediacy of being in the air, the surrender to a seat belt and somebody else's timetable. Meditation is one of the topics I plan to study when I have more time, along with ancient Sumerian literature and what is gained by spiralizing vegetables.

I chatted with the man in the seat next to me and gave him a sneak peek of the SportConch prototype I'd brought along in my carry-on. He was impressed by its energy-harvesting technology, and I convinced him to buy a regular Conch now and upgrade to SportConch when it's released. I don't have hard and fast rules about speaking with seatmates. You have to be flexible and take the gifts the world offers. I've hand-sold a lot of product by not being afraid to get conversational.

The downside of flying is the sinus pain. When the plane started to descend, it was as if someone were holding me up by icy-hot rods plunged deep into my ears. Like twin drills going in, one from each side, or electric icicles. The pain eclipsed everything else. While other people put away their laptops, wiped away drool, or watched the clouds part and Malaysia tilt below us, I leaned forward, pressed my temples, and visualized sinking into a warm bath, discomfort floating away in the form of iridescent soap bubbles. The man next to me looked concerned. When the plane hit the runway, a smattering of people in the back clapped. The agony subsided, replaced by a stuffy fullness that padded reality like a European-hotel duvet and gave me a regal detachedness as I gathered my bag and strode down the concourse.

The airport in Penang was glossy and modern. More orange and umlauts than the San Francisco airport, but the same incongruous Hyundai SUV parked in the middle of the food court, near the McDonald's and the Starbucks.

"Weather alert," my Conch said. "Rain and thunderstorms expected later. Remember your umbrella!" Swollen gray clouds hung low in the sky. My Conch buzzed with pent-up alerts, and I dismissed them all. It's Friday, I thought, the day I've been dreading, and tomorrow is my birthday, and I will be forty. Outside, the air was warm, humid, and smelled of unfamiliar fruit.

I found my driver and we lurched onto the highway. I felt as if I could fall through the floor of the car. Keep hold of the reins, I said to myself. I'm not sure where it came from, maybe a dream on the plane in which I was on a horse in a forest, riding too fast.

We drove straight to the factory, along a wide and freshly asphalted highway. We passed billboards in English, Malay, and Chinese, for phones, TV shows, "miracle berries," and some product represented by young people piggybacking each other. A bright red potato chip truck whizzed by, painted with pictures of unfamiliar yet indisputably snackable curls and twists. Skyscrapers poked above the trees. Cranes swung overhead, putting the skyline together piece by piece.

My ears were sealed fortresses. I tried to clear my nose, and there was a sound that started in my brain and sizzled outward, blotting out everything except its own sound. I like this feeling, even though it's a horrible noise, even though my ENT suggests antihistamines and can't I not fly when there's fluid in my ears, don't I realize it's not advisable? When I turned my head it sounded like crackling in a pan, like static searching for a channel, like an emergency alert on the radio, like something inside me coming into tune.

We turned off the highway. The skyscrapers fell out of view. All around were reminders of how it used to be, how a lot of it still was: a narrow palmy road, fronds obscuring the low painted cottages. Corrugated tin roofs with yellow pollen filling the channels. Plant pots lined up along a rusty metal fence.

Some bumps, an annoyed cry from the driver, and we turned again. Our surroundings became more industrial, grimier, and smokier, the sooty buildings matching the gray sky. We passed factories making car parts, chips, and semiconductors. One final turn, and at last we bumped through a gate into the walled parking lot of the factory. Birthplace of 4.5 million Conches and counting.

Mr. Tengku smiled. I smiled and inclined my head slightly, splitting the difference between a nod and a bow. We did not shake hands. That was not the custom here.

"I trust you traveled well?" he asked, politely. He invited me to sit in his office, which had one small window, and a fluorescent light overhead. It was like a shed within the big shed of the factory. He asked about my children, and I asked about his. We talked for a moment about children in general: how small they are, how resistant to our ideas. He had recently gotten, he said, a new toy for the children, for the garden. He raised and lowered his hands in opposite directions. For them to go up and down.

"A seesaw!" I said. "We have one of those too."

"Yes."

"What do you call that here?" I asked.

"A seesaw," he said, smiling.

"Ah," I said.

I held myself back from being bold, direct, or moving the conversation along; that's not the custom either. My patience level, had it been quantified, dropped to single digits. Finally, he opened a cabinet and drew out some noise-canceling headphones.

"Shall we?" he said, and I felt a flutter of excitement, as if he were asking me to dance. But it was even more exciting, because he was gesturing me through the door at the other side of his office, the one that led onto the factory floor. I put on the headphones and led the way out.

In the huge gray space, robots roared at each other. Zillions of Conches immobilized in purpose-built trays swished along on conveyor belts, up ramps and around quick turns, like dead people in very quick-moving hearses. Stripped of their housings, the pattern of circuitry made the Conches look like they were smiling. I felt dizzy with pride, or possibly jet lag plus hunger.

"So good to see you again, Mr. Tengku," I said loudly, over the roar, and with such earnestness that he blushed. We strolled through the factory, taking in the trays and trays of Conches in various stages of completion. The heart of the Conch is a flexible printed circuit board with capacitors embedded in it, made using a plastic substrate and photolithographic technology. The Conch housings are manufactured separately. Then the two components are joined. One at a time, a factory worker sets them in a custom ultrasonic welding machine and fuses them together.

The factory floor was cavernous and dim, smelling of oil and fresh plastic parts. Heat radiated from the motors of the machines. At one end of the space a robotic arm trundled back and forth, trailing lassos and bundles of wire: red, blue, green, yellow, and black. A narrow table held an open laptop, and a full glass of water. A man leaned over the computer and tapped a key.

Besides him, the room was full of thin, young-looking workers—mostly women. Or, now that I looked more closely, all women. They wore blue medical scrub pants and smocks. They were standing at long tables assembling Conches. Their hands flew, pulling components from bins at the center of each table and fitting them together. Almost all the workers had long straight hair pulled back with scrunchies—the color variation among the scrunchies being, at first glance, their starkest differentiator. It was hard to focus on any one person—there was so much noise and motion. They kept their eyes down on the worktables as I walked past. I tried to emanate friendly approachability, while knowing that none of them would approach me.

"They are good *akers*," Mr. Tengku said. "Very good, this group."

"And the staff turnover? How is it?" I wondered, and was surprised to find myself wondering, if the employees got enough to eat. Mr. Tengku noticed my eyes lingering.

"We have an attractive remuneration package for the *akers*," Mr. Tengku told me, gesturing toward the workers.

"What does that mean, in dollars?"

"It's quite competitive."

"With the other factories around here, you mean?"

He nodded. There was something so uncomfortable about talking about this in front of the workers, watching how regimented they were, thinking about how many hours a day they stood at these tables. I might be able to do their jobs. I was able to work beyond other people's outermost limits. But surely it was not good for most people to do the same tasks, over and over, or stand so long. Surely some of them would prefer a different sort of work.

I had been here before. On a previous visit, I had toured the factory, examined new prototypes, and drunk small cups of tea with Mr. Tengku in his office while congratulating him on his efficient fulfillment of our orders. I had walked the factory floor and inspected the machines, but I was spellbound by seeing the manufacturing process up close, and I'd given only cursory attention to the workers. I'd thought about how much they were paid collectively, relative to how much their equivalents would cost in the United States, and the business case for manufacturing in a country with so much cheap migrant labor. I hadn't thought about what it was like to be them.

There was a woman at the end of the row, with her hair pulled back into a stubby ponytail. She was watching me, with an expression that reminded me of Melissa's, at times: as though she knows more than I do.

"How are you?" I asked her, and I had to ask again, too loudly, before she seemed to hear me.

"She doesn't understand you," Mr. Tengku said. "She doesn't speak any English."

The woman next to her, who had a young, expressive face, looked surprised by this, and it occurred to me that it might not be true.

"Can you ask her how she is?" I said. Mr. Tengku signaled to the man who patrolled the edge of the factory floor and occasionally typed away at the laptop. He seemed to be some kind of supervisor, with keys on his belt. He stalked over, there was some back-and-forth, and finally she said something rapidly and turned back to her work.

"She is saying she likes to work here," Mr. Tengku told me, and though I felt certain that this was not what she had said, or not exactly in such utilitarian terms, I smiled and nodded with great enthusiasm.

"It's so nice to meet you," I said. I introduced myself.

This time he did not bother to translate. "She does excellent work."

"How long has she been working here?" I asked him.

There was another exchange between Mr. Tengku and the foreman. "Five years," Mr. Tengku announced proudly.

"That's wonderful," I said. "Good for you, retaining talented staff. Will she be promoted to a supervisory position soon?" I gestured to the table with the laptop to make myself clear.

Mr. Tengku laughed.

"Why not?" I said. "Has she not developed all the necessary skills yet?"

There was an air of expectancy hanging over the room, as if all the workers who were not watching me were concentrating very hard on something that was not the innards of Conches. A girl—I hope she was a woman, not a girl—at the next workstation sorted wires into tiny bundles, but she kept turning her head toward us as if she were listening. I noticed the thin gold chain she wore around her neck.

Mr. Tengku said something to the supervisor, who looked surprised. Mr. Tengku turned to me and inclined his head. "Women are so qualified to *assemble* Conches," he said kindly. "They do it so perfectly, with such patient, nimble fingers."

"Do you ever hire men?"

"Only as the manager," he said, smiling.

I felt many pairs of eyes on me. I paused, deciding whether to say something. But I needed his help, so I breathed in deeply, nodded, and we moved on.

It was uncomfortably loud, even with headphones on; not that the women were wearing any. A robotic arm scooted along a track and then swooped down to place a bit in exactly the right spot. The arm weaved and dipped and, every time it picked up a piece, detonated small flashes of blinding orange light and a sprinkle of sparks. I recognized it instantly.

"The surface-mount technology component placement system," I said happily. It assembles the sleek, paper-thin printed circuit boards.

"Yes," Mr. Tengku said, pleased. We shared pride over it. He patted its blue-gray metal strut. We stood together watching it work, pleasantly hypnotized by the seductive, subsuming rhythm of it.

Steel everywhere, and the sound of precision machinery cutting metal and spraying water. The machinery was the best in the world and imported from Italy, where they make great machinery, but all the digital components inside were from Japan. Metal, blades, wires, water—it was complicated, overwhelming, really, if you spent too much time thinking about it. Lots could, and perhaps was, going wrong. Hence the famous old adage, which everyone in industry knows too well: *manufacturing is a bitch.*

The conditions in the factory, they weren't great, I didn't delude myself. Our contract specified certain provisions, but it was hard to say if they were carried out. And the workers, the women in blue smocks, looking intent or tired or bored or avoiding my gaze, weren't my employees. Our relationship was deeply dependent, closely intertwined, of course, the way working relationships often were, but it was contractual; this wasn't Conch. These employees made Conches, but they worked for Mr. Tengku. To be even more technical about it, they'd been hired not by Mr. Tengku, but by an agency with which he contracted, which brought workers here from Nepal, Indonesia, Bangladesh, and other places. My company was a proxy employer. It wasn't up to Conch where they lived or what they were paid. It was important to remind myself of that. I twiddled part of my cheek between my teeth, biting in the reminder.

It was boring work, it was tedious, but the pay was not bad by Malay standards, or so he had said, and I chose to believe it. I had been assured that the apartment complex where these women lived, just down the road, was OK. We had never had a suicide. Not that that should be the standard, of course.

It was so loud. It was hard to believe that these workers and all of us back in Mountain View were partners in the same enterprise, creating Conches together. It did of course occur to me that it would be very different if they worked at Conch headquarters in California. We could have the factory in one wing, the offices in another, the parking garage stretching underneath, and all of us crossing paths at Making Waves on the days they served their famous wild-caught, environmentally certified scallop scampi. I thought these women would like California, and they would definitely like Making Waves' scampi. Who doesn't? But of course it was not possible. The market doesn't support those kinds of manufacturing costs.

We retreated to Mr. Tengku's office and shut the door. The quiet was a relief. So was not having to see the women working, watching me watching them. Soon I would be very far away, so absorbed in the day-to-day that it would be easy for these concerns, now so blatant, to deflate and get lost, like the beach ball we'd brought back from France in a pocket of Nova's suitcase. Mr. Tengku and I talked more about our families and how happy we were to see each other. Delicately, I brought the conversation around to why I'd come.

"We've been having some . . . issues," I ventured.

He watched my lips carefully. "Issues," he repeated. He tilted his head.

"Issues" was such an American bullshit word. I searched for a different word. Not problems. "Irregularities?" I suggested. "Not working as they are intended to work. We would like Conch to work correctly." I had taken my Conch off, and I made a gesture with my hands, turning it first one way and then the other.

He nodded slowly. "Problems," he suggested dryly.

I inclined my head. You might say that, I couldn't. "Perhaps."

"I see," he said.

"We have not been able to determine the cause. Could there

be something happening in the factory? This is what we wonder. That is why I have come here today." For this friendly visit. I have come eight thousand miles across the Pacific, just to casually inquire. "Could it be a process, a chemical, different hardware? Some change, perhaps?"

His voice was clipped and fast. "This is a very good factory." He held my eyes for a moment, waiting to see if I disputed that. "Let's talk about the good things about this factory." We did, for a very long time, while I tried not to think about Phil and Powerplex and how likely it was that Cullen might solve the Clitch on his own if I failed. It's my birthday tomorrow, I thought. What do I want for my birthday? That's easy: no more glitches.

There was a pause in our discussion of the factory's cutting-edge technology and fast turnaround. I rushed to fill it. "Of course!" I said. "It is not the quality of the factory. I meant, forgive me, could it be the parts? Have there been any changes in components or suppliers? As our trusted partner"—he permitted himself a tiny smile of gratification—"what should we do?" Talking to him, I became stilted and unfluent, as if speaking English properly would seem like I was showing off.

"We should have some refreshments. I'll ask."

There were Conches lying in a bucket beside his desk, like shrimp from a day of fishing. "Are these the new guys? Can I grab one?" I said, reaching forward.

I had asked as a formality and was surprised when he jerked the bucket aside. "Um, these are, perhaps not right. We'll find you a good one later." He moved the bucket under his desk, out of view. "Ms. Stone, we like your company." He put his hand over his heart. "We are very proud to make the Conch."

I nodded encouragingly. "I am proud to be your partner."

"Sometimes things happen." He spread his hands wide. He was sympathetic, but in a way that suggested it was impossible for me to understand.

"Sure. Let's talk about those things."

He sighed. "Have you ever opened a door thinking it would be one person, but it was someone else?"

I thought about this. "Yes, I absolutely have."

"It's like that."

I was pleased. We were making progress. "OK, great, tell me more."

He sighed. "Oh, look! This is very nice." One of the women had brought in a tray with two glasses. He offered me one. It looked like coffee and I was taken aback when I sipped. It was a creamy tea, very sweet.

"Delicious."

"*Teh tarik.*"

We sipped our tea. There was a photo on Mr. Tengku's desk of his two little daughters, each carrying a parasol and posed in front of a silver car.

I risked a look at my watch. I'd been here forever and we'd hardly gotten started. I'd hoped to make this a quick in-and-out. He noticed and adjusted his own wristwatch. It dangled slightly off his wrist, and it made a surprisingly solid thwack when it hit his teacup.

"Nice watch," I said.

He blushed and pushed it back into his sleeve. I noticed that he looked well turned out, much more than the last time I'd seen him.

"You're looking well," I said. Then I sharpened my tone: "I need an answer."

Mr. Tengku suddenly stood up and called back the woman who had brought in the tea. She came in, looking a little annoyed that we needed her again so soon. Mr. Tengku spoke to her in a burst of Malay, or maybe Manglish, but it didn't matter which because I couldn't understand anyway. I picked words out from within a rapid stream of language: "Quality," "OK," "Conch."

Malay has an agreeable rounded sound, as if the person is being conciliatory—the words land and swing upward, and there are a lot of "OKs" thrown in. It seemed this way, anyway, until I once heard two cab drivers go at it.

She hesitated, looked from him to me, and then began to speak in a language I couldn't understand. At first it seemed to me that her face had that expressionless, taut quality that people's faces get when they are trying very hard not to give anything away, and I kept looking at her, trying to make out a shadow of what was underneath. As she spoke, she grew absorbed in the intricacies of what she was saying, and she began gesturing, first toward the factory floor and then to Mr. Tengku, as if explaining two opposing positions. I could tell she was saying something that she thought was interesting or important, but I couldn't decipher any of it. I hoped that through the intensity of my eye contact I could catch what she was saying. I thought, this is clearly a very analytical person, but you get the sense they aren't using her in that capacity here.

Mr. Tengku thanked her and she left. He turned to me with a look of triumph mingled with validation. "She says there are *hantu* infecting many factories in Penang, but they are less of a problem at Conch's factory."

"Excuse me, what are *hantu*? Some kind of virus?"

"They have gotten into the factory, but not to the extent they've gotten into other factories."

I was impatient but tried not to show it. "Sorry, what has?"

"It is what you might call a delicate topic. Do you know werewolves?"

I blinked rapidly. "Not personally."

"But you know what they are? They are men who turn into wolves?"

I felt irritated that we were getting off-track. "Why not women also? I'm sure there are woman werewolves."

He considered this. "I don't think women would make good werewolves."

"I firmly disagree."

"Well. It is not relevant here," he said, even more decisively. "You see, *hantu* are not werewolves, they are were-tigers."

"Aha," I said, doubtfully.

"They infect tech factories. Very common in Kuala Langat. But especially here in Penang. They are a big problem at that factory." He pointed out the window and I leaned to the side, to get a better view. I saw no werewolves.

"So the, um, werewolves—were-tigers—they get in at night and eat the parts?"

He stared at me. "They are spirits. They infect the workers and make them lazy."

"Ah! Low worker morale. My goodness." This cross-cultural stuff was such a challenge. "Have you tried exercise breaks or improving the ergonomics of the workstations or varying tasks?"

"Herbs usually work," he said. "Also, injectable sedatives. We have a doctor who will come."

"I'm not comfortable with that." I picked up my teacup, saw it was empty, and set it back down. "Are the herbs something you give as gifts, or serve as food . . . ?"

He shook his head. "The doctor comes to do the ceremony, and uses the herbs to banish the *hantu* that are living inside the workers. He brings a goat to sacrifice . . ." He made a throat-slitting gesture. "Then all is well again."

I raised my eyebrows.

He smiled as if he were being ironic. "That's right. It is a problem you encounter everywhere here on Silicon Island. The work is difficult. Very boring. A man could not do it, the hours are too long and the work is too boring." I considered arguing with this, but I was afraid there might be something to it. "Our workers are used to simple village life, and then they leave their families to come here." He gestured toward the factory floor. "It is too much. Too exciting."

"It's too exciting? The work is too boring for men but too exciting for women?"

"Yes," he said.

I nodded, rocking back and forth in my chair, eyes cast down. I'm familiar with this body language from when I shoot down employees' passionately held ideas, and they acquiesce to my decision knowing they can't win.

"Some are weak," he said. "They are taken over by spirits."

"What's it look like?" I asked. "When the overwork gets to them . . . I mean, the spirits?"

"Oh, it depends, you know. They might see things that aren't there. They may not be able to sleep, or have awful pain as the spirit tears into their chest. They go blind for a day, perhaps. They shake and tremble, go rigid or collapse, yell—"

"That's all?" I said.

He looked hurt. "It's quite bad."

I was expecting something more extreme. "Hm," I said. "I've had that sort of thing."

"You've seen visions?"

I shrugged, noncommittally. I'd seen objects wreathed in a violet haze. Would that count?

"We had a worker a few months ago who was infected—three foremen could not hold her down during her affliction. Her eyes would not move, her body went hard. She began screaming"—he flailed his arms, in an oddly rigid way—"and then the fit came over her and she fell against a machine—" He pointed out of the office, toward the surface-mount technology component placement system.

"Oh, no," I said.

"Right there. Her clothing caught in the machine. It short-circuited." He nodded, somber. "Terrible problems. For her as well."

"Is she all right?"

"She could not work and went back to her village."

"Sorry, it's the jet lag." I had inadvertently yawned. "So what's your proposed solution?"

He held up his hands in surrender and smiled. "It's fine. I know how to take care of it. We hire a healer, we pay the price. A ceremony. Just business."

"Just business," I repeated. "That solves the problem?"

He had a poker face, hard to read. "Of course."

I thought about the last time I had not had stomach problems, sleep problems, chest-pain problems, and sinus problems. Pre-Conch, certainly. At my last job, for the first couple of days—though I was pretty driven there too. I sighed and blew air up to elevate my bangs, the way I used to do and had borrowed back from Michelle. "OK," I said, pressing my temples.

"Don't worry," he said cheerfully. "Sometimes it is important to act. You traveled a long way to be here today, so I know that it is time to act."

This seemed like smart advice and a headache was taking root in my right temple and I had an overwhelming desire to get out of this place. "Sounds like the right call. Let's do it. How soon can you arrange it?"

My car was supposed to have waited for me, but when I went out to the parking lot I didn't see it. I peeked into the windows of parked cars, trying to find my driver. A light, fine rain fell. I felt deficient in energy, stamina, and possibly zinc.

My Conch was doing its little intermittent rat-a-tat to warn that it was about to run out of power. I rooted around in my bag for the Powerplex prototype. What an opportune moment to test it out. But when I pulled it out it felt warm in my hand, like a tiny baked potato, so I dropped it back in my bag to deal with later. My phone chirped, drawing my attention to a new text.

Actually, I had a lot of texts. Mostly from work. I scrolled through:

Rafe: *Big news!*

Willow: *Something's happened back home, I might have to take off a day for personal reasons.*

Melissa: *I can't figure out how to send you a video.*

I didn't reply.

A bus squealed to a stop at the factory gate and several women carrying bags got off. A woman wearing a headcloth lugged a big bucket like the one I'd seen in Tengku's office. I squinted at her, wondering what was going on.

I did a little research on my phone, standing in the parking lot, and then called Brad to loop him in. "I'm making progress, but, bottom line up front, it's tricky going. Processes look good, but there's something happening I can't put my finger on. Our guy here blames the whole thing on spirits. Add this to the problem list: we have evil spirits in the factory and we need to pay to expunge them." I explained about the were-tigers. "There's a ghost in the machine," I intoned. "What's that from?"

"It's a Police album," Brad said. "I'd have thought you'd have known that. What's your take, that you buy their trust by paying their friends off, and then they're less likely to cheat you by using substandard parts?"

The gray sky and the heat of the asphalt parking lot were exacerbating my headache.

"More complicated than that," I said to Brad. "It's real to them. I guess? I can't be sure it isn't some kickback scheme. There are many psychological factors that affect productivity in the factory. That's my background in organizational development talking. I'm fascinated by that. But I'm proposing we do it."

"Is this going to spur them to make the Conches correctly? Is the problem even embedded at point of manufacture? Couldn't this just be a nice little werewolf-cleansing that happens to enrich somebody's brother-in-law?"

"Culture first," I reminded him. Though that's a total cliché, everyone says it now.

Despite my phone confidence, I didn't actually feel that confident. Did other companies pay spirit healers to come purify their factories? Did everyone? I might reach out to my network on this. Or not. I kept thinking of what Mr. Tengku had said about the workers' symptoms. Stress gnawed my belly, and the dark star under my breastbone began its slow, forceful rotation. Would a spirit cleansing/goat sacrifice cure me, and if not, what would? Did men in my position feel the stress as acutely? Did they internalize it the same way? They must (where else would it go?), yet I wasn't sure. You really only saw the same symptoms in the ones facing jail time.

I walked out of the factory gate, past a group of people waiting at a bus stop. Across the street was a little thatched day care, its yard full of familiar plastic toys. The day care advertised, in English, its suitability for children both left and right brained. I thought of Nova and whether she missed me. We had never talked about it. I didn't want to ask. Not that I want her to be racked with sadness, of course.

My Conch and phone buzzed. More incoming messages:

Willow: *I'll work late tonight.*

Willow: *I was already planning to work this weekend, of course.*

Rafe: *Blazer walked!!!!*

I reread that one a couple of times.

Melissa: *Here's a video for you to check out!*

Rafe: *BOOM, we have a walker!*

Rafe: *Are you getting these? It says you are.*

Every opportunity comes with transaction costs. Progress

always involves pushing through pain points. I knew this well, of course. I steered my attention back to the present moment by noticing how the rain dripped into the crevasse between my jacket and the back of my neck. I registered that I was hungry and made a deal with myself that soon I would eat. Then I tried to imagine Blazer, upright, taking a step. I couldn't. It was so inconceivable I couldn't picture it. I could only picture a false, exaggerated, pigeon-toed Charlie Chaplin walk, with Blazer wearing a bowler hat.

Rafe again: *Of course it doesn't really count till you see it.*

That sounded like something from a magazine: tips for making your workaholic spouse feel like part of the family. Not that Rafe read parenting magazines.

The rain came down harder. The video wouldn't load. I watched more messages accrue.

Rafe: *So how are you? Busy?*

Willow: *Did I do something wrong? If I did, I'm so sorry. Please ping me back!!!*

A blue bus rounded the corner. The waiting people surged toward the curb.

Rafe: *How am I? I'm ok.*

Went for ice cream with your assistant and the kids.

I have a start date.

I put my phone away and leaned back against a pole. My eyes prickled. My sinuses were streaming with an especially wet form of congestion. No, I thought: tears.

"Are you OK?" someone asked, tapping my shoulder. I pulled away, shook off the tears, and blinked. "Shelley Stone!" the woman said. "I was excited to meet you."

She pushed her umbrella back so I could see her better. She was smiling. She was very young, and her hair was highlighted with copper-colored pieces and pulled into a high ponytail. She wore a flashy raincoat with lots of zippers. At her neck was a thin gold necklace. Without her smock, it took a moment for me to recognize that I'd seen her at a workstation inside the factory.

"Hi." I wiped off my hand and extended it.

"I'm Sara," she said. "I knew you right away. I recognized you when I saw you. I rode once in your car." She positioned her umbrella to cover us both. Her English was good.

"You rode in my car?"

"Yeah, because I was the number one worker. Here when you're the number one worker, they give you a little medal, it's nothing to cherish, but at the other one they let you ride in your car."

"My car? What?"

A bus had pulled up at the stop. The crowd sorted itself into a line and began to board.

"I admire you!" she said. "I too hope to become the head of a large company one day. That's why I left the other factory, to get more experience and rise up." She glanced worriedly at the bus. Just a few stragglers were still waiting to get on.

"What other factory?"

Someone yelled to her, and she took a step backward toward the bus. She was saying something, but the rain made it hard to hear her.

"Here," she said, grabbing my arm. "Ride with me!"

We stumbled up the steps onto the bus. She showed an ID card and yelled something at the driver; I rummaged in my pocket for money, but because of the chaos or for some other reason, I didn't have to pay. Everyone seemed to be looking at me. Wedged between several people, I scrounged for a hand-hold, and gripped a pole just in time as the bus jounced off.

The ride was not butter-smooth. The bus wheezed up a hill. Far ahead, at the top of the hill, loomed a tall white building streaked with rust and smoke stains and rusty fire escapes. It would have been nice to assume it was abandoned, but clotheslines hung across the fire escapes, strung with flapping clothes. This was, I think, where some of the factory workers lived.

I felt a pinch near my hip, somebody's hand insinuating itself through the crowd. "Knock it off!" I yelled, twisting away. Sara whacked downward with her furled umbrella, clearing the space around me.

"That's better!" she said. "I won the prize for being the number one worker twice. I have lots of ideas for you."

"I can't wait to get your input," I said. As the bus jerked us around, I fished out a business card and gave it to her. "Please—be in touch."

"You should go see them at the other factory. They'll be so excited. They talk about you all the time."

The other factory. I tried to think what she meant. Perhaps she was confused.

Before I could ask her, I glanced down at my phone, and there was a new message from Willow, a long one. I sighed. That's never good news.

Willow: *Hi, sorry to bother you. It's almost midnight so I'm heading out. Wanted to let you know I'm taking tomorrow off to go see my family. There was a terrible fire back home. You know how my cousin Jerilyn installed self-charging Powerplex lights in her chicken coop? Last night there was a storm, and the whole coop burned to the ground—the firefighters said the Powerplex parts started the fire. Must've been a faulty batch.*

"Oh, no!" I said out loud, without meaning to.

In my mind's eye I saw workers making new Conches, to be cradled in paperboard inserts, packed in boxes, lidded, wafer-sealed, stacked, and shipped all over the world. I saw a goat in the factory being sacrificed in a puddle of blood, much like all the other things I didn't see that kept this operation moving. Rare earth minerals being mined by child workers. The women— girls, some of them—who left their homes and families and came on buses to this factory town, not knowing what it would be like, not knowing anyone at all, and without enough money to go home. I thought of all the people at Conch who came to work when they were sick or tired or grief-stricken, and of myself. Manufacturing is a bitch.

I called Mr. Tengku from the bus, as we rode through the streets of Penang's industrial district. I left a message, shouting to be heard over the noise. "I'm so grateful for your time and your advice, but on further consideration I don't want to move forward with the goat sacrifice." Several people on the bus who had lost interest in me went back to staring. "I'm reviewing alternatives. In the meantime, I want you to give the employees a paid day off, and I'll pay for it. I have a couple other ideas for worker-morale improvements . . . I'll be in touch."

Willow, I texted, *I'm going to need you to find me a goat sanctuary pronto near my current location.*

Willow called back right away. "OK, I just had to share. Your autocorrect did something really funny."

"Huh?" I said. "Have you found me a goat sanctuary yet? OK, so what was the autocorrect?"

"Never mind," Willow said. "I just went to bed, but I'll work on it."

I overheard Willow talking to someone (a roommate?) away from the phone. "There's really no typical day for me in this industry."

"Try the zoo," I told her. "So sorry about your cousin's farm. I've got to go. My phone's dying."

Sara gave me a gentle shove between the shoulder blades. "It's over there. Here, take this." She thrust her umbrella into my hand. I got off the bus and watched from the curb as it pulled away.

I opened the umbrella. The thin, slippery material flapped in the wind. From the underside, looking up and through, I could see beads of water plotted on its surface. The sky was gray, and the umbrella was gray too, and printed with a navy blue, wave-shaped insignia. I looked around. How was I supposed to know where to go? There were dozens of factories. I was in the middle of an island full of factories. I pointed the umbrella forward to block the wind, and I started to walk.

The bus had dropped me off high on a hill, on a wide, double-yellow-line road. Through the rain I glimpsed sky-scrapers in the distance, cranes in the port, and the factory roof-tops below. Along the roadside were walls and gates shielding tall white apartment buildings.

A couple of birds staggered across the sky. A palm tree bent over, cowed by the wind. The sky had darkened to the color of a conservative interview suit. From the trees came squawks and trills. The sound was just like the white noise recordings I used to fall asleep on strenuous business trips: the silvery high notes of rain, and underneath, the filler of wind. Rain pounded my umbrella. The light kept adjusting: dark, bright, dark.

Then thunder rumbled.

Part of me is always listening for thunder, just in case. Some-times I hear it even when it isn't there (i.e., Jacqui is vacuum-ing). But this was unmistakable.

The chances are high you'll be fine, I said to myself as I walked down a chipped sidewalk. Thunderstorms are naturally occur-ring phenomena involving warm air, moisture, and lift. Another part of me, the practical planner part, thought: OK, maybe I'll die here. Water streamed around my shoes. My mind turned to the endgame—thinking of myself dead, and the lack of an appro-priate successor for me at Conch. Laundry flapped on a line. A flagpole wrapped itself in a wet flag. Thunder clapped again.

I tried to imagine my own death as a fact: the obit in the

Times (a writer had made some proactive calls right after I came to Conch), the employees at their desks reading the message HR would send out, company-wide, the day after my death. What would the subject line be? At Conch it would be "Announcement." Or "Please Read: Message from Director of HR." There's no reason to put anything sensational in a subject line. Probably we would schedule a Conch-wide call and tell them. I could hear Cindy from HR's cigarette-graveled voice: "This is a gentle reminder to mute your phones, folks."

It was late, the streets were empty, and all the stores were closed. I passed a bank and an IVF place, with a huge baby face in the window.

Who would miss me? My kids. Well, Nova. Blazer wouldn't remember me at all. Rafe. Christine. All the employees of Conch, maybe. But not right away. They would exult for a few months and mourn me only after realizing how much worse the new person was.

I saw a lit neon sign in the distance and followed it to the top of the hill, but when I got there, the sign was bright, but the place was closed. I didn't know what to do. I stood under the awning in the doorway, and looked out. The rain streamed down. I held tight to my umbrella.

My Conch buzzed. A text from Rafe. *Thought you'd call. Going to bed now.*

A man hurried by in the distance, his suit soaked. He held a briefcase over his head to block the rain.

"Hello," I cried hopelessly, but I couldn't tell if he heard, and he didn't stop.

Lightning cracked. My Conch buzzed with an upbeat chime and a reminder. "Hey, today's a memorable day. Twenty years ago on this date, you—"

"Please stop," I said. "I'm well aware."

I braced myself against the wall as lightning cracked across the sky. Twenty years. Seemed like a lot, and also not very long.

Sheet lightning brightened the area around me. I flinched.

"Your stress level is very high," my Conch warned. "You might want to sit down."

There was nowhere to sit, and nobody else besides my Conch to talk to. "I need to find a factory," I said.

"OK," my Conch prompted. "Tell me the name of the factory you're trying to find."

"I don't know."

Conches don't get exasperated, but they aren't good at open-ended questions. Mine fell back on a recitation of general information about the area. "Welcome to this vibrant port town, full of hip nightlife and modern industry. The quay is located to your east. You may want to explore the restaurants and bars to the north. Factories are clustered in the area to the south, straight ahead of you—" The thunder hit hard and the ground vibrated. I edged closer to the building.

I gazed out at a checkerboard of roofs. And then I gasped as a lightning bolt cut against the darkness, so bright I could see it through the rain and even the umbrella in front of me. It was so bright I felt like I'd seen its jagged shape right in front of me, as if it had made the awning transparent. It seemed to slip between the buildings and surge toward me full size.

I screamed.

Then there was a series of three lightning bolts.

The first bolt, and I noticed a building with a square, flat roof.

The second bolt, and I saw something in front of the building, glinting.

And then with the third bolt, a pole of light descended from the sky. It lit everything around it in a circle of light, like a flashlight against the darkness. In that instant I saw the flat square roof, with an aerial. A pale expanse. A flagpole, which my eye descended, and in front of the building, but raised off the ground on a pedestal, a car. A car with a haze of violet surrounding it. A car I happened to recognize.

I saw first its profile, sharply cut, like my toddler silhouette, cut from black paper, framed and hung in my parents' stairwell (with exaggerated eyelashes, lips). And then the light filled in, and for the shortest length of time that seemed possible, I saw that the car was silver, and behind it, on the plain façade of the factory, was some sort of insignia, shaped like waves. Then it all went dark.

The booms came one after another, like a fusillade.

I concentrated on remembering the position of the building. It was a bit like playing a memory game with Nova, trying to hold in mind the location of a certain tile. I kept my eyes on the spot and waited for the sky to lighten and the storm to break. I didn't trust myself to move my eyes away, not wanting to lose sight of the car.

"I have to get down there," I said to myself. I picked up the umbrella and set off.

The rain had quelled, and the mass of dark clouds had moved to one side of the sky, leaving a bright, stunned field of palest gray-blue, a color often seen in the J.Crew catalog when I was young, and a shade that the catalog may even have called, misleadingly, "sky."

Asphalt and roofs were stained dark from the rain, the air felt heavy, and plants looked extra green. Droplets hung under a metal handrail in a scallop pattern. The flanks of the parked cars looked like they'd been dredged in a coating of pollen, seeds, and tiny leaves. Puddles on the road vibrated from the motion of cars driving over them. My shoes were wet.

Just when I feared I would never find the silver car, I saw a glimmer of it, at the end of the block. I sprinted toward it. Hello, old friend! Could it be? Was it? Surely not the same car I'd driven in Spain. An unusual car, it had seemed, though couldn't it just be a type I wasn't used to, which might exist plentifully in other countries, if not at home? Perhaps it was just a model I'd never seen before. Though it was hard to believe there could be many of them, with the same deep silver exterior, with its hint of depth, of shadows beneath the surface. Surely it was a coincidence that it was here.

The car was on a pedestal of poured concrete outside the factory, elevated off the ground. The concrete had been formed into a ramp at one end, presumably so that it could be driven on or off. I climbed up, tried the door (locked), and peered in the window. The upholstery, the dials: I was glad to see it again.

There was a plaque on the pedestal: "This car is reserved for our #1 employee."

What was this place? What kind of factory was this?

I Conched the query, and my Conch buzzed. "Enjoy your visit to . . . Name Suppressed Engineering." Then my Conch gave a light tremble, like the shake of an insect's tail, as its power ran out.

The building was plain white, with no sign except the wave-shaped logo. It was getting late. People had probably gone home from work. Only a few lights were on. But I tried the door and it was open. I went in.

A receptionist behind a counter was checking his phone. "Hi," I said. The room was tiny, hardly a room at all, more of a vestibule. There was a TV on the wall, broadcasting news or weather. Trees whipped on the screen.

"Hello," he said, sounding bored. Then he looked back at me and suddenly put his phone down with a start. "Excuse me!" he said, with a change of tone. "Many apologies! One moment, please."

Gratified, I introduced myself as he disappeared into the back. A moment later a man in a short-sleeved shirt came out from the inner door, beaming.

"Shelley Stone! What a tremendous honor! We weren't expecting you, but we are thrilled you are here. Do come in."

Surprised but pleased by this warmth, I left my dripping umbrella by the door and followed him back into a small, high-ceilinged factory. The factory floor was compact and well lit, with white walls. There was something familiar about it. But I haven't toured too many factories; my background was in digital-only plays, prior to coming to Conch. Most of the machines were off. There were no workers around; they'd probably gone home for the day.

"Some tea?" he said. "Or should we tour first?"

"Tour," I nodded, my throat dry, but I was already curiously examining the equipment. "A surface-mount technology component placement system," I said. My eyes widened as we strolled around.

He pressed a button and a conveyer belt thrummed past. The devices whirring by on the belt beamed at me with their inane frozen smiles. I did a double take, because I recognized those smiles. I leaned closer. They were partially assembled Conches.

Disbelief gripped me, but I strived to be no more than casually, appropriately curious as we walked around. An orange bucket of housings, like the one I'd seen at Mr. Tengku's office, sat beside a familiar machine. Much of our machinery was there, in a more compact space. It was smaller, and arranged differently, but there could be no doubt: this factory was making Conch. The manager spoke proudly of the systems, and showed me Conches in various stages of completion. "I have always wanted to visit California," he confided, and gave me his business card. I stared at it as it lay in my palm; it had our Conch logo on it, subtly askew. "I am very proud," he said, exactly as Mr. Tengku had, "to make the Conch."

His pride was touching. I was touched, although the statement was also alarming, since this was not our factory. We only had one factory, and I had just visited it. I dipped my hand through a bin of housings, stroking these incipient Conches. They felt very like the real ones. I picked one out and peered at it. It looked the same, as far as I could tell. I asked him about himself, his career here, scrabbling for clues.

"These are . . . ?" We'd come to a bin of unfamiliar housings.

"The new generation, of course," he said. "We are very excited about it."

"Of course," I said, though I had never seen the style before.

The surprise of seeing this factory was making me dizzy. I had pins and needles in my feet, and I winced as we walked. When we rounded the corner, I gasped. It was an executive-style gasp, in which my heart seemed to stop for a moment but only the subtlest shimmer of dismay crossed my face. On a wall hung a large poster featuring a photo of my head and Cullen's, pressed together against an orange-and-pink sunset. "Conch Top Team," it said below, in a script that I am certain is not one of our approved corporate fonts.

"Wow, that's amazing. Do you have an extra copy of that?"

"You should see our more advanced Conch2. These sell very well in certain markets: Asia, the Middle East . . ."

"Would you tell me a little," I said, "about the people you work with and how you established the relationship with us? Your supervisors, or contacts higher at Conch?"

"Certainly there's a lot of paperwork." He alluded to it with a gentle wave at his office. "It's a complex, sprawling company, Conch."

I nodded in extremely genuine agreement.

"But as a matter of fact the president of regional operations is here this week. Of course you must know him. You two must work closely."

I nodded, but without really paying attention, because my attention had been drawn to something on a TV monitor on the wall. I went closer. "Oh, wow," I said expressionlessly, trying to move my lips. I felt my chest go tight and my body get heavy. It's the feeling I have when grappling with an especially stressful turn of events, or possibly when I am possessed by spirits.

"It's me," I said, at the same moment he said, joyfully, "It's you!"

I gazed dully at myself. "Turn up the sound."

There I was, giving a speech. Striding into a building. Driving a car—the silver car. Then I was standing in an unfamiliar room, exhorting a diverse crowd of workers in a language I don't understand.

"What am I saying?"

He looked perplexed, and then his expression resolved, as if he thought it was some kind of test. "You're speaking of the necessity of work, how important it is to work hard." He looked sympathetic. "Perhaps the jet lag has affected your ability to speak Chinese."

I'm impressed by the ingenuity of my employees, even ones I don't realize I have.

"Every day," he reassured me. "We work hard, just like you say. It is inspiring, how you work all the time."

In the video I was at a desk in a gray room, stacks of paper in front of me, a rapturous expression on my face, demonstrating exceptionally good posture while fake-writing on papers. There I was, gliding along a production line, patting an employee's shoulder to gently urge her to greater productivity. There I was in a park as my children (not my real children) wobbled on a seesaw. Meanwhile I typed away on a phone, resolutely disengaged. "When you want to rest, that's the time to work harder," I said, turning to look at the camera. "Work more hours. Work harder."

"The regional director is here," the manager said again. "Would you like to see him?"

I would.

He led me down a back hallway of the factory past several plain, unprepossessing offices. "I don't think either of you needs me to introduce you," he said, holding the door, smiling. "I'll leave you to your talks."

I saw the regional director and nodded. "We've met."

"Oh, it's you," the man behind the desk said, in a familiar burnished voice. He half-stood and extended his hand.

"Hello, Enrique," I said.

Chapter 19

There was a prickle along the back of my scalp as I slid down into a chair. My vision went gray, narrowing until it was as if I were looking through the binoculars Nova made at preschool out of toilet paper tubes. Through the two small circles of my visual field I was able to make out a gold cuff link, the metal twisted to simulate a knot, and a small digital clock. I braced myself against the chair's armrests and willed my blood to rush through my body and oxygenate it. I don't like feeling vulnerable or weak; I don't even like sitting on the underling side of the desk. I reminded myself to stay in the conscious zone. That's where the action happens.

"I can't believe it," Enrique said. "What are you doing here? How did you find out about our operation? Are you truly a genius like *Fast Company* says? Ms. Stone, are you all right? Don't fall. Do try to sit up, you look gray. Are you going to *sleep*?"

I pried open my eyes. It wasn't sleep. It was another feeling I've had once or twice before, most recently the time I got too aggressive about leading the workplace blood drive (I went down with every department, and demonstrated, baring my green-veined forearm again and again, what a not-big deal it was to give). The key takeaway I gleaned from that experience was it's better to stay sitting until you are certain you can stand.

"What is this place?"

He smiled slyly. "Conch."

I shook my head, disputing this. My vision was coming back, the circles of sight widening enough to admit the wall, some of the window, and Enrique's face. He lifted one finger, indicating a logo on the wall behind him.

It was a vinyl decal that resembled the Conch logo, but there was something off about it. The spacing or proportion of the three scallops, or perhaps the concavity of the curves, didn't exactly comply with the Conch style guide, though even someone like me who was as familiar with Conch's logo as anyone, who has debated in meetings the pros and cons of tiny tweaks and their global repercussions, could not exactly articulate what was wrong.

"We are all so proud," he said, "to make the Conch."

"This isn't Conch."

"We make duplicates," he said pedantically. "Some of our duplicates turn out more successfully than others."

"They're not duplicates, they're violations of our intellectual property."

"Imitation is a form of—"

I broke in, with emotion, "And they aren't *duplicates*, because they don't even work right."

"Oh, don't give me that look," he said. "There is room in the global market for both of us. You, to market Conch and make it *cool*." He made a little cheerful gesture in the air. "And us, to sell it all around the world for thirty percent less."

"You make bad ones," I said.

He didn't like that. He bristled. He was touchy. I remembered that now, from the way he'd reacted when I'd criticized his video app in Barcelona. He was too proud of himself. He thought he was so much more clever than other people. I understood that point of view; I had had my own moments of feeling that way. It was dangerous, though. Because groups, when thoughtfully composed and solidly managed, can actually be smarter than the individuals who make them up. And sometimes those of us who are ultra-talented at generating and synthesizing enormous piles of information can miss something quite simple, something right in front of us.

"Ours work," he insisted. "They differ from yours, because we use our own software. But different is not worse. In fact, I think you'd be surprised by some of our novel solutions. I am certain they will appeal to an innovator such as you, Shelley." His voice turned whispery, maybe tender. "May I call you Shelley?"

An itch called to me from in front of one of my ears. I postponed scratching it and then I did: it seemed expeditious to take care of it. Another itch, on my neck. Another, at the edge of my shoulder blade, and that one I couldn't scratch. Easily, I mean. One starting on my right temple, above the initial itch. Then the flat part of my opposite ear. The back of my neck, along the skin above the spine. My nose, where the nostrils separate. My scalp, clavicle, the soft part of my belly. I looked down at my hands and arms for a rash: no rash. It was like I was being eaten by doubt. "You'll go to jail."

"Eh." He gave a contemptuous wave, as if this were the stupidest thing he'd ever heard. "You don't go to jail for counterfeiting electronics."

I was beginning to suspect that Enrique was unwilling to have a constructive discussion.

Through the window of his office I could see a tall building going up across the street. Scaffolding ringed brick walls. Empty sockets awaited window glass. The top edge of the walls was uneven: in some places the bricks had been built way up, and in others they hadn't. I blinked, and on second look I wondered if

I'd been wrong, if the building wasn't going up, but was an old one being taken apart piece by piece.

Flies buzzed around the room. I started coughing, possibly because I'd swallowed one.

It's amazing how much in life you don't see coming. For someone committed to her five- and ten-year plans, who views her life as a series of ninety-day goals, there are nevertheless so many possibilities that occur despite their infinitesimal likelihood and destroy your best efforts to knock out your priorities.

It's not just the distractions that represent a failure of self-control or will, but the distractions that oughtn't to have happened, in any logical world. Why was Enrique doing this? Who'd have thought a legacy company like Powerplex would have such unreliable quality control? The unexpectedness of life is a source of sorrow to me, but it's also a fact of which I'm aware. I'm more aware than most people. It doesn't stop these things from happening.

"It is truly a pleasure to see you again. I've looked for you so many times," he said. "And here are you, you came to me. That's funny, isn't it?" As if to prove this, he laughed. The laugh was detached from the joke, if it were a joke. It was more of a prompt, a suggestion. I didn't take him up on it; I sat stony-faced. I'm not big on laughing in business contexts, anyway—it's a distraction that gets people off-track, and if it's aimed at a particular person, that's mean and potentially could have HR implications. Plus I don't always get why it's funny.

I don't like this man, I thought. He didn't seem aware of that.

"Of course, every day—" He pushed the paper on his side. "Every day, you are who I hope to see. On trains, in restaurants, on nighttime streets . . ." He was gazing at me and the intensity of his eye contact made me uncomfortable. That's rare for me. "You have a special way about you. You must know it."

I shook my head. I felt physically weak. My mouth was dry.

I thought suddenly of my dead Conch, my dead phone, and that nobody knew where I was. Also, I had to pee. It was sudden, overwhelming, and dire. I can hold it for an extremely long time, and then I start to shake and sweat.

"May I use your bathroom?" I asked.

He showed me the way, leading me across the factory floor, past the equipment, the Conches flat on their backs on stopped conveyor belts, the bins of components. It was quiet; a solitary machine hummed.

"Just the same as your factory, so far, correct?" he said.

I forced myself to nod. "Similar."

He beamed. "Ours is more efficient."

"It's a decent space," I said neutrally. "Is it up to code?"

"Well, we do the best we can. We don't have a license to be a factory; no sprinklers for instance, but it's OK, it works all right. But here. This is what you should see. I prize this area very much."

He gestured to a tray set into a long, narrow cabinet along the wall. The tray was divided into compartments, and in each compartment was a kind of proto-Conch, varying a little in shape, size, and texture: some were crisply articulated, some embryonic. Many lay on oval discs of shiny metal. Some were vibrating against the metal, as if they were wiggling. One was flat and equipped with comb-like teeth. Some were attached to thick industrial charging cables. In a cylindrical container at the end of the row, something very like a human ear (pale, waxy, and perhaps made of silicone) bobbed in liquid, a wire running out of it and into the base.

"What are these?" I said.

"These are in development. We are always advancing our product, using the foundation laid by your Conch." I chose to ignore this. He led me past a plastic crate in which thousands of Conches lay heaped. He flattened the pile with his hand, like smoothing cake batter around a pan. "Our Conch gives many more reminders than yours. Ours uses more data, and pushes users harder. Some of your users are a little lazy, don't you think?"

"All data is actionable," I repeated to myself, quietly. As I followed him, I studied the arrangement of machinery on the factory floor, blinking hard to take it all in.

In the tiny, semi-functional factory bathroom, I executed my number one priority (peeing). The lightbulb overhead flickered. Maybe it was the storm. I rooted through my bag, pulling out the Powerplex prototype. It looked just like all the other Conches I've had the privilege of using, inspecting, touching, or evangelizing. It didn't look faulty, but one could hope. It felt a little warm. I sandwiched it in the crook of my hand, between my thumb and forefinger, and practiced holding it there in the webbing so it wasn't obvious I was holding it. I was not that good at this. Then I went out to face Enrique.

"I've been thinking," he said. "There's a lot you could learn from our operations. We had the benefit of your Conch as a model, but we have taken it further. The code your friend sent was very helpful. You should be grateful. Buy us up. Enfold our operation into yours. Here we have dozens of trained workers and product improvements. Let's be friends. We have every reason to be friends. Perhaps even, someday, more than friends. It is not impossible, would you say?" He held his jowly expression and looked at me without blinking. He had the droopy kind of eyes that let you see, at the bottom, a comma of puddled red-and-white viscera.

"What does that mean?"

"No doubt you are curious about all this. I could help you. If you remember, I have been helpful in the past." He leaned forward.

I shook my head, not trusting myself to speak.

"I helped your daughter when I found her on the beach."

Your daughter. When I found her. The words thundered inside my head, filling my chest with what felt like noxious black smoke. I could feel it curling into my shoulders and arms, and lapping at the back of my throat. *When I found her.* The briefest gallop of the mind through the horrifying preparation that "finding" must have required. I had the feeling of being in a helicopter, banking left, my body dropping before my stomach. A long downward view to Nova on the beach, in a smocked dress with a red bucket, oblivious and exposed. I couldn't stand to think about it; a great wave of pressure surged through me.

"Hm," I said. It was a groan, which only through gritting my teeth, curling my toes, and clenching my pelvic floor I was able to transmute into something that sounded a little bit open-minded and conversational. I dipped my head, which could be interpreted as a nod, to buy myself time ("Take a moment," Greer always says). I've had a lot of experience pretending to entertain terrible ideas. I drew on that well now and adopted my most relaxed facial expression, to give the impression that soliciting his help was an intriguing possibility. I clutched the Powerplex prototype tighter. It felt encouragingly warm in my hand. Hot, even.

I had never so desperately wanted a product to malfunction. Please be part of the faulty batch, I thought. Please have a glitch.

It seemed a long shot. For a moment. I felt scared and panicked about what to do, or how to do it, and then I caught sight of myself on the video monitor. There I was, or if not me, a version of me: cool, powerful, serene. It was fake but I felt a little inspired nonetheless. Everything that had ever happened to me was a long shot. I reminded myself to be optimistic, not because optimism was warranted, but because it was necessary.

"I see," I said to Enrique. "What are you thinking, roughly? Tell me more about how you'd help me."

"You might be interested?" His eyes were bright.

"I'm interested in all kinds of things. For example"—I patted his surface-mount technology component placement system. "Is this the same one we have? I think we have the nine hundred series at our factory, am I right? Yours looks newer—is this the one thousand?"

"It might be," he said. He seemed a little suspicious of my sudden enthusiasm for pick-and-place technology.

"I'm certain," I said. "Ours hasn't been working well. Could you turn this on? I'd love to see it in action."

He hesitated, but then he seemed to change his mind. He switched it on.

We waited for it to warm up. Some machines can take almost an hour to warm up. Fortunately this wasn't that slow. Still, I thought about things I could do to distract him. I could offer up Nova—we could call her. Would that be horrible? Yes.

The pick-and-place machine began to make a whistling sound. I leaned in, pretending to examine it.

"So, tell me more about what you've got over here." I gestured over to the tray.

"You're interested."

"I'm very curious."

"Well . . ." He walked up the row. "We're developing one that senses vibrations. It's very promising."

"Can I hold it?"

He turned around to pick it up, and as he did, I jammed the Powerplex prototype into the surface-mount technology component placement system. I wedged it into one of the nozzles, hoping the suction would help it get stuck in there. A torrent of golden sparks rained down from the nozzle. I glanced out the window at the bowing palm tree. Please let the storm continue, I prayed.

"This is my favorite one," he said, turning around. He seemed to be able to tell from my expression that something was up. I raised my hand and made a dramatic swishy gesture in the air. I thought about Jedi mind tricks, and I summoned up intense leadership and certainty with which to stare him down.

"That's not a Conch," I announced. "This is not a Conch factory."

He looked confused. I held the eye contact.

I saw, behind Enrique's back, a wisp of smoke coming from the machine. Aha, I thought. Good. "I need to get going," I said.

"When will I hear from you?"

A bulb in the machine flashed and popped in a blaze of white, and a thin trail of purple smoke trailed from the machine's arm toward the ceiling.

"What was that?" he said.

"I will never consider partnering with you," I said. "Your products are terrible. Especially the waxy little ear."

He looked stricken. I turned and fled.

"What's that smell?" the receptionist said as I left. "The lights are always going out in these evening storms. I apologize."

"I don't smell anything," I told him. I took a deep sniff. "That? I think that's the construction going up next door." I hurried out of the building. The factory manager and the receptionist waved me out, smiling. But even outside in the fresh rain, I could still smell the acrid scent of smoldering Conches beginning to spark.

Part 5

CALIFORNIA AGAIN

✦✦✦✦✦┼✦✦✦

Chapter 20

I looked down at my phone on the plane. I had just watched the video of Blazer toddling down the hall. He propelled himself with an expression of thrilled disbelief, as if he'd imagined many things but not this. Then he plopped down onto his bottom and looked startled, as if ending up on the floor was yet another unexpected development.

We had crossed the international date line. I would be home, and it would be Friday morning again. I was looking forward to seeing the family. Though it's too bad, when you have a traumatic anniversary, to experience it twice.

Grinding thunder from the gray cloudy sky and an answering grinding within me, like a setting on the food processor when Melissa makes baby food. A familiarly ominous ache: my period, two days early. A notification of internal gears in motion. I pressed on my abdomen and kneaded hard with a fist while pulling my suitcase through the terminal; I theorize this speeds it along. The pressure made me feel better, anyway, until I took my hand away. I swallowed an aggressive but non-liver-damaging quantity of ibuprofen. My Conch and phone, recharged after the flight, buzzed with a barrage of pent-up messages and alerts.

Thinking about you today, Christine had written, cautiously and sensitively. I tried several potential replies and then left her message there, unreplied to. She would understand.

I had an invitation from Greer to her failure party (delete!), and a message from Brad, which I read twice: *Signing's on! Great work. See you tonight.* I opened and closed my jaw a few times to clear my ears.

I'd bought an apple at the airport to tide me over on the trip to the office. The apple had come shrink-wrapped to a cardboard plate. I had to use my house keys to rip the plastic, somewhat negating its hygienic protective powers. The apple was mealy. I wished it were crisp, and thinly sliced, and fanned upon a real (not cardboard) plate. I could not wait to get home.

My ears were still stuffy, but my eyes too hadn't adjusted to being home. Everything had a tinge of the unfamiliar and looked glossy, intriguing, and at once both veiled and real, like a film. How sedately people here drive, I thought, as I glided down El Camino Real. They must be soothed by the pleasant weather and the abundance of places to buy burritos. A shiny white self-driving car glided along in the next lane, parallel to mine. The two guys inside, freed of having to drive the car, looked underutilized, with no function except to smile self-consciously at passing drivers. I had anticipated problems with my ears, but it was the visual adjustment I always forgot about, the way that travel reset your sight and recalibrated your attention.

The parking lot of the office was about half full. It was Friday night, after all, a time when non-high-achievers often go home. A few familiar cars were in their usual spots—Stefan's bus, with its gathered curtain in the window, a huge pickup truck, and in our visitor spot, Brad's car, with its surfboard strapped to the roof. People waited in line at a food truck that had pulled up near the lobby door. I scanned the menu on the side of the truck as I passed. Crepes, available with various combinations of asparagus, prosciutto, honey, walnut, lemon.

The lights in the lobby were off. Tony was away. The extruded pasta sculpture cast loopy shadows. I headed straight for the iris scanner, and there was Michelle.

She was leaning against the guard's desk, biting a fingernail. When she saw me she took her hand out of her mouth and straightened up a little. I thought she looked a little afraid to see me.

She's only an inexperienced entry-level young person, I thought, and she probably is afraid. This made me like her better.

"You came back," she said. I nodded. I wasn't sure what to do, so I gave her the quickest, skimmiest of hugs. I told her about an article I had read on the plane.

"Fascinating stuff," I said.

"Thanks for letting me stay at your house. Your kids are cute." Our eyes were at exactly the same level, which did add a feeling of intimacy to ordinary conversation—it was as if I were seeing right in. "You look dirty," she said.

"It's been a long day," I said. And then I felt entitled to press, just a little: "You're here."

She nodded. "I have a job." She blushed. "An internship, actually. Well, a job. Part-time."

"At Conch?" I no longer interview all candidates or am as involved in hiring as I used to be, but I usually review résumés over email. I felt uncomfortable with the idea of her at Conch.

She looked embarrassed. "No, no. Brad got me a job working at one of the companies he invests in. I'm going to advise on the youth audience. You know, the millennial market and what we're up to." She grinned. "I'm supposed to meet him—he's inside."

"That sounds like it could be promising." I looked inquiringly at her. "Are you comfortable working with him? He's kind of difficult . . ."

"They say stuff about you too," she said.

"OK, right."

Shouts and stomps came from above us. It sounded like someone had just won at foosball.

"People are really excited about whatever it is you're doing right now. Like, crazy excited. And they have beer and crepes. Are you going up?"

I remembered being at Gorvis the night before our launch, and how we'd all sat around on bouncy balls and speculated, with limbic shivers down our spines, about how different the world would be in the morning. Think of all those people asleep in their beds, someone had said, not knowing that when they wake up, Gorvis will have changed the world as they know it. It'll all be different. We'll remember this night forever. Well, I did remember it, as a matter of fact. I could hardly remember the product, but I remembered the feeling of belief we'd all had. We'd been so fervent then, the same as the Conch employees were now.

"They think we're doing a deal," I said. "I have to go break some bad news."

I dreaded having to go through with what I was about to do. But I had to; it was the right thing for Conch. I leaned in, waited for the beeps, and started through the door.

"Tell your husband thanks for hosting me," she called.

"I will. It's nice to see you . . ." She didn't say anything. I did a little circling gesture to elicit what I needed.

"Miranda," she admitted.

"Nice to meet you, Miranda," I said, and slipped through the door.

B rad, do you have a minute to talk?" He looked up at me, interested, glad to see me, not suspecting what I was about to say. I had a feeling much like the one I've had in the moments before giving notice at a job, when it feels as if the ground is shifting, and your perspective changes as the ground tilts, like being on an airplane.

Outside the conference room the office was in full Friday night, celebratory disarray. Conch employees ate asparagus crepes and squirted craft beer from a keg in the microkitchen. Some were even working.

"So, Shelley," Brad said. "Looks like we squeaked it out." He smiled, tired and relieved. The contract lay on the table, thick and interlaced with plastic tabs showing where to sign. You might think contracts would all be electronic now, but though all the markup and negotiation is done over email, we still sign paper. Later we upload the documents to our data center for corporate record-keeping.

I sat down on the opposite side of the conference table. Brad opened his hands, cheerful and exuberant. "No more charging," he said. "Love it." He slid the contract toward me. His attention flicked over to his phone. This was not the last problem he'd solve today. Then he noticed, belatedly, my expression. Perhaps it was that I wasn't picking up the contract.

"What's up?"

I looked into his eyes.

I gulped. Nothing to it but to do it. "I want to preface this by letting you know it may be unwelcome news." That's also my standard opening gambit when I have to fire someone. Brad's expression clouded.

I took a deep breath. "I've decided not to go forward with the Powerplex deal."

Brad stared. Then he shook his head.

I kept going. "This merger's not a good idea. There are problems with explosions from the Powerplex parts. It's not even a good goal, to encourage constant long-term Conch use. Some people can't handle continuous wear; we're already seeing the mental health impact on some users. We're not doing users any favors if we push them to the point of collapse. There's no reason to take this forward."

"Phil's on board," Brad said. "It's a done deal. You just need to sign." He jiggled his fingers in the air, as if I needed help with the concept.

"I won't."

He stood up and rubbed his forehead. "I can't believe this."

I shook my head.

"You can't make a unilateral strategy decision like that." He was pacing the room, wringing his calculator in his hands.

"Actually, I can."

"The board won't support you."

"That's their choice," I said.

"I put myself on the line for you."

"Thanks for the opportunity."

"God damn it, Shelley," he said, thumping his calculator down on the table. "I expected you to show some leadership on this."

"This is leadership," I said, steely.

Brad sighed and rolled his eyes. He slammed the door back on his way out. "This is the last time I put a woman in charge."

I could hear him moving through the office, bellowing. "Deal's off. Back to work." A whoop went up, from someone who hadn't been listening. This made Brad madder. "Get that keg out of here."

I sat for a moment at the table, looking out the window at the marshland and the hills. I stacked up the contract and all the papers on the table, and I threw them out. Then I left the room and went through the office to look for Cullen. The office was emptier already. I found Cullen in the lobby, in front of the fish tank, meditatively sprinkling fish flakes on the surface of the water. I told him about the counterfeit factory, and my trip, and how Brad had taken the news. We talked about how to scale back the productivity algorithm to reduce the number of time-optimization prompts.

"It's too much," I said. "Any of the data you're getting from my beta testing—or the beta testing of people like me—it has to go. I'm not a sustainable model. We need to take out all the real-world testing and walk it back."

"How will users take that?"

"I don't know. Maybe we should tell them that Conch is so effective you should only use it in small doses."

"That'd be a switch in our messaging."

"It's a pivot," I agreed. "You'll have to iron out the details." That's a great phrase I love. Who even irons anymore? But the very act of saying it irons out having to go into what the specific problems are. Anyway, they would be Cullen's problems now.

He understood that, and he hugged me. "I thought you'd hang in there longer. Truth be told, I've been thinking about what might be next for me. It's not as fun as it was in the beginning, you know?"

"I get it," I said, and it was the first time we had ever acknowledged to each other that we'd have lives after Conch. Some people love to start tasks, and some people like to complete them. I love both, which is the most unusual type, but I knew what he meant.

This is good," I said, turning Nova's ice cream cone, assiduously licking up the melted parts and getting it organized. Nova, ahead on her scooter, dinged her bell and glided down the path. We were near the Stanford Dish, on a trail that loops through the foothills and goes by the Dish itself, an enormous radio telescope. The weather was pleasant, as it so often is where we live; lots of zealous joggers were out, industriously completing the loop as if it were their job. A woman in a straw hat power walked past and smiled at Blazer in his stroller. Up ahead the Dish, cocked to one side, towered over the hillside.

It was what I'd once heard called "a Swiss day," which was a great rebranding of cold spring weather: a densely blue sky, buds on the trees, yet another opportunity to wear fleece. It wasn't the kind of day that made a pitch for ice cream, but knowing how scarce time was, we'd seized the moment. It was, after all, my birthday. When we reached the top of the hill I breathed in deeply; my sinuses were exquisitely clear.

Rafe stopped the stroller and gave Blazer a bite of ice cream from a plastic spoon. "And the supercharger goes . . . into the electric car," he said, as Blazer's mouth opened. With a deft turn of the spoon Rafe recaptured some of the ice cream that had dripped down Blazer's chin. "Watch out for the runner," Rafe called to Nova, picking up speed ahead. She flashed her sandal sole as she sped away. "How'd it go with Brad?" he asked.

"Not good. In fact, it was bad."

"He'll come around," Rafe said, spearing his ice cream with his spoon. "Give him time."

"It's not going to be like that. It's not going to . . ." I shook my head, to stave off any false hope he might offer. Down below us sprawled the red roofs of Stanford, with Hoover Tower poking up like a stylus. Beyond was a fuzz of treetops, a comma of Bay, and a bank of low gray mountains. I'd known the first time I'd come here that my future was in this place. Once, on a winding drive through foggy hills, struck by the possibility all around me, I'd said to Rafe: it's like a postcard here. Rafe shook his head. It's like a video game, he said, which was truer.

My phone chirped in my pocket. "It's ringing," I announced.
"Aren't you going to answer it?" Rafe said.

I shrugged.

"You don't think that the board will really . . ." Rafe didn't have to say more.

"I did the right thing," I said. "That's what leadership is. To be clear, I'm doing this for the company. It's not for me, or for us. I'm doing it because it's the right business decision for Conch. In the long term they'll realize I was right, but meanwhile . . ." I trailed off. "It's over. I'm going to be out of a job." I licked the ice cream until it was flush with the top of the cone. "Brazil, here we come." I tried to sound peppy and pleased. I had known it would come to this since before I'd boarded the plane home, but to be here and say it was different. I buried my emotion in eating my ice cream. "I bet they don't have mint chocolate chip in São Paulo. Or what do I know, maybe they do."

Rafe stopped in the middle of the path. He spoke without looking at me. "I turned it down," he said.

"I don't usually like these little chocolate bits, but—wait, you did what?"

"I said no." He was looking straight ahead, not meeting my eyes. There was a dark pink flush rising up from his neck, past his jaw and into his cheeks. He leaned on the stroller's handlebars. "I couldn't go through with it. I turned down the job."

My jaw dropped open. "How was *that*?"

"It was also bad." He attempted, with moderate success, to smile. "It means I'm done there. I'll have to find something new." He still wouldn't meet my eyes. "I wouldn't have done it if I'd known that—I'd really believed you'd make yours work. You always do."

I bit off a crisp, waffly bit of cone and crunched it. I was secretly pleased he'd assumed this. "Well, too bad we're not going. I heard they have great Japanese food there."

We looked at each other, him trying to read my tone. I touched his back gently and saw there were tears in his eyes. He didn't want me to see that. "Look, Nova," he said, turning away and pointing. "Cows!" Nova isn't interested in farm animals. She didn't slow down to look, and instead it was Rafe and I who stood there, marveling at the grazing red cows, and other things.

"We'll figure something out," I said.

We watched Nova drop her scooter by the side of the path to jump on and off a low wooden railing. We unclipped Blazer from the stroller, put him down on his feet, and he took off after her, his little plaid shirt unbuttoning from the bottom, showing a band of white diaper and pudge. He grunted as he waddled toward her. Nova, pin-thin and all angles, jumped back on the scooter and glided away, her dress and sweatshirt hood floating behind her. I could hear her calling to her brother, her high voice in instructional mode.

Rafe put his arm around me as we stood by the stroller and watched them go.

"Careful!" I yelled. "Nova, not too far! What are you doing? Nova, that's too far! Come back!"

"So," Rafe said, as if it were just dawning on him, or as if it were a truth too difficult to hold continuously in mind. "No job for me. No job for you."

I nodded, having grasped this. I ate the point of the cone.

He said, wonderingly, "What are we going to do now?"

I looked ahead, down the trail and up at the radio telescope, its antenna pointing into the sky. What was I going to do now? It was a very good question. An excellent question. A question I was absolutely going to have to answer. I was always asking myself that question, and I'd never been short of answers. But at that moment, I just wanted to do nothing.

Acknowledgments

I'm indebted to several books that informed my thinking on women and work, including Aihwa Ong's *Spirits of Resistance and Capitalist Discipline*, Leslie T. Chang's *Factory Girls: From Village to City in a Changing China*, Arlie Russell Hochschild's *The Outsourced Self*, and Anna Fels' *Necessary Dreams: Ambition in Women's Changing Lives*. Shelley cites statistics on women CEOs very like those from *Fortune*.

I'm so grateful to my incomparable agent, Alexandra Machinist, for her support and countless good ideas, and to my exceptional editor, Jenny Jackson, whose encouragement and vision took this way beyond the minimum viable product. Thanks to Hillary Jacobson and Amelia Atlas at ICM and to Zakiya Harris and everyone at Doubleday for their work on this book.

Crucial thanks to Courtenay Harris Bond, Becky Cassler Fearing, Chaitali Sen, and Kim Wall. Erin McGraw's generous advice on an early draft of this novel caused it to pivot. Thanks to my teachers Alice McDermott, John McPhee, and Edmund White, and, for friendship and encouragement, Max Abrams, Katya Andresen, Joyce Carter, Gregory Cohen, Justin Cohen, Jane Delury, Marian Heiskell, Lizzie Skurnick and the whole W. Amherst book club (and you'd see this nice mention, guys, if you ever finished a book).

Tanya Ramos' lucidity and bonus emotional intelligence have enriched these pages, as well as my life. And thanks to my colleagues—Conch has nothing on them—particularly Karen Albright, Nichole Armstrong, Trish Carrington-Adkins, Keryn Lane, Lisa McQuiston, and Abigail Seligsohn.

I am grateful to my parents, Bonnie and Jay Cohen, for so much love and practical support. To my favorite disruptors, my sons: thank you for your many ideas on how to improve this book by adding car chases. Your input on vehicles went far beyond what I needed, but thank you.

And lastly but most of all, unfathomable gratitude to James. This book is for him, and never has an honor carried with it more obligation to provide childcare. His generosity, encouragement, and partnership have made so much, including most of the good parts of this book, possible.